keep this between us

ALBANY ARCHER

Image from Anna Fury

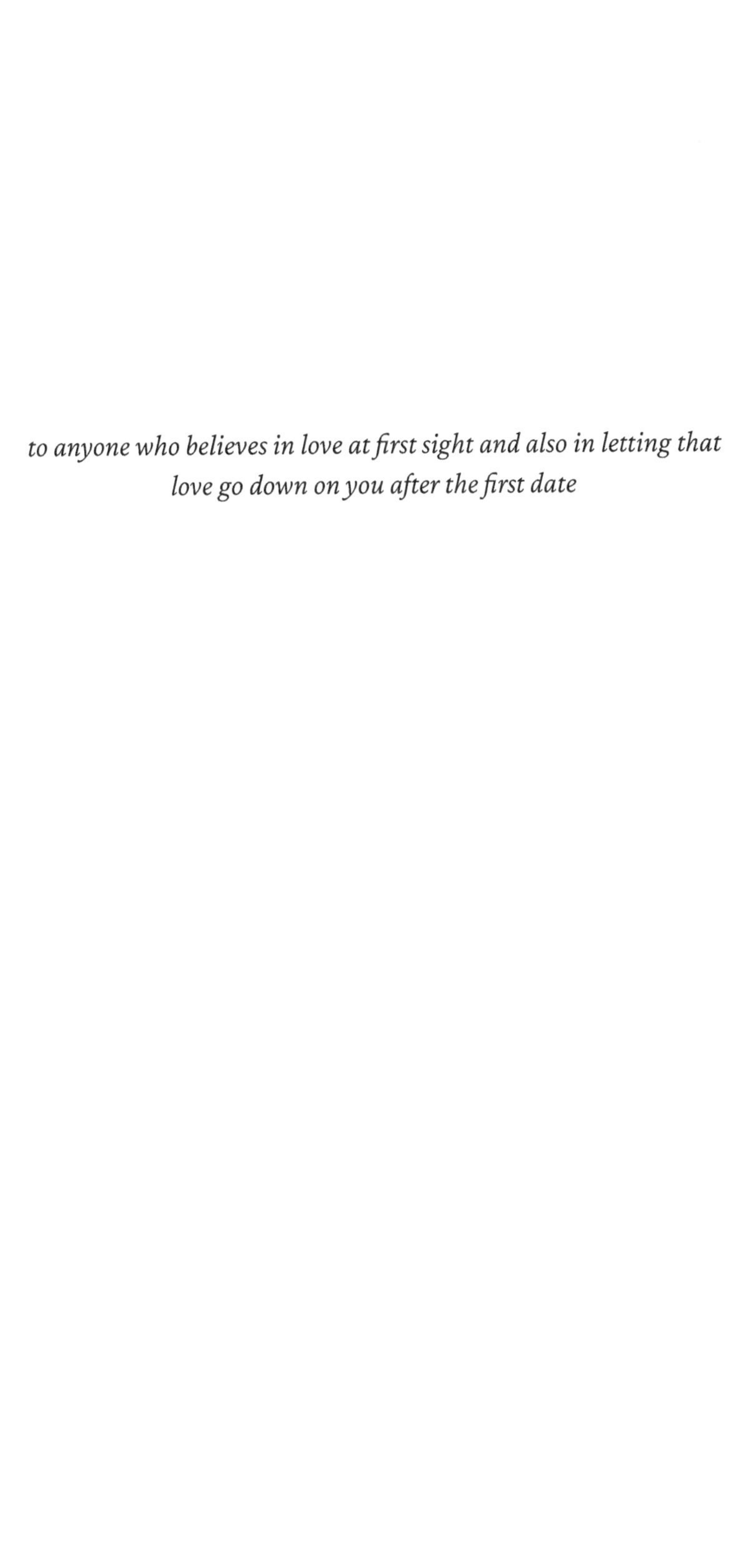

to anyone who believes in love at first sight and also in letting that love go down on you after the first date

introduction

TUESDAY

I'm making the most of my forced fresh start. Exiled by my family to a tiny mountain town, I'm going to show them I'm not the screw-up they think I am. But I never expected to love it here. To find all my missing pieces in the fresh air, quaint town, new friends, and a man who sets my soul on fire. But is seven hundred miles enough distance to keep my mistakes in the past?

BOND

I've lived in Trail Creek, New Mexico, my entire life. My plans are set: take over the family business and live my best life. Simple. Except, I never accounted for a storm like Tuesday Phillips. The moment I meet her, everything shifts, and it doesn't matter who her family is or what she's running from. There's no way I'm letting her go.

content warnings

This book is an open-door romance, meaning there will be on page explicit sexual content: (not limited to) praise, back-door play, power exchange, and toy usage. Strong, descriptive language is used throughout, including during sexual and intimate encounters between the MCs. There are on-page discussions and depictions of family estrangement, gaslighting, unwitting infidelity (in the past, discussed, NO cheating between MCs), photos taken without consent, mild on-page violence, and threatening behavior. There is also on-page alcohol consumption and one instance of getting sick.

Put this way, it sounds dark, but it isn't. Above all else, this is a love story about two people finding their forever when they least expect it.

This is not a slow burn. If instalove and explicit sexual scenes aren't your thing, you probably won't enjoy this book. But, with that said, all the scenes are full of consent and eager enthusiasm. If you're interested in which chapters have spice, you can check out the dick-tionary in the back!

Take care of your brain, your heart, and yourself!

tuesday

"Have we met?"

Startled by the interruption, I choke, dribbling my delightfully lurid pink drink down my chin and onto my cream-colored sweater. Perfect. Nothing says *welcome to your new life* like drooling on yourself in public.

Frowning at the man settling on the barstool beside me, I want to say, *Of course, we haven't met*, seeing as how I spent the past two days driving hours and hours to get to this hellhole. But my mother taught me some manners. Plus, I am new in town—no point in alienating the first person to speak to me. I refuse to count the death row escapee who checked me in at my motel or the striking—but grumpy—bartender who took my drink order before moving on to check on the other patrons.

So I simply say, "No. I don't believe we have."

He's handsome enough, kind of Ken doll-esque, with sandy brown hair and generically attractive features—with the sole exception of his eyes, which are a pale, icy gray. He's making me uncomfortable, but maybe this is a turning point? It can't hurt to give him a chance, right?

"Are you sure? Because you look exactly like the next lucky lady in my bed."

Yeah, that's going to be a no on the chance thing. Who doesn't want a side of self-important Chad with her drink? This girl.

In less than an hour in my new home, I've somehow managed to draw the attention of the exact type of guy I'm trying to avoid. So thanks for that, universe.

"I'm sure that line is usually a hit, but I'm here to enjoy a drink before crashing at the lovely local establishment up the street." Grabbing a cleanish napkin off the dingy bar, I dab at the spreading stain. Maybe if I snag a club soda from the bartender, the spot won't set. I try to wave him over, but my highly unwelcome companion opens his mouth before I can.

"I'm Jacob, Jacob Ashford."

He pauses as though I'm supposed to react to his name. When I don't, he powers on. "Since you're new, I'll happily give you the lay of the land." He waggles his eyebrows at me, a smarmy leer in place.

Studying the drink on the bar in front of me, I contemplate the life choices that brought me to this point. One mistake. One massive, blond mistake made months ago, who decided humiliating me wasn't enough. Now, here I am, banished to a northern New Mexico town, attempting to drink while dead animals and idiots with terrible pickup lines stare at me. I'd rather sit on an ant hill covered in honey than deal with this jerk.

"Jake—"

"It's Jacob."

And I'm Tuesday, not that you've bothered to ask. "Right, Jacob. I appreciate the effort you're putting into this, but it isn't going to happen. I've had a crappy day. I'm here to unwind, eat my weight in fried food, and then stumble home to my hopefully bedbug-free room. If you'll excuse me, I'm going to find a new place to sit. Have a nice night." I go to rise off my stool, but a firm grip on my shoulder halts my attempt to leave and pushes me back to my seat.

My gaze flickers around, hunting for witnesses. The bartender disappears through the double doors to the kitchen. There's a big guy a few seats away with a baseball cap pulled low over his eyes, nursing something on the rocks. Other than that, the rest of the patrons are too far away to see what's happening.

"Hey, baby, don't rush off. I'm just making small talk with the sexiest woman in this bar. Let me buy you a shot or two, loosen you up some. I'll show you a real good time, help you forget about whatever's got you so sour. Give me a smile." His hand slides down my side and squeezes my thigh. "I don't usually go for redheads, but these thick thighs make up for it," he says as if he's uttered the world's most charming line.

I stiffen at the clammy touch, the smell of beer on his breath. Can everyone else hear my heart pounding over the tinny country music playing through the scratchy ceiling speakers? A spiral of anxiety coils in my chest. I'm a single woman, in a strange bar, in a nowhere town, alone. I swear I catch a glimpse of Baseball Cap stiffening and sitting up. Maybe he's paying closer attention than I thought, or maybe my heart really is beating that loud. Good to know either way, in case things get worse, although there's an equal chance he's as bad as ol' Jakey boy here.

"Why don't you leave the lady alone, Ashford?" A glance over my shoulder shows Baseball Cap still staring at his drink, but I'm certain the deep, rumbly voice belongs to him.

"Why don't you fuck off?" the barnacle next to me spits, his hand still gripping my leg. He really is a prince among men.

Straightening my shoulders and using my best boardroom voice, the one I've perfected over years of working for my father, I turn and face Jacob. "First, get your hand off me." I glare at the offending appendage, and thankfully he removes it so I'm not forced to stab him with a fork from the olive tray behind the bar. "Second, I'm not your baby, and you certainly aren't my daddy. Like I said, I'm not interested. Maybe in some alternate universe, these lines work, but here in our current reality, there is a zero percent chance of me sleeping with you. So why don't you move on and let me drink in peace?"

A chuckle sounds from my right. Baseball Cap.

Jacob's cheeks turn red, and his gray eyes are stormy with anger. "You obviously don't know who I am, or you'd be begging me to take you home." He rises from his seat to tower over me. The screech of a barstool against the concrete floor startles me, but I don't take my eyes off Jacob.

Gone is any attempt at charming. Here's the real version of Jacob Ashford—an aggressive bastard who doesn't like the word no. That fire ant bed sounds better and better. "Jake—"

"Are you stupid or something? I told you it's Jacob."

I wipe my sweaty palms on my jeans and slide off my barstool. He's still standing over me, and his height is substantial compared to my paltry five foot two, but I've had enough. Doing my best to remove any hint of nerves from my voice, I say, "And I told you I'm not interested. If you can't bother to understand that, why should I bother to learn your name? Incidentally, you never asked for mine." I snag my sadly neglected drink and cross the bar toward the far corner, thankful to get away from that jerk.

This is not how I imagined my first evening in Trail Creek. Zero out of ten, do not recommend.

I glance around the bar, grateful to see Jacob is gone, then sink my fingers into my hair and pull against my scalp. The slight pressure helps to release a bit of tension. I roll my neck and shut my eyes, but as I'm calming down, my momentary peace dissolves with the buzzing of my phone.

> **WAR**
>
> Text when you make it to Trail Creek. If you followed the directions I put into your phone, you should have arrived an hour ago.
>
> Things are delicate right now, Tuesday. There's a lot of tension in the office, and the optics around you are problematic. But there's no need to be mad or sensitive about it. Business decisions aren't personal. It's what's best for everyone.

I snort. Yeah, there's nothing personal at all about your family voting you off the island.

> Since you're concerned, I made it. You can take off your "I'm so worried about my sister" hat.

> **WAR**
>
> I know you're upset Tuesday, but can't you see this is what's best for everyone? You're out of the spotlight, and this whole ugly affair will die down.

I cringe at his choice of words.

Another text comes in, but I don't bother responding. War knows I'm safe, and that's all he's getting for now. Maybe I'll feel more generous in the light of day, but I doubt it.

A burst of laughter from a nearby table drags me from my woe-is-me thoughts. The silver lining to this whole fiasco is that I'm over seven hundred miles away from that lying sack of crap, Duncan. Dad and War can play the heroes, putting out the fires I inadvertently set, but I'll show them. I plan on taking this job seriously and being the best thing to ever happen to Davis Designs.

As if summoned by magical thinking, another text message pops up. I flinch at what I see on the screen. Duncan.

DO NOT REPLY

So, big brother and Daddy sent you out of town. Don't forget, I still have people at Phillips who tell me things.

We can end this messy situation once I get what I'm owed.

What he's owed? What about what I'm owed?

I left behind my entire life in Dallas. Though, most of my friends abandoned me when the Duncan thing happened. My career stalled out months ago. I couldn't even go into the office without people scrutinizing me, talking about me behind my back, calling me awful names. The pictures... And of course, my family, who weighed me against the value of Phillips Construction and found me lacking.

"This is your final chance, Tuesday. You've not only ruined a man's career, but you've tarnished our family's image. Don't disappoint me again." The sting of my father's parting words has me rubbing my chest as if it can ease the ache.

I turn my phone off and slide it into my pocket, not wanting to deal with more drama. Time to bury my head in the sand—ostrich style—and pretend my problems don't exist. Between Handsy McGee, the text messages, the unwanted memories, and the exhaustion of driving eleven hours in two days, I'm due a distraction, stat.

Mindlessly flagging over the pretty server with a beautiful sleeve of tattoos, I order a shot and fried cheese. Booze and carbs—the real soldiers in the battle of keeping reality at bay.

I sip my cocktail. *Yummmm.* This must be what keeps the patrons returning because it certainly isn't the ambiance.

The Great Dane, the dive bar I stumbled into on a whim, desperately needs an update. Crackling over the speakers, some man sings about all his exes being in Texas. Hah, mine too, buddy. The worn pleather booths show years of use, and the walls are tinted gray. I'm guessing they were once white, but the previous decades' smokers changed that.

The server returns to my table with a Kamikaze shot and cheese sticks. Thanking her, I slam the shot and dive into the basket of crispy, gooey bliss. Okay, maybe this is how the bar stays in business because these cheese sticks are giving me life.

"Hey there, need anything else?" The server's sweet voice pulls me from my food-induced euphoria.

"I'm good, thank you." I smile, but it's stretched and wrong, like a grimace.

"If anything changes, flag me down." She opens her mouth as if to say more but stops before nodding and moving on to other tables.

I settle into the booth, curling my legs under me as I devour my deep-fried treat and people-watch. Thankfully, Jacob is nowhere to be seen.

Saluting the mounted deer in the jaunty Santa hat, I pick up the remainder of my fruity pink concoction. The siren song promising escape calls to me, the straw inches from my lips. So close, I can practically tas—

"You okay?" A vaguely familiar voice, gruff but warm, interrupts my self-soothing.

I stare longingly at my drink and whisper, "Someday, you and I will be together the way we are meant to be. Eventually, everyone will get that I just want to—" My words die on my tongue as I look up and into the striking, electric blue eyes of the most handsome man I've ever seen. Blue eyes almost hidden beneath a hat. "B-Baseball Cap?"

He barks out a laugh. "My friends call me Bond, but Baseball Cap works too."

tuesday

I freeze, mouth agape. How could I blurt out "Baseball Cap" like that? He's tall, broad-shouldered, and thick in all the best ways. The pushed-up sleeves of his Henley hit him at that perfect spot to highlight the corded muscles and veins.

I drag my attention away from the free forearm porn in front of me and dare a second peek at his face. Surely, he isn't *that* gorgeous.

Nope, turns out he's even better looking.

The urge to tangle my fingers in his dark hair grips me; it's a little long, curling at the nape of his neck from under his hat. I wonder, briefly, how soft it might be in my hands.

"N-nice to meet you, Bond," I stammer, my brain still trying to reconcile that the man in front of me is real and not some figment of my dry spell's imagination. I really need to shake the horny dust from my mind.

"This is usually where the other person shares their name." He gives me a friendly, encouraging grin. And holy crap, if he was handsome before, Baseball Cap with a smile is a thing of beauty.

"Uh…" *Oh, brilliant. He's going to think I don't know my own frigging name. Come on, mouth! Work!*

He holds his hands up. "Hey, I'm sorry. I wasn't trying to make you uncomfortable. Just wanted to check on you after what happened with Ashford."

Already, I'm getting a totally different vibe from Bond. No immediate ringing alarms, no stomach twisting or unease. Just plain old-fashioned nerves from meeting someone too beautiful to be real. Clearing my throat, I manage to mumble, "Thank you."

"So, are you? Okay, I mean?" His genuine concern catches me off guard. When was the last time someone asked how I was doing and meant it?

Am I okay? I'm tempted to tell him no. I'm sad, lonely, a little broken, and more upset about the asshole from earlier putting his hands on me than I let on. But Bond is as much a stranger to me as I am to him. So I say, "Yeah, I mean, yes. I'm fine. Not my greatest night out, but it's certainly one for the diary." *Hey, good job, me. That was a whole sentence.*

Now that I've regained the ability to speak coherently, I'm also aware that despite my physical attraction to this man, he's another unknown entity in an unknown place. I'm not equipped to deal with Jacob 2.0. I watch him closely, gauging his reaction to my words. "I appreciate you checking on me. It's very kind of you, but it's been a long day. If you don't mind, I'm going to finish my drink and head out of here."

His smile softens, and he nods. "Sure thing. I understand. It was nice almost meeting you, Peach. I hope I'll see you around Trail Creek again. Oh, and don't worry about your tab; it's on me."

Peach? My tab? What? Who is this guy? Maybe it's the shot and pink drink or the fried food coma, but I call out to his retreating back. "Baseball Cap!"

With a lopsided smirk, he makes his way back to my booth. "Yes?"

Warmth spreads across my cheeks. "I wouldn't mind if you stayed for another minute or two. If you want, I mean."

Bond taps on his watch. "Should I set an alarm? Wouldn't want to go over my allotted time."

I arch an eyebrow at him. "You've already eaten up thirty seconds with that question."

"Yikes, need to maximize this gift." Resting his hip on the side of my table, he's quiet for a second, then says, "I was watching the whole time."

I blink once, then twice. "Not going to lie, that's a little creepy. I'm considering rescinding my invite." I smirk, taking the sting from my words.

"Creepy! I assure you, I am a fine, upstanding citizen."

"Uh-huh, that's what all the creepers say."

"What can I do to earn your trust?" he asks, those beautiful blue eyes piercing me.

I swallow and say the first thing that comes to mind. "Tell me something true."

After a few seconds, a thoughtful look crosses his face. "Every fiber in my being rebelled at the idea of not stepping in as soon as Jacob Ashford approached you. He's a prick." His gaze never wavers from mine.

Doing my best to keep cool, I only address the second half of his statement. "I noticed that about him." Then, teasingly, I say, "So, it was marvelous meeting you. Splendid, really. But your two minutes are up."

Bond laughs, and a corresponding tingle flutters in my stomach. I remind myself I'm still recovering from the effects of my familial shunning and the encounter with Jacob. The goosebumps covering my flesh are from that, not at all from Bond's sexy laugh.

"Could I extend my time to five more minutes?"

I pretend to think it over and then give him a coy smile. "I'll allow it."

"Good. You don't need to worry about Ashford." At my obvious confusion, he adds, "I escorted him to his car, and we had an educational conversation about how he should treat others. It took him a minute, but he eventually came around to my point of view." Bond's hands flex, then close into tight fists.

"You didn't punch him, did you?" I squeak.

After a beat, he chuckles. "No, though I can't say I wasn't tempted. Believe me, Peach, that talk was a long time coming."

Okay, but seriously. Who is this guy—besides all my Luke Danes fantasies come to life with less grump and more...girth. I take in the small wrinkles near his eyes, the slight bend in his nose. I imagine scenarios about that minor imperfection. Maybe he broke it when he was younger, and it didn't get reset right away. I like that bend. It makes him more real, more rugged, but no less handsome.

Lost in my study of his face, I mumble, "So, Peach?"

"Hey, you're calling me Baseball Cap." That devastating grin is back. "Besides, you still haven't told me your name, and Peach fits. Hope you don't mind." After a moment, he knits his brows together and says, "You surprised me."

"Why? Because I didn't fall for that rusty knob goblin's charms or because I stood up for myself?"

"Did you just call..." He pauses and shakes his head. "Both, actually. Ashford is a wealthy, decent-looking guy. Even if his personality is shit, he usually gets what he wants."

"I definitely got the feeling he's not used to being turned down, given how he handled it."

"Highlight of my night."

I laugh, but there's no humor behind it. "Every *other* person

I've dated, most of my friends, and my family would say I should have removed myself from the situation instead of antagonizing him and that I caused the problem in the first place."

He contemplates me for a moment until a sly smile takes over. "Every other person you've dated? Does this mean you're dating me?"

"Wh-what? I didn't say that!"

He chuckles, "Oh, but you did. That's what we call a Freudian slip."

My mouth opens, and my cheeks burn. "Stupid handsome men with their stupid perfect smiles calling me out."

"So you think I'm handsome and have a perfect smile?" His grin is so enticing.

"I also said stupid, but you opted to ignore that part."

"Sure did."

The easy back and forth between us gives me a thrill. "I'd say it's been a delight meeting you, but that seems too generous."

"You wound me! I thought we were connecting, and I still have two minutes left."

"Must be something in the air—besides mold—making the local men think I'm interested."

He laughs again, that wonderful barking laugh. "Must be. Still waiting on your name, Peach. You ready to share it?"

"Nope. You have to earn it, Baseball Cap."

"And how would I do that when you haven't asked me to sit?"

I misread him. I assumed he was a grump, the way he'd hunched over his drink, his baseball cap low. Even the way he spoke to Jacob made me think grouch. But if the quips, grins, and easy laughter he's sharing with me now are the real him? Cue the explosion of butterflies in my stomach.

I'd like to say I play hard to get, keep things cool, but what actually happens is the words, "Would you like to join me?" tumble from my lips.

His smile kicks up those same butterflies, sending them into a giddy frenzy. "For longer than five minutes?" At my wordless nod, he slides into the booth before taking off his hat, slapping it down on the table, and running a hand through his hair. "Thought you'd never ask."

A dark brown Superman curl falls forward, and I sit on my hands to keep from reaching across the table and smoothing that stray lock away from his forehead. He turns his eyes on me, the fine laugh lines crinkling when he chuckles. "Am I one step closer to discovering your name?"

"Maybe a half step closer." I shrug, then cock my head. "Are you a fan of nicknames, Baseball Cap?"

Rubbing his hand over the stubble on his chin, he says, "I am." He studies me before leaning forward, steepling his fingers. "For the sake of research, let's talk about how you shut Ashford down for calling you baby. Not a fan of that particular endearment?"

I wrinkle my nose. "It was all in the delivery."

"Do you have a favorite nickname?"

I shift in my seat. "I'm not sure I have an actual favorite. The right one from the right person is all I can think of, but I don't know what that is. I don't think I'm explaining this well."

"You're doing better than you think you are." He shakes his head as if to clear away deep thoughts and sits back, smiling at me. "Have you had any nicknames you hated?"

"Some kids in school called me princess; I wasn't a huge fan of that." Then I say, "My parents call me ridiculous all the time, but that's less of a nickname and more of a descriptor." He meets my awkward laugh with a wrinkle of his brow and a slight frown. *Good gravy, Tuesday. Those are inside thoughts; let's keep them that way.*

Eager to get the focus off me, I ask, "What about you? I'm sure no nickname will ever trump the majesty of Baseball Cap, but have you had ones you loved or hated?"

"Oh yeah. My growth spurt didn't happen till I was sixteen. Before that, I was always small for my age. People took to calling me Runt. As a kid, I hated it. All I wanted was to be as big as my dad. He'd always seemed impossibly large." Bond pauses, seemingly lost in thoughts, before shaking himself and smiling at me. "Family and a few older friends still call me Runt, to the point I wonder if some of them know my actual name. It makes me laugh now."

"It's hard to picture you as the small one in your friend group or any group."

"You think I'm pulling your chain?"

"I mean, it's entirely possible. You could be a lying liar who lies for all I know." The truth is clear in my words as much as I try to keep the tone light and joking.

Bond lays his hand on mine. The weight of his warm, rough palm covering my much smaller hand settles something in me. His thumb circles over my knuckles, and his voice is soft, like a weighted blanket settling over me. "Guess you'll have to trust me."

"That's the second time."

He raises an eyebrow in question.

"Second time you've told me to trust you. That's a pretty big ask of someone I just met."

"My mom says I have a very trustworthy face."

I laugh, a snort escaping, which only makes me crack up harder. Bond watches me, flashing his toothpaste commercial worthy smile.

He nudges my foot with his, and that tiny point of contact

makes the base of my spine tingle. "Have we moved any closer to the big name reveal?"

"You're getting closer, but you've blown it up into this thing, and you'll probably be disappointed when I tell you."

"Impossible! But since it seems your name is still off the table, how about you tell me something else? Are you in town visiting?"

"Oh, no, I moved here. Arrived in town today. I have to admit, the welcome committee did not impress."

"Ouch, I hope you aren't lumping me in with Ashford."

Taking a sip of my cocktail, I shrug and make a noncommittal sound. "I haven't decided about you yet, Baseball Cap."

Lie. I have decided, and despite having just met him, my gut says he's nothing like Jacob Ashford. And if the universe has any kindness, nothing like Duncan Wright.

Around Duncan, my stomach hurt, and my chest ached. I felt trapped in a haze of unease, ignoring every warning my intuition threw at me. But here, with Bond? There's no nausea or anxiety. Just warmth.

"What can I do to change your mind about our fair burg and improve my standing in your lovely eyes?"

I tap my finger to my chin. "I already have this exceptionally pink drink. I've eaten a plate of fried cheese. What's left?"

"How about dessert?"

"This place has dessert?" I gesture to the rough-hewn tabletops, cracking pleather, and mounted animal heads.

"Tied with one other place for the best in town." He winks and to my disappointment, lets go of my hand, calling out to the same pretty brunette server who checked on me earlier tonight. "Hey, Clairy, can we get a Sweetheat à la mode?"

"I guess. It'll cost you, though!" the server, Clairy, chirps.

Bond groans, "Name your price."

"I'll have to think on it and get back to you." Clairy squeezes his shoulder before disappearing into the kitchen. *Hmm, nope, don't like that.*

I swallow down the wisps of jealousy blossoming in my chest because, obviously, I'm suffering from some sort of post-stress reaction making my emotions go haywire. Jealousy over a man I just met? Not today, Satan.

I nibble on my bottom lip. "She seems nice."

"Yeah, Clairy is great."

Before I can dive off the overthinking cliff deep into all the subtext of his words, Clairy is at our table, placing a skillet heaped with pie and ice cream in front of us.

"This is our best-selling pie, the Sweetheat. A mix of apple and Hatch green chile filling, topped with candied walnut streusel and freshly made ice cream. These are a Trail Creek specialty. Auntie B has been showing me—"

Bond clears his throat and looks pointedly at Clairy.

"Oh, gosh, listen to me yakking away when I've got tables to bus. You two enjoy!" She gives me a friendly wave and shoots Bond a knowing smile.

"Thanks, Clairy." Bond turns his attention to me, that sinfully sexy grin on display. He dips his spoon into the decadent dessert and offers it to me. "Dive in, Peach. Trust me, you've never had a pie like this one."

For a moment, I think he's going to feed me, and I'm torn between my desire to be a strong independent woman and wanting this sexy as hell man to spoon-feed me pie.

He gestures to the spoon, raising a dark eyebrow at me. "The spoon won't bite."

I roll my eyes and take the loaded spoon from him. Flavors like I've never experienced burst on my tastebuds. Tart, fresh apple, sticky sweet nuts, rich, creamy vanilla, and behind it, delicious slow-building heat. A moan slips from my lips, and my eyes close.

When I recover from my mini foodgasm, Bond is staring at me, his irises navy. I duck my head and cover my mouth. "Sorry."

"Don't apologize for that delicious noise or for enjoying yourself when you're with me." The timbre of his husky voice crawls up my spine, leaving a path of tremors in its wake.

I nod wordlessly. This bossy side works for me.

"Do you want more?"

He's talking about pie, but damn, if my brain doesn't jump to other types of more he might be offering. I manage to get one garbled word out that might be yes and might be please. Yease? If the universe opens a sinkhole beneath me at this exact moment, I won't even be mad about it. Yease.

He gestures toward the skillet before swallowing down a mouthful of pie. "What brings you to Trail Creek?"

I tense at his question, trying to figure out how much I want to tell him. *"My dad bought a business and sent me here under the guise of work, but truthfully, he wants me gone because he's ashamed of me. Oh, and my ex is suing the family company for workplace misconduct."* Seems more like a third date kind of answer.

Sensing my hesitation, Bond nudges some of the remaining crispy, flakey pie toward me. Apparently, he's noticed how much I'm enjoying it. "You don't have to tell me."

"What if we keep it light instead of unpacking what brought me here? Save the bigger stuff for another time. We did just meet, after all."

His beaming smile lights up his entire face. "Oh, you've deemed me worthy of more time?"

"That's what you took from what I said? Your selective listening powers are superb."

"I majored in selective listening," he deadpans before rubbing his hands together. "I have to know. Was it the pie?"

"Partly the pie, partly you." I can't resist playing along with him.

"What ratio? Did I win out over dessert?"

"Sorry, sixty/forty pie."

"Damn, bested by a pastry!" He laughs, and I join him. I haven't enjoyed myself this much in months. Maybe ever, if I'm being honest.

"So what do you say? Save the heavier topics for later? Keep tonight light?"

He smirks. "Yease, that sounds great."

I hide my face before breaking into a fit of giggles. Damn pink drink. "I was hoping you didn't hear that."

"It's adorable. I like that I fluster you."

Without my brain's okay, I blurt out, "Are you single?"

Bond's eyes are serious and focused on mine. "I wouldn't be sitting here flirting with you if I wasn't."

"Is that what you're doing? I thought this was a wellness check and an apology pie."

He chuckles. "It's those things, too, but mostly it's me wanting to talk to a beautiful, intriguing woman who rolled into this bar and captured my attention." He studies me for a moment. "How about you?"

"I'm single." As soon as I answer, an infectious smile breaks out on Bond's face but fades when I say, "My last relationship, if you want to call it that, didn't end well, and I haven't dated anyone since."

He cocks his head. "How long ago was that, if you don't mind me asking?"

"Things ended between us seven months ago and got worse after. He was the last in a long line of bad decisions."

Bond laces our hands together. "Maybe our meeting is the first step in breaking your streak of bad luck."

My voice is breathy. "You don't even know me."

"Yet. I don't know you yet. But I'd sure like to."

CHAPTER THREE

I settle against my side of the booth, holding my cocktail like a lifeline, and chug the remainder of the watered-down drink. My mind buzzes, and my stomach flutters at the potential in his words. "I'd like to know you too, Bond."

"I have to admit, meeting you tonight has been a highly unexpected but enjoyable surprise." He snags my hand, giving my knuckles a quick peck. His lips are soft against my skin, and that brief touch makes me wonder how they'd feel against my mouth.

"So, Peach, how did you end up in the Great Dane Bar and Grill?"

"The past few days have been...challenging, so when I saw this little hole in the wall I figured I'd grab a bite and a drink to take the edge off before going back to the Bates motel and crashing."

"Bates? The only motel in town is the Trail Creek Inn."

I groan. "I knew you were too good to be true. No one as handsome as you comes without serious flaws. Not a Hitchcock fan?"

Bond laughs and runs his free hand down his face. "You found me out. I hate horror movies. But even I've heard about *Psycho*—that just wasn't my brightest moment." A small smile turns up the corners of his lips. "I don't think Mr. Wester would appreciate the comparison you're making regarding his fine establishment."

He picks up his drink, and as he's taking a sip, I say, "Is Mr. Wester *The Hills Have Eyes* reject who works behind the front desk?"

"Shit," Bond coughs, choking on his whiskey. "Wasn't prepared for that."

A laugh bubbles out of me. "My bad." I spin my empty glass, giving him a chance to recover.

"Instead of talking about terrifying movies I've only seen due to peer pressure when I was young and impressionable, let's focus on the fact you've called me handsome twice now."

"You have to be aware of the effect you have on others. I mean, look at you." I gesture at his physique. "Tall, well-built, dark hair, and blue eyes? You're single lady catnip."

His laugh might be my new favorite sound. "You're too good for my ego. Keep it up, and I won't be able to let you go."

"Maybe that's what I'm aiming for." I'm trying for a playful retort, but instead, it comes out all breathy.

The idea of Bond being unable to let me go stirs up those damn butterflies again. They're practically rabid at this point. But it also quiets some of the pain from how easily my family brushed me aside.

Bond's eyes fix on mine. "Can I buy you a drink?"

I swallow. I want to take this chance. To find out if this connection is real or just a by-product of alcohol, stress, and sadness. "I'll take one more of whatever this was." I hold out my empty glass, and Bond's upper lip curls.

"Those Flocked Up Flamingos are dangerous. They taste like fruit but pack a wallop."

"Is that what it's called?"

"Didn't you order that one?"

"I asked the bartender to make me something that tasted good, and he brought me this. It's an absurdly cute name for a drink in a bar with a bighorn sheep head on the wall."

"The Great Dane is one of two bars in town, so the clientele, decor, and menu are eclectic." Hopping up from the booth, he grins at me. "Don't pick up any more knob goblins while I'm gone."

"I'll try my best, but no promises." I press my lips together, hiding my smile as I watch him walk away. Crap. I like him. He's nice and funny and so frigging handsome. Somehow, of their own accord, my eyes drift over and latch onto Bond's ass. He fills out those jeans like a champ.

Bond glances over his shoulder and catches me staring. I freeze, busted. He smirks and winks before turning to the bartender. As the two chat, Bond shifts forward until he's leaning over the bar and subtly shakes his hips back and forth, occasionally checking to see if I'm still staring.

I am.

A few minutes later, he returns, drinks in hand. "You see something at the bar you like?" he teases as he slides into the booth.

My cheeks flush as I sit up. "You know I did. Muriel and I shared a moment." I gesture toward the sheep and blow it a kiss.

"Muriel?"

I bite my lip and glance at the table before asking, "Have you ever played Two Truths and a Lie?"

Bond gives me a sly smile as he rests his elbows on the table. "You want to play a game?"

"Yease." Why do I keep saying that? It isn't even a word.

"Yease, indeed. Ladies first?"

"No, you go." I sputter around my drink. I can't think of a time I've been this flustered by someone I just met.

"I'm thirty-six years old, I wanted to be a fireman, and my family moved every two or three years when I was growing up."

"I thought for sure you were over forty." I deadpan.

"Ha ha, funny girl. Is that your guess?"

I examine him for a minute. He's so large I can very easily imagine him as a fireman—a big, sexy, axe-carrying fireman with a huge...hose. My lips quirk in a half smile.

"You still with me? You've got a glazed look and a little drool right here."

When Bond reaches for me, I playfully swat his hand away. "Sorry, I was thinking about my answer."

"Sure you were."

Okay, fine, I was thinking of you wearing nothing but a fireman's hat and a pair of those suspenders attached to a tiny pair of black briefs. Obviously, I can't say that out loud, so I go with the mature response and stick my tongue out at him. "You've got hometown boy written all over you, so the lie is that your family moved a lot."

"Winner winner, chicken dinner. Trail Creek born and raised."

"So, are you a fireman?"

"Sorry to disappoint you, but I'm not. I work for my family business."

"Do you enjoy it?"

A dark shadow passes over Bond's face. "I want nothing more than to keep my family business going for years to come."

Before I can ask him what he means, the flicker of anger is gone, and he's back to his smiling self.

"Working with family can be challenging, but I wouldn't trade it for anything. But that's enough about me. It's your turn. Let's see how good your poker face is." Bond sips his whiskey, and I follow his lead with my Flamingo.

Bright, tropical flavors coat my tongue, and I shimmy in my seat as the alcohol streams through my system. "Mmm, yummy."

"Be careful with it, Peach. Those Flamingos are popular for a reason. I swear they pour half the bar into that blasphemy."

"They do a good job hiding it." I pointedly stare at him as I take another long pull from my cocktail.

"I think you have a touch of brat in you." The way he says *brat*, as a term of endearment with laughter in his voice, warms me.

"I prefer to think of it as precociously impish. Okay, my turn. The 4th of July is totally overrated, I'm a natural redhead, and I hate gum."

He reaches out and tugs on a strand of my hair. "As pretty as this is, it's not natural."

"Sir, how dare you besmirch my natural redhead standing!" I gasp in faux outrage. "What gave it away?"

"It might be the brown eyebrows or that your hair is like a desert sunset. All these shades mixing together. It's beautiful." Bond shakes his head. "What do you have against the 4th of July?"

I hold my hand up and count. "Bugs, hot, loud, people."

"You make excellent points."

"Exactly. You go again."

Rubbing his hands together, he says, "Alright, let's see if you can figure this one out. I'm an only child, I hate my mom's brussel sprouts, and I put gum in Tracy Sinclair's hair when we were eleven."

"The last one better be the lie!"

This time, Bond's laugh is so loud a few of the bar patrons turn to stare at our table.

"Sorry, wrong. I have two sisters, one older, one younger. Listen, Tracy Sinclair and I had the same homeroom every year. From Kindergarten on. She was the meanest person I'd ever met. Used to steal my snacks, pinch me under the desk, and tell the teachers I was copying off her papers. Which I wasn't. Anyway, when I saw her in my homeroom, again, sitting in front of me this time, I couldn't pass up the opportunity for revenge."

"What happened?"

"I stuck six pieces of bubble gum in my mouth and chewed them into a sticky mess. When the bell rang for dismissal, I stood next to her desk, pretending to talk to her, while I smashed that gum into the back of her head. She ended up having to cut her hair off to her chin."

"You have officially reaffirmed my hatred of gum."

He smiles, totally unrepentant. "If it makes you feel any better, the principal called my mom before I made it home. She more than held me accountable for my actions. And Tracy Sinclair never pinched me again."

"No, I imagine she didn't!"

"It was worth losing every privilege I had and doing extra chores for three months. Also, turned out she was pretty cute with a bob. She never did grow it out."

I'm laughing now, my breath hitching. "Remind me not to get on your bad side, Baseball Cap."

Bond tugs my hair again. "Now tell me your truths."

"I graduated high school at sixteen. *I'm* an only child, and I make the best mug eggs you've ever tasted."

"Graduating at sixteen?"

"Nope, that one is true. I have a twin brother. For seven glorious minutes I was the favorite. Then the golden boy came along." My laugh is bitter. I don't add that even though I've worked my entire life to make them proud, trying my best to please them, graduating early, earning my Master's by twenty-one, going to work for the family despite what I wanted, I've never been enough to make my parents proud. The Duncan situation is one in a line of many disappointments for them.

Bond looks at me thoughtfully, seeing too much. Thankfully, giving me an out, he flags down Clairy from where she's clearing off a nearby table. "Hey, Clairy Fairy, c'mere a sec."

Clairy Fairy. Well, that's an adorable nickname. I can't help but check her out as she makes her way to our booth. She's tall, five-eight, maybe, with beautiful brown curls that fall to her mid-back. Her left arm is covered in realistic black and gray artwork, starting at her wrist and disappearing beneath her short sleeve. When she smiles, I wonder if the entire town is sponsored by the American Dental Association.

"What's up, Bond?" She rests her hip against his side of the table.

"Can we get two glasses of water, please?" He gives her one of my grins. Whoa. Not my grins. His grins. He can give them to anyone he wants.

"You've got it," Clairy says before heading to the bar.

Those same tendrils of jealousy from earlier, when she touched his shoulder with the confidence of someone who knows him well, thicken and wind around my heart. I said not today, Satan. Why doesn't he ever listen?

I don't have any cause to be jealous. Bond told me he's single, but I've learned the hard way people lie. They tell you they're single when they aren't. That they love you, but really you're just a means to an end. Or that family means everything before sending you away without a second thought.

Taking the coward's way out, I fake a yawn and stretch. "I'm going to get out of here."

Bond scans my face. "Is everything okay?"

"It was nice to meet you, Bond, but it's been a long day, and I'm ready to head to my motel." While my voice is still friendly, it's clear from the shift in his posture he isn't buying my lies.

"Hey, what's going on?" His eyes, sharp and clear, pierce my barriers and expose my fears to the light.

"Does Clairy Fairy mind you flirting with me over pie?"

Did I say that out loud? I glare at my Flamingo—stupid delicious drink making me say exactly what I'm thinking.

"What are you tal—"

Bond is cut off by Clairy arriving at the table with the water. "Can I get you guys anything else before we close the kitchen?"

"Just my tab," I mumble.

"Okay, I can do that." Looking up, I see Clairy watching me with concern. That she cares about what's happening here between Bond and me cuts those ribbons of jealousy into tatters. Clairy has been nothing but nice to me, and even if they do have a shared past, it's none of my business.

And while it's true I don't know much about Bond, I want to believe he's a good man.

Taking a deep breath, I ask, "Bond, how do you and Clairy know—"

"Clairy, put her tab on mine, please."

"Sure thing, Bond. No problem."

To her, I say, "You don't need to do that." Then I turn to Bond. "I can pay my bill."

"I offered to pay your tab earlier tonight, and I'm the kind of man who keeps his word. I'm also a firm believer in paying for my dates."

"This isn't a date."

Bond doesn't reply; he looks at Clairy, some unspoken conversation happening between them, and she smiles. "I'll leave you two alone to work this out."

He studies me for a minute, a slight frown on his full lips. "We need to clear up a couple of things. Talking is important. We're both adults. We can handle it, and I mean that regardless of whether you and I are acquaintances, friends, or something more." His voice drops when he says that last bit, and now the idea of something more burrows into my brain. I want that.

Bond places a water in my hands. "Drink." When I don't immediately pick up the glass, he nudges my leg beneath the table. "Come on, Peach, hydrate. You need to be able to make informed decisions when you leave here tonight, and that monstrosity," he gestures to the Flamingo, "is clouding your thinking."

I huff but drink the water because he's not wrong. Mid-sip, Bond says, "Clairy is my sister."

Sputtering, I spit water all over him. "Your sister?" The realization I covered Bond in my backwash hits me, and I consider climbing under the table in an attempt to disappear. *Dear universe, it's me, Tuesday, I ordered one sinkhole. Could we expedite the shipping on that, please?*

"Oh, crap, Bond, I'm sorry!"

Bond laughs as he wipes off his face. "It's okay—refreshing, actually. And yeah, she's my little sister. She works here part-time. I try to stop in a couple of nights, make sure no one messes with her. My older sister, Charli, works with me."

Sighing, I cover my face and mutter about handsome men who are friendly and funny and watch out for their sisters.

Where has he been my whole life? Oh, that's right, Trail Creek, New Mexico.

Bond smirks, probably mentally adding to his *Tuesday called me handsome* tally. He rises from his side of the booth when I stand, but I hold up my hand. "I'm not leaving, but I need to use the restroom."

He reaches out, pulling me toward where he's sitting. "Bathrooms are around the bar to the left." Then he places a chaste kiss to the tip of my nose.

I stand there, stomach swirling, pulse racing, feet glued to the floor all over a nose kiss. Good gravy, what would happen if he kissed me for real? I'd probably combust.

"Go on. I'll be here when you get back."

Finding the bathroom is no problem, but walking in a straight line is. Those damn Flamingos are making the room spin. Or maybe it's all the time with Bond. Hard to say.

As I'm drying my hands, Clairy bumps open the door.

"Hey there!"

As soon as she speaks, the connection between my brain and mouth severs, and I word vomit all over Bond's sister.

"The last guy I dated did a real number on me. I got in my head because you're beautiful, and Bond called you by that super cute nickname. And for a moment, I thought maybe the two of you...Which is silly. Right?"

Clairy's eyes are wide, her mouth open, listening to me babble.

"I don't have any say over who he talks to or anything. Not that I would want to. He's his own person. I mean, obviously. Man, he's right about those pink drinks being sneaky strong. He told me you're his sister, and I spit my drink on him. Who does that? I just moved to town, and I haven't met anyone except Bond and sort of you and that asshole Jacob Ashford, and I'm starting over all alone, and—"

"Whoa there! Take a breath."

I suck in a lungful of air, and on the exhale, my shoulders sag. "Please don't tell Bond about my verbal diarrhea. Shit, I just said diarrhea. And shit. I'm so sorry." I bury my face in my hands. My words are muffled when I say, "I'm Tuesday, and I swear, I'm not usually so...whatever this was. I blame the Flamingos."

Clairy covers her mouth with her fingers, trying her best to stifle her laugh. "Your secret is safe with me, Tuesday. This will probably sound weird, but I've been watching you and Bond. My brother is a good guy. He's not playing a game with you, I promise."

As we step out, I catch Bond taking two steps towards the restroom before turning towards the table, then repeating his actions as if he can't decide whether to come get me or wait at our booth.

"Clairy, thanks for letting me unload all that on you. It was really nice to meet you. I hope I'll see you again."

A bright smile beams on her face. "You too. I'm looking forward to it. And, Tuesday, he loves big, just so you know."

I rest my hand over my heart. Perhaps the universe is telling me that a man like Bond is what I need. Between Duncan and my family, I could use someone who loves big.

Making my way back to the table, I'm greeted by the warmth of Bond's smile. He gestures for me to join him on his side of the booth, and I hesitate for a minute.

Oh, who am I kidding? I slide in right next to him.

His sizable body takes up more than his share of the seat, and he emits heat like a living furnace. He smells so damn good; I duck my head and take a subtle inhale.

He stifles a chuckle. Crap. Maybe not so subtle after all. His thick thigh presses against mine, and even though we're both in jeans, I swear a jolt of electricity sparks where we touch.

Bond wraps one arm around my shoulder and twirls a lock of my hair around his finger. "You and Clairy have a good talk?"

"You could say that."

We sit in comfortable silence for a minute. I get lost in the weight of Bond's arm around me. The closeness between us makes me even more aware of our size difference. He's so broad and thick, like a yummy old-fashioned strong man. Though I'm short, I'm no fragile waif, but next to Bond, I'm positively tiny, and I'm here for it. Size kink activated.

"Size kink, huh?"

What is wrong with me tonight? I freeze, the water halfway to my lips. What do I do? Pretend I didn't say that out loud? Or better yet, pretend I don't exist?

A gentle touch under my chin guides me to meet his gaze. "Hey, put those pretty eyes on me. I have a favor to ask."

"Okay."

"If you start to feel some kind of way: jealous, upset, hurt, angry, horny," he shoots me a charming grin, "talk to me about it."

I nod, resembling a bobblehead in my agreement.

After a moment, he says, "I want nothing more than to kiss you. Tell me you want that."

"Bond." My voice is raspy and wanton.

At my one-word plea, his hand caresses my jaw, and I sink into his touch. He anchors me to his body as if he's afraid I'll drift away. The solid warmth he radiates seeps into my being, thawing my resistance, melting away any reasons I have to say no to this, to him.

"Need your consent, Peach. Have to hear it."

"Yes, I want you to kiss me."

He tangles his fingers in my hair, positioning my head where he wants. Myriad sensations compete for my attention. The slight tickle from the stubble on his jaw against my skin.

The sweet sting of the nip to my bottom lip. The prickle of smoke and honey from his whiskey on my tongue. Desire ignites in me, and my prediction that a kiss from this man would set me alight is confirmed.

Bond breaks the kiss, my lips chasing his for one more taste. His brilliant blue eyes scan my face. I'm not sure what he sees, but he sighs and presses a chaste kiss to my jaw before shifting us and brushing his lips against my forehead.

The warmth of his breath fans over my skin when he says, "How about you keep sipping the water and finally tell me your name? The suspense is killing me."

CHAPTER FOUR

Peach shifts, rubbing her thighs together and straightening her pretty sweater. Her skin flushes pink, and her eyes darken to the color of rich whiskey. I want to drink them down.

As she takes a sip of water, she says, "Tuesday."

Guess we're still playing games. Kind of thought after that kiss we were moving past them, but I'll play as long as she wants. Forever if that's what it takes. "Saturday."

"What?"

"What? You said Tuesday. I thought you were avoiding my question and sharing your favorite day of the week. Mine's Saturday." I'm sitting in my best friend's bar, two drinks in with the most intriguing woman I've ever met, and I still don't know her name.

"So typical. Everyone picks Saturday as their favorite day. Overrated. But actually, I was telling you my name."

My eyes trace the curve of her lips. There's no reason for her to lie, but..."Tuesday? Really? That's an interesting name."

"You're one to talk, 007."

"007. Clever. Never heard that one."

"Sarcasm noted, but my point stands. I haven't met many Bonds in my life."

"Probably as many Tuesdays as I've met."

"Probably." She holds up her water. "Here's to parents who pick crappy names and those who suffer for their uniqueness."

"Cheers to that."

Once she finishes her water, I check my watch. "Can I walk you to the motel?"

"You don't have to do that."

"I won't be able to live with myself if I don't make sure you get there safely."

"And how do I know I'm safe with you?" she asks.

"I guess you have to decide for yourself if I'm worth the risk."

The double meaning of my words isn't lost on her. Her pupils dilate, and all I can think is please say yes. Or yease. Both to the walk and the risk.

"I'd love it if you walked me home."

Standing, I grab my baseball cap off the table and slide it backward onto my head. Her eyes flit from my biceps to the hat and back; those little reactions are addictive. I settle my hand on her lower back and guide her toward the bar.

"Hey, Mendoza, I already told Clairy, but her tab's on me tonight." I jerk my chin in Tuesday's direction.

Dane nods. "Sure thing, man."

As soon as we step out of the bar and into the rapidly cooling night air, Tuesday says, "You didn't need to get my tab. I told you I could pay for it myself."

"And I told you, I pay when I'm on a date." She's so cute and stubborn, with just enough adorable brattiness to keep me on my toes.

She lets out an exasperated sigh. "It wasn't a date."

I lace our fingers together, marveling at the soft texture of her hand as we stroll down the dimly lit road toward her motel. "Wasn't it, though? We shared food. We talked and kissed. And now I'm walking you home. Sounds like a pretty solid date to me."

"I...well...I guess it was kind of a date, but I still should have paid my tab," she grumbles as she rubs her arms, picking up her pace.

"You cold?"

"Um, a little. It's probably still sixty degrees in Texas. I wasn't expecting it to be in the forties."

"Yeah, the altitude here makes a difference, especially once the sun goes down. Here, scoot closer. I'll keep you warm while we walk." I pull her into my side, snuggling her tight. It's no hardship to share a bit of my body heat. She fits perfectly against me even if I'm close to a foot taller.

"So you already know I don't do scary movies. Tell me a secret, Tuesday. A tiny one." I hold my thumb and index finger a sliver apart and make my best puppy dog eyes at her. I'm desperate for anything she'll tell me, dying to know everything I can. I want all her secrets, the good, the bad, the weird.

"I'm scared of the dark."

Wasn't expecting that. I stop walking and look at her. "Really?"

"Yeah, don't sound so surprised, *mister-I-don't-do-scary-movies*. Movies are fake; things that go bump in the night are real. Fear of the dark is a primal trait. Plus, it's creepy. I mean, look around us right now. We are in classic serial killer territory. Very few street lights, minimal traffic, tree-lined narrow roadways. We're asking to end up on someone's small-town murder podcast."

My laughter breaks the silence of the night. At her little huff, I say, "Movies may be fake, but I don't see the fun in paying someone to scare me."

"So, no haunted houses either?"

"No." I shudder.

Tuesday's face lights up with laughter, her brown eyes dancing with mirth. "Who'd have thought my great big Baseball Cap would be such a chicken?"

I don't tease her about calling me hers because she's well on her way to being right. A gentle breeze could tip me into the *property of Tuesday* camp at this point. From the moment she put Ashford into place like some kind of curvy, smart-mouthed angel, she intrigued me. After spending the evening with her, intrigue has grown to something more. Am I a damned fool for thinking this after only one night in her presence? Yep. Does it change things? Nope.

I shrug, pulling her closer. "I'd rather spend my cash on more enjoyable things. I wonder if I can convince you to like the dark. It lets us see the stars and has a certain serene stillness."

I tuck a loose strand of hair behind her ear. "It also lets me do things like this without prying eyes." I brush my lips against hers, nothing but a hint of a kiss so brief it should hardly count. But that simple promise of more is all it takes. I'm fucking hooked.

"Do that again," she whispers.

I place a feather-light kiss to one corner of her mouth, then the other. The sublime sound she makes breaks my resolve. I capture her lips, kissing her with every bit of the need pounding in my veins. Deep-seated yearning like I've never experienced shreds my control. I part my lips, sweeping my tongue along the seam of her mouth, begging without words for more. She responds beautifully, a tiny whimper slipping from her throat as I take advantage of her opening to me.

The sweet taste of her mixed with the sugary Flamingo washes over my tongue, and the heady combination gives me an instant buzz. My hands grip her hips, anchoring her to me, while hers stretch out to tangle in the hair at my nape. I bend my body over hers, enveloping her as much as I can, and kiss her for all I'm worth in the middle of the poorly lit street.

My lips blaze down her jaw to her neck, teeth nip and graze, and I fight the urge to leave my mark on her skin. Her scent floods my senses. Honey and citrus, and something that reminds me of a spring meadow.

"B-bond," she stutters, her voice raspy.

A soft growl rumbles in my chest at the sound of my name on her delicious lips.

"We're in the middle of the street."

I rest my forehead against hers. My chest rises and falls in rapid tandem with Tuesday's. My back aches and my knees scream, but I don't want to break contact with her petite frame. The minor discomfort is worth it to hold her like this. Somewhere in the distance, a car door slams, bringing me back to reality.

"I never expected to meet a wonderful mess like you, Tuesday."

"A mess!" She jerks back, but I don't let her go. Instead, I grab her hand and place it over my heart.

"A wonderful mess. Focus on the wonderful. I am."

Can she feel my heart thundering in my chest? I want nothing more than to kiss her again. The way she deserves. To see her irises eaten up by her midnight pupils as desire floods her system, doping her brain with endorphins. I wonder if she likes being called a good girl. I file that away for later. Tonight is too early to ask how she feels about dirty talk and praise. But I hope I get the opportunity to find out.

With a deep breath, I take off my hat and run my hands through my hair. "Let's get you home."

Our walk finishes in quiet comfort, arms wound around

each other. "This one is me." She gestures to number 124, a bland, bleak, brown square amongst all the identically sad rooms.

I hold out my hand. "Give me your phone."

Tuesday reaches into her pocket and flinches at the immediate influx of notifications on the screen after she powers it on. She taps away, clearing the messages. She's not ready to share, and I won't push her. I enter my number and send myself a quick text before handing it back.

"Good night, Peach." I hug her, inhaling her honey, clover, and citrus smell. I drop gentle kisses on her forehead, eyelids, cheeks, and mouth. It takes every ounce of my willpower to stop from taking the kiss further. All I want to do is fasten her to my body and taste her lips for hours. Every cell in my body thrums with a message as old as time: mine. Mine to please and pleasure. But I overpower my hindbrain and remind myself—and my cock—it's too soon for more. We need an actual date under our belts before we take them off.

After pressing a few more tender kisses to her lips, I step back and lean against the doorframe. "I'm waiting right here until you bolt the door. Wouldn't want to make it easy for the murderers. Or the podcasters."

She shoots me a smirk. "You're going to be so embarrassed if I get chopped up and sold to cannibals for their winter chili stores."

"That's oddly specific." I cock my head. Such a funny woman. I soften my voice and gently push her towards the door. "Go on, Tuesday."

Digging the antiquated key and its plastic tag out of her pocket, she opens the door and steps over the threshold into the dark room. I wait, watching as she flips on the lights. The warm glow illuminates the room's many shortcomings. Between the cracked walls, the scuffed and stained floors, and the threadbare bedding, the Trail Creek Inn could certainly use an update. Maybe I should send in an unsolicited bid.

While I trust Mr. Wester, the motel owner and manager, implicitly despite his—according to Tuesday—horror-show-worthy looks, I also know bad shit happens, even in tiny towns. And I won't be able to sleep if I leave before she's tucked in safely for the night.

She does a quick pass-through, checking the restroom and closet. Once she's done, she returns to the door and places one last kiss against my cheek. It's so fucking cute when she stands on her tiptoes to reach.

"Hey, Bond?"

"Yeah, Peach?"

"Tell me something true."

It's the same thing she said in the bar the first time I told her to trust me. Swallowing, I step forward, stealing one last kiss to tide me over. With my lips still pressed against hers, I murmur, "I came to the bar tonight mad at the world, but the moment I saw you, all other thoughts flew from my mind. You captivated me from the minute you walked in the door."

"How am I supposed to close this door when you say things like that? I'm sober, I swear. Want me to say my alphabet backward?"

I laugh and hug her. "I owe you a proper date before anything else happens between us. You deserve to be wooed."

Tuesday mumbles into my chest, words that sound suspiciously like he's too good to be true. It's clear there are things in her past coloring her perspective, and I vow to do everything in my power to show her I'm a man of my word. She deserves the moon, and I'm going to be the one to lasso it down and gift it to her. Against the top of her head, I whisper, "Welcome to Trail Creek, Tuesday."

Stepping out of my grasp, she says, "Goodnight, Bond," then slowly closes the door, her eyes never leaving mine.

Loitering against the doorframe for a moment, I replay our kiss. The taste of her tongue, fruity and sweet, lingers in my mouth. She smells so good. I pull my shirt to my nose and catch another hit of her scent. In a handful of hours, I've been reduced to standing on the side of the road, sniffing my shirt in the dark to get a fix of my new addiction.

Setting a brisk pace, I head toward Dane's. Tonight didn't go the way I expected. I'd shown up at the Great Dane pissed as hell with a plan to drink and mope, maybe bitch to Dane about my father, the business, and the clusterfuck he created when he sold our family legacy out from under me. But then in walked my gorgeous Peach with her feisty, take-no-shit attitude, wit, and luscious curves. And the cherry on top? She handed Ashford his ass.

I rub my hand over my heart, the place hers rested after our kiss. I've never been one to rush into anything, never bought into the ideas of love at first sight, instant connections, or things like that—much less wanting a relationship with someone I just met—but damn if it doesn't feel right with her. While it isn't only her looks drawing me in, her mix of tiny and thick is enticing. Getting to touch her and seeing my rough hands on her soft, lush body is the kind of memory that sustains a man for life. Add in that she's funny, clever, a spit-fire, and, as I told her, a bit of a mess, and my interest level is off the charts.

I make my way to the bar, where Clairy is flipping chairs, and Dane is closing out the register.

"How's your girl?" Dane asks.

A smile draws my lips upwards. "She's not officially my girl yet, but if things go my way, she will be soon."

"I've never seen you like this."

I can't deny what he's saying, so I stay quiet.

After another beat, he says, "About you escorting Ashford out—"

"We were just two men having a friendly talk."

Dane grunts. "Yeah, talk. I'm sure that's what happened. Need ice for those knuckles?"

"I didn't hit him. I may have helped him out of the bar and into his vehicle with more enthusiasm than it strictly required, but he left without a mark."

"I'm just saying watch your back. She embarrassed him, and you did too. He won't let this shit go."

"I'm not worried. Jacob Ashford doesn't scare me."

"Yeah, but what about your girl?"

A small pang of concern tightens my stomach. Tuesday. Alone at the motel.

Jacob is a bully, a misogynistic jerk, and a grade-A asshole, but he's also a lot of hot air and talk. Even with all the shit he put Charli through, I never worried about her physical safety. But he was pretty handsy with Tuesday tonight.

I clear my throat. "I'm heading home for the night, Clairy Fairy. You good?"

At my sister's nod, I walk out to my truck, phone in hand and Tuesday's number on the screen.

She answers on the first ring.

Before she gets a hello out, I blurt, "Have dinner with me. Tomorrow night?"

"I'm sorry, is this Baseball Cap? The man I met at a bar tonight? Because all it says in my phone is 'Sexy' and I'm not sure who that is."

"Oof, I'm hurt, Baby Girl."

Her effervescent laugh bubbles over the line. "Baby Girl? I like it. And sorry, Sexy, I didn't mean to bruise your fragile male ego, but don't think I'm not changing it to your proper nickname."

"How about a compromise? Sexy Baseball Cap has a nice ring to it, don't you think?"

She laughs again, and it's like striking oil. Each one is another gush of black gold. "So, dinner?"

"I'd love to have dinner with you, Bond."

"You just made me a very happy man. I'll text you when I get home."

"My new friends and I'll be waiting in my luxurious accommodations with bated breath."

"New friends? I'm only a few minutes down the road."

"These friends came with the room." She switches to a video call, and I immediately accept.

It's only been ten minutes, but she's makeup-free, her rose gold hair piled into a bun. I can see a smattering of freckles over the bridge of her nose. Fuck me, she's gorgeous. Then the camera flips, and I get a 360-degree tour of her motel room.

"I named this one Bruce. He has that look about him." Centered in the frame is a dead spider. At least, I think it's dead. If not, it's doing an admirable job of staying still. "And here's his cousin, Ollie." This time, she shows me an obviously dead moth. Most of it has turned to dust.

"You are delightfully strange, Peach."

The camera flips back to her, and she grins at me and shrugs. "My family would say I'm just strange, no delightful involved. But new town, new me. Or rather, same me, but working on not caring about fitting into a mold. Anyway, I'm going to call it a night. Fingers crossed I don't end up with any more unexpected roommates overnight."

"Do me a favor?" The serious tone of my voice dims the light of her smile.

"Sure, Bond. What's up?"

"Don't open your door for anyone tonight."

I expect her to say thank you, or you've got it. What I get instead is her choking back laughter.

"Bond, do you think I'd open the door? I am all about that not-getting-murdered life. Trust me; I'm deadbolt, chain latch, chair in front of the door, night light on, ready for bed."

I can't help but laugh at her as she shows me the small wooden chair pushed up against her door. "Alright, glad to see you're so prepared. You, Bruce, and Ollie have a good night. Get some sleep. I'll see you tomorrow."

"Goodnight, Bond."

Content knowing I secured at least one more opportunity for time with Tuesday, I hang up with a goofy smile. I'm smitten, like some teenager mooning over his first crush. I don't even know Tuesday's last name, but if I have my way, it'll be Davis one day.

CHAPTER FIVE

The dull buzzing in my head wakes me from a fitful night's sleep. Wait, no, that's my phone. I know who it is—no point in answering it yet. There's still plenty of time to hear how much of a disappointment I am. So instead, I opt to stay wrapped in my blankets.

The sunlight filters through the sheer curtain and shines a gentle light on the ugly motel room. Sadly, it didn't magically turn into a five-star accommodation while I was dreaming. I stretch, hoping to work a few of the kinks out of my back. Sleeping on a bed that is more coil than mattress has me feeling older than my thirty-three years.

Staring at the cracked ceiling above me, last night replays in my mind like a highlight reel starring a very handsome man. I think of the beauty and warmth of his startling blue eyes when he checked on me, his cheeky grins and raucous laughter as we traded quips, the way his energy lifted me. And the kissing.

Oh, the kissing.

Sense memories rush over me, making my lips tingle. I lick

them, hoping for a taste of Bond. It took every ounce of willpower to stop myself from flinging the door open and chasing him down after he left for the night.

Bond's admission that meeting me turned his night around, the quiet vulnerability in his voice when he told me his truth, has cracks splintering in the walls around my heart and mind.

Usually, it takes me a while to warm up to a potential partner. In my past relationships, I always felt slightly disconnected, as if I had to hold a piece of myself back to fit into the mold they expected. But with Bond, I want to tell him all my secrets, to flay myself open and let him see the parts of me that have always been somehow too much but also never enough.

I imagine Bond in my bed, his dark hair ruffled and wild, his body curled around mine, whispering sweet and filthy words in my ear while he does all sorts of wonderfully wicked things. My tongue tracing his body, drinking my fill of his broad shoulders, licking the length of his spine until I get to that perfectly biteable ass and his tree trunk thighs.

Desire pulses in me, and I squeeze my thighs together in a hunt for friction. Some stress relief could do me good. I reach over to the small side table and jerk open the unwieldy drawer. Inside lays a velvety bag full of goodies. This bag may not have been the first thing I unpacked, but it was definitely in the top ten.

Hidden in the cocoon of my blankets, I dig through the bag and find what I'm looking for. I settle in and let my mind run wild. Bond kissing me, his surprisingly soft lips parting mine. My hands burying in his dark waves as he nips and teases his way down my body. Those same curls tickling my inner thighs while he tastes every sensitive part of me. Bond on top of me, his weight pressing me into the mattress as he slides his cock, hard and ready, into me.

I tease my nipples until they pebble and ache before skimming my fingers down to my hips and thighs. Slowly, I bend one knee and slip a single finger into my warmth. I keep it shallow for a few strokes before switching to my toy. Sliding the wider end of the C-shaped vibe inside me, I place the smaller, tapered tip next to my clit. I start with it on the lowest setting, nothing more than a flutter. My daydream continues with Bond pinning me to a wall, his rough, calloused hands running up and down my body, exploring every inch of me.

My breaths and the quiet hum of the vibrator break the silence of the room. Turning my vibe up to the next setting, I moan, my eyes squeezing shut. My free hand drifts to my chest, twisting and pulling on my hardened peaks. I wish my fingers were his. I'm so close, just a little more. Pleasure unfurls in me as I tap the tip against my clit, before pressing down and kicking it up to the final setting. Flashes of Bond sweaty, hungry, and panting above me, growling my name, eyes glazed over with need combine with the toe-curling pulses of the toy to send me over the edge, and I clench around the rumbly vibrator as I ride out the last moments of my climax.

As I lie there letting my muscles uncoil, a part of me—the mischievous part, the part Bond teasingly called out as being a brat—wants to snap a quick selfie of my flushed cheeks and relaxed smile and send it to him. See if he can guess what brought me to this point.

But it's too soon for that, and I learned the hard way that private pictures don't always stay that way.

With a final stretch, I crawl out of my sleeping bag and wash my hands and face. Muscles relaxed and mind at ease, I'm ready to face my phone. The only thing that might make this less painful is coffee. But alas, I have none. Which means I get the joy of facing the family uncaffeinated. This should go well.

The number of missed calls, voicemails, and text messages makes me want to throw my phone out the window. Who's idea was it to play ostrich last night? Oh, right. Me. I'm the problem.

Thanks a lot, past Tuesday.

I scroll through the texts, deleting the ones from Duncan. No need to read them. I don't have the emotional capacity to deal with taunts and ugly names today. Next, I thumb through the messages from War. Nothing there worth replying to that I can't address when I call him. Which, I guess, is what I'm going to do now.

Hitting dial on the video chat, I weave a trail from one side of the room to the other.

War doesn't bother greeting me when he picks up. "Tuesday, you didn't reply to me last night."

My brother is dressed impeccably in a custom suit and perfectly coordinated tie, not a hair out of place. I glance down at my slouchy sweatshirt and try to straighten it. "Hi to you too, War. I'm fine, thanks for asking. And if you recall, I replied that I arrived safely. What more did you want from me?"

My mother cuts in. "Are you seriously staying in that motel? I thought it was a joke until I saw the name on the account."

Crap. I wasn't prepared to face them all at once. I also didn't think about the family account when I used my card to check into the motel. I need to stash it away and move my funds out of the shared account ASAP. Note to self: find a bank, create an account, and transfer money.

"You knew your brother and father arranged everything, including booking you in a very nice hotel thirty-five miles out of town."

I grit my teeth. "And they knew I wanted to handle my accommodations."

"Tuesday, I don't understand why you have to be so stubborn. Your father and brother have gone out of their way—"

"Out of their way?"

"Yes, you just don't see it. They've taken on this new company, given you a job—a promotion, I might add—all while trying to settle this whole ugly mess. And you haven't said thank you once."

"Why on earth would I thank them?"

Mom sighs, "You always make things harder than they have to be. We could have avoided this entire situation if you… You don't realize how difficult this has been on us."

"Difficult on you? Are you kidding?" Not expecting an answer, I power through. "Was there a reason you called?"

"Since you didn't reply to any of the messages we sent, aside from a single tart response to your brother early last night, we were concerned."

I'll take Lies We Tell Ourselves for 800, Alex.

"Good news: I'm alive and well."

"I'd hardly say you look well. Please tell me you aren't going out looking like that." She gestures to my messy bun and makeup-free face.

"I was planning—"

She cuts me off, "Remember, you represent our family. What will people think?"

All I can do is sigh.

"Have you been to the office?" my father asks, his tone curt and sharp.

Hello to you, too, Dad. If he cared about me half as much as he did his business, I'd be the most adored daughter in Texas.

"No. I got into town late last night, checked into my motel, then went out for a drink."

"You went out? Did you meet anyone?" The mention of possible social interactions brings Mom back on the line.

"Nope. Turns out this town is full of ghosts, and I'm the only living person in it."

"Oh, Tuesday."

I grant myself a half smile. They grant me full frowns.

"I'm not going to the office until Monday. I didn't see the point of going in early."

"Why am I not surprised? You never apply yourself." There's a shuffle, and as Dad walks out of view, I hear him say, "I should have let her go."

Something in me snaps. I'm so tired of being the problem. Tired of trying my best for it to never be enough. Of letting a family—who cares more about their profit margin and public profile than their flesh and blood—dictate my life.

"You've done your due diligence. We should switch to weekly texts like most estranged families."

"We aren't estranged. That's so distasteful." My mother's perfectly made-up face twists.

In the sweetest voice I can muster, I ask, "Did you think forcing me out of state would bring us closer?"

The only answer is an exasperated huff. And there goes Mom. Just one more ball to sink, and I'll have cleared the table.

My brother's voice sounds over the line. "I get it. You're mad, Tuesday. But we are your family."

"You're right, War, we are family. I wish you'd kept that in mind before you determined I was worth less to you than the company. What I need right now is space and time. I will work with you and Dad in a professional capacity, and I will text you to let you know I'm okay. Outside of that, please don't contact me."

"Tues—"

"Goodbye, War."

I faceplant into my blanket nest. It seems Trail Creek Tuesday has some bite to her. I'm proud of myself for saying what needed to be said, but sarcasm is a sharp sword, and sometimes it cuts the wielder too.

My father's parting words about firing me echo in my mind. Would that even be a bad thing at this point? It's not like I need the job. I could live off the inheritance my grandparents left me, as could War. It's just never been an option before. After all, *"How would it look if my own children don't work for the business?"* I can't win. I'm a bad daughter if I don't work for him, but somehow, a worse one when I do.

I don't realize I'm cradling my phone to my chest until it vibrates against me. Tensing, I glance at the screen. If it's anyone who shares my last name, it isn't getting answered. It might get chucked across the room, though.

> SEXY BASEBALL CAP
>
> How are you? Bruce and Ollie keep you up all
> night?

Every ounce of built-up hurt, stress, and worry melts away.

Bond.

Bruce and Ollie were perfect, but I may burn this mattress when I leave.

> SEXY BASEBALL CAP
>
> Any plans today? Besides your date with a
> very handsome man?

> Who would that be? I thought you and I had
> plans?

> SEXY BASEBALL CAP
>
> Always with the hurtful words!

> I'm using the next few days to unpack basics
> and get to know the town.

After rereading that last text seven or eight more times, I scratch out a list. Number one on my agenda is to find a local bank. Once that is taken care of, I can explore the town.

I glance at myself in the mirror. My messy bun droops to one side, and my cheeks are red. Am I going out like this? Smiling, I grab my phone and keys. Hell, yes I am.

As I make my way downtown, I realize I've been hasty in my initial assessment of Trail Creek as a hellhole. Nestled in the mountains with the city's namesake creek winding around the far edge, it's charming. Beautiful really.

The air is crisp and clean, if a little thin for my scarcely above-sea-level blood, but I'll adapt. The street is quiet, with more people walking and riding bikes than driving. I reach the main square, a collection of shops, cafes, and other locally owned businesses all settled around a majestic courthouse with a gazebo on the lawn. Have I fallen into a Southwestern Stars Hollow? If so, I'm here for it.

A giant purple building catches my eye, and I can't contain my excitement when I realize it's a bookstore. That is totally going on my must-do list. The bank is easy to find, and the clerks are beyond helpful—small town charm in the flesh. With my banking problem sorted, I cross the street to The Bee and The Bean, an adorable coffee shop and bakery.

Inside the shop, I admire the cheery yellow trim and honeycomb accents. The rich aroma of freshly roasted coffee blends perfectly with buttery baked goods. And cue Tuesday drooling in three, two, one.

"Hello! Welcome to The Bee and the Bean. How can I help you?" a pretty teenager chirps from behind the case laden with mouthwatering treats.

"What do you recommend? I'm new in town, so I have no idea what's best, but I'm betting you do."

The teen's icy gray eyes light up. "Yes! You should get a sea-salt croissant and drizzle it with our house made honey. The honey makes all the difference."

"Sold. I will take one and a cup of pecan coffee, please." While the young girl works on putting together my order, I check out the shop. The interior work is stunning. Someone has put up intricate gingerbread trim, and the cabinets behind the display case are custom.

"Here you go." The teen waves after leaving me with my coffee, croissant, and a tiny, single-serving jar of honey.

I take a few more appreciative looks around; I may have worked in land and asset acquisition, but I still enjoy good design. It only takes one bite of my treat to realize I owe that sweet girl a debt of gratitude. This is exactly what I need.

On my walk back to my motel, my realtor texts. There's nothing like buying a house sight unseen. Once I found out the family plan to cut me out of the picture, I desperately searched for a move-in ready home I could act quickly on. I wasn't leaving my living arrangements up to my father. Putting my new address into my phone, I make my way to Piñon Hills, a new home development about fifteen minutes out of town, higher up in the mountains.

As soon as I drive up to the chalet-style home, comfort washes over me. Nestled amongst a mix of pine, spruce, and aspen trees, the house has all the charm of a classic ski lodge.

After walking the house with my realtor, I happily sign all the paperwork to make this place mine. Then, I revisit each room, losing myself in the intricate details. There's the hand-built double-sided stone fireplace that separates the living space from the kitchen. The stained wood plank ceiling with inset lighting and exposed beams. Windows. So many windows. I suspect the shine from the moonlight and stars through them will be enough to keep my fear of the dark at bay. My favorite room by far is the lofted suite with its own fireplace and attached bathroom, where a massive clawfoot tub sits against a wall of windows overlooking the mountains.

If it wasn't an impossibility, I'd say the person who built this house knows me. Knows I love delicate touches and unique fixtures. That I prefer charming and homey over sleek and modern. Much like the coffee shop downtown, someone has poured themselves into crafting this place.

This is a Davis Designs home. I wonder if they did the work on The Bee and The Bean too. If both are examples of their craftsmanship, Phillips Construction scored a deal by purchasing them. This is next-level quality.

At seven on the dot, there's a sharp rap at my motel door. Excitement and nerves flutter through me. I fling the door open, and Bond stands there, a big smile on his handsome face. He's in another tight-fitting Henley, this one a deep forest green. His jeans fit perfectly around his thick thighs, and work boots complete his comfortable look.

"No baseball cap tonight?"

"Had to step it up for our date. You ready?" he asks with a dashing grin before leaning in and kissing me.

I savor the gentle press of his lips and encourage him by teasing my tongue along his bottom lip. Breaking the kiss, I say, "Only all day."

Bond takes me by the hand and leads me to his waiting pickup. He opens the door for me and then reaches over to buckle me in.

"You know I can do that myself, right?"

"I enjoy doing things like this. Does it bother you?"

I consider his question. "It's not that I don't like it. It's that I'm not used to it. No one has ever taken care of me without an ulterior motive."

"If it bothers you, I'll stop." He nuzzles the side of my neck.

I don't want him to stop. It makes me feel special and important. "No, I'm not saying to stop." I turn my head so our faces are scant inches apart and flutter my lips over his. "I promise I'll tell you if I change my mind."

"Never doubted that for a minute."

Bond shuts my door and jogs around the front before hopping in on his side.

"So, where are we headed?"

"It's a surprise."

"Is this a good time to point out that I saw you sitting in your truck for twenty minutes waiting for seven o'clock to get here?"

He shifts so his hand rests on my thigh. "I might be a little excited about seeing you."

A burst of joy soars from my toes to my stomach to my heart before settling in my brain, overriding my anxieties that my feelings for him are coming on too fast.

"You could have knocked earlier." I tease, resting my hand

on his. I want that hand to stay on my leg, to keep drawing circles against the seam of my jeans.

"You could have come out to the car."

"Touché, Baseball Cap."

This earns me one of those glorious belly laughs, and I embrace the blissful surge of endorphins it gives me.

After a few minutes spent peppering each other with random facts about ourselves, we pull up to a tiny restaurant. "This is one of my favorite restaurants. When they ask red, green, or Christmas, the answer is always Christmas. Got it?"

"Yes? But why would—"

"Trust me on this one."

A server sits us at a small, intimate table for two, an L-shaped booth built into a corner of the outdoor patio. The entire space is covered in greenery and the soft glow of fairy lights. It's magical. I'm so caught up looking around, taking in the abundance of plants draping over the pergola, I almost miss Bond ordering drinks for us.

"Sorry, this place is really cool." I smile at him, torn between staring at him and continuing to look around the patio.

"Yeah, Ava's is the best. The inside is beautiful, but it's a nice night, so I thought we'd sit outside. They'll turn on the tower heaters if you get cold."

I spot the heaters, subtly placed to blend with the decor. "Everywhere in Trail Creek, except the Great Dane, and, sadly, my motel, is so lovely. Though...I guess I've only been to a handful of other places." Oh good, Awkward Tuesday has made an appearance. *Shoo AT, shoo!*

"Where did you visit today?" Bond asks as a server brings out chips and salsa, which happens to be one of my love languages.

In between chips, I tell him about the bank, the bookstore,

and exploring downtown. His eyes light up when I mention The Bee and The Bean.

"Did you like it?"

"Yes!" The shout is out of my mouth before I can reign it in. Why am I the way I am? Taking a sip to calm myself, I try again in a quieter voice. "I plan on making it my regular morning stop for pastry and coffee. The design work in that space is amazing."

Before Bond responds, the server is back to take our orders, and sure enough, he asks me red, green, or Christmas. I follow Bond's suggestion and go for Christmas. Why not?

"Any chance you'll tell me what I did to my cheese enchiladas?"

"Made them even better."

"By..." I wave my hand to encourage him.

He scoots closer to me in the booth, and the warmth of his arm and thigh pressing against mine is addictive. I fight the urge to curl into his touch and purr like a cat.

"Are you impatient, Tuesday? Do you like things right when you want them?"

"Who doesn't want things right away?" I ask, lifting my chin in an invitation. Bond raises a single eyebrow at me and smirks, and I whisper, "Distract me until the food arrives. Then I won't have to think about mystery toppings."

Bond's fingers play with the ends of my hair. His breath fans over the sensitive skin behind my ear, and a small sound falls from my lips. I freeze. Did I just whimper? Because that's embarrassing.

His quick inhalation confirms I did let out some sort of needy sound, but the look on his face doesn't embarrass me at all. In fact, it's making me tingly and warm. When his mouth is a hairsbreadth away from my ear, he murmurs, "Peach—"

"Enchiladas?"

With a sigh, Bond places one featherlight kiss on my neck, then turns to our server. "Those are hers."

A whoosh of air leaves my lungs, the coiling heat in my stomach and between my legs lingers, but I shift my attention to the massive platter of food: enchiladas drenched in red and green chile sauces. And now the Christmas question makes sense. I dig in, savoring the spicy, cheese-laden feast. Bond watches me, chuckling. When I finally surface for air, I shrug. "What? It's delicious."

"Just enjoying the view."

I point my fork at him. "Stop staring at me and eat."

"Can't blame me for wanting to look at the prettiest thing out here, can you?"

I snort-laugh and roll my eyes. "Tell me something random. Something I'd never guess about you."

"Something silly or something real?"

"Your choice."

A huge smile breaks out on his face. "I'm a secret Swiftie."

I blink, the words taking a second to register. "Are you serious? I am extremely attracted to you right now, Baseball Cap."

He tips his head back and laughs. "Shit, I should have shared that instead of my name when we first met."

My cheeks heat. How does he do that? Make me blush without even trying?

"But to answer your question, I am serious. I have my niece, Waverly, to thank for that. She's fifteen and has been all about Taylor since she was old enough to talk. Your turn."

I push my food around and debate with myself. Do I tell him more about Duncan or keep it light?

Sensing my hesitation, Bond pulls me closer until I'm practically sitting on his knee. "You can tell me anything or nothing. No pressure. Silly or real? Your choice. Always."

CHAPTER SIX

"Do you remember talking about questionable nicknames last night?" Tuesday asks, pink spreading across her cheeks and the tip of her nose.

As I nod, she continues. "My last ex called me TD, short for Tuesday, which was fine. Cute even."

My Peach merits a better nickname than TD, but that's in the past. Tuesday inhales, then lowers her eyes to the table. Whatever she's about to say isn't good.

"Over time, it evolved into Titties, and that became just Tits."

The wince that flits over her face raises my hackles. Who is this asshole?

"Also, when I say over time, I mean over a few weeks because that's about how long the relationship lasted. It's not like I'm opposed to the word. A well-timed tits during dirty talk is one thing but as a nickname? It made me incredibly uncomfortable, especially in front of friends and cowor... mutual acquaintances." Her nervous rambling trails off.

Doing my best to keep the anger off my face, I ask, "Did you tell him?"

"Yeah. Many times." She shrugs. "What can I say? I may have missed one or two thousand massive, screaming *look-at-me* red flags before things ended." Her attempt at levity falls flat, and I wish I could take away the pain and regret on her face.

"You don't deserve to be treated that way." My fingers slide along her thigh.

"How do I deserve to be treated, Bond?"

Like you're mine, like we have forever. "Like a fucking goddess." As soon as the words leave my lips, my mouth is on hers.

I want nothing more than to take her to her room and make her forget about her asshole ex calling her those shitty nicknames, to remake her with my touch and chase away the memories of everyone who came before me.

Is it too soon for these feelings? It doesn't matter. Call me a sap, but I know in my heart Tuesday and I are written in the stars.

I break the kiss and search her brown eyes. The heat in them is the answer I need. I throw down enough money to cover the bill and tip. "Let's get out of here."

"Hell, yease." She freezes for a moment, then smirks. "Whatever, I'm owning it." The way she scrambles out of the booth and grabs my hand tells me she's as excited about dinner ending early as I am.

The drive to her motel takes twice as long as it should, or maybe that's just the palpable tension in the air between us. Tuesday's eyes flit from my face to my shoulders, down my arms. One hand grips the steering wheel, the other rests on Tuesday's thigh, and I can't stop sliding it upward.

"Just a little bit higher."

I jerk my head to the side. Did she say...When I look at her, she's staring straight ahead, an ear-to-ear grin visible in her profile. This woman.

She wiggles, shifting my hand again. One more inch and I'll be able to feel the heat of her through her jeans. Finally, the motel comes into sight, and I race into a parking spot, my desire for the touch of her skin against mine riding me hard.

I cut the engine to the truck but don't get out. I pat the seat, encouraging her to slide across the bench. I want her next to me, more contact between us, for this conversation. Twisting so I can see her, I take her hands in mine. "Before this goes any further, we need to talk. I'm not saying it will be tonight; you're in control of that. If you want, we can go in there, sit and talk, and that's it. But, if you decide you want more, you're mine. No one else gets to taste you or touch you. Only me. If this thing between us is as good as I think it's going to be, I can't stand the idea of another man having you. I don't share. It's a big ask, but Peach, you make me want to be a greedy bastard."

"Does that go both ways? Because I've been burned before."

I hate that someone out there hurt her. Good thing she's in my life now. "It does." I kiss her knuckles, then graze my teeth against the thin skin. "If you're mine, then I'm yours."

Pulling her closer, I nuzzle my nose into the juncture of her shoulder and neck and kiss her racing pulse point. "How do you feel about me holding your tiny wrists in my hands, my body pinning yours to the bed? Or my arm across your hips, banding you to the mattress? Would you like it if I whisper all the things I want to do to you in your ear? Tell you how perfect you are while I bite along your skin or spank your ass pink? What if I rest my hand on your throat, letting the weight settle there?" At her gasp, I whisper against her skin, "Does any of that turn you on?"

She squeezes her thighs together and crawls into my lap, the two of us crammed between the seat and the steering wheel. Tuesday kisses me, her tongue coiling with mine. I pull back and, between kisses, say, "Answer me. Does that turn you on? Does it make you wet?"

"Yes. Yes, it turns me on."

"Such a good girl." Tuesday shivers in my arms. Seems my girl likes praise. "If we do this, you're mine. Yes or no. Do you want this? Want me?"

With a whine, she says, "Yes, Bond, I want you. I like the idea of you being bossy even if I don't make it easy for you."

"I knew you were a brat; bring it on, sweetheart." I brush my lips against her ear.

"But..."

"But what? This only works if we talk. Tell me."

"Don't be mean. No name calling."

"Shit, Baby Girl, does me calling you a brat hurt you? I'm so fucking sorry."

She cuts me off with a kiss. "No. I actually really like it when you call me that. It doesn't feel mean." I can see the pink high in her cheeks in the dim light of the truck. "It feels...special."

"I promise I won't degrade you. Ever. You'll get nothing but praise from me. Is there anything else you don't like?"

"I'm open to trying new things." She nibbles on her lip. "I love toys."

Hell yes. I'm all about that.

Clearing my throat, I bring up one of the more awkward but important parts of dating. "I'm STI-free. Tested last a few weeks ago."

"I'm negative too, and I have an IUD." That adorable blush spreads down her neck.

I need to get her out of this damn truck and into her room. "I don't know who or what brought you here, but I owe them my thanks. If things go my way, you'll never live another day without pleasure."

I hop out, Tuesday still bundled in my arms. I throw her over my shoulder, caveman style, and swat her ass when she squirms.

"Bond!" Her tickled voice brings a smile I can't fight to my lips.

All but sprinting up to her motel room door, I swing her off my shoulder and drop her on the stoop. "Get this door open, Peach."

She fumbles for her key, hindered in no small part by my roaming hands. My hips are pressed against the swell of her ass while I suck on that sensitive spot behind her ear.

When she pushes back against me, a whimper slipping from her lips, I can't help but growl, "Tuesday, if you don't get this door open, I'm going to take you right here where anyone can see."

Her visible tremble ticks my need for her up another notch. Can't wait to have her skin against mine.

"Hey, bitch! This is for being such a cold fish last night!"

We snap apart, startled by the angry voice, as a wall of water, saturated with chopped-up fish fins and tails, douses us.

A flash of Jacob fucking Ashford sprinting to his truck, followed by the squealing of tires pulling out of the parking lot, shakes me from my stupor. I should have beaten the shit out of him when I had the chance.

Grabbing Tuesday, I run my hands over her, checking that

she isn't hurt. "Are you okay? I swear I'm going to teach that asshole a lesson."

Tuesday stands still, her eyes wide and mouth open, little bits of fish caught in her hair and clinging to her sweater. For a minute, I worry she's in shock, but then she doubles over and shakes in a fit of laughter. "He threw fish at us! Who does that? And did he seriously have truck nuts on the back of his pickup?"

I stare at her until her infectious, snorting cackle takes over, and we're both laughing, covered in fish guts, and still, there's nowhere else I'd rather be. Once we've caught our breath and calmed down, I sweep away the biggest pieces of fish from her clothes, then do the same to myself.

"This isn't quite how I saw our date ending."

"No, even with a hundred guesses, I would never have expected this." Sighing, she cocks her head and looks at me thoughtfully. "Come inside. You can rinse off here and change clothes."

"It's okay, Peach. I can go home."

Tuesday nudges me with her shoulder. "You're really going to leave me alone after that? I'm not going to let that buttmunch ruin our evening. Let's rinse off, and we can talk some more. I can't vouch for the water pressure or how long it will stay hot. I haven't tried it out yet."

"Wait, does this mean you didn't shower before our date?" At her noise of indignation, I hold up my hands in defense. "I'm not judging! I don't mind a little funk."

"Oh my gosh, Bond, stop." She gives me a horrified look as we step into the motel room.

"What? If that honey-citrusy smell is your natural scent, I can only imagine how it would be after—"

She slaps her hand over my mouth and grimaces, dropping her palm and giving me an apologetic look for touching my face with her fish hand. "First, research shows that showering every other day, or even every few days, is better for your skin. Second, I did shower. At my new house. It has no furniture, but the water is on. Third, please don't say *funk* in relation to the way I smell again if you ever want a chance of getting up close and personal with my natural scent."

I can't help it; I crack up. Here I am at the Trail Creek Inn, covered in fish guts, with a woman I'm undeniably drawn to, telling her how I'd happily sniff—and taste—her even if she hasn't showered in days. I love how interesting my life has become since Tuesday.

Peach huffs and shoves me through the bathroom door. "Go on, rinse off. I'm going to wash my face and hands in the sink and get a plastic bag for these fishy clothes. When you're done, we can swap."

My eyes shift toward the crack in the door, and I catch a glimpse of Tuesday bending over, digging through her bags. Her sweater rides up, exposing the smooth expanse of her back. I can't look away. I trace the lines of her body. The way her waist nips in and her hips flare out, twin dimples visible above the top of her jeans.

I'd love nothing more than to dip my tongue into those dimples.

Snapping back to reality, I undress and step into the warm spray before realizing there's no soap or shampoo.

As if reading my mind, Tuesday's sweet voice trickles over the sounds of the falling water. "Bond, here's my shampoo and body wash. You'll smell like me, but it's all I have."

As if that's a hardship.

Her silhouette moves along the line of the shower curtain as she sets down a pile of toiletries. "I don't think I've ever had a date quite like this one."

She means the fish, but even without the reeking bits of

leftover bait and tackle, this is still the most memorable date I've ever been on. This woman is burrowing deeper under my skin every minute we spend together.

As I wash off, we chat through the door, but she catches me off guard when she asks, "Where do you think he got it?"

"Who got what?"

"Ashford. The fish. Where do you think he got them?"

"My guess? His family's restaurant, The Blue Hill."

"Oh, is he a chef?"

"No, he doesn't do jack. Old family money. The Ashfords own a handful of random businesses in town. His dad's been mayor my entire life, and that dipshit will end up following in his footsteps."

Clean enough, I snag a towel off the rack and tie it around my waist before stepping out. I don't see us recapturing our earlier heat, but it doesn't matter. She needs to shower, and I'm still debating whether I should hunt Jacob down and shove some fish eyeballs up his nose.

Tuesday sits in one of the chairs, her feet propped against the wall. When she catches sight of me, I can't help but smile. It's a damn fine feeling knowing the person you want craves you just as much. And that's what I see in Tuesday's eyes —craving.

Maybe I'm wrong about recapturing the heat.

Her gaze follows the rivulets of water as they drip down my chest. Unable to resist the chance to tease her, I say, "You have some clothes for me, Peach, or was this all a ploy to see me in a towel?"

Without missing a beat, she deadpans back at me. "Yep, I planned this whole thing. I asked Jacob to be a giant scuzzball and do a drive-by fishing on us." She holds out a threadbare t-shirt and a pair of men's sweatpants.

"Not to be ungrateful, but these don't belong to the ex, do they?"

"No! I didn't even...no. These belonged to my brother. I borrowed them from him years ago and never gave them back. I swear, not an ex."

I grin and take the offered clothing. "You shower, and I'll change."

Tuesday nibbles on her bottom lip. "You won't leave till I get out, right?" There's a thread of worry in her voice.

That won't do. "Wouldn't dream of it."

Ten minutes later, Tuesday is freshly showered, her damp hair loosely braided down her back. The mix of colors is even more obvious: the orange, pink, red, and blonde strands twist around each other. She's dressed in an oversized sweatshirt and a tiny pair of sleep shorts that leave only the best bits to my imagination. The shirt and sweats she gave me are too small and make it very clear how I'm feeling. Peach guides us both down to the nest of blankets on her bed and sneaks a thigh between mine, her head tucked under my chin. I hug her tight, something in me growing warm and content when she rests against me.

We lie together, our hands roaming, sneaking the occasional kiss from the other. Tuesday tells me about her first pet, a scraggly pup she found and brought home despite her parents' objections. I share about the first time I drove on my own and backed into the basketball goal in our driveway. I love the overwhelming normality of sharing these silly details of our lives.

My mind drifts to her ex and the names he called her despite knowing it hurt her. She's been vulnerable, sharing more of herself tonight. It's a special sort of privilege when someone trusts you with the pieces of their story.

"You shared a serious secret tonight, but I only shared a silly one."

She lifts her head, her eyes soft in the dimly lit room. "Bond, I shared the Duncan story because you make it easy to do. You don't owe me a big secret."

I make a noncommittal humming sound and graze my knuckles up and down the side of her neck from collarbone to ear. "What if I want to tell you one?"

Tuesday kisses my chest, right over my heart, before resting her cheek there. "Then I want to hear it."

"I'm divorced."

She tenses in my arms. "For how long?"

I pause before answering, inhaling her sweet smelling hair and walking my fingers along her back until she relaxes against me. Only then do I continue. "A long time, almost fourteen years."

"What happened? I...you don't have to answer that. It's none of my—"

Cutting her off with a tender kiss, I say, "I was young. We both were. Young and dumb. She was my high school girlfriend; we thought we knew everything at eighteen. But it was painfully clear by the time we were twenty-two, we knew nothing. That heat we had as teenagers faded, and as we grew up, we grew apart."

"What's her name?"

"Darcy. She lives in California with her husband; they have two kids together. Best thing either of us ever did was agree that we weren't the ones for each other."

"Di-did the two of you have kids?" She twists the strings on the waistband of her sleep shorts.

"No, no kids. Not even a dog."

When she doesn't say anything, I worry it's too much too soon, but then her lips graze against my jaw.

"Thank you for sharing that with me, Baseball Cap." She kisses higher until her soft lips are on mine. The kiss starts gently, her tongue runs along the seam of my mouth, but as we cling to each other, Tuesday climbing me to straddle my hips, it deepens and becomes hungry, wanting. Her hands pluck at my borrowed shirt, urging me to take it off. Giving in to her, I reach back, pull the thin white tee over my head, and savor Tuesday's noise of appreciation.

She tracks me like a cat stalking a bird, her eyes gliding over my chest, up and down my arms, toward the dark line of hair on my lower stomach. The cocky bastard who lives deep within me preens under her gaze.

I sweep her into a crushing kiss. "When you walked into Dane's, everything else disappeared. I kept my eyes on the bottom of my glass so I wouldn't make a fool of myself drooling over you."

Tuesday's nails scrape along my skin, her fingers skimming my chest. "Is that another truth for me?"

"You know it is." I take her hand and cover my heart, marveling again at how small she is in my arms. "Do you have one for me?"

"I never really wanted you to walk away, but it meant so much that you did. And it meant even more when you came back."

Primal desire rises within me, and I grip her hips and roll, repositioning us so her body is beneath mine. Once I thoroughly taste her mouth, exploring the contours of her lips with my tongue, I trail a path of kisses down the column of her neck. I nip at the center of her throat and lick along her collarbone, staking my claim on her skin.

"You remember what I said earlier?" I whisper the words into her neck, my lips never stopping their quest to taste each exquisite inch of her. "Do you want this?"

She nods, but that won't work. I need that yes from her. For her to say she wants this as badly as I do. "Words, sweetheart, words."

"Yes."

With her one-word whimper, I crush her mouth to mine, branding her from the inside out with my searing need. Pulling back, I drink her in—pink lips swollen, braid mussed, cheeks flushed—she's everything. "Tell me what you want."

"I want…"

My patience walks a razor-thin wire, but I need her words. "Say it, Tuesday. Do you want me to stop right now and hold you? Because I will. Or do you want me to make you come? Because I will, but only if you say what I need to hear."

She gasps as I run my tongue along the shell of her ear. "I w-want you to kiss me."

"Kiss you where?"

"Everywhere."

CHAPTER SEVEN

"Take this off." I tug on Tuesday's sweatshirt. I should stop there. Savor this moment. Slow things down and have some self-control. I only get one first glimpse of the majesty that is Tuesday's bare body.

But I don't.

"And then these." I slip a finger between the elastic waist of her sleep shorts and her stomach before snapping it against her skin.

Without question, she pulls her top over her head, then shimmies the tiny shorts down her shapely hips. Fuck me, no panties. Taking over when the pajama bottoms reach her knees, I glide the silky material over her calves and ankles. I note each place I touch that elicits a reaction.

My palms ghost the length of her smooth legs, over her rounded hips, and the dip of her waist. She feels so fucking good. Like she's mine. My fingers inch along her ribcage, moving closer and closer to her chest, navigating her supple curves. She is the most beautiful creature I've ever seen.

I sit and drink in her body, bare before me, a gift from the universe. She flushes, the pink spreading from her cheeks to her chest.

"You're staring."

"I am."

She wiggles and goes to cover herself, but I snag her arms and pin them above her head. I kiss a path from her sternum, hovering my lips over hers. "Don't hide from me. Don't hide what's mine."

Her arms relax in my hold, and I let them go. She's free to touch me, at least this time. My hands roam her body while my kisses reverse their prior path. When I reach the swell of her teardrop breasts, I thank the universe before locking my mouth onto one of her hardened peaks.

Tuesday arches into my mouth. Goosebumps erupt over her skin. My fingers mirror the actions of my tongue and teeth, pinching and twisting until she's whimpering for more, for less, for me. There's nothing more divine than my Peach panting my name between desperate breaths.

"B-Bond, please."

"So needy, aren't you?" I murmur as I let the abused pink tip pop from my mouth. "I'm not done with these beautiful tits yet. Such an abundance here, filling my hands." I bite down around her nipple, enough to make her moan.

I twist and pull while my teeth nip. I like finding that little lick of pain, the kind that curls up beside pleasure and coexists in harmony. Tuesday writhes beneath me until she cries out and tries pushing my head away.

"Too much."

"I'm in charge of your pleasure. Yes or no?"

"Yes." Her desperate one-word answer pumps heady satisfaction into my bloodstream.

"Then I get to decide if it's too much unless you say stop. Are you saying stop?"

"No." She digs her fingers into my hair, holding me fast to her chest.

I bite down again, harder this time, gloating when she shouts out my name. Each action of mine causes a reaction in her, and from it, I learn which buttons make her fall apart in my arms.

"You have the perfect tits for kissing, sucking, and biting. Look at how pretty they are with my marks on them," I whisper against her breastbone, giving each rosy tip one last gentle kiss before licking a line down her stomach, taking the time to appreciate the softness of her skin, grazing her navel, and sucking on both hips before continuing lower.

As I settle in the cradle of her thighs, kissing that sexy-as-sin crease between her leg and pussy, I pause and take in the bounty before me. I memorize her body, highlight each scar and stretch mark, each flawless flaw that makes her uniquely beautiful.

She wiggles in my hold, and I tsk. "Such an impatient little thing, aren't you?" I slide my palms under each leg, gripping the muscles and splaying her wide before hooking her legs around my shoulders. "I'm about to worship at this altar spread for me. So fucking pretty. Peachy pink and perfect, like I knew you'd be. And so wet. You're dripping for me, aren't you?"

When she doesn't answer, I nip the soft skin of her inner thigh, a low chuckle rumbling from the depths of my throat when she whines and pulls my hair.

"Answer me, Baby Girl. Who has this pussy so wet you're soaking the sheets?"

"You, Bond! You!"

"Good girl."

She shudders when I say the words, making me even harder. My cock throbs in the confines of the too-tight sweatpants, and I grind my hips into the bed, trying to ease my desperation. At this rate, I'll come in my pants before I see if she tastes as tempting here as she does everywhere else.

"Look at me, Tuesday."

Her honey-brown gaze snaps to mine, and I don't break eye contact as I lower my face and lick her from opening to clit. She's beyond anything I could ever imagine. I explore her depths, long, flat licks from bottom to top, tasting every inch in between, her desire drenching my tongue. She tastes like a dream, and every noise she makes feels like the stroke of her hand around my cock.

"Licking this pussy is my new addiction. I'm gonna do this every day."

Her back curves as I slip my tongue inside her, thrusting in and out, showing her what I plan to do with my fingers. She rolls her hips, and I put my palm on her lower stomach to keep her from moving before wrapping my lips around her clit, my teeth grazing the sensitive bundle of nerves. Then, I suck.

"Bond!" She tries to buck upwards, but I keep her firmly in place.

"Are you asking for something? Good girls ask nicely." I hum against her.

"Pl-please make me co-come."

I press a single finger into her entrance, sliding it in and out of her tight opening before adding a second. Once both are buried to the knuckle, I scissor and curl them inside her while her hot center grips around me. I keep working her, searching for the tiny, textured place inside that will shatter her into pieces. She feels amazing, and my hips buck into the mattress again, the thought of my cock inside her lush heat riding me hard.

Tuesday's body sings to me, her pussy quivering against my lips, stomach tensing under my palm, thighs shaking against my ears. She's so close. I crave her orgasm. It's mine. I ache to savor the burst of her release, to roll her flavor on my tongue and sate my thirst.

"Come on my face, sweetheart. Soak me. Want your scent and taste all over." I slide my hand higher up her body, releasing my hold on her hip and pressing against her breastbone, loving the hammering of her heart against my palm.

With a cry of my name, she comes, her hips jerking upward, drawing my fingers in deeper as she seizes around me. Thick thighs lock around my head, but I never stop sucking, licking, stroking—liberating a second smaller release from her before she begs me off.

Tuesday's legs fall away as she melts into the bed. My chin and mouth drip with the proof of a job well done. Is there anything better than pleasing your partner? No, there sure as shit isn't.

"Holy crap. Th-that was…" She trails off, her eyes closed and voice shaky. "Incredible."

"Taste yourself, how delicious you are. Open for me." I move up her body and hold out my fingers, shining with her wetness.

She parts her lips, trust and warmth in her hooded eyes. I slip one soaked finger into her mouth, then the other. While Tuesday sucks my fingers clean, she reaches into my sweats and grips my cock. It throbs in need, and a mere handful of strokes is all it takes before I'm spilling all over her stomach, one last marking claim laid tonight. Then I kiss her, my tongue coiling with hers, sharing the remnants of her flavor before collapsing, my borrowed pants still low on my hips.

When she goes to move, I grab her wrist. "You stay. Let me clean us up." Taking care to not crush her, I roll, kissing the tip of her nose before striding the two steps to the bathroom, snagging a washcloth, and returning. With all the tenderness I can express, I sweep the warm cloth against her skin, cleaning her and myself before tossing it away. Lying on my side and pulling her so she's resting against me, I press her ear to my pounding heart. Can she hear that it beats for her now?

"It's time for you to get some sleep."

"Are you real?"

I kiss the top of her head and chuckle. "Have to convince you to see me again somehow, right?"

"You've outdone yourself." Her sweet voice is slow and sleepy. It won't be long until she's out cold. She fiddles with the blankets and whispers, "Thank you, Baseball Cap."

"Peach, you never have to thank me for this." As we lie there, her body tangled with mine, I run my fingers through her hair, trying my best to tame the snarls and knots back into her ruined braid while she snuggles against me. I never want to stop touching her. In no time at all, she's rapidly becoming my entire world.

We fall into easy conversation, whispering secrets in the shadowy room. It's nothing serious like before, but important all the same. I learn she hates country music and wishes Firefly had more seasons. In return, I share about my love of skiing, both water and snow. Each secret, big and small, ties another thread thickening the string connecting us together.

Before long, she's asleep—her dark lashes fanning over her cheeks, her breathing deep and even. Careful not to wake her, I gently tuck the blankets around us. I take another greedy minute, appreciating her beauty before brushing my lips against her forehead. A soft snore slips from her lips, and fuck me, it's the cutest thing I've ever heard.

God, I'm gone over this woman.

I wake the next morning with Tuesday nestled in my arms.

Her pretty hair is a tangled mess surrounding her face, and her cheeks are ruddy and creased from the pillowcase. She's so beautiful.

"Peach? Sweetheart, wake up."

A snore tumbles from her mouth, and she turns onto her side.

Looks like someone isn't a morning person. Chuckling, I whisper, "I've got to go, but I'll text you later, okay?"

Without bothering to open her eyes, she grumbles, "Shhh, sleeping." A brat even in her sleep.

I drop one last kiss to the top of her head and crawl out of bed. The last thing I want to deal with is work. I'd much rather stay here holding her, but we've got all the time in the world for that. After all, we're only getting started.

"What do you have to be so happy about? We're here on a Saturday," my older sister says as she throws her bag on my desk.

The smile on my face is obnoxious. It has been since I left Tuesday's motel room this morning.

Charli snaps at me again as she sinks into the chair across from me. "Bond! One, why are you so damn happy, and two, why are we here today?"

I shrug, wishing we could ignore that we're here to meet the men who bought our future out from under us. "It's the only time the new owners can fit us in, so it's not like we have a lot of choice, considering Davis Designs doesn't belong to the Davis family anymore. I still can't believe Dad pulled this shit, especially without telling us about it. You and I have been running Davis Designs for six years with him in the wings. It's supposed to be our future. Wavey's future..."

"Bond." Charli's voice softens, and she reaches out, squeezing my shoulder. "This is hard for all of us. The entire sale and restructure came out of nowhere, but Dad did it for us."

"Yeah, sure."

"Think about it. The money guarantees we never have to struggle. And he negotiated for us to stay on and kept the name from changing. We're still Davis Designs. We still get to do what we do best. The differences are we're getting a new team member, and a portion of our profits funnel to them."

"Oh, that's all?" I'm being a shit. It isn't Charli's fault. She's as shocked, hurt, and angry about the sale of our family business as I am.

"We're still here. We still get to do what we love, but we have the added benefit of more money in our accounts than we've ever had before. I don't have to worry about paying for college for Wavey. You can afford to buy your dream house in Piñon Hills. Mom and Dad can travel, and Clairy can do whatever it is Clairy wants to do."

A quick pang rattles in my chest at the thought of the last house I designed and helped build in Piñon Hills. I poured myself into that house. The hard part of creating beautiful things is sometimes they don't end up yours. That house, more than any other, I built for myself.

"The house sold," I say too quietly for her to hear. "Easy on Clairy Fairy. She's here for good now and trying. Also, when did you become such an optimist?" I study my big sister. The irony isn't lost on me. She's the smallest in the family, maybe an inch taller than Tuesday, and her hair is a light butterscotch color. Clairy, on the other hand, is tall and dark-haired like me. We tease Charli that Mom must have had another life before

Dad and brought her along, which neither Mom nor Dad ever appreciates.

"I'm not dunking on Clairy," Charli says, glaring at me when I snort. "I didn't mean that literally, you lunkhead. She spent the last ten years floating on the wind. If that's what she wants, now she has the means to do it safely. If she wants to stay and take over Auntie B's bakery, she can do that too. Anyway, my point is it's not optimism. It's pragmatism. These are factual benefits. You can't argue with facts."

"We weren't hurting, Charli. You and I were making it work. Look at Piñon Hills. And The Bee and the Bean. Our footprint has grown like crazy, and now we're taking a step back. Will they honor their word? What if they implement sweeping changes or cut corners to save on costs? Phillips Construction is a huge multi-million dollar company. They aren't building someone's dream, spending months ensuring every detail is perfect. I won't compromise on our work. And more than that, they don't care that you have a daughter, that our employees have struggles of their own. You think they know our employees' names, much less anything about them? Like how Cal and Morgan have gone through three rounds of fertility treatments trying to build their family? We are nothing but an asset to them, and I don't understand why we ended up in this position." I finish, deflated.

Charli's eyes—the one thing my parents say proves she's a Davis through and through—soften. "You need to ask those questions today. We have to make the best of this. What other choice do we have?"

Closing my eyes, I inhale and nod. "I guess being the oldest also makes you the smartest."

"Watch it, Runt." She reaches over the desk and flicks me on the forehead, her favorite way to torture me growing up. "Is the new guy joining us?"

"No, apparently, he's coming in next week. The Warrens didn't offer me any other details. Only one crappy, brief email."

"The Warrens?" Charli lifts a single brow at me.

"Yeah, Warren the Elder and Warren the Younger. Dad and son."

"What time is this call again?"

I check my watch. "We've got about half an hour."

Charli rubs her hands together and levels an evil grin my way. "Let's table the business talk for a minute or two. Instead, tell me about the cheek-cracking smile you walked in with. Does it have anything to do with a pretty newcomer?"

Groaning, I run my hand over my face. "Clairy?"

"Clairy."

"Is nothing sacred in this family?"

"What did you expect? You spent Thursday night with a beautiful stranger at Dane's."

"Fine, no point in denying it. Yes, Peach and I were together last night."

"Uh oh, already to nickname status? This must be serious. Clairy said you were a total mush over this mystery woman even though you just met her."

"I've never met anyone like Tuesday. She's funny and smart."

"Oh, you don't know anyone funny and smart?"

"Present company excluded, of course."

At Charli's eye roll, I continue, "It's that gut feeling you get when something is right or wrong, and when I'm with her, right is all I feel. And there's something inside me, screaming, hey, you big dope, don't fuck this up."

Only three years older than me, Charli and I grew up close. And that's continued as we've aged. We were there for each other when I went through my divorce, when she found out she was pregnant and raising a baby alone, and when Clairy left us behind, flitting off at nineteen to explore the world, returning ten years later. And now, as we navigate these unexpected business changes.

"It's fast. And I don't know much about her, I admit it. But I wish I did. Every little mundane thing. I want to be the leading expert on all things Tuesday. How she takes her coffee; if she likes her toast whole, cut in rectangles, or triangles. If she eats ice cream in bed. All the piddly crap that makes up a life together. When I'm with her, Charli, I'm settled. Happy."

Tears glisten in my sister's eyes, and I panic. Call me a sap, but seeing any of the women in my life crying kills me. I swoop around the desk and crush her to me in a rib-cracking hug.

"I'm so happy for you. That's all. Now let go of me. You're suffocating me." Charli wipes away a few stray tears, then says, "Finish telling me about the date. You said things went well?"

"Yes, except…"

"Except what? Did you make an ass of yourself?"

"Not me. But thanks for the vote of confidence."

"If not you, then what?"

My look conveys more than words can, and it's obvious when she interprets my silent message.

"Ah. Not a what, a who." At my nod, she sits on the edge of my desk. "Did *he* do something? Because Clairy told me about the fiasco at Dane's. I'm surprised you didn't tell me, to be honest."

I shrug. Jacob Ashford is a touchy subject in our home.

"Bond, he's nothing. He has no power over my life, emotions, or mental well-being anymore and hasn't for a long time. It's okay to tell me things. Especially if those things end in you punching him in his rude mouth."

"Why does everyone assume I hit him?" She raises one eyebrow, and I sigh. "I haven't punched that asshole in the face in four years."

"What about two years ago when he told me he'd be willing to *'give me another turn on his joystick'* at Dane's?"

"That wasn't me. That was Griff."

Charli's face lights up at the mention of Griffin Anderson. Those two need to figure it out already.

"But, after last night's trouble, I more than owe him one."

"What did he do?" she asks.

"He threw fish at us."

Charli blinks. "Fish? Did you say fish? Like frozen fish or goldfish or whole cans of tuna?"

"Chopped up fish tails and fins and other parts."

At my sour explanation, Charli clamps her hands over her mouth, laughter bubbling out. I can't help but join in because it's as absurd in the light of day as last night when it happened. I'm still pissed, but in the end, it didn't derail my night, and thankfully, Tuesday wasn't hurt. Still think I should pop him in the nose the next time I see him.

"He really is a prick, isn't he?" Charli manages to say once she's calm. "Don't get yourself in trouble for beating him up, Runt. He's not worth it. How did your new friend handle it?"

"Laughed as hard as you did."

"See, no reason to bother with him. You're right, though. If it's been two years since anyone punched him, he's due."

Seizing the opportunity for some good-natured teasing, I say, "So how is Griff anyway? You two finally figure out that you're in love or what?"

If looks could kill, Charli would be up on murder charges in a minute. "We're just friends."

"I know you both say you're just friends, but I also know you're both stupid."

"Bond!"

I wave her off. "Come on, Charli Horse. Let's get ready for this video call."

"Don't call me that," she grumbles as she knocks over a stack of invoices on my desk before stomping to the door, a very insincere, 'Oops' thrown over her shoulder.

My laugh echoes in the empty office. Sisters. Gotta love 'em.

CHAPTER EIGHT

I steeple my fingers and exhale slowly. "Mr. Phillips, I've asked you three straightforward questions, and you've skirted around them all so far. I want firm, clear answers. Why did you reach out to my father? What are your long-term plans for Davis Designs? What are the expected roles of each of us here in the office? If you can't answer me, then there's no point in continuing our conversation."

Warren the Younger says, "Please call me War, Porter. May I call you Porter?"

"Actua—"

"Listen, Porter." *Nice of him to give me time to tell him no.* "There's no reason to be suspicious of Phillips Construction. We made a more than generous offer to your father, which he accepted. Within that offer, we placed certain provisions that afford you and Davis Designs a fair amount of freedom. Far more than our traditional acquisitions retain."

"And why is that? What about a custom home builder in Trail Creek, New Mexico caught the attention of a Dallas large-scale construction company? Why was the buyout so fast and sudden? Usually, things like this take months."

Charli interrupts my line of questioning. "We aren't accusing you or the company of anything, but this situation surprised us."

Warren's eyes soften, and for a moment, I'm weirdly reminded of Tuesday. I shake my head, needing to focus on this meeting and not let the memory of her golden whiskey gaze distract me.

"Sometimes, families make difficult choices. Choices that are hard to explain but truly are in everyone's best interest." I hear a muffled voice off-screen, Warren the Elder, if I was guessing. He hasn't spoken to us or appeared on screen during the meeting. War's face hardens, his voice formal and detached when he says, "Phillips Construction saw an opportunity to break into a niche market, and we were aggressive in our attempts. We are in the position to move quickly due to our ample capital, and your father was more than happy to accept the terms of our proposal. Perhaps you should raise these questions with him."

"Perhaps." The single word comes out little more than a grunt.

"As to your other concerns, the long-term plan is for you to continue as you have. We'll explore different options as needed when we next meet. You will continue in your capacity as Director of Design and Construction. Ms. Davis will continue as Director of Finances, and TJ will transition into the previously unfulfilled role of Marketing and Acquisitions. How you choose to handle your day-to-day operations is up to you. This is an opportunity for you to grow. We encourage you to embrace it."

Again, the voice of an older man sounds off-screen. War clears his throat. "Yes, well, if that's all?" When neither Charli nor I speak, he nods. "We will communicate via email unless a problem arises. Have a nice day." The screen goes black.

"Well, it could have gone worse." Charli offers as we sit, still staring at the blank screen.

"I don't know what I expected, but I thought I would get some kind of answer from them. Why us, Charli? Why Davis Designs and why now?"

Charli goes to answer me, though I already know what she's going to say. The same thing Warren the Younger, War, did. I need to talk to Dad. Before she can say anything, our debrief is interrupted by the buzzing of an incoming video call.

Glancing at the screen, I see my niece's picture. "Waverly?"

Charli nods as she answers. "Wavey? What's going on?"

"Before you freak out, I'm fine."

All the color drains from my sister's face. "What happened?"

"I had a little accident."

The phone drops onto my desk, and I scoop it up. "Wavey, we need details. Are you hurt?"

She rolls her eyes. "No, Uncle Bond. The first thing I said was I'm fine."

"Care to share what happened, Wavey Gravy?" I ask.

"Ugh, don't call me that, Uncle Bond. And yes, I do care." Her tone goes from whiny to petulant in a matter of seconds. Behold the power of a teenager.

"Waverly Claire Davis, tell us what happened." Charli cradles her head in her hands, not looking at the phone.

I faux whisper, "Oooh, you got middle named. You're in trouble."

"Mom, I'm sorry. It was an accident! I swear. I got home from The Bee and The Bean and decided to make something to eat. But I forgot you can't put foil in the microwave."

"Waverly, is the house on fire?" I worry any dogs in the area will go deaf from the pitch of her voice.

"Don't you think I would have started with that?"

Charli purses her lips and inhales deeply. "You're sure you're okay?"

"Yeah, my burrito can't say the same, and the kitchen smells funky. But I'm good."

"Alright. Let me pack up here, and I'll head home so we can clean up. I'm so glad you're okay."

I can hear the exhaustion in my sister's voice. Wavey is a great kid, but being a single mom is hard, or at least I imagine it is. Lord knows I don't have any hands-on experience, but Charli works her ass off raising Waverly on her own—all without an ounce of help or support from that bastard who donated his sperm. I make an involuntary fist when I think about how much Charli has done over the last fifteen years to give Waverly an amazing life. My big sister is a badass.

"You want to hang with me tonight, Wavey?"

Twin expressions of confusion stare at me, one in person the other over a phone screen. Charli says, "Bond, I'm sure you have plans. It's a Saturday night."

"Nope. No plans." To Waverly, I say, "What do you think? You and me, plus junk food, cokes, and bad TV? Maybe your mom and Aunt Clairy can go out and enjoy themselves?"

"Bond, I'm sure Waverly would rather—"

"That sounds kind of cool. You should go out, Mom."

She's such a good kid. I shoot Waverly a covert wink, and she smiles at me in return.

Charli chews on her thumbnail. "Clairy's probably busy."

"She's off today. Even if she was busy, you could always ask Griff."

"Oh, yeah! Mom, you should totally ask Griff out."

The sound of grinding teeth makes me laugh. Anticipating

Charli's defense, I beat her to the punch. "Now, Waverly, you know Griff and your mom are 'just friends' even though neither has seriously dated anyone else over the last five years since they met."

Grinning at Charli, I say, "Call Clairy and Griff. Go out, convince Dane to let you do karaoke, have a Flocked Up Flamingo, and enjoy yourself. Take advantage of a Wavey-free night. I can handle her for the evening."

"You know I can hear you, right?" my niece snarks. When I laugh, she huffs at me in annoyance. She looks so much like Charli at that moment, except for her eyes, which are pale gray like her dad's.

Despite being on my mind all day, I haven't had a chance to talk to Tuesday. I picked Wavey up from Charli's, risking my life by letting her drive us into town. The two of us headed to Up a Creek Without a Book, the local bookstore, where she conned me into buying her another album. I swear all the women in my life know exactly how to get what they want from me. And I'm counting my Peach on that list too.

I'm itching to call her, and while I'm sure Wavey wouldn't mind, I don't relish having a fifteen-year-old—or as she likes to remind me, *I'm practically sixteen, Uncle Bond*, flourished with a dramatic eye roll—eavesdropping on my conversation. We're on hour two of some terrible singing competition show Wavey loves, and a pint of ice cream and a large pizza deep into our junk food journey.

Faced with potential teenage mocking, I slink into the

kitchen, leaving Waverly engrossed in an off-key rendition of *Shake It Off* and text Tuesday.

> Hey, Baby Girl, I know you start your new job Monday, but any chance you'd want to Netflix and chill tomorrow night?
>
> Thought it'd be fun. If you're interested. No pressure

The triple dots bounce on my screen, but no reply comes in. Groaning, I run my hands over my face. What is wrong with me? I'm like a nervous teenager trying to find out if a girl likes me. It's like I've never dated before.

But, to be honest, I've never cared this much.

My phone buzzes in my hand, the unease churning in my stomach growing when her replies come in.

> PEACH
>
> I'm sure it would be very fun. I mean, if that's all you want.
>
> I thought after what you said, we were both looking for more than casual.
>
> I understand if you changed your mind.

I set my phone down and run my fingers through my hair. What's she talking about? Changed my mind? I thought I made it pretty clear she's mine. Shit. I'm asking her out again less than twenty-four hours after seeing her. What about that says casual?

Behind me, girlish giggles chime. A small hand yanks my cell phone off the counter.

"Uncle Bond, you know what Netflix and chill means, right?" Waverly chirps around a mouthful of potato chips.

"Yeah, watch a movie and hang out. A date."

She snorts, "OMG, you're old. That's not what it means. It's slang for um..." She tilts her head to one side and raises her eyebrows. "Don't make me say it."

"Don't make you say what?"

My niece's cheeks redden, and I watch her thumbs fly across my phone screen. "Here." She shoves the phone back at me.

> Aunt Clairy? It's Wavey. Uncle Bond has a super awkward question for you.

CLAIRY FAIRY

> What's going on?

> Can you please explain what Netflix and chill actually means to him so I don't die of embarrassment before I get my license?

As I'm reading, my phone rings. "Yeah?"

"Hey there, Waverly says you've got a question?"

"I asked Tuesday if she wanted to Netflix and chill, and now, here I am. Where did I go wrong?"

Clairy's hiccup-checkered laugh rolls over the line. The amount of glee evident in her voice stings. "Yeah, you basically told your dream girl you're looking for a casual hookup. Hope you straighten it out. I like her. She's just the right amount of weird." The sudden disappearance of the bar noise is the sole indicator she's gone.

Well, shit. A casual hookup isn't what I want from Tuesday, not by a long shot. Jerking my chin at Waverly, I snag a few chips from her. "Maybe I should call her? Try to straighten this out. Wait, how do *you* know about this, anyway?"

Her eyes roll so hard I worry they won't come back around. "Everyone knows what it means. You and Papaw are probably the only people on the planet who don't. And call her? Jeez, you really are old."

"Wavey Gravy, I love you, but get out of my kitchen."

Her laugh taunts me as she grabs her chips and goes back to the living room. Taking a deep breath, I grab my phone.

> I had a very enlightening conversation with my niece and one of my sisters. I've concluded I gave you the wrong impression.

PEACH 🍑

> It's fine, Bond. We just met. I understand if you want to keep things casual.

I'm fucking this up. This is why *old* people call each other.

> Nipping this in the bud now, sweetheart. I'm asking you on a date. Because I want to date you. Everything I said last night was and is true. We started this thing, and I have no plans of backing off.

> See you tomorrow night—my place at 6. I'll take care of the food. You pick the movie.

> And Peach, this thing brewing between us? Not casual. Not even a little bit.

"Netflix and chill, huh?" Tuesday stands on my porch, arms crossed, a playful smile on her lips. "You really didn't know what it means?"

"I do now, following a very informative and uncomfortable conversation with my fifteen-year-old niece and both sisters, followed by hours of merciless teasing that I'd rather never talk about again."

I love her rollicking laugh. It's not dainty or delicate. No, each snort and uncontrolled guffaw from her beautiful lips feeds my obsession with her. I want to make her laugh like this every day: her cheeks red, clutching her side and gasping in delight—a creature of pure mirth, unrestrained and free.

Unable to resist, I pull her to me and kiss the smile off her face. Kissing Tuesday is becoming an integral part of my day.

Breaking the kiss far too soon, I pull us over my threshold and into my living room. I follow her gaze as she studies my small two-bedroom bungalow. It's a far cry from my dream home, but I've made it my own. Leading her into the kitchen, I grab two plates.

"I kept it simple tonight. Burgers and fries from Dane's."

Her eyes widen, and her eyebrows jump almost to her hairline. "Bond, um, I'm a vegetarian."

Fuck. Shit. Hell. This is a reminder of how much we still need to learn about each other.

Tuesday's words are soft as she hugs me. "Hey, it's okay, this is on me. I should've said something when you offered to take care of the food."

I run my hands over my face. First date, she says it's not a date. Second first date: fish. Third date, I bring her meat. I'm batting a thousand here. Maybe this will be a funny story we tell our kids one day. *Gather round while I share how I wooed your mom with a pile of meat she couldn't eat.*

Tuesday plops the food on the table and paws through the bags. She pulls out the burgers, their wrappers gone clear from the grease. That cute nose wrinkle is back, and she drops them onto a waiting plate before digging deeper. A noise of elation meshes with the rustling of the brown bag when she finds the basket at the bottom.

"I may not eat burgers, but I love fries." Acting as though she uncovered gold, she pops a french fry into her mouth, and my cock perks up at the indecent sound she makes.

I carry dinner to my couch, and we curl up next to each other, the opening notes of some superhero movie playing in the background. I give her most of the fries, which is no hardship considering I've got two burgers to eat, but the adorable brat swipes a fry off my plate.

"You've got an entire plate of your own fries, Peach."

"They're better off yours."

"So you're telling me if I took those same fries off your plate and put them on mine, it would magically alter the taste?"

"Yes."

At my skeptical stare, she shrugs. "I don't control science, Bond."

I laugh. Hard. Then I grab our plates and push them to the coffee table before tackling her into the couch cushions and tickling her until she cries out for mercy.

"Bond." Tuesday's breathy voice pauses me in my perusal of her secretly sensitive spots.

"Yeah, Peach?"

She leans in, lips grazing my ear. "I really want more of those french fries."

Once the food is gone and the movie over, Tuesday stretches, laying on the couch so her head is in my lap. "So, how was yesterday? Did you do anything exciting?"

"Nope. Unless you count the drunk girl parade that came through my house at two in the morning." I press my thumb into a knot in her shoulder, the immediate moan she makes my reward.

"Mmm, that feels good. And drunk girl parade? Dare I ask?"

"Both sisters, too many Flamingos, a late-night pickup call, and a junk food run."

"Sounds like way more fun than my night of reality TV and popcorn."

"Clairy and Charli may have had more fun last night, but they woke up this morning worse for the wear. I was as loud as possible while making breakfast, some middle sibling payback with support from Charli's daughter, Waverly."

"Do you always take care of everyone?"

I consider her question, and as I'm about to answer, her phone buzzes. Tuesday sits up, takes one look at the screen, and blanches.

"Do you need to reply to that?" I ask, catching a quick glance of a notification from what looks like *Do Not Reply* before she swipes it away.

"No. Absolutely not."

Tuesday doesn't say anything else. I can't help but wonder what it's about, but I won't push her. She rolls her shoulders and exhales through her nose, tossing her phone onto the coffee table. The urge to erase the disappointment off her face propels me into action. I guide her into my lap and kiss her, parting her soft lips with my tongue, relishing her sigh as she melts into my arms.

Against her mouth, I mutter, "Tell me something true, Tuesday."

It's become my favorite game with her. Each truth, big or small, reveals another piece of my Peach puzzle.

As Tuesday kisses her way along my jaw, I shut my eyes, the featherlight brush of her lips against my skin somehow innocent and intense. Then her hand grazes the front of my pants.

"I want this." Her whispered words curl in my ear.

I didn't expect that as her truth. I bury my fingers in her silky hair and pull to hold her attention. "You want *what*? Tell me. Be specific." The demanding tone of my voice leaves no room for argument.

"To taste you." She tilts her head forward, resuming her teasing kisses, even with me holding her hair. Her mouth is hot against my neck, the kisses turning to grazes, the grazes to nips. My hips buck at the sensation of teeth against flesh.

"Tuesday..." My voice is steady, belying the tremors coursing through my body. She pulls my fist to her lips, delivering chaste kisses that morph into tiny nibbles. Then she opens her mouth, enticing me to dip my finger between her lips. I accept the invitation and groan as her tongue rolls and twirls around my finger, a wet promise of what her talented mouth can do.

She grabs a throw pillow off the couch and tosses it to the

floor before dropping to her knees. Fuck. The way she peers up at me through her thick lashes has my heart racing.

"Stand up, Bond."

"You gonna show me what that pouty mouth can do, Baby Girl?"

There's no hiding the physical impact she has on me. My cock pushes against the confines of my pants, and I let out a grunt of relief as Tuesday loosens my belt and unzips my jeans, lowering them to my thighs.

With a coy grin, she traces the outline of my bulge through my boxer briefs with her tongue before pressing her lips against the black cotton in a sweet kiss. "I'm so glad to see things aren't just bigger in Texas."

I flex my hands, the urge to grab her head and direct her where I need aching in my veins. This moment I've fantasized about since meeting her is now my reality.

She kisses the lowest part of my stomach as she pulls out my cock, and all I can think is, *please don't stop*. Her pouty lips are so close, a fraction of an inch, and I'll be in her mouth.

"Go on, Peach, taste me."

I can't tear my eyes away from her. She runs her thumb over the crown, and the sexy smirk she gives me is my undoing. When she takes the droplet of precum and brings it to her mouth, sucking on the pad of her thumb with relish, I almost come apart. She licks her lips like she's eaten the most delicious snack ever, then winks.

A small groan of disappointment crawls from my chest when she skips my cock and kisses my thigh instead. "Patience Bond, it isn't time yet." Her words, mirroring ones I said to her two nights ago, make my skin prickle in anticipation. My little brat.

She teases me, ghosting over my cock, lightly scratching at my legs, pressing into the muscle of my ass. I throw my head back. Whatever this spell is between us, I hope it never ends.

My fingers tangle in her hair, relief and excitement racing through me when her tongue finally swirls around my head. Her lips wrap around me, and she sucks the crown.

I roll forward enough to slip half my length into her mouth, my muscles flexing at her happy humming sound.

"You look so beautiful with my cock in your mouth. Fuck, that feels so good. Take me deeper now. You can do it. Such a good girl, sucking my cock." At my praise, she whimpers and eagerly lowers her head.

"Gorgeous. Now lick me, sweetheart, like I'm the best ice cream you've ever had."

Tuesday pulls back, my cock falling from her mouth. Following my direction, she licks me from base to tip, tracing the veins of my cock with her tongue before lapping at my head.

I curse and snap my hips towards her face, desperate to be enveloped in her hot, wet mouth again. "More." I slide back between her swollen, slick lips, lightly thrusting so she takes me deeper each time.

"Touch yourself, Tuesday. Slide those fingers deep inside your pussy, and don't you dare stop until we both come. Do you understand?" I pull back so she can answer.

"Yes, Bond." Her breathless agreement hardens my cock almost to the point of pain.

She shimmies out of her jeans and yanks her pale blue panties to the side. "Go on, start with one finger. Then, when you're nice and ready, add another. I want to hear your fingers fucking that pretty pussy."

She whimpers, following my instructions perfectly before opening for me. I take myself in hand and give a few rough pumps before pushing it into her waiting mouth. My heart thrums, and my mouth goes dry as she pleasures herself in front of me, all while my cock glides between her lips.

The sucking and slurping meld with our alternating moans and groans, creating a symphony of lust. I'm about to warn her of my impending release when she pulls her mouth away and goes back to kissing my thighs and hips. I growl in frustration.

Twisting her hair around my fist, I tilt her head back. "Stop teasing."

With a mischievous grin, she toys with my head, swirling her tongue around me like I'm a lollipop. Tuesday moans in earnest now, still touching herself, and the vibrations plus the wet noises from her pussy make me groan.

When my cock hits the back of her throat she makes a soft gagging sound, and I can't help the surge of masculine pride that courses through me. "Right there. So fucking pretty taking all of me."

I ease back, a long, sloppy string of saliva stretching between her mouth and my cock. I shouldn't find that so sexy. She looks up at me expectantly, waiting. If Tuesday wants all of me I'll gladly give it to her, but she has to say it.

As if she's reading my mind, she guides me forward while kissing my thighs and nuzzling her cheek against me. "Don't hold back on me, Baseball Cap." Then she grazes her teeth down my length and slides my cock back into her mouth.

"Fuck, I love that little bit of teeth. You want me to fuck your throat, sweetheart? You want to choke on my cock while you finger your pretty pussy?"

She nods her consent, and I thrust, no longer holding anything back. The deeper I go, the more tears stream from her watering eyes, but she moans out a mumbled yes, hollowing her cheeks. I set a feral pace, both hands on her head, pulling her to me as I thrust into her mouth.

"Look at you drinking me down. My good girl." Coiling tension builds to overflowing. I'm so close.

A high-pitched keening sound rings out when she comes, and the vibrations have my eyes rolling back in my head. Tuesday pulls her soaked fingers out from between her legs and uses them to palm my balls and tickle that sensitive spot behind them.

"Shit. Yease, give them a tug. Just like that."

She makes a gurgling sound when I say yease; I love that it's become our inside joke. That we have inside jokes.

"Baby Girl, I'm gonna come. If you want me to pull out—"

She shakes her head and keeps going. I shudder, trying to piece together how asking for a truth ended with me getting my cock sucked by this goddess on her knees. My hips jerk forward of their own accord, and I moan out her name as my balls tighten.

"Yes, Tuesday, don't waste it, not a drop. Swallow it all." I'm buried deep, hips stuttering as I spill into her perfect mouth.

Empty and spent, I nudge her, begging her off, but she laves my length once more, cleaning any remaining spit and cum from my cock. I collapse against the couch, eyes closed, heart pounding, and panting.

If she wasn't mine before, she abso-fucking-lutley is now.

"Tuesday, do you need help—"

All the air whooshes from my body when she drops into my lap. "Nope, just need you to hold me."

"Anything you want, Peach, anything you want." And I mean it. I kiss her, not even remotely bothered by my taste on her tongue. I pick her up and carry her to my bedroom. Repeating my steps from the last time we were together, I make sure she's comfortable while I get a warm washcloth to clean us. When I crawl into my bed, Tuesday twines her body around mine so the pair of us—half-dressed, holding tight to one another—drift off to sleep.

CHAPTER TEN

I jolt awake from a nightmare. In it, I show up at Davis Designs, where my father and Duncan wait for me. A group of faceless employees stand behind them, copies of *the pictures* in their hands. I swallow. Stupid anxiety.

The glow of a digital clock on the nightstand next to me shows that it's a little after four. Soft light spills into the unfamiliar room from a cracked door, and I spend a few confused minutes trying to place where I am. It's not until I feel the warm puff of Bond's breath against my shoulder that my brain comes online. Along with the realization he left a light on for me. The tension from my nightmare melts away, and my heart flutters. I so don't deserve someone like Bond.

"Go back to sleep, Peach."

"How'd you know I was awake?"

His lips caress the back of my neck. "No more cute little snores."

"I do not snore!"

Bond pulls me tighter into his chest and mumbles, "You do, but they're fucking adorable."

I snuggle against him, soaking in the heat radiating off his bare skin. When he invited me to his place, it quieted so many of my lingering fears about him. About us. It was something Duncan never did. Not once in the eleven weeks we were together.

Who's the idiot who missed the red flags sprouting all over like tiny toxic mushrooms? Oh, right. Me.

No, Bond definitely isn't him. I'm in a new place. A new office. No one here knows about Duncan, the pictures, the lawsuit. I'm a blank slate. This is a fresh start.

Rolling over, I kiss Bond, my lips brushing his. As much as I want to stay here, the people-pleaser bred into me by years of unattainable parental expectations and subsequent disappointment can't stand the thought of not making a good first impression at work today. Sighing, I kiss him again and whisper, "Baseball Cap, I have to go. Thank you for last night."

Bond's eyes open. "Told you that you never have to thank me, and I think you can stay a little longer." He presses his lips to the hollow of my throat before making his way higher to tease my mouth open. God, kissing him feels like coming home in a way I've never known.

Five minutes later, I'm still in bed, grinding against Bond's thigh while he sucks on my neck. "B-bond, I have to go." I moan.

"Can't go till you come." He guides my hips so they rock harder against his leg, the pressure on my clit hitting me in the best way. His lips and teeth travel along my skin, the sharp nips soothed by the sweet kisses. "Let me have it, Peach. Soak those panties. Come on my leg like a good girl."

My hands curl around his neck, desperate to pull him closer, and my pace quickens as I chase my pleasure. The muscles in my body tense, and heat spreads through me.

"Yes, so perfect when you come. I need to see it. Use me,

sweetheart," Bond murmurs as I cry out, and then I'm there, falling off the cliff. My toes curl, and my thighs lock around his, the final refrain of my release playing through me. I melt into him, chasing his lips with mine.

Good gravy, Bond just dry humped an orgasm out of me before the sun rose.

"You are so fucking beautiful," he says as he kisses my forehead. "You're going to have a great day."

I card my fingers through his tousled hair. "You can't know that, but I appreciate it."

"Well, I say it's going to be great, and I haven't steered you wrong yet."

I bite my bottom lip and graze my fingertips over the outline of his cock visible in his black boxer briefs. "I really do have to go, but—"

He lifts my hand to his lips. "I'm all good, Peach. Don't worry about me. Let me walk you to your car." He grins. "Then I'll hop in the shower and replay the way you fell apart until I'm coming all over my shower tiles."

I blush and snort-laugh before laying a kiss over his heart. This man.

Back at my motel, I put the finishing touches on my *I'm new here, let's be friends* work outfit. The single-cup coffee maker I picked up is hard at work, as is my phone playing my favorite playlist. With each song, I perk up, dancing and singing along until any nerves and concerns melt away. Not even the cracks in the ceiling or chips in the tile can get me down. Bond said it's going to be a great day, and I believe him.

Mid hair toss, a loud knock at the door startles me. Sucking in a stray strand of hair along with a shock of air, I run to the door, nearly crashing into it. Sitting on the stoop is a bright yellow box. The embossed lid showcases The Bee and The Bean's logo, delicately raised and velvety smooth under my fingertips. With bated breath, I open it, the decadent scent of buttery pastry filling my senses. There, nestled in cream wax paper, lays a sea-salt croissant, a tiny dipper, and one miniature jar of honey. How did he know?

Surely he just ordered the house specialty. Maybe the helpful teen is working again this morning and recommended it. It's doubtful he's aware it's my favorite item or that I've frequented the little bakery slash coffee shop four times in the past three days, ordering a new item plus a croissant each time. But either way, the sight of the delicious pastry makes me feel special and cared for.

In my rush to devour my precious—yep, totally going full Gollum on my carby treat—I almost overlook the folded slip of paper tucked inside the box.

My Peach,

Good luck on your first day. I stand by my claim that it will be a good one. I can't believe I haven't asked you what you're doing. That's dating 101, isn't it? Right beside knowing if your girlfriend eats meat or not. You can tell me about it over dinner. I promise it will be hamburger free.

Last night was one of the best nights I've ever had. Currently tied for first with the other two nights spent with you. Shit, that sounds like a line, doesn't it?

Enjoy your croissant. The trick is to drizzle it in honey.

I'm self-aware enough to know I have trust issues and that my experiences with Duncan and my family's less-than-optimal response only exacerbate them. I've got to stop lumping Bond in with them. Stop letting my past color my future. Clutching the note to my chest, I fall onto my back on the mattress, undeniable happiness written on my face.

I stand outside Davis Designs, an adorable miniature ski lodge-style office in the center of Trail Creek. It resembles the same style of homes in the Piñon Hills neighborhood on a smaller scale serving as a perfect example of what Davis Designs does. They, we, are selling the apres-ski dream and doing it well.

As I make my way up the stairs, I smooth the front of my chambray shirt, ensuring it's tucked into my burnt orange pencil skirt. Years of training from my mother have me wanting to put my best foot forward. My hand is on the door when my phone buzzes in my pocket. I eagerly reach for it, hoping it's Bond, but my blood goes cold when I see the message.

DO NOT REPLY

Try not to sleep with an employee on your first day, Tits. Wouldn't want to disappoint Daddy again. Besides, we both know they won't compare to me.

That piece of garbage includes a dick pic because, of course, he does. My stomach turns, and I swallow the dread and panic threatening to take over. No. I'm not letting him ruin my day. I reach into my cardigan pocket. I grip the folded—and already worn from multiple reads—note from Bond. Today is going to be a good day. Duncan isn't here. He's just trying to get in my head. This is my fresh start. With a deep, calming breath, I delete the message and the picture. Out of sight, out of mind.

You can do this, Tuesday.

"Hi, I'm Morgan. How can I help you?" A perky, blond, twenty-something chirps at me as I step through the door.

I return her friendly smile and extend my hand. "I'm Tuesday Phillips. It's my first day here at Davis Designs."

Confusion colors her expression. "Tuesday? Um, I'm expecting a TJ Phillips, but no Tuesday."

"That's me. I'm TJ, though I'd prefer to be called Tuesday." Frigging Dad and War strike again. How did I not anticipate this? It's been a long time since I've used my initials, but my father insisted on it when I first started. He justified it as protection against the misogyny of the business and construction worlds. I suspected he enjoyed people thinking he had two sons, not one son and an embarrassment of a daughter. It doesn't surprise me one bit that he pulled the same crap here.

"Oh gosh, I feel your pain! I get calls all the time for Mr. Morgan Collins. People always make assumptions." I find myself at ease with her, her cheery demeanor welcoming and uplifting. "Let me take you on a tour!" She points out the departments and their corresponding offices as we walk.

"I'm not sure what you've been told, but we only have two private offices. The rest are come-and-go workspaces. People use them as needed, but given your position and title, we arranged for you to share the larger of the two offices. Unfortunately, the extra furniture won't be here till tomorrow."

"Ah, so I'll have a roommate?"

"Porter isn't in right now. He's an early bird. Likes to pop in while the office is quiet and work for an hour or so before heading out to check on the builds. He usually shows up again around ten. I can introduce you to Charlotte, though. Her office is down the hall."

"Do you mind showing me the office I'll be sharing?"

"Of course not. It's this one."

The sign on the door reads Porter Davis. I peek my head into the oversized space, taking in the beautiful detail work I've come to expect where Davis Designs is concerned. One wall is entirely built-ins, while windows cover the entire east-facing wall, providing a breathtaking view of the mountains.

"What did you do before coming here?" Morgan asks.

I freeze, my brain sputtering at the unknowingly loaded question. Work, Tuesday, she means work!

Putting on my brightest smile, I say, "I worked primarily in land and asset acquisition." This brings back the reminder of how sneaky my brother and father were about the Davis Design deal. Because it never crossed my desk. Bitterness coats my tongue with the realization. How many other deals did they broker without me knowing? How long have they been actively working to cut me out? Did it start before Duncan? Was that just the excuse they needed to oust me?

Before I can spiral anymore, Morgan's sunny voice breaks through the clouds in my mind. "Oh, that sounds like Porter now!"

"Morgan, where are you? Has our wayward new teammate arrived?" A loud, friendly baritone calls from out in the hall. It, it can't be.

That voice.

I know that voice.

I purred to the sound of that voice calling me a good girl hours ago.

Moving as though I'm stuck in syrup, I turn, my startled gaze settling on a pair of electric blue eyes. "B-baseball Cap?"

"Peach?"

This has to be a mistake. Bond can't be Porter Davis. I can't do this again. I can't handle the lies. The gossip. The disappointment. What are the odds my dad will buy another company when this relationship fails?

No, this has to be a nightmare. I'm still asleep in Bond's bed. "Ouch!" I yelp at the sting of the pinch I gave my inner arm.

"Tuesday?"

Bond's voice is muted, drowned out by my twin storms of panic and shame. I've already ruined everything. My father is right about me. Duncan is right about me. I'm a walking disaster. Making the wrong choices at every turn. Falling for anyone who shows me kindness. My first night in town and I ended up in the arms of another coworker. Is Bond using me? Just this morning, I was thinking how he'd proven to be so different from Duncan. But is he?

"Tuesday," he says again, gently touching my shoulder.

I stare at him wide-eyed, unspeaking.

"This is a welcome surprise. What brings you here?" He wrinkles his brow. "Not that I'm complaining, but how did you find me? I thought you started work today."

His words serve as a stark reminder of how little we know about each other. Despite having an undeniable connection, I don't even know his full name, and he doesn't know mine. For all the secrets and intimacies we've shared, it's painfully clear we skipped a few key details along the way.

I swallow. "I'm here for work."

"What do you mean?"

"I mean, I'm the new Davis Designs employee, sent here by Phillips Construction."

"Oh god. TJ. Tuesday. Tuesday..." He looks at Morgan, then me.

I give him a small, sad smile. "Tuesday Jane Phillips. I haven't gone by TJ in over eight years. My father is the only one who uses my initials as my name." Letting a sliver of ice slip into my voice, I extend my hand. "It's nice to meet you. Porter, I believe it was?"

When I call him Porter, a frown mars his face. "Morgan, could you please give Tuesday and me a few minutes?"

Morgan scurries toward the reception desk with an apologetic smile, leaving us alone.

Bond ushers me into his office—our office—the one we will share because, of course. As soon as the door snicks shut, I pounce.

"Was this some sort of game? Pretend to like the new owner's daughter and use her to grow your career? Because I won't fall for that again." I choke on the bitter words. Doubt, fear, and sadness coat my tongue like bile.

Bond jerks. "Again?" he repeats, his brows knitting together in confusion. Giving his head a slight shake, he says, "Tuesday, how can you think that? I've been nothing but honest from the moment I met you."

"Honest? Really, Porter?" I snort. "Let's explore that. Are you in the habit of giving fake names to women you meet in bars?" I let him lick me inside and out and returned the favor; all the while, I didn't even know his actual name.

"Technically, I said my friends call me Bond."

Wrong answer. Though I'm not sure what the right one would be. Unless it's *I have a neural disrupter in my pocket and can wipe this entire moment from your memory.*

"Oh, you want to play the 'technically' game? Fine. Technically, I find you handsome and funny and charming. Technically, I can see myself falling for you. Technically, I came here for a new job and to escape the mistakes of my past. Technically, I report to you, making you my boss. Technically, my father is your boss. And do you know what all these things technically mean? You and I are done before we even have a chance to begin."

"Tuesday, that's ridiculous."

"Maybe I'm ridiculous. It's not like I haven't heard that before. My mom. My dad. War. Duncan. And now you. You're too much, Tuesday. You're so sensitive and dramatic, Tuesday. How could you do this to the company, Tuesday? You're such a ridiculous mess, Tuesday."

Bond stiffens. Crap. I've said entirely too much.

"Tuesday, please. I don't think you're ridiculous. I said it in frustration, and I'm sorry."

I have to get out of here, but Bond moves so he's standing in front of me, blocking my path to the door. "Fuck, look at me, sweetheart. Can you tell me more about—"

I crumple into his arms, giving in to the need for his touch. I brush my lips against his and whisper, "No."

Hugging him like this might be my last chance—because truly it may be—I breathe him in. Absorb all that warmth and strength and kindness he exudes.

Then, I straighten my spine and throw my shoulders back. "My desk and chair will be ready tomorrow, correct?" At his wordless nod, I slap on my best boardroom, press-friendly smile. The one that doesn't meet my eyes and makes me feel hollow. "It was nice to meet you, officially. I look forward to our future collaborations as part of the Davis Designs branch of Phillips Construction."

I slip around him and take ten steps down the hall toward

the front door before he pulls me back. "Wait, where are you going?"

Loud enough for Morgan to hear, I say, "Since there's no actual desk for me here today, I'll be working from home."

Jerking my arm from his grasp, I walk away, not wanting him to see the tears running down my cheeks. Where am I going? To my motel to bury myself in blankets and cry for my future with Bond, lost before it even began.

CHAPTER ELEVEN

The look on Bond's face when I left haunts me. This has to be some sort of fever dream. It can't be real. Channeling my discontent into action, I call my brother.

"What the hell, War! You couldn't have given me a heads up? A dossier? A frigging full name? Anything?" In a fit of annoyance, I fling my pillow across the room, then run to scoop it up when it lands on the disgusting motel floor. I am so over this place. One or two more nights here. I can do it.

"Tuesday, what are you talking about? You're supposed to be at work." War's brusque tone stiffens my spine. We haven't spoken since the awful call when I told them there was no need to reach out unless it's work related. Which this is.

At the very least, it's work adjacent.

I take a deep breath. "I wish I'd known more about the people I'm working with here."

"We felt you had all the necessary information."

"Well, I feel like you're a giant turd, so here we are."

War's weary sigh comes through the phone. "What's this really about?"

I close my eyes and swallow. There's no way I'm going to tell him I hooked up with a fellow employee. Not when that was a key contributor in my exile to Trail Creek in the first place. Granted, Bond isn't married, which is a considerable improvement over Duncan, but he's still a coworker and, therefore, off-limits. I can't go through another round of people talking about me, calling me a homewrecker, proving my family's opinions about me right.

"It's nothing. I wasn't prepared when I went in today. That's all." The lie rolls off my tongue with ease.

"You're making something out of nothing. All new employees deal with those nerves. You'll be fine."

Knowing I won't get anywhere else with War, I hang up. No point in drawing out the conversation.

Half a dozen missed calls and text notifications fill up my phone screen. All from Bond.

SEXY BASEBALL CAP

Are you okay? At least tell me that.

You were crying when you left. I'm worried.

I know the situation is unexpected, but it doesn't change how I feel about you. We can make this work.

No one in the office will care if we're together if that's what worries you.

Come on, Baby Girl, answer me, please.

I'll be at your place at seven.

Why does he have to be so sweet? So perfect? He's kind, playful, and sexy as hell. He sees my quirks and finds them charming. No one in my life cares about me the way Bond does, despite him, as today brutally showed, knowing virtually nothing about me.

I let myself hope for too much. I should have known it was too good to be true.

I'm breaking my heart, but what other choice do I have?

After changing into my grubbiest sweats, I spend the rest of the day at my future home. The shipping containers with my furniture arrived this morning while I was mid-meltdown, and they're the distraction I need. I take my time unpacking, doing everything in my power to not think about Bond.

Of course, it's a miserable failure, but I multitask like a boss. I overthink while unloading most of the items still in my car. Cry while putting away a chunk of my clothes. And rage sing while arranging my kitchen items. I'm talented like that.

My conversations with Bond replay in my mind, and I search them for signs of deceit on his part. Nowhere do I see indications he knew about my connection to Phillips Construction. My heart says name thing aside, Bond truly is nothing like Duncan. He wouldn't see me as a ticket to a better job. Or as nothing but a burden and embarrassment, like my dad.

Eventually, the growl of my stomach is too loud to ignore, so I call it a day. Tonight should have been a celebratory dinner between Bond and myself, where I shared details of my first day of work, and we continued our ravenous explorations of each other. Instead, I'll eat a granola bar alone in my depressing motel room and read some sappy romance with a guaranteed HEA for the perfect man and the imperfect woman he loves.

We all have our coping mechanisms.

To my surprise, when I pull into the parking spot I've claimed as mine over the past several days, I see Bond leaning against the door to my room. I glance at the dashboard clock: seven-twenty.

Do I chicken out and run? I can always pretend I don't see him and retreat to my Piñon Hills house. The floor wouldn't be that much worse than the mattress here. Before I can decide, he spots me and jogs over to my car.

Holding his hands up as though he's approaching a skittish animal, Bond makes his way around to my window and waits, an easy smile on his face. Does anything ruffle this man? With a huff, I roll the window down.

"You're late for our date, Peach."

"Our date? After everything that happened this morning?"

"Yes."

"I replied to your text, Porter. Told you I didn't want to see you tonight."

"And I ignored it. Also, don't call me that." He leans his elbows against the windowsill, ducking his head into the car. "Not you."

"It's your name, isn't it?"

"Two truths and a lie, Tuesday. I'll go first. My name is Porter Bond Davis, but only acquaintances, employees, and my parents call me Porter. I met a beautiful woman a few nights ago, and despite it being fast, we connected. On the stoop outside your door is a bag full of terrible food I plan to eat alone."

"I'm an employee."

"Not to me, not when it comes to this. You call me Bond or Baseball Cap or yours. I don't want to hear Porter out of your beautiful mouth."

When I don't respond, Bond straightens, studies me, and nods. "If you want me to leave, I will."

He gets two steps into the dark of the parking lot before I

call him back. "Baseball Cap, wait!" As quick as the words are out of my mouth, he's opening my car door.

Despite fearing this road and its potential for heartache, embarrassment, and disappointment, I step into his arms and say, "I used my initials at work when I first started because my father said I would get further if people thought they were dealing with a man. I'm here because of a scandal back home. I wish you hadn't come here tonight."

"Baby Girl…"

I fight back the rush of tears. "I'm sorry. But, whatever this is, might have been…"

He presses me to his chest, the two of us still standing next to my car in the busted and broken parking lot of the Trail Creek Inn. It's too on the nose, too symbolic.

The turmoil in Bond's voice is like a fist gripping my heart. "Don't you finish that sentence. I'm not entertaining talk of us ending now. Tuesday, I never lied. I had no idea you were TJ Phillips."

"It's not that. I promise," I whisper, "I just can't date anyone who works for Phillips Construction."

"I don't work for your dad's company. I work for Davis Designs," he says as if that solves the problem. How I wish it did.

"Bond, that's splitting hairs. Phillips owns Davis Designs, and we'll be working side by side, sharing an office. If anything goes wrong—"

"Nothing's going to go wrong, and even if for some unforeseen reason it did, I trust that we're both mature enough to deal with it like professionals." He kisses me, a tender sipping of my lips. "I don't want to lose you. I only just found you."

A small sob breaks from me, and Bond pulls me tighter. "I don't want to lose you either, but you don't understand."

"Then help me understand."

"I…I can't." I blink, trying to stop the tears before they fall, my breath hitching as I answer.

Bond studies me like he's looking for the secret to life, his face pensive when he finally says, "We can keep this between us. Our secret."

"There's no such thing as a secret in a town like this or an office the size of Davis Designs. I couldn't even keep my secrets in Dallas."

"We'll stay professional at work, and then after, we'll go out of town or back and forth to our houses. No one will see us, and if, by chance, someone does, we play it off as a business meeting. It's worth exploring, Tuesday. This thing between us? This connection? I've never felt this way about another person, and you can't tell me it's not the same for you. Don't you think it's worth it?"

"Yes, yes, I feel that way. But there's so much I haven't told you."

"Then tell me. Make me understand. Lay it all out, Peach. You won't run me off. But we can't fix this if we don't talk."

When I don't answer, he sighs, running his hands through his hair. "Let's at least go inside and eat. I can hear your stomach. The two things I can't abide are my girl crying or hungry, and now you're both. Let me take care of you." He laces our fingers together, and I follow him to my waiting motel room.

I catch sight of my red-ringed eyes, clumpy eyelashes, and pink nose. Pretty when I cry? That's a no.

Bond moves straight to the small table, splitting up the food he brought—a bounty of Indian vegetarian delights that smell heavenly. I don't even bother looking for my cardboard granola bars. My plate has a bit of everything, from the surprising green chile pakora to traditional spinach paneer.

Taking a deep breath, I try for what passes in the normal

world as casual conversation. "I'm impressed a town the size of Trail Creek has so many high-caliber restaurants."

"We're lucky to attract an eclectic mix of people who come out this way thanks to our proximity to the slopes." He nudges a perfect piece of naan toward me. "This came from a vegetarian food truck with a rotating global menu."

The food is another way Bond shows his feelings. He's a caretaker. From the moment we met, he's shared this side of himself—escorting Jacob from the bar, walking me home, opening my door, bringing me pleasure.

It's been nice having someone who cares about me.

Bond sets his plate to the side, our brief reprieve from real talk over.

"Will you tell me what you meant when you said you were sent here? When I talked to Warren the Youn…War. Your brother." He pauses and cocks his head at me. "It's funny. His eyes reminded me of yours during our video call. I thought I just had you on my mind. He's your twin, right? The golden boy you mentioned?"

"Yeah, that's him."

"Besides your eyes, you two don't look much alike. I pegged your brother at close to my height, and he's pretty broad-shouldered."

"Oh, we aren't those kinds of twins. We're more of the Danny DeVito/Arnold Schwarzenegger type of twins. War is the perfect one. I'm the disaster." My laugh comes out harsh.

"You aren't a disaster, Tuesday." When I don't reply, Bond clears his throat. "War said sometimes families make tough choices in everyone's best interest. Your dad cut him off when I asked him to explain what he meant. Was he talking about you?"

"Yep. Me. Black sheep extraordinaire."

"Remember when you agreed to tell me if you were feeling some kind of way? I'm holding you to that, Peach."

"I'm not ready to go into all the details yet, Bond. I owe you an answer, but...it's hard to talk about."

Bond grabs my plate, sets it on the side table, and pulls me so I'm straddling his lap. We're face to face, his hands on my hips, anchoring me to him. He sneaks a quick kiss to the tip of my nose. "Tell me what you can. I'll take that."

"My last relationship, the ex who called me the awful nicknames, he was a coworker. We dated for almost three months, and it didn't turn out well. Like epically unwell. And after it ended, it somehow got worse."

Bond's eyebrows draw together. "He didn't hurt you, did he?"

"Physically, no. But there are a lot of ways to hurt people when you have power and leverage over them."

"I'm not him."

A tear rolls down my cheek, and he swipes it away with his thumb. "From the moment I met you, my heart said you aren't like him. But my brain...I want to trust you more than anything, but this is all so new. Until today, we didn't even know each other's last names or jobs. You see how well that turned out."

"You aren't going to talk me out of wanting you, Tuesday. There's nothing you can say that will make me run."

"You can't promise that." My whisper is full of sadness. This beautiful, charming man deserves a beautiful, charming life.

With every ounce of internal strength I have, I pull Bond's hands away and climb out of his lap. I place a kiss on his lips, hoping it conveys the truth of what I feel for him despite what I'm about to say. "I think you should go now, Bond. I need time to think. Can you give me that?"

"I can, but I want to be clear." His gentle grip on my chin guides my eyes to his. "I'm not leaving because this is over. The conversation or us. It isn't. Not by a long shot. I told you that you were mine, and I mean it, Tuesday Jane Phillips. I will prove to you that this thing between us is more than just a physical attraction. I don't care if it's sudden or new. I know it's right, and so do you. I'll go tonight, but come tomorrow, I'll be right back in your life, showing you how much I want this."

Clutching my shirt over my aching heart, I sink into a chair. Bond has given me what I asked for, and nothing ever hurt so much.

CHAPTER TWELVE

"Tuesday? Are you okay?"

I attempt to smile before a tear snakes down my cheek. "No. I'm not."

A warm hug envelopes me, Clairy's taller frame surrounding mine. "What happened?"

"Bond and I...it turns out we have more in common than either of us expected."

"What do you mean?" Clairy asks as she takes the empty barstool next to me.

Before I can answer, Dane comes up. "Clairy, you're still on the clock."

She rolls her eyes at him and yanks off her apron, tossing it at him. "Then clock me out. Tuesday needs me more than Mr. Cahill and the other regulars in here."

"Um, Clairy, it's okay. I'm going to have a drink and then head back to my motel. Don't get fired over me."

"Dane won't fire me." She laughs like I've told some hilarious joke, with Dane standing there watching us.

With a long breath in, then out, Dane gives us a tight, closed-lip smile. "What can I get you, ladies?"

"Two Flocked Up Flamingos," we say at the same time. I look over at Clairy, and this time, the smile I give her is genuine.

Once our drinks are served, Dane mumbling under his breath about not being able to find good help, Clairy asks me again, "So, what do you mean it turns out you and Bond have more in common than you expected? I would think that's a positive."

"Normally, you'd be right, but in this case...I'm the newest Davis Designs employee, the one sent here from Phillips Construction headquarters."

Clairy spits and hot pink mist lands all over the bar top. "Oh shit! You're TJ? Charli and Bond had a lot to say..." She trails off when I wince.

"Yep, that's me."

"Okay, admittedly, that's a twist I didn't see coming, but what about it brought you here?" She sweeps her arm around the room dramatically.

"I can't date him. We're coworkers. And my dad is his boss. Plus, um, other reasons I'd rather not get into since I haven't even told Bond."

"It's not my business, Tuesday, but I'm going to ask anyway. Why are you here instead of talking to him?"

"Because I needed some space to think, and when he's around me, I lose about half my higher brain function."

She curls her lip and mumbles, "That's a feeling I know all too well." Her pretty blue eyes, so much like her brother's, cut over to where Dane is frowning at us. Clairy turns her attention back to me, searching my face. "You can talk to me. We don't know each other well yet, but you're important to Bond, which makes you important to me. Plus, you're a little weird, and I like that in people."

An unexpected laugh bubbles up from my chest. "I am a little weird. You're right. And thank you, Clairy. I appreciate those words. You have no idea. For now, though, I just want to enjoy this drink." We clink our glasses together and slip into comfortable conversation.

A couple of hours later, I look up from my fourth Flocked Up Flamingo and into the frowning face of Dane. "Hello there, Grumpy Puppy. The Clairys and I want another drink." I jerk my head toward Clairy One, then Clairy Two. I don't remember there being two Clairys before, but there they are.

"No more drinks. I told you the last two times you asked," Grumpy Puppy says, so grumpily.

"Babes, I told you he doesn't like having fun, so no more Flamingos."

"Oh, babes! I like that. Are we friends, Clairy? I hope so. I need a friend. I don't have any. Because I'm a ruiner, Clairy. You're so pretty and tall. I wish I was tall, but I'm not. My perfect brother is tall. Asshole." I lower my lips to my straw, slurping as I drain my cocktail.

To Dane, I say, "This bar could be so clool with a makeover. The food and drinks are delickcious." I lift my drink in a toast, proud of my excellent conversational skills. "Hey, Muriel, how's it going? Probably not that great since your head is hanging on a wall. Does this place have karaoke? Because I need some sad girl karaoke."

"That sounds so fun! Daney wouldn't let us sing on Saturday. Said we are menaces, and no one in his bar wants to listen to the two of us caterwaul," Pretty Clairy says, her voice low, imitating Grumpy Puppy. She nails it.

"You're just like your brother. All caring and beautiful. I haven't met Charli yet, but I bet she's perfect too." I frown at her. "Clairys, in the grand scheme of karma, kismet, whatever." I wave my hands, gesturing around me. "I'm ave-rage." Stupid hiccups. "I'm not a monster who kicks puppies or spits on babies. I did one terrible thing—without knowing—but still terrible. As soon as I found out the truth, I broke up with him. But the universe keeps reaching out and bitch slapping me."

"Hey, Bond." The mention of Bond's name catches my somewhat fractured attention. Through the blur in the bar I see Dane frowning into his phone. "Yeah, I know what time it is. No, stop interrupting me. You need to come down to the bar."

"Are you calling Bond?" I go for the phone, pouting when Grumpy Puppy glares at me, his dark brown eyes narrowing as he steps out of my reach. Stupid T-Rex arms. "I like Bond so much, maybe even more than like him. It's too bad I ru... ruint everything with him. I always ruin everything. It's my special gift. I want to kiss Bond. He's so handsome and funny. And the right amount of bossy while we—"

Dane frowns at me again. "Tuesday, do not finish that sentence. Yeah, look, she's beyond drunk, as is your sister. She came in almost three hours ago, and now the two of them... well, you need to come get her. No, I'll take care of Clairy. Uh-huh, I will. See you in five."

I snort. Come get me? I'm not drunk. Maybe slightly tipsy, but as soon as all these Clairys move, I'll be fine.

"You said all that out loud." Dane grumbles, "Fuck, how did the two of you end up so drunk? I told Val not to serve you anything else after your second Flamingo."

Hiccuping, I grin at him. "Oh yeah, but I'm sma-smark. I poured one I found on the bar into my glass, and then I got that boy," I point across the bar, "to buy us another one."

Dane curses under his breath, a very creative mix of words.

"Wow, that was a lot of swearing."

The Clairys giggle. "Oh yeah, Grumpy Puppy has a naughty mouth."

I'm pretty sure his ears turn pink. So cute.

"You just admitted to drinking someone's leftovers, and that 'boy' is Mr. Cahill, a former professional wrestler who is pushing sixty. Also, did you say smark?"

"Yep. Smark like a fox." I point to my temple right as someone pokes me in the eye. "Ouch, who did that?"

The Clairys laugh, so I do too. I'm not sure why we're laughing, but it's fun. I like laughing. It's so much better than crying.

With a grunt, Dane pushes off the bar. "I'll be right back. If either of you goes anywhere, I'll track you down and spank your asses red."

"Oh, Bond won't like that. He's the only one who gets to spank me." I say with as much gravity as I can muster. A wave of sleepiness hits me, and I rest my forehead on the bar for a second. Yuck, it's sticky.

When I raise my head, both Clairys are gone. "Ooooo, snap! She's going to get a spanking!" I laugh at myself because I'm very funny.

A glass of water is placed in front of me, and my Flamingo disappears. I pout—those drinks are so damn tasty—but it's just as well since the room is spinning now—an ugly off-white carousel of animal heads.

Clairy is leaning against Dane, a happy smile on her face. Wonder if she already got her spanking...the thought of Bond giving me one sends a charge through my veins. I swear I can practically smell him, all fresh air and damp earth. I shift on the barstool, imagining running my nose up his neck and breathing him in.

"Peach?"

My head snaps up, and I promptly slide off my stool.

CHAPTER THIRTEEN

I grip the steering wheel tighter, my knuckles white. If today hadn't gone so sideways, Tuesday and I would probably be in bed together right now. The two of us sleeping out this storm, Tuesday curled up against me, her pretty hair tickling my bare chest. What kind of idiot doesn't ask the woman he's falling for what her goddamn last name is?

Whatever she's running from, finding out we work together brought it all to the forefront. Now, she's trying to put walls between us. Good thing I'm a home builder.

When I said there's nothing she can say that will scare me off, I meant it. I don't fall easily, but I know what's in front of me is too special to let go. I'll show her how much she means to me. How serious I am about making things between us work, no matter her reservations.

As soon as I walk into the Great Dane, I see her, half leaning on the bar laughing. She's spectacularly disheveled, but it does nothing to detract from the fact she's still the most beautiful woman I've ever met.

I sneak behind the bar, quickly replacing her Flamingo

with a glass of water, watching her perfect lips turn down in a pout. Brats gonna brat.

A smile tugs on my lips as her glazed eyes flit from Clairy and Dane and then back to the floor. She's grumbling to herself while rubbing her forehead.

"Peach?"

As soon as I say her nickname, her head snaps up, a startled yelp coming from her as she slides off her barstool onto the floor. I spring into action, darting around the bar top and across the slick floor.

"Are you okay?" I pull her from where she's sprawled on the ground and into my arms, running my hands over her.

As she squeezes me tight, a cacophony of giggles burst from her, along with the cloying scent of too many Flocked Up Flamingos. "Of course I'm okay, Bossy Baseball Cap. You're here. Did you see someone push me? So rude! I think it was Clairy Two. She's not as nice as Clairy One."

I glance at my sister, singular, and Dane, who shrugs. "You should have called me earlier," I say as Tuesday nuzzles her nose against my chest.

"Mmmm, you smell yummy. Like home."

"Before you accuse me of over-serving, it's not true." Dane glares at Clairy, who stares at him with a look a lot like the one Tuesday is angling at me. "After the Davis sisters' epic Saturday night, I changed the limit on Flamingos to two per customer. But apparently, your girl is creative. She snagged an abandoned Flamingo off the bar and talked old man Cahill into buying them another round."

"So this is four Flamingo Tuesday." I gesture to where she's wrapped around me.

"Four Flamingo Tuesday sounds like a premontional day for the bar. I give you permission to use my name, Grumpy Puppy."

Premontional? Shit, she's hammered. Raising my eyebrows at Dane, I mouth, "*Grumpy Puppy?*"

He rolls his eyes and shakes his head. "It's been a long night. Ask her later about how 'smark' she is." Dane's a grumpy bastard most days, and I know he's annoyed, but a sliver of laughter slips through when he says that.

"I'm very smark. It's a known fact. Bond, why are you so tall? And handsome? Why do you like me? I'm a run, a roon, a... what am I?"

"A ruiner," Dane says, voice dry as a bone.

"Yes!" She scrunches her nose. "It's a hard word."

Kissing the crown of her head, I stifle a chuckle. "Yes, Baby Girl, it's a very hard word."

"I love it when you call me Baby Girl and sweetheart. So much better than Tits." She looks at Dane. "You better not call my best friend Clairy any mean names unless that's what she's into."

Dane's groan rings over the general hum of the bar.

Tuesday slumps against me, cheek pressed to my chest, eyes closed. "Take me home, Baseball Cap. You can even boss me around. I like it when you say all those dirt—"

"Hey!" I interject, stopping her from finishing that thought. I do not need my little sister, drunk as she may be, or my best friend privy to what happens in my bedroom. "Okay, on that note, Dane, if she has a tab open, I'll settle it tomorrow."

"She's good. Just get her home."

A bright smile lights up Tuesday's face as she pushes back a tangle of sunset-colored hair. "Goodbye, Grumpy Puppy. Goodbye, Clairys. Enjoy your spankings."

I raise an eyebrow at Dane, whose ears are pink. Dane spanking my sister? I need brain bleach.

"Clairy, you sure you're good with Dane taking you home?"

"Yes, that's what I want." She's leaning heavily against Dane, his arm around her waist.

"I'll call you first thing in the morning."

Clairy nods, snuggling deeper into Dane's touch as he looks at me. "I'm taking her straight home. You know I would never take advantage of a drunk girl. But especially not Clairy." A soft look passes over his normally harsh features before disappearing. "She's always safe with me."

Catching the question on my face, Dane clears his throat. "She's your sister. I'd never do anything to hurt her. You've got your hands full with that one, anyway." He nods at Tuesday, who's straining to stay standing on her tiptoes as she kisses my neck.

He's not wrong. And I trust Dane with Clairy. He won't take advantage of her being drunk, even with the mention of spankings. He's a good man, but I'd be remiss in my brotherly duty if I didn't check with her.

Dane and Clairy actually make a lot of sense. Clairy needs someone with roots, and Dane needs someone to lighten his spirit.

"I'm ready to go home, my Bond." In the span of a sentence, I'm no longer thinking about my sister and my best friend. Despite slurring her words, Tuesday called me hers.

With a mumbled goodbye, I find myself pulled along by Hurricane Tuesday, straight into the rain. She attempts to run but stumbles, my grip on her hand the only thing keeping her from crashing to the asphalt. Not taking any chances, I swing her into my arms to carry her the rest of the way to the truck.

This is a good idea in theory, but in reality, the weight of her soft curves against me is a temptation I'm hard-pressed to resist. Small hands caress my back and shoulders before they tangle in the hair at the nape of my neck. Then sweet lips nibble my earlobe down to my jaw.

And it feels good. Really fucking good.

But she's also in no frame of mind to consent to anything. Not to mention, she was in tears a few hours ago, trying to break things off. So as much as I want—and trust me, I want—to thrust my hips up against her and hear my girl purr, I don't.

"Bond." Tuesday's voice is a whine in my ear, and she pulls me tighter, using her thighs like dual vise grips. "Touch me."

I falter, almost slipping on the rain-soaked ground. Two or three steps max, and I'll be to the truck. "I am touching you, Peach." To stress my point, I pat her back before striding the remaining steps and opening the door to the cab.

When I pry her arms and legs off me and drop her into the cab, the little brat blows a raspberry at me. "That's not what I mean! I mean touuuuch me."

"Can't, Tuesday. Have to get us home." Saying *us home* seems to pacify her for the moment, and I buckle her in, mindful of her grabby hands. She wiggles her shoulders back into the seat cushion, eyes closed, and a happy smile on her lips. I take a few seconds, rubbing my hands down my face and laughing. I can't help it. Not one dull moment where this woman is concerned, and I wouldn't trade it for anything.

We make it back to my place without issue because I keep her entertained with the radio. It doesn't seem to matter which station it's on because, apparently, my girl knows all the songs. She sings loud and proud and incredibly off-key. And like everything about her, I find it charming as hell.

"Come on, let's go inside." I grab her from the truck, her silky hair tickling my nose when she rubs her head against my chin.

Sprinting through the rain to my door stoop, I set her down and grip her hips to steady her. Which is a mistake. She circles her hips, grinding back against me, and a moan slips from her lips. My cock responds, which makes her push back harder.

Jesus fucking crackers.

I cue up the mental playlist of all the unsexy things I've experienced in my thirty-six years. Breaking my nose in eighth grade, my divorce, the pea-soup scene from *The Exorcist*... Willing my blood to redistribute amongst my other organs, I say, "Tuesday, it's pouring. Let's get inside."

Tuesday stumbles in and lands face-first on the couch. With one cheek pressed into the cushion, she tries to kick off her shoes. I guide her up to sitting and pull them off for her. Then I loop her arms around my neck and carry her to my bedroom.

"Let me get you some dry clothes, and then you can change."

I search through my drawers and get as far as a pair of boxers that are too small when I feel her hands slip under my damp shirt. Fuck. Me. I'm going to have to jerk off in the shower once she's asleep.

"Hands off." I'm gruffer than normal, but if she keeps touching me, I'll lose the last shred of my control.

Her hands fall away, and she huffs. "Fine."

She's silent for a few seconds, which I take as a good sign. I should know better. I hear a faint mumbling of *Alexa play* right when I find a shirt. Then, the distinctive opening notes of Ginuwine's *Pony* blast into the formerly quiet room.

"You said hands off, but that doesn't mean I can't give you a show." Her words are a slurred jumble, and she attempts a wink before moving her body to the beat. She drags her sweater over her head, getting tangled, before throwing it to the ground in annoyance.

"What are you doing?" I ask, even though it's pretty damn obvious what she's doing. I need to distract her before she takes her pants—well, shit, too late. Her jeans land in a puddle at my feet.

"Come on, Caseball Bap, you know you want to touch me. Feel my skin on yours." Tuesday staggers closer, her chest brushing against me. She snakes her arms around my waist, shifting her hips against mine.

All I want to do is trail my fingers down the back of her thighs, wrap those legs around me, and grind against her until we both come. Instead, I gently push her back, putting space between us. But when she reaches back to unclasp her bra, I grab her arms and bark, "Tuesday, stop."

She freezes, big brown eyes filling with tears. Fucking fuck.

"You don't want me? Is this b-because of our fight today? You said you weren't g-giving up on me. I knew this wou-ld happen." Her broken words mix with drunken hiccups and teary sobs.

"Tuesday, look at me."

"No."

Sighing, I lift her chin. "Tuesday. Look. At. Me." My voice is commanding, leaving no room for debate. With a pout, she lifts her bleary eyes to mine.

"Peach." I wipe a tear from her cheek and pull her head so it's resting over my heart. "I want you. So much. But you need to drink some water, change clothes, and get some sleep."

"But—"

"No. Be a good girl. Do those things, and I'll hold you while you sleep."

"Okay," she says, that lower lip sticking out, asking for a nip from my teeth.

With a heavy exhale, I pass her the dry clothes. She fumbles them, then looks up at me, eyes wide, skin stark white. With a gurgle, she slaps her hand over her mouth.

Oh, shit. Grabbing Tuesday and moving as quickly as possible, I maneuver her around the bed to the bathroom— just in time for her to unload a violent, pink stream of vomit.

"Shhh, it's okay, sweetheart." Gathering her hair into a loose ponytail, I rub small circles against her back while she heaves the contents of her night out into the toilet.

"Go away. I d-don't want you t-to see this," she whimpers. Her muffled voice echoes inside the bowl.

"I'm not going anywhere. I meant it this afternoon, and I mean it now." She has no idea how much I mean it. It'll take more than a little puke to run me off.

"But I'm gross." No sooner have the words left her mouth than another flock of Flamingos makes their appearance.

"You're perfect. Go on, get the rest out; you'll feel better." Fucking Dane. I love the guy, he's like a brother to me, but he should ban those damn drinks. I hope he's faring better with Clairy.

"Let me wipe your face, Baby Girl. Come here." Her head lolls to the side, and I grab a nearby washcloth, gently wiping her eyes, cheeks, and mouth before gathering her in my arms. "Do you think you're going to be sick again?"

She shakes her head and sniffles, looking up at me with red eyes and tear-streaked cheeks. Even now, my girl is nothing less than flawless.

Between the two of us, we get her teeth brushed and her face washed. But looking at her, I make a decision. I walk to the shower and adjust the temperature so it's nice and warm. Tuesday is all but passed out in my arms, pliable like a rag doll. Without bothering to undress, I step under the spray and carefully prop her between my body and the wall.

Seeing her like this, vulnerable and sick, awakens my primal side. It demands I protect and care for what's mine. And make no mistake, Tuesday Phillips is mine. Nothing that happened today changes that fact.

I grab my shampoo and massage it into her scalp. The side

of me that wants to be a possessive asshole struts like a rooster knowing she'll smell like me tonight.

Tuesday's eyes flutter but stay closed. I shift her slightly, giving myself a better angle to rinse the suds from her hair. I study her pretty features as drops of water slide down her skin —the curve of her lips, the smattering of freckles across the bridge of her nose.

She's so beautiful. A messy, funny, stubborn whirlwind of a woman. Refocusing on her, I repeat those same actions, this time with conditioner, working it through, ensuring her hair is tangle free before rinsing.

Snagging a fluffy towel off the rack, I dry her off. Then I set her on the bed, and in the most gentlemanly way possible, I slip off her wet bra and panties and tug an oversized t-shirt over her head.

Tuesday never stirs.

I gently kiss her forehead and lower her head to her pillow. Once I'm certain she isn't going anywhere, I strip out of my soaked clothes, dim the lights—not all the way because my girl doesn't like the dark—and climb under the covers next to her.

As I'm about to drift off, Tuesday whispers, "I'm sorry." Her voice is raspy and worn.

"Hey, I thought you were asleep. Why are you apologizing?"

"Because I roone, run, mess everything up. Just ask my family; they'll tell y-you."

She's breaking my heart. Hugging her tight, I say, "I promise you haven't messed anything up. Tomorrow, we'll figure everything out. Find a way to make this work."

Tiny fingers reach out and pinch my side. "You shouldn't make promises you can't keep. Are you sure you're real?"

Chuckling, I say, "Yeah, sweetheart, I'm real, and ruin is a hard word to say."

With a sigh, Tuesday's body relaxes against mine. "See, you get it. That's why you're my Bond."

Her words trail off, but I catch her once again calling me hers. She has no idea. No idea at all how well and truly gone I am for her. Fuck it being too fast. Fuck all the things we don't know about each other. Fuck what people may say.

"Truth. You're my future, Tuesday Phillips." I drop one last kiss on her head before closing my eyes.

I wake with Tuesday snuggled against my chest, and it's so right. This is how my life should be every day.

With eyes half-closed, Tuesday kisses my skin, her lips so soft. She yawns and stretches, a sweet, sleepy smile on her face. Then she blinks at me. Once. Twice. Before a wrinkle forms between her brows.

"Bond?" Her gaze drops down to the worn t-shirt. "Why am I only wearing a shirt?"

"Because last night, you needed a shower. I promise nothing funny happened. You—"

Tuesday cuts me off, groaning, covering her eyes with her hands. "Oh no. No. No, no, no. The striptease. The throwing up. That wasn't a dream?"

"No, Peach, it was real." I do my best to stifle my laughter.

She sinks back into the bed, pulling the blankets over her head and wiggling her way downwards.

I lift them, peering at her. "Where are you going? You know you can't get out that way."

"Leave me here to die in peace," she says, face buried in my thighs. My half-hard cock twitches at the warmth of her breath so close but now is not the time.

Reaching down, I haul her up into my arms. "Never, Baby Girl."

"Please don't be nice to me. I can't take it if you're nice."

"I'm always nice."

"I know. That's part of the problem." She hides her face in my neck. "I can't believe I got that drunk. Did I do anything else I'll have to skip town for?"

"Naw, nothing the Great Dane hasn't seen before."

"So I got drunk, acted like a fool, stripped, then threw up on you?"

I nod. "Though you didn't throw up on me, just near me, if that makes you feel better."

She folds her lips into a thin line. "It does not." Then tears well in her eyes.

"Fuck, please don't cry."

"I'm sorry. For all of it. I made a mess of everything."

I hold her against my chest, tangling her legs with mine, immobilizing her. "No apologies. Nothing is broken." I pause. "Or ruined. Bet you can say that word like a champ now, huh, Peach?" I kiss the tip of her nose and grin when she glares at me. Love seeing a little of her fire back.

"Today, we are going to work. You'll meet the team, get to know the office and our systems. We'll be completely professional, nothing more than two very attractive colleagues sharing a workspace." That earns me a small smile, and I soak it in. "Then tonight, we'll have dinner and talk until we agree to keep seeing each other."

"Ha, there's that bossy side again."

"I thought you liked my bossy side?"

Her laugh is like a balm to my bristling nerves. "Oh, I do."

I press my forehead to hers and murmur, "Don't say goodbye. Promise me."

"I'm not." Her lips graze mine. "But we have to be at work in an hour. I need to get back to my motel, and I feel like someone sucked all the moisture out of my body and replaced it with sand." She pries my hands apart and slips out of my grasp. Counting on her fingers, she says, "I desperately need food, coffee, water, and triple thick concealer to have even a chance of looking presentable today."

With a teasing wink, I reply, "Guess I'll get you back to your place then, Ms. Phillips."

I blow her one last kiss when I drop her off at her motel. My heart screams that I'm an idiot who should pin her to the wall and kiss her until she's breathless, but my brain reminds me I have work and a plan. I can be professional from nine to five, but at 5:01 Tuesday Phillips and I are settling this because she's dead wrong if she thinks I'm letting her go.

CHAPTER FOURTEEN

At promptly nine o'clock, Bond meets me at the Davis Designs door, pecan coffee and sea-salt croissant in hand. When I raise an eyebrow in surprise, he shrugs.

"This is our way of making up for not having your desk ready yesterday. But if you don't want it..." A teasing smile lights his blue eyes.

There is no way I'm turning down my favorite buttery, flakey treat. So, like the carb and caffeine addict I am, I snatch both from his outstretched hands. "Thank you," I say loud enough for everyone to hear. But to him, I whisper, "Even if I don't fully believe these are '*Sorry we didn't have a chair for you*' gifts."

He shoots me his most innocent smile. "Come on, Tuesday, let's finish up that tour Morgan started yesterday. I'll make sure to introduce you to the other employees."

They have a great thing going on here. Though there aren't many, the employees are all friendly, seem genuinely happy to be working at Davis Designs—and more surprisingly—happy to meet me. There's an easy camaraderie, something I never experienced at Phillips HQ.

Reaching our shared office, Bond sweeps open the door and bows at the waist like he's some sort of fairytale prince. They've brought in a matching desk, attaching it to the end of Bond's, putting us in an L configuration. It gives me a fantastic view of the mountains.

Cutting my eyes to him, I say, "This is a lovely workspace."

"Glad you like it." Bond grins before settling at his desk and diving into work.

I unpack my meager office supplies, acquaint myself with my new laptop, and finish some paperwork. Then I start pulling comps and land deeds, the familiarity of the process oddly comforting. After doing that for a while, I switch modes, settling into brainstorming possible ways to increase Davis Designs' social media presence.

Around two that afternoon, I stand and stretch, my half-eaten lunch lying forgotten on my desk. Turns out that in addition to having a wonderful view of the mountains, the placement of my desk also gives me a perfect view of Bond. Which is equally amazing and distracting, to say the least.

He's seemingly unaffected, typing away on his laptop. Meanwhile, I'm sitting here excruciatingly aware that it's been six hours since Bond dropped me off at my motel room. Six hours in which I've displayed perfect work decorum—no flirting, no lingering touches, no longing stares...well, a few longing stares, but I'm a paragon of discretion. Totally subtle and sneaky. Nothing at all that would make anyone suspect the two of us are more than colleagues sharing an office.

I study his face, the strength of his square jaw, the shadow of his stubble, that wonderfully imperfect nose, his full lips. He's so handsome. So funny. So kind.

So professional.

True to his words, Bond has been the picture of propriety since we arrived at work. Which is great.

Perfect.

Precisely what I want.

I am one hundred percent on board with him treating me like any other coworker.

Eighty-five percent fine with it.

Maybe forty percent.

Who am I kidding? I am zero percent happy about this, but it's my own doing.

I'm suddenly gripped with the overwhelming urge to crawl across our shared workspace and kiss him silly.

Or, even better, crawl under our desks and kiss him in other not work-appropriate places until he's moaning my name and everyone here knows exactly what he means to me.

I want to get so caught up in him that all my doubts and fears melt away. Tell him that despite the speed, he already means everything to me. Share why I'm afraid, and lay all my secrets on the table between us.

"You're staring." Bond's deep voice startles me from where I am, in fact, staring.

"What?"

"You're staring at me. Have been off and on all day."

"No, I'm not." Brilliant retort, Tuesday.

"It's okay, I don't mind." His nonchalant shrug brings my shoulders up to my ears.

"I wasn't staring...at you. I, um, there was a deer." Yes. Totally believable.

Bond swivels in his chair, studying the wall of windows before glancing back at me. "A deer? At two in the afternoon? In the center of town?" He chops through my fabrication as if it's squishy fruit.

Bond-one, Tuesday-zero.

"It could have been a big dog." I nod my head as if that will convince him.

That delicious, teasing smile is on his face. "A deer-sized dog." He tries and fails to smother his laughter.

"I thought I was the bratty one in this relationship." Then I jerk my head up, eyebrows lifted, eyes wide, and mouth agape. Crap. Not a relationship. It might be after we talk tonight, but it sure isn't right now. Because work.

"Relatio—" Bond cuts off when a sliver of balsamic-dressed tomato flies across the desk and hits him on the cheek.

Holy balls. I threw a tomato at my for sure boss and maybe boyfriend. Professionalism? Don't know her.

What is wrong with me? Who behaves this way? Why can't I admit I was staring at him like a cartoon character with heart eyes? I roll my lips and look down at my desk to keep from laughing. Because as horrified as I am by my behavior, the sight of a stunned Bond peeling a tomato slice off his rugged face will stay with me for a long, long time.

"Did you throw a tomato at me?"

Still looking at the desk, I say, "No."

He snorts. "No? It flew over here of its own accord?"

"Yes?" I grimace, chancing a look at him. He's smiling, a mischievous twinkle in his eyes. A gasp of surprise puffs from my lips when the same slice of tomato nails me in the fore-head. My voice goes ultrasonic. "Is this you being work appropriate?"

The hypocrisy demon is alive and well inside me.

Grabbing the twice-thrown tomato and the remains of my lunch, I rush over to the trash can, thinking about stupid, perfect men with infuriatingly soft lips and idiotically thick thighs.

Wiping the slimy remnants from my hands, I freeze. Despite no noise indicating movement, I know he's near. An undercurrent of electricity buzzes through me, all the proof I need. The large hand coming to rest on the wall next to my head confirms it.

For a millisecond, I tense before melting into his touch when he sweeps my hair to the side. Whispers of his breath tickle the nape of my neck when, in a faux innocent voice, Bond says, "Was I being inappropriate? I was simply returning your lunch to you."

His free hand settles on my hip, the warmth seeping into my skin even through the dual layers of my skirt and tights, setting all my nerve endings alight. A whimper slips from my lips when his hand comes off the wall, sliding up the entire length of my arm, across my collarbone, to rest against my throat.

"Is this okay, Peach? My hand here?"

I swallow. "Y-yes." Can he feel how my pulse races? Hear how it drums? Anticipation spreads out from my stomach, upwards to my pounding heart, and down towards...other parts. I push into his touch, my eyes closing at the press of his broad chest to my back. He smells so good, like crisp air and hints of something earthy and sweet.

Bond's grip on my hip and throat tighten, holding me so close I couldn't get away even if I wanted to. Which I emphatically do not.

Lips, softer than they have any right to be, brush the shell of my ear. "If I was being unprofessional, I might say the way you've been staring at me all day has me hard as a fucking rock." Bond rolls his hips into my ass, punctuating his point. "Or that your tight little skirt is driving me up the wall and has me imagining hundreds of ways I can make you scream my name."

A hand slides down my thigh before snaking under my skirt, fingers skimming ever so lightly over the clenching heat between my thighs. "Maybe I'd say I've been imagining you bent over my desk since 9:01 this morning, my face buried in your ass, licking you while you writhe in pleasure. You're mine. My good girl. And pretending you're nothing but a coworker feels so fucking wrong." His teeth graze that sensitive spot behind my ear, and his hips thrust forward again. "That would be unprofessional."

My high-pitched whine pierces the air around us, and my eyes cut to the door, thankful it's firmly closed.

"Shhh, Baby Girl."

Spinning me in his arms, Bond kisses me as though he's a man dying of thirst and I'm the lone source of water. Tongues twine, breaths heave, lips chase. He holds me firm, my soft curves melding to his solid frame. Then, the kiss slows, and he savors me like I'm fine wine.

"Tuesday."

My name on his lips sounds like a prayer. An exquisite psalm from him to me.

"Bond," my answering purr spurs him on as he places hot, open-mouthed kisses haphazardly on my neck. When his thigh slips between mine, I can't help but grind against him. All I can do is feel. All I am is need.

His lips skate over mine, a gossamer-light caress, before drawing back. Our mouths barely touch as we breathe. His chest rises and falls, my aching heat still resting on his thigh. My fingers dig into his wide shoulders while his keep me rocking against him. As I'm about to speak? Kiss him? Ride his thigh until I come? Before I can decide, a knock at the door snaps us away from each other like a broken rubber band.

A thousand thoughts fire through my mind in rapid succession. They range from the absurd: my father being the one at the door here to berate me in front of my new team. My mom with a stylist to pick apart my outfit. All the way to the more likely scenario of Morgan bringing papers to sign, but the one thing they all have in common? They make my chest tighten and my blood pressure spike.

Frantically smoothing my hair and clothes, I rush to put distance between us, my heart in my throat.

Bond coughs out a choked, "Just a sec!" before striding across the room and dropping into his chair, strategically placing himself behind his desk to hide his hard-on. Acting as if he didn't cause me to soak my panties like a human firehose, he calls out, "Come in."

I want nothing more than to wipe that damn delicious grin off his face, preferably by sitting on it.

"Hello." A beautiful woman about my height, with generous curves, honey-blonde hair, and eyes the same shade as Bond's, walks into our office. She's either oblivious to my flushed cheeks and heaving chest, or she's too polite to say anything. Fingers crossed for option one.

"Charli? What are you—"

"I came to meet Tuesday. She's all anyone is talking about."

Her words make me cringe, but I keep my smile fixed firmly in place.

"I'm Charlotte or Charli. Most employees call me Charlotte, but obviously, the situation with you is different." Charli smiles at Bond and me, her head tilted and blue eyes flicking back and forth between the two of us.

Waving my hands in her direction, I say, "No, no. Nothing different, please. If you'd prefer I call you Charlotte, that is totally fine. I'm a regular employee like everyone else. Not looking for any special treatment because of who my dad and brother are." I smile, hoping it comes off bright and confident, not anxious and flustered. I don't want the specter of my family hanging over my head. Yes, nepotism of the highest order is at play—my dad literally bought their company to stick me here—but I'm committed to making things work in Trail Creek. And no small part of that is helping Davis Designs become an even bigger success.

Charli frowns, and her brow furrows. "Um, I didn't mean because of the Phillips. I meant because you and Bond...well, you know." She laughs. "I feel pretty confident that you are the only Tuesday in town and the same one Bond and Clairy have been talking about."

I open my mouth and then close it. It makes sense. Bond told me his sisters teased him about the Netflix and chill text. I got drunk with Clairy last night. Bond talked about Clairy and Charli with me. Why wouldn't he also talk to them about me? Of course, Charli knows who I am.

However, rational thought swan dives out of my head, clearing a path for Irrational Tuesday to shine. Beads of sweat form on my forehead and, unfortunately, other places. The rosy, picturesque image of my fresh start shrivels and dies before me. If Charli knows who I am and what's going on between her brother and me, it's only a matter of time before the entire office is aware. If they aren't already. She did say I'm all anyone can talk about.

Past experience tells me this is a bad thing. A very bad thing.

My morning interactions, brief as they were, flit through my mind. Was Morgan's smile friendly or knowing? Did Cal notice I stood too close to Bond when we went into the workshop? I analyze them, looking for any sign the other employees know. Each conversation, look, laugh. Were they genuine or already tainted by the knowledge I'm not only the new owner's daughter but also all but sleeping with Bond?

Bond and Charli are watching me, curiosity on her face and trepidation on his. Crap. It's been too long since anyone has spoken. I will my brain and mouth to get on the same page, but alas, those traitorous bitches betray me.

I make a noise similar to a deflating balloon. My flight or fight response kicks in, and I bolt.

Thankful I'm wearing my usual flats, I spring toward the door, fling it open, and rush out of the office. Bond calls my name, but it's white noise. I scour the small hallway for anywhere I can hide. I just need a minute. Or twenty. Yanking on the handle to the small supply closet, I scurry in, slamming it shut behind me. There's no lock, but there is a small over-head bulb. I'll take it. I stumble over the surplus paper towels and other cleaning accouterments before crashing to the floor under the weak light.

With a groan, I bang my head against the wall and replay the last few minutes, watching it in abject horror, like some sort of terrible B-movie. I want to yell at the Tuesday in my mind, *No, you dummy! Don't go in there!*

There being this closet.

This isn't me. Tuesday Jane Phillips doesn't hide in supply closets. She stands up for herself. She doesn't let what people think or say about her make her feel less than. She doesn't slink off to lick her wounded pride.

Except...that's not really true, is it? I mean, I ran away to a whole new state, for crying out loud. Granted, I didn't have a lot of choice in the matter.

No, even that's not true. I did have a choice. I could have quit.

Trail Creek Tuesday threatened to stab Jacob Ashford with an olive fork. She stood up to her family with a classic, *Don't call us, we'll call you.* And she is rapidly falling for a wonderful man who treats her like something precious.

Dallas Tuesday is the one who hides in closets, scared of

possibilities, but it's time she lets go and gives Trail Creek Tuesday the reins.

With three deep breaths, I stand. Shoulders back, head up, I'm ready to face Bond, Charli, and anyone else who comes my way. TCT is on the job.

Or at least she will be once I get out of this hiding spot.

I'm ready to let myself fall, trusting Bond will catch me. With a deep breath, I open the closet door and smash directly into a familiar chest.

CHAPTER FIFTEEN

I watch, stunned, as Tuesday darts from the room.

"Tuesday!" I call after her, but she doesn't stop, disappearing through our office door in a blur. Shit.

Charli turns to me, blue eyes wide. "Bond, what's going on?"

"Sorry, I've gotta go. I'll catch you up later, I promise."

"Yeah, of course; anything I can do?"

"Nothing, but please keep what went down quiet." At Charli's fretful nod, I shoot her a half grin. "Don't worry, Charli Horse. I'm not giving up." With that, I stride from the office in search of my girl.

I've never been more thankful our office isn't massive. There are only a few places Tuesday could have gone, but given how she reacted yesterday, there's always the chance she left the building.

"Hey, Morgan?" I stick my head around the corner, getting the younger woman's attention.

"Yes?"

"Has Tuesday come through here by chance?"

"No, sorry. I haven't seen her since I brought lunch around to everyone."

"Thanks." I keep it at that—no need to stir anything, especially knowing how Tuesday feels about office gossip.

She's still in the building. That soothes some of the ache in me. I doubt she's in Charli's office. The breakroom, shared workroom, and workshop are also unlikely because they have people in them. I beeline to the two storage closets, but the first one is locked.

"Gotcha, Peach," I say as I jerk open the door to the small space we use to hold our janitorial supplies.

An *oomph* slips through my lips when Tuesday's small, soft body crashes into mine. Without thinking, I wrap my arms around her and bury my nose in her hair. My instinct is to comfort her, hold her. I don't care who sees us.

But she does.

So I bear hug her and walk us both back into the supply closet, shutting the door behind me. Running my hands over her, partly to check she's okay but mostly to make sure she's real, I say, "You ran."

"I-I did."

I place a quick kiss on her lips. "Where you headed?"

"Could you set me down?"

I'm still crushing her to me, her tiny feet barely touching the ground.

"Oh, shit yeah, sorry, sweetheart." While I loosen my grip enough for her to stand, I don't let go completely. Her bolting spooked me, as much as I don't want to admit it, and I'm not ready for her to be out of my sight or arms.

"I was coming back to apologize to you and Charli for running away." Her voice is quiet but strong.

"You don't need to apologize, Peach, but we do need to talk."

Before she can say anything else, I sink to the floor, pulling her into my lap. I need my hands on her. Need to feel the beat of her pulse, the warmth of her skin, the silk of her hair.

"Bond, we can't stay in here."

"The way I see it, we have two options." I squeeze her thighs as they straddle my lap. "Option one, we have this talk right here, right now, in this closet. You tell me your truth, and I tell you why it's not enough to end this. Option two, same as the first."

She huffs with a hint of laughter. "So by two options, you mean..." Tuesday raises her eyebrows at me.

"I mean, I'm being an asshole and only giving you one. I'm not waiting until after work. I'm a relentless man, Peach, and what we have is worth being stubborn for."

"I can't have this talk here. Someone could walk in and find us."

"No one's walking in. Morgan and Charli are the only other people here now. Everyone else is out in the field, and Sally, our cleaning lady, comes in after six."

Tuesday goes to talk, but I cover her lips with mine. This conversation is too important to put off even a second longer. So if it has to happen on a storeroom floor, so be it. I need to know why she's running, and for her to understand I'm going to keep giving chase.

With my lips against her skin, I whisper, "I'm so fucking sorry. I'd already told Charli about you, mooned over you to her, actually. Days before I found out you were TJ. I didn't get to tell her about everything else that happened."

Her small hands push against my chest, putting another half-inch of space between us. It's too far.

"I overreacted."

"No, Tues—" The pillowy brush of her lips against mine cut me off.

"Shhh, you big wonderful man. Let me talk."

"Sorry."

Tuesday wiggles, moving around so her back is to my chest. "It'll be easier if I'm not looking at you."

"Because looking at me is so distracting, you can't think?" I tease, using my most cocksure voice.

"Good gravy."

"Okay, sweetheart. If that's what you need." I rub my hands up and down her arms until she relaxes against me.

"So, obviously, we were failing at being professional before Charli walked in. We only made it through two-thirds of the day before we gave in."

"I take full responsibility for that, Tuesday. I told you I'd be professional; I took it too far. That's not on you."

Tuesday's words temper the memory of that heated kiss, how good she felt pressed up against me.

"It's on both of us. I wanted everything you did and more. If Charli hadn't walked in," she sighs, "I don't think I would have stopped. Which is part of the problem."

"Wanting me too much is a problem?" I tickle her a little to make sure there's no sting in my words.

"No tickling! And yes, in a way, it's a huge problem. We have to work together. No matter what happens after we talk, we'll still be office mates tomorrow. Do you think we can maintain a professional environment when we couldn't even go a full day without making out in our office?"

"It's no one's business what you and I do in our personal lives so long as it doesn't impact the job."

"But it does impact the job, Bond. Did you get everything done you needed to with me in there?"

"Actually, I got more done. I was so focused on not flirting with you that I did a full day's worth of paperwork in three hours."

"You are impossibly perfect; you know that?" Tuesday thumps her head against my chest. "I wasn't as productive."

"That's the learning curve. You'll find your adorable little feet here soon."

Her snort makes me chuckle.

"Anyway, when Charli made it clear she knew about us, I panicked. I saw everything that happened over the past seven months happening again and my fresh start here in Trail Creek," her words speed up, and I almost miss when she says, "here with you, slipping through my fingers."

"I'll say it until you believe me. Every day, if that's what it takes, but you aren't losing me."

"Are you real?"

I throw my head back, laughing, "You asked me that last night. Even pinched me, though I'm pretty sure I'm supposed to pinch you."

Tuesday's honeyed laugh curls in my ear and down to my chest.

"I was a disaster. Am a disaster. Bond, you deserve—"

"Stopping you right there, sweetheart. I deserve *you*. That's all there is to it." I kiss the crown of her head. "Now. Tell me your story. Tell me what's got you running from me. What brought you here."

I watch her long lashes shadow her cheeks as she closes her eyes. *Come on, Tuesday, trust me.*

"I already told you that my last relationship was with a coworker."

Her voice is small, and I make a quick decision. "Hold on, Peach. Stand up for a sec." Tuesday rises as I shuffle and rearrange the stacks of supplies around us until I have a clear spot from wall to wall. I click the lock on the door, then reach up, pulling the string to turn off the overhead bulb. Darkness envelops us, the only light a tiny sliver coming from the crack between the door and the floor.

"Bond, if your goal is to calm me, this is not helping." Tuesday's voice is brittle, her breathing gaining speed.

"Easy, Baby Girl. Easy." I flip on the flashlight on my phone, propping it up so it shines on the wall. Though our faces are still in the dark, I can make out Tuesday's delicate features in the shadows. I drop to the floor, snagging a roll of paper towels, then guide Tuesday down. It's a tight fit, my wide, six-one frame not meant for hiding in storage closets, but I'm going with my gut. I prop my head on the paper towel roll, then snag Tuesday so she's lying against my chest.

"Selfishly, this lets me touch more of you." To emphasize my point, I grab one of her legs and haul it over mine, setting my hand on her curvy ass.

"Bond, this is for sure not keeping it colleagues only."

The tinge of worry in her voice makes me wish I could purr like an alpha in those Omegaverse romance novels my sisters love. I briefly wonder if Tuesday reads those. Adding that to my list of things to learn.

"Trust me, Peach." Giving her a quick squeeze of encouragement, I wait. I've pushed her to stay while settling her as much as I can. Now, I need to give her the space to talk.

"It started the way a lot of relationships at work do. Unintentionally. I was working on the purchase of a lot with a standing building. Phillips Construction wanted to demolish the building and use the foundation for a new warehouse. The seller made all these demands and constantly tried to amend the purchase price. It was a lot of back and forth, so I spent extra time in the legal department."

"Phillips has its own legal department?"

"Yeah, legal, marketing, finance, acquisitions, interior design, landscaping, etc. Depending on the size, each department has a director or executive director who reports to Dad and War."

"But not you?"

She shakes with silent laughter against me. "Oh gosh, no. I wasn't a director there. Just a regular office drone."

I don't like her seeing herself as a drone. Tuesday is a queen.

Her slim fingers tap against my chest, and I brace myself when she takes a deep breath and says, "Dating Duncan Wright was the worst mistake I ever made."

CHAPTER SIXTEEN

Curling around Bond like he's my personal body pillow in the darkened room—and knowing the door is locked—makes it easier to breathe. The feeling of a hand clutching my heart lessens, and I relax against him, the words spilling from my lips.

I walk into legal, a smile on my face. Duncan and I are coming up on three months together, and while things aren't going great, they are at least going. He's been with Phillips Construction for about nine months, and during that time, he aggressively pursued me. I resisted for months until he wore me down.

He's kind of a jerk, if I'm being totally honest, but he's older, good-looking, and can be charming.

Sometimes.

When he wants something.

The clearing of a throat pauses my story. "Yes?"

"How good-looking?"

I smile into Bond's chest. "A troll compared to you, Baseball Cap."

Bond's rumbly chuckle vibrates my ear, and I let out a happy sigh before diving back in.

"Hey, Tits, what brings you here?"

I cringe at the horrible nickname, glancing around to see who's listening. "Duncan, I've asked you not to call me that. Especially in the office. I need you to sign these forms for the Bradshaw lot."

"Relax. You're always so sensitive." He signs off on the documents without looking them over, then punctuates his reply with a quick slap to my ass. My cheeks burn when one or two employees turn to watch us. Duncan, seemingly unaware or simply uncaring, turns his hazel eyes on me. "So, have you heard anything about the possible new Executive Director position?"

"No, I told you. Dad and War never talk shop with me unless it's specifically about a new lot or small company acquisition my team is handling."

He reaches out, patting my head like I'm a child. "It would mean a lot to me if you would talk to your dad about it. You know how much I want this."

"Tuesday, this guy is a dick."

I bury my face deeper into Bond's broad chest. "I told you I ignored the red flags despite them practically slapping me in the face."

"I swear if I ever meet him..."

The way his words growl from deep in his throat makes me want to stop telling this horrible story and instead let him kiss me senseless. But if I don't get it all out now, I'll find more excuses not to talk about it.

Bond's fingers walk up and down my side, from my hip to my shoulder, and I lose myself in the soothing pattern and my story once again.

In an attempt to change the conversation, I ask, "Are you going to the company thing on Saturday?"

"Yes, it's required. But we have to stay away from each other."

I nod. I'm the one who suggested we keep things quiet.

After he said it would look bad if people knew we were together.

Duncan dismisses me by turning his attention back to his monitor. I flip him off behind the screen before going down to my floor. Despite the momentary smile it brings me, the discomfort in my chest and ache in my stomach don't ebb. Just like they haven't for the eleven weeks Duncan and I have been together.

The following day, I wake up not feeling well, so I text him to let him know I probably won't be at the company picnic. He sends back a thumbs up. No asking if I'm okay or anything else. With a sigh, I send the same message to my father, who immediately sends me a paragraph-long reply about my familial obligations and how irresponsible and disappointing I am.

So I suck it up, and Saturday morning, I arrive at the Phillips Family Fish Fry—insert internal eye roll here—alongside my mom, dad, and War, doing my best dutiful daughter song and dance. I make it through two miserable hours of forced social interactions before wandering away. My head pounds, and I need space.

I'm aimlessly wandering when I see him. Well, them—Duncan, a beautiful brunette, and two small children. At first, I think, hope, delude myself that they are just people he knows. A colleague's family, maybe. But then, he kisses her with a tenderness he's never shown me, and I know. Know how foolish I am. How he's played me all along. A way to get what he wants, all while already having more than he deserves.

The blinders I have in place regarding Duncan fall away with a clatter. This is why we never go to his place—not because he thinks I'm more comfortable in my apartment or because hotels make it feel like a getaway. Why his replies are spotty after eight at night. The real reason we have to keep things secret. It's not about protecting our work reputations. How could I be so stupid?

It's about his picture-perfect family. Complete with loving wife and two-point-five children.

"Two-point-five? She was preg—"

"Yep. Easily six months along."

"Shit." He squeezes me as though he can fight away the shame coursing through me with his bare hands. How I wish he could.

A couple of tears drip down my cheeks. Not over Duncan, never over him, but over her and the kids, how selfish he is, and how many lives he ruined with his gluttony.

"What did you do?" Bond brushes away a tear, and I sink deeper into his touch. At this point, I'm pressing as much of myself to him as I can. Burrowing into his warmth, kindness, and strength.

"I left. Ran." A mirthless laugh fills the tiny storage space. "No shocker there."

"Hey, Baby Girl, look at me."

I lift myself enough to make out Bond's face in the dimly lit room.

"We can stop. You don't have to tell me anymore." He presses his palm to my cheek, and I can't help but turn my face into his touch.

"No, I told you I would tell you. I want to." Despite the shake in my voice, I mean my words.

Three days, a massive number of unanswered text messages, and five deleted voicemails later, Duncan corners me in my small work-space. "Why are you ignoring me, Tuesday?"

He's angry. That much is clear. The absolute irony of him being mad at me makes me want to fall over laughing.

"I stop dating guys when I find out they're married. So sorry I didn't get back to you. Guess you'll have to find someone else to pretend to care about." I lean into the snark and embrace the sarcasm. It hides the hurt so well.

"Are you going to act like you didn't know?"

"I didn't!"

"Come on, Tits. You aren't stupid. Did you really think all that time spent at your place and the hotels was to make it special?"

"Do you really think I would be okay with finding out you are married?"

His derisive snort tells me everything. "I think you'll take love anywhere you can find it."

I jerk back like he's slapped me. "Get out of my cubicle, Duncan, and don't call me again."

Weeks pass, and I manage to avoid him entirely, pawning any jobs with him onto my team. Until…

"Did you tell my wife we were sleeping together?"

I glance up from where I'm working to find a red-faced Duncan standing in my cubicle. "What?"

"Did you tell my wife about us, you dumb slut?"

"Stop right there, Tuesday. He called you a dumb slut?" Bond's voice is dangerous and dark. The last word nothing more than a bark.

"Remember when I said I don't like being called names? Now you have a better understanding of why."

His arms are iron bands around me, and his legs twine around mine until we are coiled together like the snakes on a caduceus.

Through gritted teeth, Bond says, "Go on."

"Yes, of course, I told her, you skeezeball. In fact, I took her to lunch and offered to pay for her lawyer." For a moment, I think he might hit me. Instead, he goes deathly quiet.

After a few agonizing seconds, he says, "You're going to regret this," before storming away.

The next few times I see Duncan, he smiles at me in a way that makes my stomach ache, but he doesn't speak to me, and for that, I'm thankful. Then, the first email arrives.

I'm checking my messages, and there in my inbox is one from Unknown. The subject mentions an acquisition I'm working on, so like an idiot, I assume it's actually work-related. Imagine my surprise when I open it to find a picture of myself naked and in a very compromising position. A picture I did not consent to take.

"Bond!" I yelp when he sits straight up, me still in his arms.

"Need to drive. Need to do something with my hands and mind. Let's go, Peach."

"Go? We can't go."

Bond presses his forehead to mine. "I'm begging, please, Tuesday. I need to get out of this room."

Swallowing, I say, "Okay, Baseball Cap. Why don't you drive me out to my new house? That's a good fifteen minutes from here."

He gives me a jerky nod of assent before flinging the door open. He looks both ways down the hall. "Morgan isn't at her desk. We're going."

I'm practically jogging to keep up with his long-legged stride. When we reach his truck, he yanks open the door and all but tosses me in. Only then do I get a chance to see his face. He's furious. I've seen silly Bond, happy Bond, worried, smug, and post blow job Bond. But angry Bond is a truly terrible, beautiful sight.

"Bond?"

"Not mad at you, sweetheart. Never at you." The furious line of his brow softens, and his lips search out mine, brushing over them in a feather-light kiss.

Bond climbs in and peels out of the Davis Designs parking lot. His hands grip the wheel, knuckles white, veins visible in his forearms.

The pretty vista of Trail Creek is nothing but a blur as we speed through town. I can't help but reach over and stroke his arm, wanting to ease some of his tension and take away the hurt and anger on his face.

At my touch, he closes his eyes briefly before giving me a slight nod. I guess that's my cue to continue on with this horror show of a story.

I print out the email, grab my phone, and head to the bank of elevators, intending to go to Human Resources. But as soon as the elevator doors open, Duncan steps out. He grabs my arm and steers me into the closest empty cubicle.

"You said he never physically hurt you."

In a soft voice, I say, "He didn't. I swear." Pausing, I try to smirk, but it comes out more like a snarl. "Though the emotional damage is clearly long-lasting."

My weak attempt at a joke falls flat in the tension of the cab.

"Not funny, sweetheart."

With a huff at the ceiling, I continue.

Jerking my arm from his grasp, I stare him down. "What the hell do you think you're doing?" I hiss.

"I'm giving you a warning. It'd be a real shame if everyone in the office gets ahold of these photos." As the color drains from my face, he sneers. "Yes, there are more. You really should be more careful about who you trust, Tuesday."

I set my jaw, unwilling to give him any more emotion.

"You want this to go away? It's easy. I'm on the shortlist for the Executive Director position. All you have to do is convince Daddy to give me the job," he pauses and, almost as an afterthought, adds, "and tell my wife you lied."

With that, he walks away, leaving me alone, clutching the printed email. I sprint down the stairs, five flights, to HR. I come clean about everything. Dating him, finding out he's married, telling his wife, the email, and his threat to post the pictures if I don't give him what he wants.

I get called into my father's office almost as soon as I leave HR. He's furious, not for me, but at me. Not over me being lied to or extorted, but because I dared to date someone in the company and then admitted it to HR. He spends hours berating me.

His words seem chosen to deliver the most pain. "Don't you understand how this makes me look? My daughter galavanting with employees, sleeping around with married men. You should be ashamed of yourself, Tuesday. How could you be so irresponsible? Get out of my office."

Bond's jaw ticks, and his hands flex around the steering wheel.

HR, in their benevolence, puts us both on administrative leave while they conduct their investigation. Six weeks later, because things like this take forever to move forward, I'm invited back to work. Duncan isn't.

However, it turns out he isn't actually fired. He's given the opportunity to resign without penalty and a cushy severance package. HR says since the email was sent from an anonymous sender and it's my word against his, they don't have cause to terminate him. My dad even gives him a glowing referral to help him secure a new job because, according to him, my mistake cost Phillips Construction a valuable employee.

"What. The. Fuck." Bond's voice is almost feral.

A week later, the pictures, four total, end up all over the Phillips Construction listserv and then start to pop up on various websites.

"Four?"

"Yes."

"Want to make sure I break the right number of bones."

I unbuckle my seatbelt, scoot to the center of the bench seat, and kiss him on the cheek.

"Put that seatbelt back on, Peach, hate to have to pull over and spank you."

Ah, there's my Bond. I do as he asks but stay in the middle, looping my arm through his and resting my palm on his thigh.

"It was bad enough that everyone at work saw them." I

cringe, embarrassment heating my cheeks. "At least *those* we could delete and remove from the company intranet and devices. It's worse knowing the pics are still out there on the Internet, and I'll never be able to find them all."

The moment the pictures leak, it's like one of those movie scenes you think never happens in real life. No one will talk to me, but they love to talk about me. Anytime I walk by a group, the whispering stops or gets just loud enough for me to hear. Homewrecker. Whore. Office slut. Knew she was only here because of her father.

Bond's hand slips off the steering wheel and grasps mine.

My presence is "requested" at family dinner. It's like being sent to the gallows. Mom is in crisis mode, her wine glass spending far more time at her lips than her food. According to her, my reputation is in shambles, and no respectable man will ever want to marry me. As if that's the biggest problem with this whole thing.

My father turns his dark brown eyes on me. "You will take a break while Phillips Construction navigates this issue."

"What? I didn't do anything wr—"

"Mr. Wright had amazing potential, but you've ruined that."

My jaw drops.

"We all agree it would be best," my brother says, his eyes locked on the ground.

"Who the hell is we? I certainly wasn't consulted." I spit the words, crossing my arms over my chest.

"This isn't up for negotiation. You will take a month-long leave of absence." And with that, my father leaves the room, his meal untouched.

I spend the month trying to get into my father's graces. Trying to make him proud of me. I volunteer and do work off the books so when I come back, I can hit the ground running.

Not long after that, the messages start. First, they are flirty and talk about how we can be together now that he's single. Then they shift to bragging about how well he's doing at his new company.

How they gave him the job he deserves and he is no longer being held back by petty women with jealousy issues.

That should be my first clue that he is working hard to flip the story. When I don't reply, he gets progressively more aggressive and ugly. Calling me names, saying I owe him for ruining his marriage. Then, suddenly, they stop. Nothing for weeks. I think that's the end of it.

Until I get served.

"What do you mean?"

"I was out at lunch alone—since most of my so-called friends dropped me when the pictures leaked—bemoaning my life, when a well-dressed man asked if I was Tuesday Phillips before slapping a stack of papers in my hands and telling me I'd been served. Turns out Duncan was, is, suing Phillips Construction for creating a hostile work environment and misconduct in the workplace."

Bond looks over at me, lip curled up in disgust. "You've got to be shitting me. I thought he was bragging about doing well. Why sue unless he needs the money?"

"I guess his severance isn't going as far as he expected. What with paying out half in divorce court and child support for three kids. Plus, he's a vindictive bastard. His argument is that I pursued him, using my position as the owner's daughter to force him into a relationship. Seduced him with promises of a promotion and asked him to leave his wife. When he refused because he's such a strong, morally upstanding man, I blocked his promotion and forced him out. He, of course, neglected to include the part where that entire story is bullshit, and he blackmailed me with intimate photos taken without my knowledge."

"Why didn't you take legal action against him? Revenge porn is illegal."

The truck comes to a stop outside the sign for Piñon Hills.

Unbuckling, I climb into Bond's lap. I need to feel his hands on me while I get through this last bit.

"That's the most messed up part of this entire thing. I wanted to. I should have...but my family. They talked me out of it. Claimed it would be bad for the business and our name if I *'keep making such a stink about things that are my own fault.'* That no one would believe I didn't know the pictures were being taken. The minute Duncan's lawsuit reared its ugly head, their entire focus shifted to covering the company's ass. They knew how hard the last seven months had been for me. The humiliation and betrayal I'd gone through. But it didn't matter. I didn't matter."

"You matter to me, Tuesday."

I kiss him, relishing the comfort of Bond's lips against mine. Thankful for his perfectly timed words.

"We've made arrangements for you to leave town."

"You've got to be kidding. You can't just make me disappear."

My mother, father, and brother sit across from me at the oversized conference table inside Phillips Construction headquarters. I face them. Alone. My black sheep status never more apparent than in this moment. We are literally on opposing sides.

War gives me an uncomfortable look. "Tuesday, you will be the new Director of Marketing and Acquisitions for Davis Designs, a small custom home builder in Trail Creek, New Mexico."

"Director of Marketing and Acquisitions..." Bond repeats, his voice laced with confusion. His arms tighten around me, but I plow ahead.

My father turns his stern gaze on me. "You have an obligation to this family. To this company. Don't you want to do what's best for the family? Think of all we've done for you."

"All you've done for me?"

"Let's not pretend this is anything but a courtesy. You owe your brother a debt. Without him pleading your case, I'd have fired you.

Frankly, it would make my life easier. We could distance ourselves from this embarrassment you've caused."

My mouth drops open. "Are you serious? This is bullshit, and you know it."

"Tuesday Jane Phillips, language!"

"It's fine," my father says softly, squeezing my mother's hand. "Tuesday has always been temperamental." All the kindness he has for my mother is gone when he looks at me. He's never been one to raise his voice—cold and indifferent has always been his MO—but I've pushed too far. His eyes flash, rage written on his face. "I poured my entire life into building Phillips Construction from the ground up. It's your brother's legacy, and I will not see it torn to pieces because you were too vapid to see through some man's lies. You've embarrassed and disappointed us again and again."

His barbed words cut me, and I stare at him, momentarily speechless.

His familiarly cold affectation returns as he straightens the knot on his tie. "You've always been too sensitive for your own good. This is a business decision, nothing more. This conversation is over."

War, ever the public relations master, attempts to break the tension in the room. "The pictures, plus the ethical implications from the affair, have the board questioning how we are handling the situation. Dad and I looked at all the avenues, weighed the pros and cons, and came to the agreement that this is the best fit for you."

"You'll have to excuse me for not dropping to my knees in gratitude."

My mother sighs. "Tuesday, please. Don't be ridiculous."

I take a measured breath and look at each member of my family, studying them one by one. "I have one thing I need to know." Swallowing my nerves, I lower my head and whisper, "Do you believe me? That I didn't know. About his wife? About the pictures?"

No one speaks. It feels like hours pass, the weight of the time crawling across my skin like ants.

There's my answer. Their cold betrayal is like being stabbed in the back. With a rusty spoon. Dipped in acid.

Taking a deep breath, I bury my nose in Bond's neck, sucking in his soothing scent. "The first night at Dane's, you asked me what brought me to Trail Creek? Now you know. My dad bought Davis Designs as a place to hide me, a way to get me out of Dallas until they can resolve the suit."

Bond's muscles tense beneath my touch, but when I go to pick my head up, he cups it back to his shoulder, locking me in place against him. He doesn't say anything, just holds me, his muscles taught and rigid.

"Bond?"

No answer.

Time slows, and I replay his every reaction to my story. Where did I lose him? Was it when he found out Duncan was married? About the pictures?

Why isn't he saying anything?

CHAPTER SEVENTEEN

Fucking. Fuck.

The woman I'm falling for is the reason my dreams of passing down Davis Designs to a third generation are gone.

The quiet droning of sports talk from the radio and the hum of the circulating air are the only sounds in the cab of my truck. I'm still clutching Tuesday's head to the crook of my neck, afraid to let her see the mix of anger, pain, and confusion on my face.

I'm beyond pissed. That ex of hers is a piece of shit. What kind of person treats another that way? The fact he cheated on his pregnant wife, all while using Tuesday to further his career? Fucking disgraceful. Not to mention what he did when she ended things with him. I'm not kidding when I say if I meet him, he owes me four bones. One for each picture he took and shared of my girl without her consent.

Nose, index finger, jaw, and whichever wrist is dominant will do nicely.

Her family too. The way they treat her makes my blood boil. I'll be lucky if I come out the other side of knowing all this even working for Davis Designs because I'm liable to say something to both Warrens at the next video call. Heaven fucking forbid I ever meet any of them in person.

The Phillips men deserve nothing less than a fist to the eye. I'd like to set my mom loose on hers. That woman needs a good talking to. Tuesday is smart, kind, caring, and funny. She made a mistake. A mistake she rectified as soon as she found out about it. None of what that asshole decided to do after is her fault. How they don't see that baffles me.

But it's no wonder she ran scared when she found out who I was.

Layering in with the fury on her behalf is disbelief. My dad sold Davis Designs, without consulting me or even telling me until it was a done deal, to a man looking for a place to stash his daughter while riding out a lawsuit.

The same daughter who walked into my life like a breath of fresh fall air after a sweltering summer.

Was it really an hour ago that I had her sweet body pressed against mine in our office, whispering all the filthy things I wanted to do to her in her ear? The worst thing I was worried about was convincing Tuesday to date in secret because of a shitty office breakup.

Talk about underestimating the problem.

But now that I know the truth? Do I pretend my lifelong dreams didn't disintegrate the moment her dad decided to pick a company at random and buy it? That her being sent to Trail Creek and Davis Designs didn't derail all my plans?

"Bond?"

Tuesday's voice is muffled, and she squirms in my lap. I don't say anything; every muscle in my body is taut like the string of a bow.

"Bond, I'm getting a little claustrophobic here."

Shit.

"Sorry, Peach." I pry my palm off the back of her head and let her up. Her cheeks are flushed pink, her eyes watery, and her small smile fades to nothing when she searches my face. Worry overtakes her countenance at the uncertainty written on mine.

Double shit.

What the hell is wrong with me?

The words in my heart won't come out. She did everything I asked. Trusted me enough to give me her story. The story I demanded she share after swearing nothing she could say would drive me away. I should be kissing her, wiping away the last dregs of those ugly memories and replacing them with new ones. Yet here I am, stewing in silence over the truth of how I lost my company.

Tuesday working for my business and being related to the new owners is a shock, but hearing exactly why they opted to purchase Davis Designs is a slap in the face. The hurt I felt when Dad sold the company, the hurt I felt the night I met Tuesday—wallowing in my misery until she turned my entire world on its head—comes roaring back.

"Bond?"

I need to talk to my dad. Find out why he agreed to sell to her awful family.

She says my name louder. It's a question, a plea, a desperate appeal to not leave her alone at the edge of this suddenly growing chasm between us. A chasm I'm creating one unspoken word at a time. All I have to do is tell her why I'm upset, why knowing the full details of her arrival in my life is throwing me, and that it isn't because of anything she did.

But my mouth fails me.

Giving me a sad smile, she untangles herself from my lap and slides across the bench seat. "It looks like we still have an hour until the end of the day. Could you please take me back to the office?"

Her voice is stiff, full of hurt, and I know I'm fucking up.

All I manage is a strangled, "Tuesday."

"It's okay, Baseball Cap. You took it better than I expected, honestly."

Her nickname for me makes me close my eyes. Regret and shame for the way I'm handling this rise up like bile. Tuesday doesn't look at me, her gaze focused out the passenger window as if the subdivision sign is the most interesting thing she's ever seen.

Goddamn fucking shit.

I yank on the ends of my hair, pulling the too-long waves into a tangle. My throat tightens, and everything I need to say dies on my tongue, coating my taste buds like a bitter film. With a heavy sigh, I lower my head to the steering wheel and mutter, "I just need some time."

"I understand."

"I need to talk to my dad, it's not you—"

"If you finish that with it's me, I swear I'm walking back to the office." For a second, she sounds like herself. My fiery, bratty, teasing temptress.

But then silence falls back over us like a wool blanket. Itchy and stifling.

When another minute passes with neither of us speaking, I throw the truck into drive and head back to town, cursing myself the entire way. I open my mouth, but the words won't come out.

My dream of passing down Davis Designs, the version I've known my whole life, to my children one day, of growing this business with my sisters at my side, is gone. All because Warren Phillips has too much money and not enough care for his daughter. A growl threatens to slip from me at the thought of her dad sending her away rather than believing her. Her family doesn't deserve her.

It's not her fault. She didn't ask for this. No more than she's asking for me to cut her out now.

As soon as I pull into the parking lot, Tuesday's voice cracks. "Will you at least tell me which part was the deal-breaker for you?"

The resigned misery as she speaks breaks my heart. There's too much to process, and I don't know how to answer. "It's nothing you need to worry about."

"I am, though. Please talk to me. Is it because Duncan was married? Because I swear, Bond, I didn't know."

"No, of course not."

"Because of the pictures of me that are out there? We tried to get them taken down, but you know how the Inter—"

"No," I grunt, cutting her off. The thought of others seeing my girl, vulnerable, naked, unknowingly fueling their fantasies....I grip the steering wheel so tight it creaks against the pressure.

"Then what is it?" She's almost begging.

"There's a new layer to it I didn't expect." My lips twist like I've eaten a whole lemon.

"What do you mean?"

"I mean, your dad threw a goddamn dart on the wall and stole my dream!" My anger rings in the closed cab of the truck. Tuesday's flinch is automatic.

Fuck.

I never want her scared of me. With each silent second, my stomach drops, and cold fingers grip my heart. I was too loud. Too harsh. I shouldn't have yelled at her. The steps we've taken together over the last week wash away like sand in the surf.

Closing my eyes, I lean my head back against the seat. "All I ever wanted was to pass Davis Designs down someday. To see it go from my dad, to me, to my children, and beyond. And now, it doesn't even belong to my family anymore."

"The night we met. You said you'd come to the bar mad at the world. And you wanted nothing more than to keep your family business." Her chin wobbles. "It's my fault. I'm the reason you were there that night."

"Peach, I…" My words trail off. What can I say? Am I breaking us? All for a dream I already lost? Righting myself, I whisper, "Give me tonight. Please."

Tears gather in Tuesday's whiskey eyes before they cut to the door handle. When I don't move, she deflates, curling in on herself.

The squeak of the truck door and her quiet sniffles are the only sounds as she steps out. "You know, that's the first time I've opened my own door since we met."

Her words land like a punch to the gut, and I stare at my hands, head hanging in shame.

Wrapping her arms around herself, her hesitant voice rises over the wind. "Y-you told me I'm yours, and Porter Bond Davis, you strike me as a man of your word. Since the night we met, you've been certain of us. I've been the one running scared. I know it's asking too much for you to always chase me, so this is me chasing you. Being the one to stand up for us. I panicked today, but I was coming out of that closet to find you. Because I do want you. Want us. I'm sorry my being here disrupted your dreams, Bond. But…" She takes a deep breath and looks at me. "Maybe we can be each other's dream?"

The hopefulness shining on her face flickers when I don't move or speak. And then she's gone. Running towards her car, not looking back.

I'm a fucking idiot with only my shitty thoughts for company.

Who am I even mad at? Myself mostly for being mad in the first place.

I need to talk to my dad.

Racing through town, right back to Piñon Hills for the second time in thirty minutes, I slam open my parent's front door. "Dad! Where are you?"

"Porter? What's going on?" Mom greets me, stepping into the kitchen through the back door, wiping her muddy hands on a dish towel. Her dark hair has streaks of gray, and her face shows years of laughter and happiness. The badges of a well-lived life.

"Where's Dad? I need to talk to him. Now."

"He's out in his little shed. You're all sweaty and flushed. Are you feeling alright?"

"No, Momma, I'm not."

"What's this about?"

I sigh, rubbing the scruff on my chin. "Need to talk to Dad about some things."

She frowns, a slight thinning of her lips before nodding. "Okay, I'll be in the garden if you need me; otherwise, I'll give you two some privacy."

Planting a kiss on her cheek and muttering my thanks, I make my way out the back door toward my dad's shed, nestled in a copse of pine trees and built in our signature ski-villa style but on a much smaller scale.

I need answers. To settle this disquiet growing in my chest. To get my mind right so I can crawl back to Tuesday and apologize properly from my knees.

Not bothering to knock, I bulldoze through the door.

"I wondered when you'd finally come see me." My dad's deep voice is calm and confident, and he continues leveling the board with his hand planer as if I didn't bust into his personal space uninvited.

Scott Davis isn't a small man. Almost my height and just as broad, he always seemed larger than life when I was growing up. He poured his heart into his family and his sweat into building Davis Designs.

"How could you do it?" They're the only words I can form, and right now, the only ones that matter. I have to know. "How could you sell it to—"

"To a man like Warren Phillips?"

"So you knew why he was buying us out? That we don't matter to him, and he's using us as some sort of modern castle and keep? Hiding his daughter away, shuffling her off the board like a game piece?"

Dad stops working and turns to me. His sharp blue eyes lock onto mine. Steady and strong, like they've been my entire life.

"Why don't you have a seat, son."

Gritting my teeth, I say, "I'd rather stand."

"I wasn't asking, Porter. Sit."

"You didn't come to me to discuss this beforehand, and now I'm cleaning up the fallout from the decision you made without explaining anything. So forgive me if I don't sit."

Dad drops to an oversized wooden chair, reclining as he crosses his arms over his barrel chest. "What fallout?"

My relationship with the woman I'm head over heels with to start.

When I don't answer him, he gives me a knowing smirk. "Fine. You want to know why I didn't discuss it with you?"

I nod stiffly.

"Because I knew you'd try and talk me out of it without listening," he says.

"And because as soon as we spoke to that awful man, we knew Davis Designs would be good for her." Mom's soft voice interrupts Dad before he can say more.

Without my permission, my body sags into the closest chair. "What? You knew about this too?"

Mom sighs. "Porter, her father told us everything. All about how his, and I'm quoting him here, *his ridiculous daughter was ruining everything he'd built.* How he'd pay us twice what our, again quoting him, *little no-name house-building company* was worth if we'd take her off his hands."

My fists slam down on the wooden table that separates me from my father, rattling it with the force of my blow. "He said that about her?"

Dad appraises me before reaching across the table and patting one of my still clenched fists. "Your mom and I didn't do it to hurt you. The way I see it, we're doing you a favor. You and your sisters no longer have to struggle; you don't have to worry about making payroll or keeping yourself afloat. You and Charlotte get to stay on, keep the job without the stress. Like you said, Phillips Construction doesn't care what you do."

"Plus, coming here gives Tuesday a fresh start. You know how much the Davis Designs team supports one another. If anyone needs that, it's her."

"Exactly." Dad nods, pulling Mom to sit in his lap. "It's a win-win."

"But our legacy. Couldn't we have offered Tuesday the job without selling the company? What do I have to pass down now?"

"If you think the business is my legacy or yours, I've done a piss poor job raising you."

Dad's words catch me off guard. "What?"

"The business is just that: a business. Hell, son, start your own. What I hope I passed down to you is how much I love your mom. How much I love you and your sisters, how important being your dad is. That life is more than work. It's all the small moments and memories you and the people who matter to you build together. That's what I want as my legacy."

My anger has all but receded, and now I'm left with confusion and regret.

His strong voice softens. "And no, Porter. When her dad made the offer, he made it clear he would only send her to a company under his control."

"Tuesday needs people like you and your sisters in her life." Mom reaches out and squeezes my hand. "We raised you three to be kind and supportive, and I couldn't be more proud of you. To hear her father talk about her, tell us everything she's been through is her fault...Well, I wanted to crawl through the phone and throttle him."

Mom holds her hand up before I can say anything. "You're a good man, son. A man capable of deep love. A man worthy of your father's true legacy. A man who sees those things her family calls flaws as part of what makes her precious. Surely you're not so caught up in your name being on a business that you're willing to let her go?"

At my silence, Dad chuckles. "Don't think we don't know about the two of you. Clarissa ran home the night you met Tuesday, telling us all about how you were head over heels for this pretty, new-in-town woman."

I snort, thinking of Clairy coming home and tattling on me to Mom, Dad, and Charli.

A thoughtful grin lights up Dad's face. "You truly are my son. I told your mom I loved her on our second date, and we were married two weeks later. The Davises are no strangers to love at first sight. It just took you a strange set of circumstances to meet the one."

I can't fight my matching grin. "Two weeks?"

"He's right. Forty-one wonderful years later, and he's still the love of my life." Mom kisses Dad's cheek. They've been this way my whole life. A united team of two. Affectionate with each other, open, and honest. I immediately picture myself and Tuesday that same way. I want a life like they have.

With his arm still slung around Mom's waist, Dad says, "Tuesday's brother reached out the day after I agreed to sell the company and thanked me. Said sometimes families make—"

"Difficult choices that are hard to explain, but truly are in everyone's best interest." The unspoken question is raised along with a single eyebrow when I finish Dad's sentence. "He said the same thing to me at our video call."

"He's not wrong, Runt."

Kissing Mom and hugging Dad, I say my goodbyes and run back to my truck, phone already in hand.

Where are you?

Watching those triple dots appear and disappear gives me gray hair.

PEACH 🍑

I thought you needed the night?

Nope. Got my head on straight, and now I'm back.

PEACH 🍑

Back for what?

Always you, Baby Girl. Now answer the question.

It's like light breaking through the clouds when I see the address.

Throwing my truck into drive, I head back to town. As

quickly as possible, I shower and pack an overnight bag. It may seem presumptuous, but I have a plan. It's simple, really. Feed my Peach. Apologize to her. Then wring so many orgasms out of her that she has no choice but to sleep the night away in my arms.

tuesday

Bond's silence after my boombox over the head moment outside his truck this afternoon was deafening. His not wanting to talk was the absolute worst part of everything today. *Even worse than telling him about the lousiest ex to ever ex? Yes, even worse than that.*

From night one, Bond has been open, pushing the importance of communication. To see him close himself off shocked me. The reality that I could lose him was stone-cold sobering and exactly what drove me to tell him how I feel.

I'm his.

I have been since he said how nice it was to almost meet me in the Great Dane.

But now?

God, the devastating hurt, anger, and confusion on his face. How can he want me knowing I'm the reason all his dreams derailed? My drunk ramblings at the Great Dane flash through my mind. I am a ruiner. Today simply reconfirms it.

The only silver lining to this rat crap day? The movers call while I'm mid-meltdown to say my house is ready. At least I don't have to go back to the Trail Creek Inn. No more cracked walls and mystery stains. No more of the Marquis de Sade's mattress.

Any relief I have from thoughts of upgraded accommodations fizzle. In its place, acute pain radiates from my chest outward. I feel more loss for a man I've known for a week than I did at the end of my relationship with Duncan—that says a lot about both men.

I pull into the driveway and stumble into the house, not seeing it. This should be a happy afternoon, enjoying being in my new home with my things. Instead, I fully intended to spend the rest of the day collapsed in my new tub getting nice and pruney, stewing in scalding hot water. And my feelings.

I need bubbles, booze, and *Ice Planet Barbarians*. Stat.

Ten minutes later, I'm submerged up to my neck in the fragrant scent of a sweet clover field. I can practically hear the bees and smell the honey. I'm also almost to the best part of my book, where the human woman stranded on an ice planet with a big blue alien discovers just what that spur can do.

Buzz. Buzz.

SEXY BASEBALL CAP

Where are you?

My heart seizes. And in my rush to reply, I bobble my phone, almost losing it to the mountain of bubbles. Phone saved, I take two deep breaths, then send my reply.

I thought you needed the night?

SEXY BASEBALL CAP

Nope. Got my head on straight, and now I'm back.

Back for what?

Is he coming here to end things? To tell me he doesn't want to be with me anymore?

Letting my thumbs do my thinking, I fire off my address. *Please let him come back to me.*

This relationship, as quick and chaotic as it's been, is not something I'm willing to give up. If Bond thinks he can get away from me now, he's in for a shock. TCT—*Trail Creek Tuesday*— knows what she wants, and what she wants is Bond.

I scurry out of the bath, my novel forgotten as I race to get ready for my real-life romance to come home.

All cards on the table? I'm one romantic gesture away from falling in love with this man.

Bond is my ten. Everyone has their checkboxes, and I know anyone with eyes would see him and think, *Why yease, I would like to ride that slightly crooked nose into the sunset*, but it's so much more than that. He sees me, flaws and all, and doesn't think I'm too much or not enough. When he makes me laugh, comforts or challenges me, it's like the universe opened my brain and poured him into existence purely from my thoughts.

In no time at all, I'm cozied up on my overstuffed couch, a chenille blanket draped over my lap, my damp hair hanging loose down my back as I pretend to enjoy the growing dusk through my giant bank of windows. Pins and needles thread through my bones while I watch the clock—I swear, it's moving backward.

I'm trying not to doomscroll through my brain about all the ways tonight could go wrong. So instead, I busy myself with important things like old TV show quotes, the epic comebacks I should have said to Lacy Hill in seventh grade when she called me a bra-stuffing biotch, and what it is about tacos that makes them so unanimously beloved.

Then, I hear a knock at my door.

In my rush to answer it, I almost trip over the blanket tangled around my legs. Righting myself and attempting to smooth out my rumpled hair, I fling open the door.

There he stands, dressed in what I've come to think of as standard issue Bond—Henley, perfectly worn jeans, boots, and that baseball cap—with bags of food in his hands.

"Baby Girl." Bond's broad shoulders droop. The words are out of his mouth before I can even greet him. "I'll never hurt you again. I'm not them, and I know walking away from you today...Fuck, I swear, I'll never hurt you like they did. Never again."

"Bond," I breathe his name. Without thinking, I jump, causing him to drop the bags of food at his feet as I wrap my legs around his waist, wind my arms around his neck, and open my mouth to his.

No more running. This is what I want. He is what I want.

He breaks the kiss, the bill of his hat brushing against my temple as he nuzzles me. "This was my house."

I pull back, my brows knitting together. "What do you mean?"

"I mean, Davis Designs built every house in Piñon Hills, but this one was, is, special. My pet project. I poured myself into this house. It sold, and I thought I'd lost it forever. "

Goosebumps rise on the back of my neck. My perfect house, the house I knew was designed just for me? He's the one who built it?

The cosmos have a twisted sense of humor.

I crush my lips to his. My fingers sink into the curls that peek out beneath his cap. I trace the outline of his mouth, moaning when our tongues brush against each other. Bond takes control, and suddenly, I'm no longer the one doing the kissing but being kissed.

His lips are like a cleansing fire, leaving me with a brand I'll carry for the rest of my life. I pant his name, spilling it like a desperate devotion from between my lips.

I'm still wound around him as he staggers through the door, bags of food forgotten in the desperation to feed another kind of hunger. Together, we tumble onto my couch, Bond's large body blanketing mine.

"I'm so fucking sorry, sweetheart."

"For what?" I ask, breathy and yearning.

"For what you went through with that asshole. For how your family treated you after. But most of all, for letting that seed of anger about the company take me away from you. You had no way of knowing what the family business meant to me, and instead of talking to you, I shut down. But even a moment of doubt about us is too much. From the moment you showed up in Dane's bar, my sunset-haired girl, sassing that dickhead Jacob Ashford and telling me to leave you alone before begging me to come back—"

"I did not beg you to come back."

"Shhh, Peach." Bond spins his hat around backward, then presses his mouth to mine, dropping teasing kisses onto my pout. "Not done. Got a lot of things to say. Need you to hear them. What you said this afternoon is true. I am a man of my word, and you are abso-fucking-lutely mine."

Kisses pepper his words as if he can't physically bear for his lips to be off me. "Before you, I saw only Davis Designs. My scope was too small, my view too narrow. I said your dad stole my dreams. But I was dead wrong. My dreams aren't gone; they've just grown. Grown to five foot two. Tuesday, you are my new dream."

My eyes widen, and I suck in a ragged breath. My hand flies to brush along the stubble on his jaw. "Say it again," I demand.

Bond anchors me beneath him, one hand gripping my hip, the other buried in my hair. He runs his nose down my neck, inhaling my scent as he speaks. "You're my new dream."

"And you're mine." I pull his face toward me, looking into those beautiful blue eyes of his, swimming in the truth of us. "When I'm in your arms, Bond, everything I've been missing fades away, and all that's left are possibilities and you."

Our sweet words and touches turn into making out with a side of heavy petting, and endorphins rush to my brain. *Ahhh, dopamine, my old friend. So nice to see you again.*

I close my eyes and rock my hips against his, but he holds me still, keeping me from the friction I crave. I tilt my head, giving him more access, and let out a squeal when he sucks hard enough to leave a mark. The breath of his sexy chuckle skims along my skin before Bond busies his mouth, kissing my shoulder, collarbone, and neck.

With a breathy laugh, I say, "So...day two at the new job didn't go as planned. Objective for tomorrow? Make it through an entire eight hours of work without an emotional meltdown."

Bond sits up, a bright grin on his face. "It's important to have goals, but, sweetheart, I'm doing some quality work here. Need you to focus."

A loud laugh rips from me, and I cover my face in embarrassment. At least I didn't snort.

"Love that loud laugh. Don't hold back. You laughing loud and proud and not caring who hears is sexy as hell." His lips trace lower, and my nipples harden. When his mouth closes over a peaked tip, sucking it through the thin fabric of my tank top, an ocean's worth of need floods my system.

I arch in his arms, silently begging him to keep his lips on me. Bond whispers, punctuating each statement with a soft, open-mouthed kiss along the curves of my chest and up the line of my throat. "I'm allergic to shellfish, I'm a cat person, and I'd love nothing more than to spend the rest of the night making you scream in pleasure."

So that's how he wants to play it. I squirm closer to him. "You have dog person written all over you. I'm right, aren't I?"

Bond murmurs his assent and continues kissing along my jaw, nipping and soothing in equal turns. The wet, hot sensation of his lips has me all but purring. Desire, delicious and decadent, surges through my body until my pussy throbs. All this from a few well-placed kisses.

When his teeth graze that sensitive place below my ear, I gasp and stutter, "I'm left-handed, my favorite color is the blue of your eyes, and I do not want you to take me to bed right now."

"Tuesday, you better be left-handed," Bond growls before he scoops me off the couch and strides across the room. His arms band around me as if he's afraid I'll float away, and he traverses my home as only someone intimately familiar with the floor plan could. There's no asking me for directions, nothing but pure sexy-as-hell confidence that he's going exactly where we want. The two of us are a tangle of limbs when he bursts through my bedroom door.

I reach a hand out to turn off the overhead lights, but Bond stops me. "No, Baby Girl. We leave the lights on for this."

He draws me to the foot of my bed and sets me on my feet. His fingers skim over my jaw and neck, brushing against my collarbone and shoulders before trailing up and down my arms, leaving a path of goosebumps in their wake. Every teasing touch feeds the flame of want flickering inside me. I need him. Desperately.

Bond buries his hands in my hair, the slight pressure

drawing me tighter to him. When he licks the seam of my mouth, I part my lips, welcoming his tongue with mine. A quick nip to my bottom lip makes me whine before Bond soothes the sting away with a gentle kiss.

When he pulls back, his blue eyes, practically gone navy, search my own. "This is what you want?"

I nod.

"Words. Have to have them. Need them."

"Yes, I want this. I want you."

Zigging when I expect him to zag, Bond tugs me away from the bed, and I find my back pinned to his chest, my full-length wall mirror in front of me.

"Look at us. How good we look together. How perfectly you fit against me."

He's right. We do look good together. A million different futures zip through my mind, each one centering on Bond and I together in this house.

My eyes cut to our reflection. Our size difference is blatant standing like this. He towers over me, my head hitting just below his shoulders. His tan skin is a striking contrast to my creamy complexion. He's wide and firm, and I'm soft and thick.

"All these luscious curves. I have to see them." Bond wastes no time, pulling my tank top over my head and dragging my leggings down my thighs, trapping me in a lycra cage.

"No panties? You're killing me, Peach." Bond's hips buck against me.

His hands roam my thighs, hips, stomach, ribs. The caress of his rough palms against my overheated body makes me shiver. Lips brush against the nape of my neck, and I'm ready to explode from desperation.

I whimper when he thumbs my nipples, deftly rolling and pulling until I think I might come from that stimulation alone.

When he pinches both nipples and bites that spot between my neck and shoulder, I can't help crying out.

"Yes, scream my name. No one's going to hear you, so shout down these walls."

One large hand glides down the length of my body before slipping between my legs. "You're so goddamn gorgeous. Look at you. Flushed and pink and wanting in my arms. You going to soak my fingers? Is this pussy hungry? So empty right now, needing something to fill it up."

I stare at our reflection and nod, too turned on to speak. Bond is still fully clothed, the soft material of his Henley rubbing against my shoulders while the rougher denim of his jeans scrapes against my bare skin. My hair is mussed, my cheeks, neck, and chest blotchy, but I've never felt more beautiful. He keeps circling my clit, the pressure firmer with each repeated pass he makes. I try to widen my legs to give him better access, but my leggings restrict how far I can spread. In a fit, I squirm until I can get them to my ankles and kick them off. Bond's dark chuckle in my ear sends licks of fire down my spine, and my eyes close as waves of pleasure crash over me.

"Eyes on us, Tuesday," Bond snaps, the command in his voice forcing my gaze to our reflection. "You focus on what you feel and us in that mirror. Nothing else." He locks an arm around my chest, keeping me anchored to him.

He toys with me, giving me just enough to be desperate for more. I dig my fingers into his thighs as my hips rub back against his cock. Then, two blessedly thick fingers plunge inside me, making me go up on my tiptoes in pleasure.

"Yeah? You like that?"

"Y-yes, Bond." I bite my lip as I moan.

"Tell me."

When I don't immediately do as he asks, he pulls his

fingers out of me and goes back to lightly teasing my entrance and clit.

"I said tell me. Tell me how it feels when I finger fuck you. How wet you are for me. I want to hear all your words."

"You feel so good, Bond; your fingers stretch me in the best way. I need it; I need you."

"More," he growls against my ear before nibbling the lobe. Thankfully, his fingers slip back inside me, curling forward in search of that spot that will make me break.

"I can feel how hard you are against my back, so big."

"Yeah? You can feel my big cock? You imagining it's in you right now?" He bends his knees, widening his gait and grinding his hips against my ass.

My words melt into whimpers as he thrusts his fingers in and out of me, the heel of his hand pressing against my clit. The room is filled with the wet sounds of Bond working my pussy, my heavy breathing, and his dirty murmurs against my neck.

"You are so beautiful with my fingers inside you. Can you take another one? Can this little pussy handle three of my fingers? Tell me."

"Yes! Give me more!" The stretch borders the blissful line between pain and pleasure as he works a third finger inside me. I'm coming up to the edge, the intensity between us pushing me along so I have no choice but to fall.

"When you come, you say my name. Do you hear me, Baby Girl?"

A quick slap to my ass makes me cry out. "Yes, Bond!"

"I know you're close. I can feel it. Smell it. Give it to me, Tuesday. Come for me."

The tight string within me snaps as if waiting for his command, and a euphoric thrill spirals through my body. My walls clamp around his fingers, trapping them inside me as aftershocks ripple over me.

Coming down from my high, I stare at us in the mirror, rapt, until Bond snaps me from my steamy stupor and pins me between his body and the mirror, bending me forward. "Hands on the frame. Don't let go."

"Wh-what are you—"

"Not done apologizing. I need to get on my knees and show you how sorry I am."

"I don't think—"

"You can and you will."

Leaving no room for debate, Bond sinks down behind me, pushing on the small of my back. He buries his face in me, still wearing that backward baseball cap, making good on his teasing taunt from our time in the office that if he had his way, he'd lick me from front to back.

The sounds in the room are positively indecent, and I've never been more turned on. Moans, whimpers, groans—it's our own erotic soundtrack.

"Is there anywhere I can't touch you, Baby Girl?

My breath catches in my chest. "No, touch me. Anywhere. Everywhere."

Bond rises off his knees and, in a stern voice, says, "Open your mouth."

I do as he demands, and he slips his thumb between my lips.

"Suck."

That one-word command has me trembling against him, but I can't resist nipping at the pad of his thumb. His dark chuckle rumbles over me like thunder in the distance. I bookmark everything about this moment, never wanting to forget a second of what's happening, what's going to happen, between us.

When Bond's thumb presses against the tight pucker between my cheeks, I cry out his name as heady pleasure floods my senses. The slight pressure has me pushing back against him, hunting for more.

"Does my delicious good girl like that? Like having her pretty asshole filled? I bet you'd love it even more if I used one of your toys and fucked both these tight holes at once. Tell me, Tuesday, would you like that?"

"Oh my god." My words are slurred, drunk on him, as Bond continues his explorations of all my most sensitive spots. I reach back, knocking his hat off his head and digging my fingers into his chestnut curls.

"Get that hand back on the mirror, sweetheart." Bond punctuates his demand with a nip to the back of my thigh and another sharp smack to my ass.

I suck in a lungful of air and grasp the ornate gold frame, my arms trembling and tears filling my eyes. Bond redoubles his efforts, his tongue like a heat-seeking missile targeting the exact places to make me fall apart. Two fingers slip back inside me, and my second climax of the night rocks me, my knees buckling from the intensity.

Bond keeps me from collapsing to the floor as I fold into the mirror, my cheek pressed against the cool glass. He places a delicate kiss to the base of my spine as I quiver against him; then, as if I'm some fragile, precious thing, he slowly spins me and places a few gentle kisses to my lower stomach.

I try to stabilize myself with one hand on his head and the other on his shoulder, but thanks to the adrenaline crash from the bone-shattering orgasms he gave me, I need more support to keep myself upright.

Bond wraps his arms around the back of my thighs and grins up at me like a devil. "Hope you're ready for more, Peach, because you and I are just getting started."

tuesday

I stare down at Bond, the grin on his face melting into something more heated—a promise of soul-shaking satisfaction. How is this my life?

His eyes rake over me, taking in my very naked and flushed form. "I still need to show you how I feel. How sorry I am."

Wrinkling my brow, I cock my head. "You've already apologized and made me come twice."

"And that's not nearly enough. I'm going to wring every ounce of pleasure from your body until you're nothing but a crying mess."

Mouth agape, I nod. "I want that." The most beautiful man I've ever met wants me, and I'm going to let him have me.

As soon as the words are out of my mouth, he snatches me up and carries me to the bed, tossing me into my fluffy mattress like I weigh nothing. With a squeak, I clamber upright, tucking my legs beneath me.

"Be right back." With a wink, he steps into the bathroom, and I hear the sink run. Then he's at the foot of my bed. "You ready?"

He does that mouthwatering thing where he uses one hand to pull his shirt off from behind—the effect of which causes spontaneous ovarian eruptions. Bond toes off his boots and socks, then his hands go to his pants, where he pauses.

Crooking a single finger, he beckons me. And as if I'm under his spell, I crawl to him.

I've never crawled for a man in my life, but here we are, and I don't have a single hesitation. I reach for the waist of his jeans, but he grabs my hands and brings them to his lips, chastely kissing my knuckles.

Bond guides my fingers to his pants. With a coy smile, I toy with the button and the zipper, going one tooth at a time, enjoying the strain of his bulge behind the denim.

"Peach, you better hurry up before I lose my patience."

Tugging his jeans down his hips, I fight back a smile when I see he's commando.

I drink my fill of his barrel chest, broad shoulders, thick thighs, and solid stomach. Once again, I'm reminded of an old-fashioned strong man.

Biting my lips, I let my eyes follow the thin line of dark hair below his navel. A happy trail indeed. His cock is the perfect length and girth, ruddy and delectable with veins running along the underside—it's like the mythical creature of peens. A unicock.

And it's mine.

"No panties? You're killing me, Baseball Cap."

He throws his head back, laughing. Then, the laughter stops, and I'm under Bond, my back on the bed, arms pinned above my head. Despite being trapped beneath him, the kiss is soft and sweet. A mix of feather-light brushes of his mouth and tender flicks of his tongue. As the kiss heats up, his cock presses against me, drips of precum pooling on my belly, and his hips press down, effectively locking me in place.

I love it. Love the feeling of being restrained beneath him, his heavy body resting on top of me.

The kiss goes from gentle and light to deep and bruising. The kind of kiss that steals the air from my lungs and fans the flames inside me.

"Hands flat on the headboard, Baby Girl, and don't let them move."

Without hesitation, I stretch, pushing my palms against the upholstered headboard. I love giving him control. It's not something I've felt comfortable with in the past. But with Bond? There's no questioning my trust. I want to let go for him.

My hands on the headboard make my back arch, and Bond takes advantage, his lips tracing a trail down my neck to my chest, where he captures my nipple in his teeth, rolling his tongue until it hardens. His relentless warpath continues, switching between my aching peaks until I whimper.

"That feels so good."

"Yeah?" He props himself up on one arm, running his knuckles up and down my breastbone.

Nodding, I squirm, trying to get friction, pressure, anything, but his unyielding heft holds me in place.

"Please, Bond."

"Please, Bond, what?" His eyes burn down my body, scalding a path of want and need as he drinks me in.

"I want to feel all of you." My voice breaks.

"I'll give you what you want, I promise, but you better not take your hands off the headboard. Unless you're looking for a spanking."

I consider the pros and cons. The few random spankings Bond's given me in our time together are the only ones I've ever had, and I like them. A lot.

"I see you trying to decide, but time's up." He nips my bottom lip and grips my thighs, splaying me wide. After giving me another wanton look, he lines himself up between my legs and lets the head of his cock glide against my pussy. I'm wet. Soaking. Ready. He bumps against my clit before easing an inch into me. Then he's gone, and I'm left clenching at nothing.

My mixed moan of desperation and desire rings in the air, and then his cock is back, rubbing against my clit before repeating his shallow entrance—teasing me with the crown when I want the whole thing.

"Bond, I need more. I need all of you."

"You sure that's what you want? I don't know if I believe you."

"Yes, it is! Please!"

With a throaty chuckle that melts into a groan, Bond sinks into me, stretching me as he goes deeper—just to the brink of pain, that perfect bite of pressure. Once he's fully seated, he stills, letting me adjust to his width.

Into my neck, he murmurs, "God, you have no idea how fucking amazing you are. Knew it would be this way. You feel so goddamn good. Tight and hot, like something out of my best dreams. I could spend the rest of my life inside this pussy, and it wouldn't be enough."

Who has a praise kink and loves Bond's bossy, filthy mouth?

Me. I do.

I let out a strangled cry as I rock against him, trying to coax him into action.

"Need me to move, Peach? Need to feel my cock as it works you open, spreads you wide?"

My head nods up and down like I'm a bobblehead. I dig my fingers into the material of my upholstered headboard.

He sets a leisurely, languid pace, slowly rolling into me as if we have all the time in the world. Making love to me like I'm something delicate, and while it feels amazing, it's also not what I want.

"Fa-faster."

"Not yet." Bond's lips punctuate his reply, capturing my own, keeping me from making any more requests. He's in charge of our pace, and he's not going to let me forget it.

Fire coils in my stomach, an unquenchable blaze flaring with each deep, drawn-out thrust.

"Do you love how I feel fucking in and out of you? Stroking every nerve and sensitive spot inside this gorgeous pussy?"

That's exactly what he's doing. Each thick inch of his cock, each vein of that velvet-wrapped steel sets my nerve endings alight.

But still. I'm greedy, and I want to come. "Please," I pant.

"You want more? Don't like this speed?" As he asks, Bond slows, so he's hardly moving at all.

"Bond, please!" I cry as I fasten my legs around his ass, anchoring myself to him. "I need you!"

"Need me to what? Say it. Say you want me to fuck you."

"I need you to fuck me!"

He lets out a dark laugh, and then, with a jolt, he changes the pace. Going from slow and tender to hungry and unrelenting. I'm lost in the pounding rhythm of his hips, his pelvis rubbing against my clit, stimulating me inside and out. Those electric blue eyes lock onto mine, refusing to let me look away, flashes of forever lurking in their depths.

My hands are firm against the headboard, and despite the ache in my shoulders, I don't dare let them slip. Because if he stops, I may cry. Or die.

Sweat drips down Bond's chest, leaving the smattering of dark hair plastered against his skin and a glistening sheen in its wake. He continues his frenetic tempo. Words, panting and strained, fall from his lips, and I know he's at the limit of his control. "Tuesday, be a good girl and come for me. Right. Fucking. Now."

I can't help but obey his command, my release crashing over me. I throw my head back in ecstasy as I ride out the rippling waves of my orgasm. My hands twist in the cool sheets as my climax crests, and I shout out his name.

Bond licks the sweat from my neck. I spasm around him once more, and goosebumps prickle on my skin. He nips and kisses his way to my ear, praising me.

"You're so beautiful like this. I'm gonna remember this forever. I'm gonna come in your perfect pussy now. Claim it. Cause it's mine. All. Mine."

My muscles clamp around his thick cock, and he spills inside me. His hot spend pours into me, wringing out another smaller orgasm despite how spent I am. Bond sinks, his forearms bracing his weight. His chest rises and falls like he just finished a marathon. Which, in a way, he did.

"You are amazing." Bond rubs his nose against mine. Then his sexy chuckle crawls up my spine. "You can let go of the headboard now."

As he speaks, he rolls us so he isn't crushing me but doesn't pull out. The feel of his softening cock inside me, the connection, is a balm to my overstimulated nerves.

We lie there, our breath hitching, as Bond gently rubs my shoulders to coax the blood back into them. My body gives one last involuntary quiver, and he groans against my skin.

Spent and satisfied, we lie tangled and entwined in the most intimate way possible. Only once the sweat on my skin cools and I shiver does he ease out of me.

He tenderly kisses my shoulder before sliding out of the bed. "Let me take care of you."

I raise an eyebrow in question, but Bond simply captures my lips with his and leads me towards the bathroom.

"This is my favorite room in the whole place."

"Mine too," I say, scarcely louder than a whisper, glancing around me at the claw foot tub, the massive shower, and the wall of windows where starlight streams in.

The dazzling grin Bond gives me kicks up the butterflies living in my stomach full time these days. He runs the water in the stand-alone, big-enough-for-three shower. I can't stop myself from pressing against the expanse of his turned back.

He is magnetic.

"Hey there." The dulcet timbre of his voice is like a sedative, and I find myself all but collapsing into his waiting arms. "Come on. I've got you."

Bond maneuvers me into the shower, the steady streams of water from the double shower heads raining down on my worn-out body. It's the best kind of fatigue. I'm loose-limbed and malleable, letting Bond move me where he wants. I close my eyes, lost in the calming pressure and heat of the water and the brace of Bond's chest against my back. When he sinks his fingers into my hair and massages my scalp, I practically melt into a puddle of satisfied goo.

Once we're sex and sweat-free, Bond dries us both off, taking care with my shoulders and hips. The adoration and affection in his touch make my heart swell. Never have I had a partner so attentive.

"Could you give me a minute?" I ask.

He tilts his head, reminding me of an adorable puppy. "Sure. Anything you need?"

"Um…" I gesture towards the toilet because I'm not about to get a UTI.

His barking laugh echoes across the tile. "Sweetheart, after everything we've done, you shouldn't be scared of letting me see you pee."

Grumbling under my breath, I shove him out of the bathroom.

Once I'm finished, I climb into bed, burrowing into my fluffy blanket. It doesn't escape my notice that Bond swapped out my messy comforter with one from the linen closet.

Seriously. Who is this man? *Come for the sex, stay for the attention to bedding.*

A few minutes later, Bond returns with the long-abandoned bags and my phone. "I locked up. Figure we're in for the night." Despite being utterly spent, I take the time to appreciate the sight of Bond's biteable ass as he pads across the room. There's something about a man in bare feet and gray sweatpants. I'm not saying it's a foot fetish or anything, but damn, it does it for me. It's so familiar and comfortable.

He rummages through the bags and pulls out a charcuterie platter with bread, cheese, fruit, and dips. That one romantic gesture away from falling in love? Yeah, I think I'm there.

Nibbling at his fingers, I let him feed me grapes and strawberries, apples and cheddar. Once the food is finished, Bond cuddles me to his chest. I never want this night to end. I want to stay here with him forever. Where nothing can hurt us or tear us apart.

As we snuggle in the dim glow of my night light and downy comfort of my blankets, I whisper my looming fear against his skin. "Bond, what do you think my dad will do if he finds out about us?"

His strong arms squeeze me, and his lips brush against my forehead. "We'll just have to make sure no one finds out. Get some sleep, Peach. We have work tomorrow, and it's going to be hard as hell to pretend we're just friends."

The combination of our sexual escapades, Bond's warm body pressed to mine, and the rhythmic rise and fall of his breathing lull me into the safe comfort of sleep. As I drift off, I bask in the rush of tenderness. The soul-soothing pleasure. The connection. I'm falling fast and hard, and there's nothing to stop me.

The buzzing of an alarm sounds in the distance. Without thinking, I reach a hand out and swat.

"Oomph."

Blinking open a bleary eye, I startle at the solid wall of warmth under my head.

"Not exactly the loving morning wakeup I was expecting." Bond chuckles as he rubs his chest where I hit him.

"Oh, crap. I'm sorry. It was a reflex. What time is it?"

"It's five."

"In the morning?" With a groan, I bury my head in the crook of Bond's neck. "I take my sorry back. Why are you up so early?"

The rumble of his laugh vibrates beneath me. "I get up this early every weekday. I like to get in a quick workout and be in the office by seven to work while it's quiet. Then I usually pop out to the active sites."

I mutter, "This relationship is doomed to fail," before closing my eyes. I feel a quick kiss on my forehead and then nothing but peaceful sleep. The next thing I know, my alarm is going off under my head, and Bond is back, standing in my bedroom in a towel.

He grins at me. "Do you always get up this late?"

"Late? It's six-thirty." I yawn and rub my sleep-swollen eyes. "I have plenty of time to get ready. In fact, if we weren't talking, I'd have already hit snooze."

"Need that beauty sleep?"

I throw a pillow at his head and squeal when he catches it and throws it back at me. I clutch the pillow to my naked chest and study Bond as he drops the towel and slips into a pair of black briefs.

"Are you sure you're okay with keeping us a secret?" I ask.

"You aren't ashamed to be seen with me, right?" There's a teasing tone to his voice, and he walks to the bed before crawling up it like a big cat stalking its prey until I'm caged between his arms and the bed.

"Yeah, that's it. Can't take a mug like yours anywhere." I kiss him and run my fingers through the sparse hair on his chest.

He huffs, "I'll have you know I was voted cutest smile in first grade."

A giggle bubbles up from my lips. "Too bad you grew out of it."

"That's it." Bond tickles my sides and blows raspberries against my neck until I'm begging him to stop.

I brush that Superman curl off his brow as he nips my chin.

"Peach, I promise, if keeping this between us is what you need, it's the absolute least I'm willing to do. I never want you to feel like you're exposed or put you in a situation that makes you uncomfortable."

"How'd I get so lucky?"

"I am a catch, aren't I?"

Giving him a playful shove, I roll my eyes. "You're going to be late, *mister seven o'clock start time.*"

"Worth it." Bond peppers me with blistering kisses and doesn't let up until we're both in danger of being late.

CHAPTER TWENTY

Tuesday's green SUV pulls into the spot next to mine. Fuck she looks pretty. All I want to do is press her up against the hood of her car, whisper in her ear how much I adore her while I sink into her from behind until she cries out my name. But that would probably skirt the line of professionalism. So instead, I get out, give her a quick nod, and move on as if she's not the brightest star in my sky.

Bypassing our office, I go straight to the workshop. There's no way I can be in that small space with her without giving in to my baser desires.

Usually, I'm like a machine. Monday through Friday, I wake up at five, run, hike, or hit the boxing gym, shower, and get to the office by seven. After knocking out emails, I check in on any live builds. If we're between jobs, I draft new designs or learn skills from our contracted masons and woodcutters. Everyone knows this. So when I walk into the workshop two hours later than usual, people have jokes.

I take their ribbing with a good-natured smile. Every joke cracked at my expense is worth it. *Hey Porter, what's up with the*

Smoothing out my drafting paper, I swivel in my seat. If they only knew how true the last one was. Watching Tuesday come in the mirror, feeling it with my fingers, tasting it on my tongue, was mind-blowing. But finally sliding into the tight heat of her pussy. Well, that? That was indescribable.

Then I got the pleasure of cuddling her while we slept and waking up to her beautiful—if slightly grumpy—face this morning. Nothing compares to the soft press of her body against mine. The smell of her honey-sweet hair. The flavor of her skin and delicious pussy as I lick her from tip to toe.

If I don't stop thinking about her, I'm going to get hard in the middle of the workshop.

"What's got you all starry-eyed?"

The sound of Cal's voice snaps me out of my Tuesday fantasy. With a grin, I shrug. "Nothing. Just enjoying being alive."

"As a person lucky enough to spend every day with the love of my life, I have to say, you've got it bad, Boss."

"Can't a guy just be in a good mood?"

"Sure. But that look isn't you in a good mood. That look is you married by the end of the year."

My ears burn. Am I that obvious? I thought I had a decent poker face. "Cal, we aren't all as fortunate as you and Morgan. Stop rubbing it in."

"Sure thing, Boss. Just make sure whoever she is, Morgan and I get an invite to the wedding!" he laughs, slapping me on the back as he leaves.

Resituating myself at the drafting station, I sketch out a few random designs, but instead of home elevations, they're all of a beautiful woman with full lips, big brown eyes, and a cute freckled nose. Shit. She's permeating every part of me.

Cal is right. I do have it bad.

A sudden primal need to show the world she's mine crawls through me. I meant it when I told her I'll keep things between us for as long as she needs. But, damn, if I don't wish I could shout it out. Maybe take out a billboard. Let the whole world know she's mine, and I'm hers.

While I can't do that yet, I can still remind her. With a satisfied grin, I grab my phone and pull up The Pinkest Petal's website. I scroll, looking at different options, and then stop when I see the peonies. There in the description is their scent profile: *Our peonies range from sweet and rosy to citrusy and spicy.* Citrusy and spicy. If that isn't a perfect match for my Peach, I don't know what is. Without hesitation, I place the order. When it comes time to enter the card details, I keep it simple.

I keep it true.

Yours — B

PEACH

Did you get a summons for a 10:30 meeting from Mr. Phillips?

Yep. Any idea what it's about?

PEACH

None.

I frown. This doesn't bode well.

Ten minutes before the meeting is scheduled, I walk into

the conference room and find Tuesday already there. The way it's arranged, with the video screen on one wall and the chairs on the far side of the table, puts us next to each other. Technically, there are other empty seats, but I use this to my advantage and pick one next to her. Even though it's a dangerous game, I can't stop myself from brushing my fingers over her nape. Her hair is up today, a different look from the usual, and I love the view it offers me of her jaw and neck.

She leans into my touch, her eyes fluttering closed. A small smile tugs on her lips, and she whispers, "Thank you for the flowers."

Giving the back of her neck a quick squeeze, I drop my hand as Cal, Charli, and Morgan walk in. Clearing my throat when I feel their eyes on me, I say, "Good morning. If you'll take your seats, we'll get started."

Once everyone is settled, I pull up the video chat, and soon the imposing image of Warren Phillips fills the screen.

His dark brown eyes, eyes that hold none of the warmth of Tuesday's, assess each of us. My guess? We don't pass.

"Is this the entire team?"

Pursing my lips, I say, "Yes. As you know, we are a small company. Cal is our lead foreman, Morgan is our receptionist and admin assistant, and you know the rest of us."

Warren Phillips stares at his daughter as though she's a bug under a microscope. "Yes. Everyone but Porter and Tuesday may leave."

Charli turns to us, eyebrows raised. I give a slight shrug. I'm as clueless as she is.

Cal crosses his arms, studying Tuesday, the screen, and me, but before he can ask any questions, Morgan pats him on the arm and pulls him up from the table. Now, it's just me, the woman of my dreams, and her dad.

"Is there anything going on that I need to be briefed on?" Tuesday's father glowers at us from the screen.

Everything about this man is formal and stiff, from his perfectly parted salt and pepper hair to his hard brown eyes. There's no sign of kindness or even respect as he surveys us. I think of my own father, his warm laugh, and the steady strength of his stare. I can only imagine what growing up with this man was like for her.

Swallowing my bitterness and prickle of worry, I say, "No, there's nothing to report. Things are progressing as usual. My understanding from our one and only meeting is that we would contact you if there's an issue."

"Yes, well, Tuesday called War two days ago, having some ridiculous meltdown over not having your full name, so I can only assume she's been problematic since."

Tuesday stiffens next to me, and without thinking, I reach under the table and cover her hand with my own. The action is instinctual. My girl is hurting; it's my job to comfort her. Luckily, our hands are out of view.

"Listen, Mr. Phillips, I assure you, Tuesday has been nothing but professional. She's learning the ropes here quickly and has already proven herself a valuable member of the team."

When he scoffs, I wonder how much it would cost me to fly to Texas and snatch that scoff right out of his throat.

"Porter, I hope you'll keep a clear head where Tuesday's concerned. She's often irrational and muddies the professional waters with personal matters."

"Dad," Tuesday snaps, her face red and her fingers tightening on mine in an almost painful grip, "you made your point. I'm the problem. But as Bo...Porter assured you, things are going fine. Did you actually need something, or was this just a call to belittle me in front of my new coworkers?"

I skim my thumb across her knuckles, small circles that I hope will express how I'm feeling while I'm unable to say it.

Warren narrows his eyes. "Be mindful of your behavior, Tuesday. There will not be another chance for you."

"Mr. Phillips, you owe your daughter an apology. You will not speak to her like that. Beyond the fact that she is, in fact, your flesh and blood, I certainly hope you would never speak to an employee this way."

"How I speak to Tuesday is none of your concern. You'd do well to remember who owns your company, young man." With that, he cuts off the call.

A fine tremble of anger courses through me, tightening my muscles. I have to consciously force myself to lower my shoulders and breathe.

Tuesday sags against me, rocking her head back and forth against my chest. "I'm so sorry."

"Why are you apologizing?"

"Because he's awful. And he wouldn't be in your life, threatening the company, if it wasn't for me."

Lifting her chin, I brush my lips against hers. "Hey, look at me, Peach. We settled this last night. The life we're building together is our new legacy."

"One normal day. That's all I hoped for. Guess I need to lower my expectations."

I nip the tip of her nose. "Plus side? You didn't end up in a storage closet."

She swats me but smiles, so I take the win. I press my forehead to hers once more, getting one last hit of *Tuesday* to get me through the day. As I rise, the weight of her small hand on my arm stops me.

"I...this is probably..." She huffs and stares at the ceiling. Clearly, something's on her mind.

"Go on, sweetheart."

Tuesday lays a gold key on the conference table. "This is a key to my place. No pressure or anything, and it's no big deal if you think it's too soon. I just thought it might make things easier. For us. For the coming and going. If you wanted to come and go, I mean. And really, if it feels like some—"

I cut off her adorable nervous ramble with my lips. It's a dangerous game, kissing her in the office, but in this moment, she needs that physical reassurance. Then I grin at her before grabbing the key. My eyes on hers, making sure she's watching every move I make, I slowly slide my new greatest treasure onto my keyring.

"I'll see you after work, Peach. At 5:01, you're mine."

Her beautiful smile is the only reply I need.

I'm sitting in Ava's, munching on chips as I wait for my best friends to show up for our weekly lunch. The abysmal meeting from this morning consumes my thoughts. Warren Phillips is a piece of shit. His thinly veiled threat against the company was the icing on the dickhead cake.

"Hey, man, good to see you."

Griffin Anderson's deep, booming voice pulls me from my thoughts. The six-three, blond, tattooed behemoth slaps my back as he greets me. It's not often I still feel like Runt, but with two inches and over twenty pounds on me, Griff is a massive man. Like a Viking or some shit.

"Griff, how are things going at Flora and Fauna?"

"Fucking fantastic. Best move I ever made was to this place." As he sits and reaches for the chips and salsa, he gives me a smirk. "When are you coming in and getting inked? You're the only Davis sibling I haven't worked on."

Laughing, I shake my head. "No time soon. I'll leave the tattoos to Clairy and Charli."

A slight blush forms on Griff's cheeks at the mention of my older sister's name. Dumbass. Those two are so into each other it's ridiculous. Before I can call him on it, Dane plops down at our table.

"Hey."

"Chatty as always, Mendoza," Griff snarks.

Dane raises one eyebrow before shrugging and diving into the chips. "Did you want a soliloquy, Anderson?"

Griff's loud laugh echoes across the small restaurant.

Ignoring our tattooed friend, Dane turns his attention to me, his dark brown eyes scanning me from head to toe. "So, how're things going with your girl?"

"Your girl? What's all this?" Griff asks.

Shit. I haven't seen Griff since meeting Tuesday, but I should have known it would come up. My friends aren't stupid, and with everything Dane saw between us at his bar, I'm going to have to work to convince them we aren't together.

Bracing myself to lie, I say, "Not my girl. We work together. It's a conflict of interest."

"Bullshit."

Dane's one-word snort has Griff looking at him in surprise. "Clearly, I've missed some key pieces here. I need Charli to get better at gossip."

"Long story short, I met a woman at the Great Dane. We had a good time together, but it turns out her dad is the guy who bought Davis Designs. So we ended things. No big deal. We'd barely gotten started."

"Bullshit."

I glare at Dane. "Is that all you're going to say?"

"Calling it like I see it. Bond, you were head over fucking heels for her the night you met her. There's no way you let her go without a fight."

Griffin grins. "Head over heels? Damn, who is this woman? I've known you for, what, five years? I've never seen you gone for anyone in that time."

"I haven't seen him like this ever, even with Darcy in high school," Dane says.

"I thought there was something there, but it isn't going to work. Her dad is my boss. I'm her boss. It's complicated." The lie tastes like sludge, miring on my tongue and oozing down my throat into my chest.

The stares from the two men across the table prickle over my skin, and I take the coward's way out and peruse my menu. Fuck. This is harder than I thought it would be. How will I keep this up when all I want to do is tell everyone how I feel?

"Sometimes you don't get what you want. It's a fact of life," I say.

"You're an idiot." Dane's flat voice has me setting the menu down to frown at him.

"What's going on with you and Clairy, Dane?" I ask. Partly because I'm getting pissed and partly because I'm curious what he'll say.

Dane's eyes narrow, and he rubs his clean-shaven chin. "Nothing. You know that." He bends his head, not looking at me. "She's your baby sister."

"And if she wasn't?"

When he doesn't answer, I turn to Griff. "What about you and Charli?"

"It's not like that. We're just friends."

"Looks like I'm not the only idiot at the table." *Or liar.*

My friends glower at me. A lesser man might break, but I swore to Tuesday I'd keep us a secret, and I will not hurt her.

Ready to change the topic and move away from the uncomfortable air settling over us, I give them my best shit-eating grin and tap the menu. "So what are you assholes ordering?"

Griff opens his mouth, but a familiar voice calling my name interrupts him.

"Bond!" Clairy jogs up to our table. "Oh, you're out with the guys. Great, Charli and I will join." She immediately squishes into the empty chair next to Dane. No sooner does she sit than she snags the chip out of his hand and pops it into her mouth.

Charli stands next to the table, shifting her weight back and forth. "You don't mind if we crash?" Griff hops to his feet, offering his chair to her.

"Here, Lottie, sit."

Lottie? I raise my eyebrows at her, but all that gets me is an elbow to the side.

"Thanks, Griff." A faint blush colors Charli's cheeks as she cuts her gaze away from him.

"Where's Tuesday?" Clairy asks, helping herself to Dane's water while he frowns at her.

I scratch my temple and shrug. "At the office, I guess."

Clairy's eyes narrow, and she jerks her head towards me. "Why do you sound weird?"

Shit. "I don't."

"Why isn't she at lunch with you?"

Dane crosses his arms and leans back in his chair. "That's an excellent question, Clairy. Why isn't she at lunch, Bond?"

Asshole. The sharp, pointy toe of my sister's boot catches me in the shin. "Ow! What was that for, Charli Horse?"

My older sister outright glares at me. "Did you screw things up? You were supposed to fix them."

"What does she mean? What happened?" Clairy asks.

Every eye at the table fixes on me. Waiting.

Sighing, I throw my head back and stare at the ceiling. All I wanted was some Mexican food with my friends. I should have eaten in my truck. Or snuck under Tuesday's desk and had her for lunch.

"Bond? You going to answer?"

"Yeah, sorry, Griff, just lost in my thoughts. Tuesday and I... we aren't...after talking it out..."

"Are you serious? You guys aren't together?" Clairy asks. "What the hell happened between the two of you?"

Trying to come up with a viable lie is too much pressure, so I lean into the truth that almost tore us apart—at least as much of it as I can share without overstepping Tuesday's privacy.

"Her dad bought Davis Designs on a whim. He picked us at random. We were nothing but a name in a hat to him."

"So? Call it kismet and move on." My little sister waves her hand, dismissing my words.

"Tuesday's family stole our legacy out from under us."

"Oh my god, not this again, Bond." Charli pinches the bridge of her nose. "Dad agreed to sell. If you're mad at anyone, it should be him. Tuesday had nothing to do with that."

"It's not that. There's a lot to it—"

"Fix it. Get some food, show up, and tell her you're a moron. You haven't been this happy in years." Charli's piercing gaze steadies on me, unblinking.

I give a noncommittal shrug and shove a chip in my mouth.

"Porter Bond Davis, you're an idiot. You were talking about making her a Davis. And now, you're sitting here all whatever about giving up?"

"Clairy, there are things you don't understand."

"I am so tired of the words, Clairy, you don't understand." She turns and pokes Dane in the chest. "From you." Then she stands and does the same to me. "And you." Eyeballing Griffin, she gives him a quick poke. "I'm not sure about you, but I bet you deserve that. I'm just so tired of all you...you men! None of you know what the hell you want, even when it's right in front of your dumbasses. Come on, Charli, let's go check on Tuesday. She's probably hurt and upset, and she doesn't have anyone else in town."

As my sisters storm out, Dane sits there, a stunned look on his face, holding his hand over his heart where Clairy jabbed him with her finger.

I definitely should have eaten at the office.

CHAPTER TWENTY-ONE

DO NOT REPLY

You're going to have to come back to TX eventually, Tits. We have unfinished business.

I delete the message. Duncan's texts are coming in more frequently, each one more unhinged than the one before. They range from taunts to vague threats about making me pay for ruining his marriage. As if it's my fault he decided to cheat on his now ex-wife and take photos of me without my permission. Asshole. Rolling my neck and unclenching my jaw, I refocus.

After that cluster of a meeting with my father, I desperately need to stay busy. Otherwise, I'll fall into a spiral, wondering what I can do to make myself worthy in Dad's eyes. Thirty-three years' worth of evidence would suggest the answer is nothing.

Shake it off, Tuesday. You're in another state. You're doing your job. You're enough.

Okay, that's enough mantras. Kicking my pointy-toe flats off beneath my desk, I pull open my laptop. Priority for today? Determine a plan of attack to approach Davis Designs' abysmal digital footprint. Between the quality of their work and the kind and attractive staff, our greatest asset is ourselves. So I'm starting an employee of the week social media takeover. Each week I'll highlight a staff member, have them share what they love about working at Davis Designs, recap their favorite projects they've worked on, and what they hope to see in the future.

I go through the list of all our employees, full and part-time. Then I sort them out by years of experience and position, webbing those who are connected together. Some by blood, some by age, some by role, until I have a woven tapestry of the story of Davis Designs. My messy grid would make a bystander go cross-eyed, but it makes perfect sense to my brain. And there, buried in the threads, is the answer to who should be first.

Morgan.

She's the face who greets you at the door; she's beautiful and bubbly, and she's worked at Davis Designs for years with easy connections to everyone else. Sliding my shoes back on, I snag my phone, a notepad, and my lunch. Time to work.

"Morgan, any chance you'd be willing to eat lunch with me and let me pitch an idea to you?" I ask, interrupting her mid-bite as I walk into the break room.

Swallowing, she grins at me. "I'd love to have lunch with you." She gestures to the empty chair across from her.

"So, I'm looking at ways to increase our social media presence, and I thought, what better way to start than with who we are?" I sit and situate myself to eat and take notes. "You're the first person who came to mind."

"Really? Me?" The gold flecks of Morgan's wide hazel eyes shine with excitement. "But I'm just the receptionist and administrative assistant. Wouldn't it make more sense to start with Porter or Charlotte?"

"No, you're the perfect person to start with. Are you interested?"

With an eager nod, Morgan smiles. "Yes. Very! What do I have to do?"

"Let me take a few pictures of you or share any of your favorites from your years here at Davis Designs that you would be okay with me posting online. Then I'll ask you a few questions to work into the posts."

"I can do that." Her serious tone belies the brilliant grin on her face.

"Perfect." I snag my phone and capture a quick picture of her, catching her off guard.

"Tuesday! I wasn't ready."

"You're beautiful, and candids do well. I would never post anything to embarrass you. I promise. I understand how cruel social media can be."

Morgan raises a delicate blonde eyebrow but doesn't push.

"Okay, so, tell me how long you've been at Davis Designs and how you got your start here."

"I've been here for nine years. Porter and Charlotte's dad, Scott, hired me right out of high school. This job changed my life."

"What do you mean?" I ask, leaning forward, my interest piqued.

"Not only did it give me financial stability at eighteen, but it also introduced me to the love of my life and helped me build my family."

I do a double-take at her words. "Wh-what do you mean it introduced you to the love of your life?"

"Cal is my husband."

My mouth drops open, a little of my sweet tea dribbling out. How did I not know that?

"We've been married for seven years. We met my first day on the job, and I fell head over heels for him. But he thought I was too young." She waves her hand dismissively. "After over a year of pining and tiptoeing around each other, he finally asked me out. Everyone in the office told him he was a dummy for waiting so long when it was clear we were perfect for each other."

Love radiates from her, and my heart aches for what she has and is free to share and show to the world. There's a pulling sensation in my stomach that feels suspiciously like envy. If things were different, would the entire office be rooting for Bond and me the same way they did for Morgan and Cal?

I wrinkle and then smooth out my napkin. "And the two of you weren't worried about how it would impact your work relationship or the office? Especially if things didn't work out?"

"Well, Cal had some concerns at first, but most of those were because he's a few years older than me. Hence, the making us wait a year before asking me out." She laughs and shakes her head. "When we first started dating, we had our hiccups. What couple doesn't? But no, nothing that could keep us apart. We agreed early on to be honest with everyone here and with each other. And if, for some horrible reason, things didn't work out, we could both be professional. But honestly? When I think back on those early months, we both recognized that the feelings between us were for forever," she says, a thoughtful look on her face.

A lump forms in my throat. This could be Bond and me.

I smile at her because, despite my jealousy, I'm incredibly happy for her and Cal. "So besides meeting the man of your dreams, what else do you love about working for Davis Designs?"

I'm back in my office, reviewing the photos Morgan sent me and matching them up with the quotes from my note-taking. A picture of her and Cal, Morgan sitting behind the reception desk, Cal leaning against it and looking at her instead of the camera, draws my attention. It perfectly captures his love for her. I have to use it in my post.

Everyone loves a Jim and Pam story, right?

Taking a final look at the picture, another stab of envy flutters through me. Bond and I don't have any photos together. I need to remedy this ASAP. Agenda item for the evening? Convince Bond to snap a few selfies with me through any means possible.

I smile, thinking of all the ways I might persuade him. One specific toy comes to the front of my mind. Biting my lip, I lose myself for a few minutes, imagining all the fun he and I can have together.

The clamor of footsteps and two voices bursting into my office snap me from my daydream.

"Tuesday, tell us everything."

Both Davis sisters stand at my desk, matching blue eyes filled with curiosity and concern.

"Clairy? Charli? Um, hi?"

"No time for hi's. What happened? Are you okay?" Clairy continues, her tall frame bending over my desk.

Charli frowns at me, the soft piney green of her sweater a beautiful compliment to her butterscotch hair. "Is this my fault? Because of what I said yesterday? I swear, Tuesday, I wasn't trying to put you in a bad spot."

"What are you—" Oh crap. This is about Bond and me.

Clearing my throat, I say, "I'm not sure what all Bond told you."

"We ran into him, Dane, and Griff at lunch, and when we asked where you were, he told us you two aren't together anymore."

I hate lying. I want nothing more than to be friends with them. Even if things work out between Bond and me, am I ruining our chance for friendship? Why does this have to be so complicated? Why couldn't Bond and I have no connections other than the romantic ones?

C-Squared watch me, patiently waiting for my answer, but the lie sticks in my mouth. I decide the best course of action is the truth up to a certain point. With a sigh, I say, "I have a complicated past. Things with my ex ended poorly, and it was an office romance. Not to mention, there's an extra layer of complications because of who my family is."

"You know that's total horse crap, right?" Clairy asks. With her chestnut hair, blue eyes, and tan skin, she and Bond favor each other a lot.

"Um...I mean...no?"

Charli's clever eyes narrow, studying me. "Are you sure that's what you want? I know I didn't really get to see the two of you together, but from the way he talked about you and what I heard from Clairy, there was more to what you had than just a physical connection. And I saw the determination in his eyes when he went after you yesterday."

Swallowing, I try to decide how best to answer her. "It's true. Bond and I have a genuine connection. He's the sweetest, most caring man I've ever had the pleasure of meeting. He's smart, funny, se...um, handsome, and the way he loves those around him is something to behold. Anyone would be lucky to be with him. But it doesn't change the fact that we work together or that my dad owns this company."

"Are you okay?" Clairy asks quietly.

"I'm taking things one day at a time." Not a lie.

I find myself enveloped in a Davis sister sandwich. "We hope you'll still spend time with us. We've been itching to hang out and get to know you."

"I'd love that." Another not-lie.

"How about brunch on Saturday at Ava's?"

Charli's suggestion perks me right up. Both because of the brunch invite and the thought of returning to Ava's. "Yes, that sounds amazing!"

We stay hugging for a moment more when Charli catches sight of my post draft. "Is that Morgan?"

"Yeah, I'm starting a new social media series to help our online presence. I want to highlight employees along with the projects. Really show people the talent behind the company. If people feel like they know us, they're more likely to let us build their dreams. At least that's my working theory."

"I love it." Charli cocks her head and speaks as though she's weighing her words. "Maybe we weren't expecting you, but I think you're exactly what we need."

"Okay, that's enough sappy stuff. Tuesday, if you really are single and certain things won't work out between you and Bond, which we aren't buying, by the way, why don't you tell us what you look for in a guy? We can give you the lowdown on the locals."

Unsure where to begin with Clairy's question, I stutter, "Um...wh-what I look for?"

"Yeah." She waves her hand in the air. "Black hair, dark brown eyes, tan skin, compact build, grumpy attitude—"

Charli gives a delicate cough. "That sounds very specific."

Clairy's cheeks flush. "No. It was an example."

"Uh-huh. Sure." To me, Charli says, "And don't think that gets you out of answering the question."

"You really want to know?" Both sisters nod at me. With a deep breath, I answer honestly. "Looks are negotiable, but the mix of chestnut hair and blue eyes holds a certain appeal. The most important things, though, aren't physical. It's someone kind and caring who sees me as I am and likes that person." I pause. "And if they happen to be six-one with a Superman curl and a smile that lights up a room, that's a bonus."

"Superman curl?" Clairy gives me a grin that rivals the Cheshire cat's.

Ducking my head, I backtrack. "I mean, you know, some hair I can grab onto."

"You like grabbing hair?" Charli's eyebrows jump as she fights her laughter.

"Oh my gosh," I groan.

All three of us break out in a fit of giggles until we recover enough to breathe and talk. They stay another hour, talking about everything and nothing like we've known each other for years. I learn Charli is a single mom, and Clairy returned to Trail Creek about six months before I arrived after being gone for ten years.

They are brilliant, funny, kind women, and I want them in my life.

After Charli and Clairy clear out of my office, I soak in their words. My heart warms at them racing over here to check on me and their desire to grow our friendship. I really hope this whole secret thing doesn't blow up in my face. If things don't work out, I stand to lose more than Bond.

The incoming sound of a video call plays out over my laptop. With a groan, I realize it's coming from my brother. Why is War calling? Maybe Dad didn't fill him in on my morning belittling.

Straightening the random items on my desk and my

blouse, I sit up and paste on my fake smile, the one I used daily in Dallas and have only had to rely on a handful of times here.

"Tuesday."

"War, how can I help you?"

"How are you settling into the Davis Designs office?"

"I'm settling in well. Thank you for asking." The warmth of this conversation couldn't melt an ice cube. I think of how Bond talks about Clairy and Charli and how close they are. What must that be like? "I assume you were privy to the conversation between Mr. Phillips and myself this morning?"

I can't mask the sarcasm, disdain, or hurt when I snarl, *Mr. Phillips.*

"Yes. I heard it. You know how he is, though, Tuesday. You should have expected his questions."

"I can't believe you told him I called you having a meltdown. Actually, I can believe it, but it was still a crappy thing to do."

"What did you expect? You called me in a panic. I figured things had gone off the rails."

"Ah, yes, because that's the only way things go when I'm involved, right?"

When he doesn't answer, I pinch the bridge of my nose and say, "Is there anything I can help you with?"

"Mom wants to know how you're doing outside the office."

"So this is a perfunctory well-check under the guise of a work call?"

War has the good sense to look away from me. "We all want to make sure you're okay."

"I'm fine." My voice is flat and empty. "If that changes, I will be sure to let Mr. Phillip's administrative assistant know."

"Tuesday, don't be so difficult."

Wrong thing to say. "Have a nice day, War. Let Mom know

you did your due diligence." With that, I disconnect from the video call and bury my face in my hands.

Why can't things be easy with them? Am I truly so hard for them to love? I mean, the three of them all seem to get along with each other just fine. I'm the odd one out.

Diving back into work, I immerse myself in checking our social media channels and researching marketing trends.

When my back grows stiff, and my eyes start to cross, I glance at the clock. Holy balls, it's five. I made it through an entire day of work with minimal issue. I didn't throw fruit or veg at anyone, hide in a supply closet, or storm out in a fit of tears.

Yay, me!

The desire to see Bond, snuggle with him, and learn more of his secrets overwhelms me. I haphazardly throw my things into my bag and run to my car. My fingers fly over the letters as I text him.

Missed you today.

Stopping at High Country grocery store. Then headed to my place. Hope to see you there

winky face emoji

His reply pings almost as soon as I hit send.

SEXY BASEBALL CAP

Been dying to see you all damn day, Baby Girl.

You're a local now. Call it the HiCo

winky face emoji

I don't even bother fighting the grin. I love the way he teases me, love how open he is with his feelings. I love...

Shaking my head, I connect my phone to the Bluetooth in my car and tuck it under my thigh. Embracing my younger self, I sing along to Avril Lavinge as I drive closer to the outskirts of town. I zip into a parking spot in front of the tiny Mom and Pop store. It would never survive in Dallas, but here it thrives. It's another plus in the Trail Creek column, as far as I'm concerned. I hop out, pop in my earbuds, and continue with my Millennial nostalgia playlist, waving to an older couple coming out.

As I browse the aisles inside *HiCo*, I lose myself in the beat of the music. I shop quickly, eager to get home to Bond, grabbing anything that nabs my fancy. Nearing the baked goods section because, duh, carbs, I startle when a large hand seizes my arm. I can't help but jerk, both from the unexpected touch and the force of the grip. But all pulling my arm away does is make the person tighten their hold. Whirling around, I find myself nose to shoulder with Jacob Ashford.

Chills sweep over me, and I cringe away from him.

With a sneer, he flexes his fingers, digging them into the muscle of my arm. "You embarrassed me in the bar that night. Why don't you make it up to me by letting me show you what a real man can do?"

I cover up my panic with a derisive snort, which makes his face turn red. I yank my arm, but he still won't let go. Adrenaline pumps through my veins, and my heartbeat pounds behind my eyes, in my ears, on my tongue. Giving one more hard jerk, relief floods me when I free myself from his grasp.

"You embarrassed yourself in the bar. Learn how to take no for an answer." Summoning courage I don't actually feel, I say, "If you touch me again, you'll be sorry."

Jacob goes to say something but stops when a massive man steps up beside us.

"Everything okay here?" The Viking—because seriously,

that's exactly what he looks like—asks, his green eyes narrowing on Jacob before flicking to me.

"Yes, thank you. Jakey-boy here was just leaving." Fighting the quiver in my voice, I will it to fill with ice as I stare him down.

Muttering under his breath, Jacob stalks away, leaving the Viking and me standing next to each other and the freshly baked bread.

"You sure you're okay?"

I blink back tears of anger and pain. My arm throbs from where he grabbed me. "Yeah, thank you."

The Viking's lips thin into a line, like he wants to say something else, but then he gives me a nod before leaving. I power walk to the self-checkout lane and pay, my brain functioning at a rote level. *Scan. Bag. Scan. Bag. Pay.*

Outside, the cool air and rapidly approaching dark are enough to pull me back to the here and now, and I regret not asking the Viking to walk me to my car. A stupid trickle of fear grips me. So I do what any self-respecting thirty-something would do and sprint to my car, the few bags of groceries swinging at my side.

All I want is to get home and wash this interaction off. For Bond to burn the remnants of Ashford's touch away and replace it with his own.

CHAPTER TWENTY-TWO

I'm impatiently waiting down the road from Tuesday's house for her to arrive home. Adrenaline surges through me as I sit in the darkened cab, hiding in plain sight. There's something sexy about the idea of getting caught. This is the upside of sneaking around.

But it's been almost an hour since she texted me. And even with the drive to Piñon Hills from town and a stop at the grocery store, I thought she'd be here by now.

> Hey, Peach. I'm here, parked a couple of lots down.

After ten minutes with no reply, my nerves get the best of me. Phone in hand, I'm about to hit the call button when the flash of headlights catches my attention. Tuesday pulls into her driveway, climbs from her car, and—bags in hand—trudges to the door. Tension radiates from the lines of her body.

Something's wrong.

I jerk open the door to my truck and jump down, jogging my way to Tuesday's.

My two quick knocks go unanswered. Giving the knob a tentative turn, I find it locked, which doesn't surprise me. I think back to the small barrier she built in her room at the Trail Creek Inn. Reaching into my pocket, I fish out my keys, the new, small gold one she gave me today shining in the glint of the porch light.

She gave it to me to use, right? Right. I knock once more before sliding the key into the lock and letting myself in. "Tuesday? Baby Girl, where are you?"

Locking the door behind me, I scan the living room and kitchen. The familiar brown paper bags from HiCo sit on her island, but she's nowhere to be seen. What the hell is going on?

In a handful of strides, I'm heading to Tuesday's lofted bedroom. As I lumber up the stairs, I hear the faint sound of water running.

A wicked grin lights my face. A naked, wet, soapy Tuesday in my arms? Sign me up.

Shedding my clothes as I walk through her bedroom, I tap on the bathroom door to avoid spooking her. Once again, though, my knock goes unanswered.

With a frown, I open the door and step into the steamy room. I can just make out the silhouette of Tuesday's curvy frame behind the fogged glass.

I pull the shower door open and step into the warm spray, but what I see stops all thoughts of fun, sexy times dead in their tracks.

My girl washes her hair, her eyes squeezed shut as tears drip down her cheeks. And there, on her left arm, is a large red handprint. Someone touched my Peach. Someone put their goddamn hands on her and made her cry.

"Tuesday?" My voice is a rough rasp, barely audible over the multiple shower heads raining down.

Her eyes fly open, and I curse myself for startling her, but an instant later, she melts into my arms, burying her head into my chest, her hair still full of suds.

I hug her close. Running my hands over her body, I check for any other marks. When I don't find any, I focus my gaze on her arm. Everything else disappears, my entire field of vision narrowing to the red marks marring her skin.

Those will be bruises by the morning.

Bruises.

On my Tuesday.

"Are you okay? Who did this?"

Her voice is soft. "I'm okay. More mad than anything. Sorry, I didn't answer your text."

"Don't you apologize to me, Baby Girl." I gently tip her head back, rinsing the shampoo from her hair and placing a careful kiss on her lips. When her eyes close and she sighs, putting more weight against me, I grab her citrus-honey conditioner and run it through her strands. "Tuesday, talk to me. Who did it?"

"Jacob."

My fists give an involuntary clench. "Shit, sorry. Did I pull your hair?"

"No, but honestly, I wish you would."

"What?" I freeze, processing her words.

"I need you to replace his touch with yours. I want you to leave your marks on me." She stands on her tiptoes and presses her pillowy lips to mine.

"Tuesday..."

"I promise I'm okay. Please, Bond." She trails kisses down my neck before her pink tongue licks a drop of water off my chest.

On the one hand, I live to give Peach anything she wants. On the other, I can't imagine being rough with her right now.

Rising to her full, adorable height, she takes one of my hands and places it on her throat. "Please. Make me forget his touch."

Tilting her head back, I say, "Tell me what happened."

She swallows, and I can feel the motion under my palm. My grip tightens, and Tuesday lets out a breathy moan. "After. I'll tell you everything. But right now, I need you."

I give her throat one more squeeze before sliding my hands down her sides. Reaching around her, I shut off the water and after a quick peck to her nose, gather her in my arms. Quickly toweling us both off, I take a moment to nuzzle my face into her neck and graze my teeth over her soft skin. I could stay with her like this forever.

Tuesday shudders, her eyes closed and lips parted. We step into her bedroom, and I guide her to sit on the edge of the bed. Dropping to my knees, I rest my forehead against hers.

"Are you sure this is what you want? I can hold you, and we can talk."

"No, Bond. I need you to reclaim me. To drown everything else out in our desire and pleasure."

How the hell can I say no to that?

The kiss between us starts sweet and soft, but then my little brat nips my lips. "Harder, Bond."

Tuesday's tongue slides along the seam of my lips, enticing me to open to her. She explores my mouth, tangling her tongue with mine. I lightly trace her tempting curves before trailing my hand up and down her back. Her skin is like silk against my calloused palm.

"Please, I need more," she whispers.

I gingerly lift her arm and brush my lips against the angry red mark on her skin. Fighting back a surge of anger, I refocus all my energy on her. "If that's what you want, I'll give it to you."

"Yes, that's what I want."

With that, I push her back against the bed before burying my face between her thighs. My hot breath ghosts over her delicate flesh, raising goosebumps, and all the blood rushes to my cock. Every reaction she gives me only makes me hungrier for more. Dragging her hips up, I smile before parting her legs wide and diving in to taste her.

That particular sweetness that only comes from between my Peach's legs coats my tongue. My hands ache with the need to explore her, and I soon give in to the urge, plunging two fingers knuckle deep as I bite down on her inner thigh. When she squirms and tries to plant her feet on the bed and push away, I growl and press my palm to her lower stomach, locking her in place. She's not getting away from me tonight.

Tuesday whimpers, and I curl my fingers forward in a come hither motion as if I'm calling her pleasure to me. My tongue moves in slow circles over her clit, and my fingers stroke her from the inside. Her walls tighten, but instead of bringing her to release, I stop. My fingers go still inside her, and I lift my mouth from her pussy. Her reaction doesn't disappoint.

"Bond!" She looks practically scandalized that I dared deny her an orgasm. So fucking sassy.

Lowering my head, I chuckle and graze my teeth against her clit. Her snarl of frustration has me smiling against her sex. "I may give you what you want, Baby Girl, but it doesn't mean you're in charge. I own your orgasms. I'm the one who makes you come. And it's not time yet."

When she starts to squirm, looking for any relief she can, I sink two fingers back inside her and press my thumb to her clit. The hand holding her down slides higher until I can count time to the wild beating of her heart beneath my palm.

Tuesday's hands twist in the sheets. "Please, let me come!"

"Trust me, sweetheart. When I finally let you come, it'll be worth the wait."

I bring her to the edge again and again until tears stream down her cheeks. Each time she gets close, I stop. No movement, no release. But fuck me, she looks beautiful. Her eyes are glassy, her pupils blown. My cock aches to sink into her, to fill her pussy. To leave a piece of myself inside her.

"Bond, I can't wait!" Her fingers clench the sheets, and her thighs clamp around my head.

Finally, I give her what she wants and consume her like a man eating his last meal. It's wet and sloppy and perfect. No stopping this time. My hips move against nothing, my cock seeking out pressure it won't find. Yet.

Like a bird breaking free from a cage, Tuesday's orgasm explodes on my tongue as she cries out, shivering and twitching beneath me. "Bond!"

I lap at her release, cleaning all traces of it from her skin until her thighs fall away from my ears. Legs akimbo, she lays melted into the mattress, her chest rising and falling in heavy pants. Rising to my feet, I stand over her, drinking in the sight of her spent, beatific glow. My goal is always to make her come first, and I aim to be a gold-star student.

"Tell me what else you want."

A wild look lights up her eyes, and she crawls to the side of her bed and digs into the side table. A moment later, she clambers back toward me, a small clear bottle and a set of graduated pink beads in her hand.

Fuck yes.

"What do you have planned for this, Peach? Tell me everything you want me to do to you."

A playful smile spreads across her face. "What do you think I want you to do with them?"

So fucking sassy. "I think you want me to slide those into your tight asshole while I fuck you. To fill both your pretty holes and make you forget every person you've been with before."

She rises to her knees and kisses me, and I lose myself in her lips. "Yes, that's what I want."

"Anything else?" There's something mischievous in her eyes, and I need all her secrets.

"I want you to break my back like a glow stick."

Holy. Shit. Her answer stuns me momentarily, but then my primal side takes over, and I'm pushing her head down and guiding her ass up.

"Fuck. I love it." Bringing my hand down against one plump cheek, the crack of my palm makes her moan.

I grip my cock and slide it along the seam of her pussy, letting her dripping wetness coat me before teasing the head against her clit. She feels so good, and I'm not even in her yet.

Gritting my teeth, I bark, "Keep your head down and your ass up. You hear me?" Another sharp spank has her skin blossoming pink. Seeing the rosy glow on her ass from my hand urges my hips forward of their own accord.

She nods.

"Not good enough. Words." I spank her again to punctuate my point.

"Y-yes, I hear you."

Popping the lid on the bottle of lube, I pour some over my fingers before gliding them down her spine. I move lower, tracing soft, lazy circles before gently slipping my thumb into the tightness of her ass, just enough to tease her. A needy noise, more akin to an animal than the articulate woman I know, fills the air as my finger sinks deeper. When she starts working back and forth against me, I know she's ready for more.

"Gonna put those pretty pink beads in this pretty pink ass now. You ready for that, Baby Girl?"

"Ple-please!" she pleads, wriggling her perfect ass at me.

I fucking love it when she embraces her bratty side. I can't resist bending over and placing a trail of kisses against her skin, the draw of touching her too much to resist. Tuesday's responding shiver has me craving this connection for the rest of my life.

I lube the beads and slip the first one into her cute rosebud. One by one, each sphere disappears, and Tuesday moans beneath me. Every sound she makes is a delicacy, and I'm dining so fucking well tonight. When half the beads are in, I stop and pull them back out, each pop eliciting a whimper from her.

While she's mid-clench, I sink my cock into her pussy, relishing the stretch of her around my girth. "Fuck, Tuesday, you feel like a dream," I grunt.

She looks like one, too, some kind of wet dream come to life. Her long hair is a tangled mess of snarled waves across her back and shoulders. The swell of her hips gives way to the nip of her waist, her curves a visual treat. I trace the constellation of freckles across her lower back, mapping the skies on her skin as I work my way as deep into her as I can go.

Once I'm fully seated, I push the beads in once more, this time going all the way to the end. The last one is considerably thicker than my thumb. She tenses for a moment, but I pet her back. "Relax, sweetheart. Breathe," I say in a low, calm voice.

"Oh, god, Bond," she pants, desire in her exhale.

Her walls quiver and tighten around me as I push past that ring of muscle to bury the entire tapered strand inside her. My eyes roll back in my head at the feel of my cock encased in her silken heat.

"How does that feel, sweetheart."

A long moan of pleasure is her only reply.

Gritting my teeth, I pause for as long as I can stand, letting her adjust to the fullness of the beads in one hole and my cock in the other. She pulses around me, shifting, trying to take control.

"Move, Bond."

"You're being bossy tonight, my beautiful brat. Luckily, I'm feeling generous." I spank her, the sound of skin on skin ringing out. I move, but instead of pushing in, I ease out, one inch at a time.

"No!"

I chuckle, deep and low, and wait until she's clenching on nothing. "So impatient. Beg for me, Baby Girl."

"Pl-please, please make me feel good. Please move."

I love seeing her so needy, knowing she wants me so much she's aching.

Only when she's desperate do I slam into her, hard and deep, filling every glorious inch of her pussy. Then I do it again. Inch out, slam in. Over and over until she's mindlessly crying out.

"Yes, Bond, yes. That's ex-exactly what I want. M-make me ache."

"You want to be sore when we're done? Does my good girl like being filled and fucked?"

"Yes, I love it. You f-feel so good."

I grasp her hips tight enough to leave marks of my own. "Only one person gets to mark this body. No one else. My fingerprints are the only ones. I'm going to leave an imprint on you, another reminder of our secret."

"Yes, mark me, Bond!"

"Gonna bruise you, sweetheart, but make it feel so good. So fucking good." The words come from between my teeth, and my tempo is frantic. Brutal. Punishing.

A pounding need to shatter her and put her back together comes over me. I'm a man consumed, and I won't fail.

With each snap of my hips, Tuesday sinks into the mattress. She stretches an arm back, her fingertips searching for me. When her hand grazes my thigh, I buck forward. My name is a whimper on her lips, and she's a beautiful, sobbing mess.

"God, you're so fucking responsive for me, Peach."

My deeper moans meld with hers, harmonizing in a hymn of carnal worship. I keep thrusting into her, lost in the rhythmic slap of our bodies. We're caught in an endless loop of give and take. She gives me everything, and I fucking take it.

"B-Bond!"

She cries my name, and I grab the loop on the beads and pull, each one popping out from between her cheeks as her pussy strangles my cock. "You can come, but I'm not stopping. You said you wanted me to break your back? Well, I want more than that." A ragged pant tears from my lips. "I want to undo you. To unravel you. To watch you come apart in my arms until there's nothing left but what I give you." Every slide out destroys us both. Each plunge in rebuilds us stronger than before.

Tuesday's orgasm soaks my cock, and my head falls back, the intoxicating pleasure better than any buzz I've ever had.

"Stroke your clit." When she doesn't follow my directions, I give her already pink ass another quick smack, and her core spasms around me in response.

She snakes an arm beneath her body, and I know when she touches herself because her already strangling grasp on my cock grows even tighter. It's like she's a living vise grip. She's shaking beneath me, her entire body twitching and trembling. We're both coated in a fine sheen of sweat, the smell of sex heavy in the air around us.

Tuesday is past words, reduced to nothing but putty in my hands. Her pussy constricts around my cock again, lighting a fuse within me. With a growl of her name, I explode, coming inside her. The rush of my release, the satisfaction of leaving Tuesday a blissed-out mess, and my faltering muscles have me collapsing over her.

I rest my face at the nape of her neck, my cock still inside her. I graze my teeth over her skin, enjoying how she shivers and pulses around me. Giving myself another moment to savor the warmth of her core and the feel of her body beneath mine, I kiss the back of her neck and whisper, "Are you okay?"

When she doesn't answer right away, a tiny surge of panic grips my heart. "Answer me. Are you okay?"

"I'm okay. I just need a minute."

"Did I hurt you?" If I hurt her, I'll never forgive myself. She asked for everything we did, but what if I took it too far? Shifting my weight and pulling out of her, I look over her ravaged body. Her hips and ass are red, her entire body shakes with exhaustion, her hair is matted, and the side of her face is ruddy from being rubbed against the sheets.

My caveman side takes over, beating his chest with pride. She's mine, he grunts. She wears my marks, my scent, my spend. Which means she's mine to protect. To nurture. To love.

Without opening her eyes, she smiles softly, her legs tangled in the jumble of sheets and blankets. "I think I might be dickmatized, Baseball Cap, but I asked for it. You gave me exactly what I wanted, but I may have underestimated how good you'd be at it."

Her breathless laugh erases the lingering unease in my chest, and I roll her over before pulling her close. Tuesday squints at me, like the effort of fully opening her eyes is too much, then reaches out a hand to caress my cheek. "I'll likely be sore, but it's worth it."

She kisses my furrowed brow, and I scoop her up and carry her to the bathroom.

"Bond, I can walk!"

"You sure about that, Peach?" I raise both eyebrows at her and give her a cocky grin.

Tuesday rolls her eyes but doesn't resist when I sit her on the toilet and step out, giving her privacy to take care of her business. While she does that, I fill the claw foot tub.

"Baby Girl, I'm hopping in the shower, but I ran you a bath so you can soak. I'll rinse quickly, then put some food together for us."

Through the water closet door, I hear her muffled *please* and *thank you*. As I step under the steady stream from the multiple shower heads, I consider taking a play from Tuesday's book and pinching myself because I can't believe this is real.

I knot a towel around my waist and kiss Tuesday's forehead while she bathes. Then, with a dopey, lovesick grin, I slip on a pair of joggers and head downstairs.

Tuesday's grocery store haul consists mostly of sweets, breads, and cheese. She did warn me she wasn't a chef. Pulling out a loaf of French bread, I dig through the fridge and find some brie. As quickly as possible, I slice up the loaf, spreading the brie over the top before popping it into the oven. I'm opening the lid on a jar of fig jam when Tuesday stumbles into the kitchen, looking like a baby deer discovering its legs. I open my arms to her, and contentment settles over me when she sinks into them.

"Thank you," she whispers into my chest.

Holding her waist, I lift her onto the island. A surge of possessive pride sweeps through me when I notice she's wearing my t-shirt. It doesn't hurt that I can see a pair of pink panties peeking out from beneath. Pulling the toasted bread from the oven, I snag the jam off the counter. After placing it over the top of the melted brie, I blow on it and hold it to her lips.

"Eat."

Tuesday opens her mouth and takes a bite, doing a little dance on the countertop as she chews. "That's delicious, Bond."

"Ready to tell me what happened?"

Her eyes drop to the ground before she straightens her back and nods. "Yes, but can we go back to bed? I want you to hold me."

I don't even bother answering. I just turn and squat in front of her. Tuesday figures out what I want, and with that noisy, ungraceful laugh I love, she jumps onto my back. I grab our food and a couple of bottles of water, then carry her up the stairs.

Once we're fed, rehydrated, and settled, I tuck Tuesday under my chin and run my fingers through her hair. Her bedroom is downright cozy; the two of us twined together, faintly illuminated by the flickering flames from the fireplace. The pillow cradling my head entices me to sleep, but she has a story to tell.

"Start talking, sweetheart."

"I was at the grocery store picking up a few random things. My headphones were in, so I didn't know Jacob was there until he grabbed me. He squeezed my arm harder when I tried to pull out of his grasp. Started talking some nonsense about how I embarrassed him and how I could make it up to him—"

A low, thrumming sound rises from my chest. That bastard.

"Bond?"

Swallowing, I kiss the top of her head. "Keep going."

"I told him exactly what I thought of him. That he's nothing more than a sad, pathetic loser. Before anything else could happen, a good samaritan ran Jacob off. I pretty much drove home on autopilot. And as soon as I got here, I showered. I had to get his touch off me."

The next time I see Jacob Ashford, he's getting everything he deserves and more. Consequences be damned.

Tuesday slides one of her legs between mine, curling against me so there's no space between our bodies. "Tell me your second favorite food."

"What?" I ask, my hands sliding to knead and massage her hips and lower back.

"Your second favorite food? What is it?"

I let out a rumbly laugh. "That's a strange question."

Her lips brush over my Adam's apple. "Anyone off the street is worthy of knowing your favorite food, but only people who matter know your second, third, and fourth favorites."

Chuckling at her logic, I say, "Ava's stuffed sopapilla, Christmas style."

"Ah, yes, Christmas style. I'm familiar with it now."

"You're practically a local," I say with a laugh. "What's your second favorite food?"

"Strawberry shortcake, though I have to say The Bee and the Bean's sea-salt croissant is quickly climbing my list."

We fall into easy conversation, sharing more silly secrets. The lightness is much needed after the intensity of our love-making and everything that led up to it.

Just as we are drifting off, a buzzing fills the air. Tuesday grabs her phone, grimacing at what she sees.

"Everything okay?"

She hands it to me without speaking.

Her ex. That stupid piece of shit is still texting her? She doesn't need this ever, but certainly not tonight. Before I can think, I'm responding to him.

"Bond! What are you doing?"

Shit. The phone drops between us, vibrating as another message comes in. "I shouldn't have answered him, but the fact that he keeps texting you has me seeing red."

"I ignore them. Interacting with him only makes it worse." Her chin trembles, and I swear to all that is holy, if she cries again tonight, I'm following through on my threat to him.

Cradling her, I ask, "I'm sorry. Is there anything I can do?"

Taking a deep breath, Tuesday closes her eyes for a moment. Then she gestures towards the fallen phone. "Go ahead and read what he sent. In for a penny, in for a pound, right?"

"Are you sure?"

She gives me a crooked smile. "I trust you, Baseball Cap."

Make sure you pass along my messages. Remind Tuesday if they don't settle, she has to come back and face me in court.

That could be ugly for her. All those pictures resurfacing. The sordid details of our affair and how she ruined my marriage and tried to ruin my career all out of petty spite because I wouldn't leave my wife for her.

It paints a compelling story, don't you think?

My eye twitches when I read his last message. That lying piece of shit.

Her voice is small in the dimly lit room. "Truth, Baseball Cap? I'm scared my family won't settle with Duncan and even more scared they will."

I didn't even think about the rock and hard place she's in as far as the lawsuit goes. If her dad and War don't settle with him, the case will go to court, and Tuesday will be called back to Texas. But if they do settle, it tells the world the Phillipses agree with Duncan over her.

My lips brush her forehead, and I hug her tight. "Truth, Peach. If that happens, I'll be right by your side."

"You'd do that for me?"

"I'd do anything for you, Baby Girl. Anything." I hold her, memorizing the pattern of her breathing as she drifts off to sleep.

CHAPTER TWENTY-THREE

Saturday morning, I wake to the warmth of the sun on my face, soft kisses on my neck, and the press of Bond's firm body against my back. It's official; this is the only way I want to wake up from now on. *Get thee behind me, alarm clock.*

"Morning, Peach." Bond's husky, half-asleep voice brushes my ear before sinking into my soul.

"Good morning, Baseball Cap." I roll over and smooth a lock of hair back from his forehead as I scan his face, soaking him in and thinking about the past few days.

Thankfully, the rest of the work week flew by with no issues. The secret to keeping our hands off each other at the office? Stay busy, stay apart. We purposefully avoided each other, making excuses to not be in the office when the other was there. Bond spent his time in the workshop and at the active build sites while I hopped out to look at possible land tracts.

But the minute we're off the clock, we collide. Drowning in each other, never coming up for air.

"What's on that beautiful mind of yours, sweetheart?" Bond asks, rubbing his stubbly cheek against my own.

"I was thinking about the week and how nice it is waking up with you."

He grins. "My bed is losing my indentation."

I wrinkle my nose. "If your mattress has the shape of your body imprinted into it, it's time for a new one."

He throws his head back, giving me one of those booming, boisterous laughs I crave. I stare, transfixed, at how his Adam's apple bobs, the way his eyes crinkle, and how he's so unabashedly happy and in the moment. I love him. The thought is like a drumline pounding in my mind.

Swallowing, I push the thought away. "I'm meeting your sisters at nine downtown."

"Really? That's great. I love that you three are getting along."

"Me too. They're amazing women."

Bond smiles. "Clairy and Charli are pretty awesome. But don't tell them I agree with you. I'll never live it down."

"It's hard keeping this from them. Especially when they want to see us together. I hate lying to them."

"If you want to tell them—" Bond's fingers lightly trail over the deep purple bruises Jack left on my arm.

"No. Not yet. I'm sorry, I just need more time." I rest my palm against his cheek, and he turns into my touch, gently kissing the center of my hand.

"As much time as you need. It's yours."

Bond's calm confidence gives me the courage to ask for a picture. Being brave and asking for pictures hardly go in the same categories. But I'm admittedly, and I think understandably, gun-shy about cameras being involved in my dating life. Plus, selfies are proof we're dating. Which can come back and bite us in the end.

But then the photos of Morgan and Cal flash through my mind.

"I can practically hear you thinking. Spill it, Peach." He twirls a strand of my hair around his finger with a smirk.

How does he read me so easily? And why does it make me so happy that he can?

"I have a favor to ask. It's silly but important, and you'll probably think I'm being ridiculous—"

"Stopping you right there. Not using that word when it comes to you. I may not be the smartest man, but I know how it makes you feel." As he speaks, he runs his thumb across my lower lip, rescuing it from being shredded by my anxious teeth. "You can ask me for anything, and I'll do my best to give it to you. So what is it you want, Tuesday? The sky? A rock from the top of a mountain? For me to eat that pretty pussy one more time?"

I slap his shoulder, stopping him from kissing a trail down my neck because we both know good and well if he gets past my collarbone, there's no going back. I hesitate despite his reassurances, and then I get mad at myself because, once again, I'm letting my past dictate my present. With a deep breath, I ask, "Can you take a selfie with me?"

Bond's head lifts from the crook of my neck, and his blue eyes study me. Then I get one of those Colgate-worthy smiles. "That's what you want? A picture with me? Afraid you'll forget how good-looking I am?"

I blink and then narrow my eyes before pinching his nipple. His yelp is my just reward.

Sticking out my lower lip. I full-on sulk. "You know what, never mind. I don't even want one anymore."

Cutting me off, he kisses the pouty words out of my mouth, only stopping when I'm glassy-eyed and flushed. "Oh, you're getting a picture. A hundred. A thousand."

"One will do for now." I run my fingers through his beautiful chestnut hair. "I just...I want proof that this is really my life."

"Those bruises on your hips aren't proof enough?" Bond asks, raising one dark eyebrow at me, a cocky smirk on his face.

"As wonderful as those are, they'll fade. I want something that lasts."

"Something that lasts? You've got it, Baby Girl."

Blushing, I snag my phone and open the camera. "Ready?"

"Since the moment we met."

The crisp weather bolsters my spirit as I stroll down Main Street. I still can't get over how pretty Trail Creek is. When I found out I was coming to New Mexico, I imagined scrub brush and sage, not aspens and pines.

Pulling my light puffy jacket tighter around me, I add purchasing a heavy-duty coat with a hood to my list. It's hard for me to wrap my North Texas born-and-bred brain around the possibility of snow this early in the season, but the cold nip and fresh, clean scent make my heart hope it's possible. Frankly, after sweating through years of autumn and even some winters, I am all about highs in the forties. Or at least I will be once I'm properly outfitted.

Neither Charli nor Clairy are here when I pause outside Up a Creek Without a Book, the giant purple bookstore downtown. So being the responsible adult I am, I pull up the photo Bond and I took this morning. I'm smiling into the camera, but he's staring at me.

My fingers run over his glassy image, and I admire his

profile. The way his gaze is locked on me. How did I get so lucky that a man like Bond—kind, caring, handsome to boot—looks at me like I hung every star in the sky? It's strange being openly adored and cherished.

Before Bond, my world was cold and empty. Gray and bleak. Slowly shattering and fracturing around me. And now? It's like I'm in *Bizarro Tuesday's* universe, where things are happy and shiny. Whole. I'm whole.

Holding the phone to my chest, I sigh.

I'm irrevocably, undeniably, head over heels in love with Bond Davis.

"Tuesday!"

The sound of my name has me hurrying to close out the picture. Turning, I run smack dab into Clairy's arms.

"Babes, I'm so glad you agreed to meet Charli and me for a little pre-brunch shopping. We can show you all the best places."

"How could I possibly say no? I'll never turn down the opportunity to get to know you better. Plus, I need a couple of things, so the timing on this is perfect."

"What do you need?"

"A better coat and some boots. And I desperately need some new books."

Charli's eyes light up. "Oh, are you a reader?"

When I nod, Clairy pumps one hand in the air. "Yesssss. I knew you were good people." She winks as she slings an arm over my shoulder. "Please tell me you're a romance fan."

"All romance, all the time," I answer honestly.

"You're going to love the bookstore," Charli says. "It has a huge selection of new and used books, including ones by indie authors you can't always find in other places."

"What are we waiting for? We only have a couple of hours

until our brunch reservation." Clairy steers me through the door as she speaks.

C-Squared aren't lying when they say Up a Creek has tons of romance books. The shelves overflow with used and new goodies, from traditional bodice rippers to contemporary romcoms to monsters and aliens. If I wasn't already Team Trail Creek, seeing the aisles of love stories would put me firmly there.

Even better than the selection, though, is how much Clairy, Charli, and I have in common. We chat as we browse, pointing out books we've read, what we liked about them, and what we loved about them.

"So I think we should all buy one of the same book and do a book club, then we should each buy a different one to trade after we read. We can annotate and pass it on. Thoughts?" Charli asks, her brow wrinkling.

"I love that idea." And I truly do. It's amazing how comfortable I feel with the Davis sisters. Just like with Bond, there's some weird instant connection like I've known them for years rather than days. They belong in my life.

"Hello, ladies." An older man with white hair and a full Santa beard beams at us from behind the counter.

"Hi, Saul, how are you?" Charli asks as she stacks our books next to the old-fashioned cash register.

"Trying to finalize the town fair and the fundraiser for the library, with no help from anyone else on the council, of course. I don't suppose you'd like to volunteer, Charlotte?"

"Sorry, Saul. I'll leave running the town to you, but you know Davis Designs will purchase a table."

"Aren't you going to ask me, Saul?" Clairy asks, looking like butter wouldn't melt in her mouth.

He makes a *hmph* sound and studies the stack of books. "Clarissa, you know we sell more than romances, right?"

Clairy laughs. "I don't know why. It's what keeps your business afloat."

Saul's cheeks pinken. "Yes, well, you can thank Sheila for the inventory." Turning his attention to me, he says, "I'm Saul, co-owner of Up a Creek Without a Book. You must be Tuesday."

"Um...yes, that's me."

The question in my voice must be evident because Saul gives me a calculating smile. "As the head of the town council, I make it my business to know who's new in town. You're quite the hot topic, Ms. Phillips."

I stiffen. "Wh-what do you mean?"

"Davis Designs is a Trail Creek staple, and the Davis family is well-known and liked. So, of course, when news spread that some big Dallas company bought the business, I had to keep a close eye on things. We don't want Trail Creek to lose its small-town appeal." He leans in as though we are co-conspirators. "Plus, everyone's been all abuzz since spotting you and Porter together at the Great Dane. On two separate occasions. And once at Ava's."

"Jeez, Saul, stalker much?" Clairy says, her forehead and nose wrinkling.

My blood pressure rises, and I can practically taste my pulse. "Bond and I are colleagues."

Saul raises one bushy white eyebrow and holds up both hands. "Of course." The older man gives us our total, and Charli picks up the tab.

"Consider it a welcome gift," she says when I try to pay my share. She shoots Saul a sour look as he hands her the bagged books.

Clairy isn't so subtle. "Don't worry about Saul, Tuesday. He's got his nose in everyone's business under the guise of being on the town council, but he's really just a gossip. I promise he's making it seem like more people are talking about you than really are."

"A pleasure as always, Clarissa," Saul calls out after us.

"Clarissa?"

"Oh, yeah, our parents, I swear. Charlotte, Porter, and Clarissa, we sound like a trio of nineteenth-century railroad barons."

Laughter bubbles out of my mouth. "That's not true. But I do think you're more of a Clairy than a Clarissa. Same for Charli and Bond."

Putting on a fake high society accent, Clairy sweeps one of her long arms out wide. "Come along, we mustn't tarry."

Charli and I can't fight our laughter as we trail behind her.

My arms ache from carrying bags, my side aches from laughing, but my soul is more whole than it's been in years. My morning girl time with C-Squared scrapes another layer of pain from the thick varnish around my heart. War and I might be twins, but we've never been close. In the few hours I've spent with the Davis sisters, I already feel more connected to them than I ever have to him.

But it also itches at the guilt under my skin. For my part in the buy-out of their family business. For lying to them. For keeping my relationship with their brother a secret.

"Earth to T! Are you coming into Ava's or what?" Clairy's bright voice calls me back.

Laughing, I shake my head. "Sorry, I got lost in my head for a moment."

"Hello, girls, so good to see you." A tiny woman with tan

skin wizened with decades' worth of laugh lines and silver hair greets Clairy and Charli with matching hugs.

"Ava, you look amazing as always," Charli says.

"And this is why you've always been my favorite, Charlotte. So sweet. Come on, your table is waiting."

The restaurant is busy, the inside as magical as the outdoor patio where I had my date with Bond. Colorful murals cover the walls in shades of turquoise, red, rust, and gold. I'm so caught up in looking around I run into Charli's back when she freezes.

"Mom? Dad? Wavey? What on earth is going on?"

A beautiful woman with Clairy and Bond's dark hair streaked with gray and a man with the same blue eyes as all three Davis siblings stand to greet us. The man offers his hand to me. "Hello, Tuesday, I'm Scott Davis. This is my wife, Lynn."

"It's nice to meet you," I say, stunned by the unexpected introduction.

Next to Scott and Lynn sits the pretty teenager from The Bee and the Bean, and across the table from her are Dane, the Viking from HiCo, and Bond. I realize I'm still gripping Scott's hand and drop it like it's hot.

What is happening?

Clairy's exasperated voice asks, "What are you guys doing here?"

"When you mentioned you and your sister were taking Tuesday to brunch, it seemed like the perfect chance to get to know her. And, of course, I couldn't not invite Porter and the boys." Lynn smiles at me.

"In my defense, I told her we shouldn't intrude on your morning," Bond says from the far end of the table, an apologetic look on his face.

"Oh, nonsense. They don't mind. Right?" Lynn's cheery

chirp makes it hard to argue. "Tuesday, we've heard so much about you. You're absolutely lovely. How are you and P—"

Bond motions for us all to sit. "Let's not overwhelm Tuesday."

"Yes." Charli claps her hands and motions for everyone to sit. "We can do introductions while we sip on mimosas."

"Even me?" the teen, who must be Charli's daughter, asks.

"Nice try, Wavey Gravy," the Viking says with all the affection of a parent. Interesting.

Once alcoholic breakfast beverages are in hand, the attention turns back to me. I formally introduce myself to Waverly and the Viking, who I learn is actually named Griffin. I give Dane a quick nod and can't help but notice he's staring at Clairy, who is decidedly not looking in his direction.

I shift so I'm face to face with Bond. The only thing between us? A few reclaimed wood pieces making up the width of the table. Smiling pleasantly, I greet him, giving no indication he had his tongue buried inside my body a few hours ago.

Deciding it's probably best if I engage with the others at the table, I lean around Charli and say, "Hello, Waverly, thank you again for the sea-salt croissant and honey recommendation. I love it."

Bond snorts. "That's an understatement. It's practically become a staple of your diet."

My head jerks up, and I stare at him, mouth agape.

Next to him, Dane chuckles. "And how would you know that?"

Shrugging, Bond ducks his head. "She eats one every day at her desk. In the office we share. I'd be a pretty poor teammate if I didn't notice."

Dane crosses his muscular arms and smirks, showcasing impossibly white teeth. *Seriously, what's in the water here?* His dark brown eyes glint. "So what does Charli eat every day?"

Before Bond can answer, Griff calls out, "Vanilla yogurt with strawberries and granola."

Every head at the table turns to the massive blond man. Though the skin of his ears and cheeks are scarcely visible beneath his long hair and beard, what I can see is pink.

"That asshole didn't give you any more problems after I left you the other night, did he?" Griff asks, his deep voice cracking as he performs a hail-mary attempt to get the attention off of him knowing Charli's daily breakfast of choice.

Without thinking, I brush my hand over where Jacob grabbed me.

Bond's eyes narrow and lock onto my movement. "Griff, you saw what happened?"

"Yeah, that prick, Ash—" A quiet cough from Charli has Griff glancing her way. "Yeah, I was there."

Lynn leans forward so she can see me past her grand-daughter and daughters. "Tuesday, are you okay?"

"Um, I ran into a little trouble in the HiCo with—" I catch the subtle shake of Bond's head, similar to the warning Charli gave Griff. "With a man." I finish. "He grabbed my arm and left a mark. It really wasn't a big deal, and thankfully, Griff stepped in as soon as he saw us."

"Tuesday, that's awful. Are you sure you're okay?" The concern in Lynn's voice and the worry in her eyes make my heart skip a beat. Scott, too, looks at me with a warm regard I'm not expecting. Is this what having loving parents is like? Because if so, it's pretty frigging awesome.

"I'm sure, Mrs. Davis."

"Call me Lynn, honey."

I give her a small smile before glancing around the table. Clairy, Dane, and Bond all have matching scowls. Griff's brow wrinkles as his green eyes flick from me to Charli to Waverly.

Charli looks embarrassed. Clearly, I'm missing some pieces of the Davis family and friends puzzle.

Competing emotions tangle inside me. On the one hand, I don't want to rehash the incident any further. On the other hand, that these people—some I've met for the first time today—have actual concern for me makes me ache for a family like this one.

As our food arrives, Waverly, who has sat quietly during the entire exchange, sighs and says, "I'm fifteen, not an idiot."

Charli's hand drops from where she's reaching for her plate, and she turns to her daughter. "Wavey? What do you mean?"

"I know you're talking about Jacob. You don't have to hide it from me, Mom. I know he's not a nice man."

"Wavey, sweetie, what makes you think they're talking about him?" Lynn asks, a bite of chicken and waffles stalling halfway to her mouth.

"No one wanted to say the man's name. Why would anyone care unless you were trying to hide it from me?" The teen rolls her gray eyes. And suddenly, the pieces click. Jacob Ashford is Waverly's bio-dad.

Charli hugs Waverly to her—the tight kind of mom hug I've only witnessed and never experienced—while whispering something into her ear. Waverly nods and ducks her head. Once she's done, Griff reaches across the table, his thumb brushing against Charli's knuckles until she pulls her hand away, pink creeping up her cheeks.

Pushing around the whipped cream on her chocolate chip pancakes, Waverly smiles and says, "I'm so glad you liked the croissant. It's Auntie B's bestseller. She lets me work there a few times a month."

Charli has a good egg in this one.

In the next breath, Waverly cuts her eyes to me, and that

innocent girlish grin morphs into all teeth. "So what's the deal with you and Uncle Bond?"

I just about choke on my green chile cheese grits. "Um, no-nothing. We're coworkers."

"Nuh-uh. He texted you the night he and I hung out. You're the lady he wants to Netflix and chill with."

Innocent and sweet? My dear Aunt Fanny.

"Waverly Lynn Davis." Charli's voice is sharp and one hundred percent mom. I'm in awe and a little worried I might be in trouble too.

"What? He did," Waverly says as though she isn't busting down our carefully constructed *we're just coworkers* story.

Charli pinches the bridge of her nose and looks at Lynn in exasperation. "I'm putting this on you, Momma." To me, she mouths, *Sorry.*

Lynn chuckles and waves her hands as if she can poo-poo the last twenty minutes' worth of awkward and terrible interactions away. "We're all family here, Charlotte. And we all know everyone at this table, with the exception of Scott and I, are just friends." She gives us a teasing wink before turning back to her food.

I have to salvage the brunch-ravaged shields we've built around our relationship. A quick glance at Bond has my chest tightening. His eyes beg me to say it, admit what everyone at the table already seems to know. But, like the world's fourth biggest jerk—coming in after my father, Duncan, and Jacob Ashford—I take a long, *long* sip of my mimosa before saying, "Lynn, I want to clarify. Bond and I *are* just friends. While we may have wanted more, after much discussion, we decided since we work together, it's simply too complicated." Once again, the lie burns as I force it out.

Every pair of eyes at the table turns on me, the looks a mix of questions, disbelief, and *Bless your heart.*

Guilt eats me up from the inside, especially at the visible disappointment etched on Bond's face. This was a prime chance to share one of the greatest joys of my life, and I ran from it straight back to the cloak of secrecy and fear. The Davises have welcomed me with more warmth than my family has ever shown. Why am I holding on to this secret so tight? I'm starting to forget my reasons with each act of love this family shows me. I don't breathe until Bond smiles softly at me, his understanding more than I deserve.

With that grin I adore, he says, "So, how about those Cowboys?" A series of resounding groans are his only answer.

Brunch lasts approximately 438 years, or possibly closer to two hours. I honestly can't tell. Thankfully, after evading Waverly's wrecking ball of a question, the conversation settled into much more neutral territory.

At one point, my foot brushed against Bond's under the table, and he snapped his head, staring at me like I'd done it on purpose.

Which I did the second and third times, but definitely not the first.

As the waiter clears the last of our plates away, I sigh in relief. We survived brunch. Acquaintances at work. Friends socially. Lovers in private. No problem.

Ha. Sure. No problem at all.

CHAPTER TWENTY-FOUR

A heavy knock, followed by a deep voice calling out *Peach*, has me sitting up on the couch with a jolt. I peer around my living room, trying to get my brain online. When did I fall asleep?

I flip on the nearest lamp, banishing the dark, just as Bond pulls me to my feet. He used his key. My heart jumps a little at that. As far as I'm concerned, this is as much his place as it is mine.

His eyes fly over my body, relief and worry swirling in his electric gaze. "Are you okay?"

"Yes. What time is it?"

"After seven. I've been calling and texting you for hours, Baby Girl."

I grab my phone, and sure enough, I have several missed calls and texts. "Sorry, I crashed. I didn't hear them."

"No need to apologize. Had me worried, Peach, that's all. After what happened with..." He glowers at my arm as though he can see the bruises through my clothes before nuzzling his cheek against my hair and pressing me to his chest. "So...brunch..."

My muscles lock. Is he mad I lied to his family? The flashes of disappointment and hurt from brunch when I adamantly denied we were a couple flicker in my mind. I'd expected him to come over as soon as we finished. When he didn't, I may have had the eensiest little spiral before passing out from emotional exhaustion.

"I didn't mean to hurt you, Bond. We agreed to keep things secret for now, and then we were at brunch with everyone you love. They all looked at us like they knew, and I panicked. I had to get them off our scent. You understand, right? Please tell me you do?"

The heavy flow of words spilling from my mouth is staunched by Bond's lips on mine. I melt into the kiss, shivering when he nips the tip of my tongue. "Tuesday, I understand. Would I love to walk around the courthouse square with a sandwich board and a bell shouting about us to the town? Fuck, yes. Will I keep this between us until you're ready? Also, yes."

I love him.

"Bond?"

"Peach?"

Just say it, Tuesday. "I, um, so Charli and Jacob..." My words trail off. I really hate me sometimes. But I'm also infinitely curious about how that happened.

"Yeah. It's Charli's story to tell, but yes. He hasn't had a lick of involvement in raising Waverly, though. Charli became her mother and father when those two pink lines showed up."

I let that sink in. Charli has raised that beautiful girl on her own for over fifteen years. "He never wanted to be a part of her life?"

"Nope. Fucking asshole."

"But you and your family stepped up. Of that I'm certain."

Bond leads the two of us in a gentle sway, though there's

no music playing. "Yeah, watching Charli go through being pregnant and having Waverly on her own had me promising to be there for them no matter what. I had a cot in Wavey's nursery for the first six months to make things easier on Charli at night. And of course Mom and Dad went all in on being Pops and Lolli."

First of all, calm down ovaries. I swear they jumped to attention and saluted when Bond admitted to taking over night-time diaper duty so Charli could sleep. "Hold up, your mom and dad go by Lolli and Pops? As in lollipops? They are the cutest."

He chuckles, the sound resonating in his chest before fading away. His grip on me tightens, and we do a small spin in my living room. "Clairy was going through her own things; she's ten years younger than Charli and seven years younger than me, so she was still a kid herself when Wavey was born. But she was just as head over heels for Waverly as the rest of us. While she was gone, she'd video chat three times a week because she didn't want to miss anything."

"Why was she gone so long? I can't imagine leaving your family." It couldn't have always been sunshine and roses, but if Scott and Lynn had raised me, I'd probably still live at home.

"Clairy's always been a wild one. She wanted to travel, to go places she'd only read about. She worked odd jobs wherever the wind took her. Sometimes Mom and Dad would go stay with her for weeks at a time, especially after Charli and I took over more responsibilities at the company."

"And what brought her home?"

"I'm still not sure." Bond squeezes me as we slow dance to nothing. "She had a haunted look when she first got back. A look that's thankfully fading each day she's here."

"But she's okay? I wonder if a certain dark-haired bar owner has anything to do with that?" Bond may not want to admit it, but the tension and pull between Clairy and Dane every time I'm around them is practically corporeal.

"She says she's fine, but having two sisters, a niece, a mom, and an ex-wife, I'm well aware that fine rarely means it is. But, like with Charli, that's her story to tell." Bond groans, "And as far as Dane and Clairy go, let's pretend we don't know anything about those two. Deal?"

"Deal," I laugh. From where I'm crushed against him, I spy a familiar yellow box on my end table. Pulling back, I raise one eyebrow, "What's in the box, Baseball Cap?"

His teasing grin makes my heart flutter. "Trying to change the subject on me?"

"Yes," I say as I make grabby hands toward him.

He chuckles, snatching The Bee and the Bean box and holding it over his head, well out of my reach.

When I jut my lip out, he nips it.

"Quit that pouting. My last round of apology pie was pretty successful, so I figured I'd try again."

"Why would you need to apologize?"

"For the brunch ambush."

"Oh." I grin. "I humbly accept your *please forgive me, Tuesday,* pie."

"You're so benevolent."

"And don't you forget it. Now, gimme." I climb into his lap, where he's settled into the corner of my oversized dark gray couch.

"Close your eyes, Peach."

I raise one eyebrow.

"You trust me?"

"Always." My one-word answer is breathy and one hundred percent true.

Bond's eyes flash with want and warmth. "You have no idea how much I love hearing that."

Shutting my eyes, I sit perfectly still until Bond says, "Open your mouth, Baby Girl."

Without hesitating, I part my lips and moan when a medley of flavors burst on my tongue: cake, cream, strawberries, and something with a hint of heat.

"It's not pie this time. Strawberry shortcake with homemade whipped cream. It is your second favorite food, after all."

Around a mouth full of cake, I say, "Holy crap, it's delicious. What's the spice?"

"Serrano strawberry sauce. It's on the side, but knowing how much you enjoyed the Sweetheat at Dane's, I figured you'd be game."

"More, please." I tap my open mouth and flutter my lashes at him, impatiently waiting for him to feed me.

Bond slices through the moist cake and dips it into the dark pink sauce before sliding the loaded spoon between my lips.

"Mmmmm."

"You keep making those sounds and licking your lips like that, and I won't be responsible for what happens."

"Really?" I shoot him an impish smile and grab his index finger, dipping it into the massive pile of whipped cream atop the cake. I keep my eyes locked on his as I put his finger in my mouth, swirling my tongue around it, sucking it clean. The way his eyes go navy as his pupils expand gives me a thrill. I repeat the action, but this time, bring the cream to his lips, leaving a dab of the sticky sweet topping in the center of his mouth before licking it off.

Bond sets the cake to the side and pounces on me. His lips go to mine, and I savor the remnants of the sugar on his tongue. Grabbing my wrists, he pins my arms above my head and holds them there in one large hand. His free hand snakes under my shirt, fingers walking over my ribs to the swell of my chest.

The firm caress of his hands on my skin, his weight settling over me, and the grind of his hard cock between my thighs all work in perfect harmony to steal my breath. When his hand lightly grips my throat, giving it a gentle squeeze, I swear I spontaneously combust. Heat drowns out all other sensations, and Bond is the inferno burning me with each loving gesture, each intimate touch.

I push him back, desperate to get out of my clothes. The salacious grin I get in response has me thinking of all the mind-melting things he can do with his mouth. Standing, I slip out of my sweater dress, which leaves me clad in only my sadly non-matching bra and panties. But it's clear Bond doesn't mind the view. His blue eyes fix on the sheer lace cups of my bra and the way my already aching nipples strain against the thin material.

His gaze drops lower to my green silk panties. I watch him as he sinks to his knees before me, not daring to speak outside of the breathy noises I can't control. He spreads my legs wide, hooking one in the crook of his elbow. My hands fly to his shoulders to steady myself as he presses his nose against my soaking panties. His tongue darts out to taste me through the wet material, ensuring it's drenched from both sides.

Everything about his touch makes my body sing. I thought I knew what desire was, but I was wrong.

Desire is this man on his knees.

Bond's wicked mouth sucks and nips and teases my clit and core through the saturated material. I can't help but shiver at the mix of the heat from his mouth, the rapidly cooling damp silk, and the throbbing need coursing through me.

My hands go to his hair, and I hear myself begging. "Please, Bond, please touch me."

He lowers my leg and hooks a finger into the waistband of my panties before slipping them down to my ankles. "Get back on that couch, Peach. Arms above your head, one leg over the back of the couch."

I rush to comply.

Once I'm in place, Bond slips his shirt off and leans over me. His warm lips graze mine before peppering my jaw, cheeks, eyelids, and forehead with sweet kisses. "I want to try something, but I know you don't like the dark. Would you be comfortable with me covering your eyes?"

"Yease." The answer is simple. Knowing Bond is here takes any fears I may have away. He chuckles at my use of *yease*. It might have started because Bond had me tongue-tied, but now it's our special joke.

With delicate hands, Bond drapes the thick cotton of his shirt over my eyes and knots it around my head.

"Can you hear me?"

"Yes, Baseball Cap."

"Can you see anything?"

My lashes brush against the soft material. "No."

"Are you comfortable?"

"Very." I love that he checks in with me each step of the way. He makes it so easy to give him all my trust.

"Perfect." The subtle brush of his lips against mine raises goosebumps along my skin.

With my eyesight taken, I focus on my other senses. Bond's shirt smells like him, and the comforting scent fills my nose. The couch shifts beneath me, and the warmth of Bond's skin against mine makes me tremble in anticipation.

"Gonna kiss and touch you now. Such a good girl." Bond's knuckles skim between my breasts.

His praise sinks into the empty, dark places in my soul, lighting little torches and creating a soft glow within me.

"You look so fucking beautiful right now. Your hands

tucked into the cushion, cheeks flushed, back arched, and legs spread. All your soft curves on display for me."

The sound of rustling paper has me turning my head as if I can see anything.

"Lift your hips for me."

The plush cushion of a throw pillow being placed beneath me changes the angle of my body, opening me wider to the air.

A feather-light touch, nothing but the faintest stroke of his fingertips against my ankle, has me clenching my innermost muscles. Then his lips are on me, burning a trail of hot, wet kisses from the bone of my ankle up to my knee. When his teeth graze the back of my knee, I wonder how I never knew that was an erogenous zone. My toes curl as Bond kisses and licks higher, pausing when he gets to the apex of my thighs.

Something lands on my stomach, and I can't help but suck in as the sensation shifts from cool and sticky to hot and wet.

"Mmm, so fucking good."

A dollop of whipped cream lands above my chest. As he licks, Bond's hands snake under my back and unclasp my bra, peeling it away from my body.

"Need more of my dessert," his voice rumbles over me like thunder in a summer storm.

He places more sticky topping on me, then promptly licks it away. My nipples ache from the beautiful torment of Bond's lips and teeth. I wonder if I could come from this alone?

Before I find out, he's gone, making his way back down my body before coating my lower lips in the sugary sweet treat. Here, he licks me like a man starved. Hungry. Desperate. His tongue slips inside me, leaving no part of me untasted.

My leg falls from the couch, landing on his shoulder, my heel digging into his broad back. "Bond!" My cry melts into a moan as he drives two fingers into me.

He shifts my leg back over the lip of the couch. "Keep these legs spread for me." As he talks, his thumb circles my clit, and the two fingers still inside me curl and twist.

Soon I'm lost in the battling sensations of sucking and flicking and curling and gliding.

"You better come for me, Peach. Need your sugar with this cream. Drench me. I want you dripping from my lips."

God, his filthy mouth. I come with a cry, my walls clenching around his fingers.

Bond's weight shifts, and then his lips are on mine, the taste of myself, shortcake, and strawberries mixing as he winds his tongue in my mouth. Gently, like I'm something precious, he slides his shirt off my eyes and untucks my hands from where I've buried them in the cushion. As he rubs my shoulders, he trails kisses along my skin.

Without waiting for him to carry me to the bedroom, I stretch to reach the end table, shuddering at the way the movement makes my lower muscles clench before scooping a generous amount of whipped cream onto my fingers.

With a smirk, I flutter my lashes. "My turn, Baseball Cap. Pants off."

Once he's naked before me, standing tall and proud—and thick and long—I sit up and touch him, leaving a sugary trail on his stomach, hips, and thighs. Then I work my way back up that trail, licking him clean.

My fingers ghost over his hard cock as I kiss his inner thigh before placing my lips chastely against him and indulging myself. I swirl my tongue over his head before moving to lick him from the base of his shaft to the crown. I do it again. Teasing him. Savoring him. The subtly tart flavor of his skin mixes with the dessert into salty-sweet perfection.

"Peach..."

"Just making sure I get all the delicious cream, Baseball Cap," I say as I lap my tongue against the slit of his tip.

"You want my cream, Peach? I'll cover you in it."

Bobbing my head up and down, I take him as deep as I can while toying and tugging between his legs. Bond groans my name and bucks against me. I pull off his cock with a pop and give him a mischievous grin.

He helps me to my feet and crushes my mouth to his. "I need to fuck you now, feel you on the inside." Bond sinks onto the couch, and I sink onto his cock, my knees on either side of his thick thighs. With one fluid snap of his hips, he reminds me I may be on top, but he's still in charge.

I whimper as we work in tandem to move me up and down his rigid shaft. My head lolls backward, and I use his strong shoulders to anchor myself as I grind my hips in deliberate circles.

"Fuck, the way your pussy grips me. I'm addicted to you. My own personal drug." Gritting his teeth, Bond rolls his hips beneath me, thrusting upwards. "You're so perfect for me. Like something out of my best fantasies."

My eyes close, my head thrown back, as bliss, burning and bright, erupts through me, spreading from my core outwards to my limbs. I call out Bond's name, praising him the way he always does me. "I love the way you fill me. You always know what I need."

His hold on my waist tightens as he drives into me, his pace faltering. Bond groans as he comes inside me, my walls quivering and clenching around him. At our shared release, I collapse forward, my forehead resting against his collarbone. His large hands drift up and down my back as tiny aftershocks rock my body. I'm overstimulated and wrecked in the best way possible.

"Hang on, sweetheart. You did so well. Such a good girl." Bond gathers me into his arms, carrying me up the stairs to my bathroom. "Take care of you, then we'll both soak." He kisses the top of my head and pulls the door so it's mostly closed.

I love how open Bond is about all things sex, before, during, and after. Prioritizing my comfort and care is another way Bond stands head and shoulders above all my prior partners. A girl could get used to this.

Bond helps me step into the warm water laced with soothing Epsom salts and bubbles. He's taken the time to light a few candles, leaving the room bathed in the soft flickering glow of firelight and the ambient glitter of the stars shining over us from the bank of windows.

I love him.

As he slides in behind me, his breath tickles my ear. "Look at all those stars. Do you see those two right there?" He grabs my hand, pointing our fingers toward the sky. "Those two are Luna and Sol, named for the sun and the moon because they shine so bright."

I rest my head against his bare chest as he talks, his baritone voice lulling me into a tranquil haze.

"The story goes, if you climb to the highest mountain top and make a wish on them, your heart's deepest desire will come true."

My voice is thick with sleep when I say, "Do you believe that?"

"No need to wish, sweetheart. Mine already came true."

I swoon and snort. "Okay, that was incredibly romantic and incredibly cheesy. I love y...it." *Nice job, Chicken Tuesday.* God, I want to tell him how I feel, but how can I when I'm asking him to keep our relationship quiet? Am I asking too much? Taking too much?

Bond doesn't call me on my almost I love you; rather, he continues pointing out more constellations and telling me stories as we clean each other, soap and water sluicing over our skin.

Only when the water cools and the bubbles melt away do we climb out. Bond crawls into the bed, lying on his back, one hand tucked beneath his head, his wide, brawny chest on display, the sheet coming to a stop below his navel. I lean against the door frame, admiring him.

"Come to bed, Peach."

"I'm enjoying the view."

Bond laughs. "I noticed. Promise, it's even better over here. Besides, I need to hold you."

"Who am I to argue with that?" With a laugh, I run and jump on the bed, collapsing on top of Bond like he's my personal body pillow.

Once he's tickled me until I beg for mercy, I snuggle up to him, my head resting against his heart. I walk my fingers in paths up and down the length of his arm. This is perfect.

Too perfect.

I know it can't last. Our secret will get out, or my dad will cause problems. Or Duncan...Anxiety sprouts in my chest like a weed after rain.

"Hey, Peach?"

"Yeah, Baseball Cap?" I swallow the fear and focus on the beautiful man lying in my bed.

"Ask me to tell you a truth."

Chuckling, I say, "Okay...Tell me a truth."

He's quiet for a moment. Beneath my ear, I swear his heart beats louder. I raise my head and find him staring at me, his blue eyes sparkling even in the dim light of my bedroom.

"I love you."

Everything stops—time, my heart, the world. "What?"

"I love you. Pretty much since the moment I met you. Not

going to apologize for it or say it's too soon because that diminishes it. It's true. It's real. I love you, Tuesday."

I close the inches between his mouth and mine and pour every ounce of my feelings and love for him into that kiss. With a smile so wide it pulls at the muscles in my face, I cup his cheek in my palm and rest my forehead on his. "I love you too, Bond."

"Best thing I've ever heard, sweetheart."

My mouth opens; I'm about to ask for a picture. But at the last second, I chicken out and slide back down into his arms, burying my head into the crook of his neck.

"You want a pic?"

When I don't immediately answer, he chuckles, his chest shaking beneath me. "I can feel you smiling into my skin, Peach. Grab your phone. I think our first out loud I love yous should be commemorated. Don't you?"

Grabbing my phone, I settle back against Bond and capture this perfect moment with this perfect man.

CHAPTER TWENTY-FIVE

I've been riding high since Saturday night. Hearing Tuesday say she loves me? Pure fucking gold.

Would I love it even more if I could wear a shirt with her face on it announcing to the world that she's mine? Hell yes. Would it be worth the maiming Tuesday would give me when she saw it? One hundred percent.

But until she's ready, I have to play it cool.

That euphoric feeling carries me through the entire week. Tuesday and I spend every night together, only separating to arrive at the office, work, and drive home. It's replaced my old pattern of waking early, working out, and getting to the office by seven. I still wake up early and work up a sweat—for a much better reason. Then I roll in at nine, Tuesday hot on my heels.

If I had my way, she'd sit naked in my lap while we worked, but I suppose most places frown on cockwarming on the clock. The vivid image of my girl flushed and sweaty as she straddles me, one hand tangled in my hair while the other trails down her body, pops into my head, and all the blood in my body speeds south.

I need to get a grip and not the kind that brings relief. Forcing my attention back to the design I'm drafting, I will all Tuesday fantasies from my mind. With a steadying breath, I shake out my arms and pick up my pencil, resuming my sketch, losing myself in the graphite's flow. I worried when I finished my degree, I'd miss being on-site, miss working with my hands. Thankfully, drafting and sketching proved to be soothing alternatives.

Some song plays in the background. Couldn't tell you what, though; it's nothing but white noise. I'm in the zone. The layout and design come together as I create multiple new elevation options for a family building on a Piñon Hills home site. Time loses its grip on me as I meticulously draw.

"Anything you want to tell me?"

My pencil slips, ruining my line, as my dad comes up behind me.

"Shit, you scared the crap out of me, Dad."

He shrugs in a non-apology. "I said, anything you want to tell me?"

"No?"

"Are you asking or answering?"

How many times did I hear that growing up? Crossing my arms, I narrow my eyes at him. "Answering."

He snorts. "Son, it is abundantly clear you and Tuesday are together."

"Dad, shhh." I jump to my feet, checking that no one is listening.

"It's just the two of us. I sent the rest of the team out to an early lunch. You were so lost in your work you didn't notice."

I raise my eyebrows. "Last time I checked, you retired."

"Eh, they threw me a bone." Dad's easy-going chuckle is contagious, and soon, I'm laughing along with him.

Pulling another stool up to the drafting station, I motion for him to join me.

"Porter, it's obvious the two of you are lying about being together. No one who was at brunch is stupid."

When I don't answer, he smirks at me and drops his ace. "Plus, your truck has been in my neighborhood every night for the last week."

My shoulders tense. Well, shit. There's no point in denying it. "You saw that, huh?"

Slapping me on the back, Dad nods. "You aren't as sneaky as you think. What I don't understand is why."

"You know the backstory. What happened to send her here. She wants it to stay private, and I'm honoring her wishes."

Dad says, "I think it's admirable you're giving her what she needs, but what about what you want?"

"I want to paint our names on the water tower and marry her in front of everyone I know. But she's scared of her dad finding out. There's also some misguided fear that she'll somehow make me look bad."

Groaning, I run my hands down my face. "Do me a favor?"

"Sure."

"Keep up the act. For me. For her."

He deliberates for a moment. "It won't be the same for her here. People will support the two of you. People practically threw Cal and Morgan a party when they finally started dating. Your mom and I, your sisters, the team, we'd all be on board."

A twinge of something like sadness pings in my chest. It never crossed my mind to doubt that my family would be all in. Tuesday, though, she doesn't have that same trust net. Her family has taught her to expect their disappointment, and even if she trusts me, that expectation still has hold. With a sigh, I rub the back of my head. "It doesn't change how she feels. Give us some time."

"Of course. I'll talk to your mom."

We sit in comfortable silence when an idea hits me. "Dad, your shed. You modeled that on an early design, right?"

"The very first. Built it myself."

"Hmmm. I need to write some things down." I grab my phone and pull up the Davis Designs Instagram account. "Here, check out our social media. What Tuesday's done will blow you away."

"Oh, yeah?"

"Yeah. It's pretty amazing." I hand Dad the phone and watch as he scrolls through Tuesday's posts. While he's browsing, I jot down my ideas, wrangling the slender thread of an idea forming in my mind.

"Hey, there's Morgan. Look at those pictures of her and Cal."

Tuesday has outdone herself on our social media. She's got all kinds of posts. Pictures from her house, a few long-range land tract shots, and videos of the team working and goofing off around the office.

"Wait till you see the newest post." I grin at him. "It's a spotlight on Charli."

Tuesday took a mix of work and personal photos and wove them into a riveting story about Charli's life as a single working mom and the head of our finance department. I think finding out about Jacob and Charli's past inspired her. The post's comments are all positive, appreciating seeing the real-life side of our employees.

"We've had more drop-ins and inquiries since she started posting, including queries from as far away as Knoll," I say as Dad stares at my phone.

His voice is soft and cracks with emotion. "This. This is

your legacy, son. She's captured everything I wanted Davis Designs to mean. Building people's dreams. Family. Love. I knew she was special. Don't you let her go, Porter."

"Not a chance in hell, Dad."

"Thanks for meeting with me on a Friday afternoon, guys. It's late notice, but I have an idea, and the timeline is tight."

"What's up?" Cal asks, reclining back in his chair. The Davis Designs core team sits around our small conference table.

"What do you think about doing miniatures?" I ask.

Charli's brow furrows. "Miniatures?"

"Yeah, like Dad's shack in the backyard."

My sister tilts her head. I can practically see the wheels turning in her mind. "I'm listening."

"For those of us who aren't Davises?" Tuesday asks, her tone light with a hint of teasing.

"Right, sorry. Our dad has this workshop slash shed in the backyard, and it's a replica of the very first house Davis Designs built. Business slows during winter; the snow makes the conditions less than ideal. I thought we could supplement the work by selling sheds, playhouses, hell, even dollhouses in the classic Davis Design styles."

Tuesday leans forward, excitement lighting her intelligent eyes. "I think that's a brilliant idea. Sheds are super popular with people looking for little spaces to claim as their own. Expanding that to playhouses and dollhouses reinforces the idea that Davis Designs is a family-focused company. I wonder if you could even offer a line of treehouses? Using the older designs plays on that feeling of nostalgia, especially for people who've lived in Trail Creek since the company began. It's genius, Bond."

I bask in her enthusiasm and belief in my pitch. Her stamp of approval makes me feel like I can't fail.

"I love the idea, Porter," Morgan chirps, her cheery voice pulling my attention away from Tuesday.

"Same," Cal adds, smiling at Morgan. "We can be the first customers for a playhouse." His hand rests protectively on her stomach. Morgan's fair skin turns red, and she ducks her head, laying her hands over his.

Charli stares at them, her mouth a little *o*.

"Are you two—"

"Yes! Fourteen weeks!" Morgan squeals, cutting off my question. "We've been dying to tell everyone but wanted to wait until after the first trimester, then the buyout happened. Anyway, we're over the moon."

Tuesday and Charli are up and around the table, hugging Morgan between them almost as quickly as the words are out of her mouth. Rising from my seat, I give Cal a clap on the back. "Congrats, man. That's huge. I know how long you two have been trying."

"I'm glad it happened before Phillips took over. While things haven't changed yet, the health care coverage, matched FSA, and help you and your family gave us made it possible. We've wanted this for so long." He looks at Morgan like she's the reason the earth spins on its axis.

My chest burns, a pang of jealousy pulsing through me. I want what Morgan and Cal have with Tuesday. To openly show the world our connection. A vivid image of her, belly rounded with my baby, flashes in my mind. Fuck, how I want that.

"Alright, alright, let's finish this meeting so we can take

these two out to celebrate their happy news," I say, my voice loud enough to get everyone's attention.

"We have potential for a healthy market on this, and it's not cost-prohibitive." Charli makes notes as she talks, no doubt scribbling figures and to-dos. "The materials are things we already have, but on a much smaller scale, and like you said, this gives us a chance to provide some of the seasonal workers a larger year-round income. I'll need to run numbers, but my vote is yes."

"You mentioned this being time-sensitive. What did you mean by that?" Tuesday asks.

"One, the snowy season will be here in a couple of weeks. It's already snowing in the mountains. I bet by the Twinkling Trail Gala, it hits town. Two, I want to display a model at the Trail Creek Carnival."

Charli balks. "Bond, the carnival starts Thursday. That's less than a week."

"The timeline is tight, but we wouldn't need the model until Saturday night. We could make do with specs, pricing sheets, and our normal booth setup for Thursday and Friday. Maybe encourage people to come back. Cal, thoughts?"

Cal scratches his chin before answering. "No, on a full-scale shed. Maybe, on a playhouse. For sure, the dollhouse size."

Tuesday perks up at the mention of the dollhouse. "We could raffle the model off. People who stop by the booth can sign up. I can take pictures and videos of you guys working on it and post teasers. Also, what are these events?"

"You remember Saul at the bookstore?" Charli asks. When Tuesday nods, she goes on. "The town council puts on a town-wide carnival, then turns around and throws a fancy fundraiser two weeks later. I swear if we go a month without some activity, Saul thinks we've lost the *Trail Creek spirit.*" Charli rolls her eyes, and I can't help but chuckle.

Saul means well, but he can also be abrasive. He isn't a fan of change or scenes. He pours a lot of time and energy into all these town-wide events, but it also makes him a control freak, ensuring they go to plan.

"Yeah, Davis Designs always has a booth at the carnival and buys a table for the gala," I say.

"And chips in or participates in every other wackadoo event that man dreams up," Charli grumbles.

The growl of Morgan's stomach concludes our meeting better than I ever could.

I stare at my clean-shaven face in Tuesday's bathroom mirror, the steam from my shower slowly dissipating. My nerves are getting the better of me, which is not normal. But I want this new product launch to go well. It's mine and Tuesday's first public event too, which adds another layer of tension to my shoulders—even if we are playing friends only tonight.

"The dollhouse looks amazing." Tuesday wraps her arms around me, burying her face between my shoulder blades and kissing my bare back.

"Baby Girl, we don't have time for this."

"We don't have time for me to compliment you? What kind of world do we live in?" she asks in faux outrage before her tongue flicks against me, lapping at the droplets of water clinging to my skin.

When her fingers sneak inside the towel around my hips, I suck in a deep breath. Which I hold when those same fingers glide up and down the length of my cock.

"Peach?"

"Just helping you release a little tension before tonight." She disappears for a moment, but before I can gather my wits, she's back, and I hear the familiar click of the bottle of lube.

"Fuck. What are you doing to me?"

"Like I said, tension release. Let me take care of you this time, Baseball Cap."

At first, it's her fingertips grazing over me, then her flat palm slides down my length. Her nails lightly scratch at my inner thighs before she reaches to cup me. Fuck. My head tips back, and I close my eyes, relishing each teasing stroke. Heat radiates from the center of my body outward as need builds in me, and my hips roll, searching for more.

Taking her hand in my own, I set a quicker pace, twisting our joined hands at the crown, mixing the precum dripping from my tip with the slick lube. My free hand rests against the wall as I struggle to not turn around and fuck my girl silly.

Between the sweet trail of kisses she's placing down my spine, the caress of her hands on my cock and skin, and her desire to care for me, I'm close to losing control.

When her knuckle rubs that sensitive spot behind my balls, I come, panting her name. The release is instantaneous, all the worry shooting from my body as I empty myself.

Spinning around, I capture her lips, pouring every ounce of love I have for her into that kiss. "You didn't need to—"

"Shhh, Bond. It's okay to let the people who love you take care of you sometimes."

Resting my forehead against hers, I whisper, "I love you." Then, with a teasing grin, I swat her plump ass, enjoying the jiggle against my palm and her squeak. "Go get ready. I wasn't kidding when I said we didn't have time."

Pouting at me, she sulks as she rubs her cheek. "And after I was so nice to you. I think you should kiss it and make it better."

"Fucking hell, Peach. We're never going to make it to the carnival."

"Look at that, Baseball Cap, right on time." Tuesday grins at me as I carefully set the dollhouse on the table in front of our booth.

My girl's bratty side is out in full force tonight. I love it.

"You're lucky I'm a highly dexterous and determined man, or we would've been late."

"I'm a lucky lady indeed."

"Why are you lucky?" Clairy asks, coming up behind us, Charli, Waverly, and Griff hot on her heels.

Tuesday takes two steps away from me, and while this is what we agreed to, I can't help but frown at the distance between us.

"Lucky to be here in Trail Creek on a beautiful crisp night like this. Dallas and the Metroplex have all kinds of fairs and events, but there's something extra special in the air here." The words roll off Tuesday's tongue so smoothly. As much as I hate hiding what we have, it does my heart good to hear her talk about how much she likes it here.

My sisters stare at Tuesday, watching her inch further away from me, a half-step at a time.

"Right..." Clairy narrows her eyes before shrugging. "So, what does everyone want to do first?"

Wavey suggests ten different things in one breath.

Griff grins. "Lottie, let's go hit the food booths. Wavey Gravy, lead the way."

Charli blushes as Griff's hand settles on her lower back. "You're always hungry, I swear."

If those two are just friends, I'll eat my baseball cap.

"What about you, Clairy? Not going with them?" Tuesday asks as she straightens the displays.

"I'm meeting up with Mom and Dad."

"Playing the youngest child card?" I tease, yanking her toboggan down over her eyes.

"For every funnel cake I can get." She swats my hand away, grinning as she fixes her knit cap. But the smile drops off her face as she looks over my shoulder.

"Is that a dollhouse?" Dane bumps my shoulder as he speaks, but he only has eyes for Clairy.

"New potential line of products. Sheds, workshops, playhouses. I'm surprised you're here. These things aren't your usual scene."

"Nothing wrong with wanting to be involved in town events," he grumbles.

"Sure, man. Whatever you say." I can't help but smirk as he strides past me and whispers something to Clairy. She crosses her arms before huffing and stomping off, Dane trailing after her, hands in his pockets.

"Those two need to kiss already," Tuesday says, her honey-brown eyes studying Dane and Clairy's retreating backs.

I laugh. "As much as I hate to agree with you, I agree with you."

Saul's booming voice over the loudspeakers, welcoming everyone to the Trail Creek Carnival, draws the attention of those around us. I use the distraction to my advantage, sneaking closer until Tuesday's body is between me and the booth. My lips skim her ear as I whisper, "I don't like it when you inch away from me, Peach. Not one bit. Do you have any idea how badly I want them all to know you're mine?"

"Bond, we—"

I cut her off with a look full of heat and promises before walking away. "I know."

We fall into an easy rhythm, Tuesday taking advantage of the carnival to introduce herself to the town. However, most already know her, at least by name. Thanks to our date at Ava's and being spotted at the Great Dane, a few locals make comments about the two of us. Each time someone asks, though, Tuesday politely but firmly tells them we're coworkers and redirects them to the product and price specs we printed for the new line.

Thankfully, our shift flies by, and Morgan and Cal arrive to relieve us. Tuesday looks around the open space, filled with random vendor booths, food carts, game tents, and fairway rides.

"Come on, Peach, let's grab some dinner." I nudge her with my hip.

"Do you think it's alright for us to hang out? There are so many people here, and you heard the questions."

"I also heard you put them all off our scent. It's more suspect if we never interact at all, don't you think?"

Tuesday nibbles her lip, the internal debate written across her face. "Okay, but I don't like carnival rides."

I grab my chest. "What? You don't like carnival rides? How is that possible?" Closing the small gap between us, I brush my pinky against hers.

She stares at where our fingers touch and swallows. "Um, I can't really explain it, but I have a terrible memory of a banana slide and a burlap sack. The exact details are fuzzy, but let's just say I had a bad experience."

"I won't let anything bad happen to you. I promise we will avoid any and all burlap sacks. Deal?" I pause for a second. "No funhouse either."

Tuesday laughs at my look of revulsion. "Too close to a haunted house for you? Fine. No banana slides and no funhouses. What does that leave us?"

As she asks, she links the pinky I brushed with mine, and that one tiny action makes me fall in love with her all over again.

Grinning, I jerk my head. "Fried food nirvana."

While we debate the pros and cons of various fair staples, I try to convince her to ride the Ferris Wheel with me. "No burlap is involved at all."

"Yeah, but they put that thing up two days ago. How do you know it's safe? It arrived here in pieces."

"I trust all the people who work on putting the carnival together. If nothing else, Saul is such a stickler I guarantee it's been quadruple checked."

"This is going to cost you, Baseball Cap."

"I look forward to paying my penance. You go get in line, and I'll grab some food."

The timing is perfect, and I snag our food fresh from the fryer and make it back to Tuesday as she steps to the front of the line. Once the lap bar is locked, she eyes the offerings in my hands with serious distrust.

"Happy anniversary, Peach."

"What?" I love the way she scrunches her nose.

"Three weeks. Well, three weeks on Thursday, so technically, three weeks and two days." I grin at her, offering her the corny dog. "Don't worry, it's vegetarian."

For a second, I think she's going to cry. The caramel and whiskey flecks in her eyes mist over, but she clears her throat and bumps my knee with hers. "Ah yes, the traditional three-week anniversary gift. A vegetarian corny dog."

"Correction, a foot-long vegetarian corny dog with mustard and ketchup."

"So you're counting from the day we met and not our first date?"

"They are one and the same. We've been over this."

She smiles, shaking her head, but snuggles into my side.

We're almost to the top of the Ferris wheel's circuit when the ride pauses. Tuesday rests her head on my shoulder and says, "This ride isn't so bad. Do you think we're high enough for our wishes on Luna and Sol to come true?"

"Yeah, sweetheart, I do. Make your wish."

She's quiet for a moment, and in the soft glow of the carnival lights below and stars above, I watch her lashes rest on her cheeks. Her words slide against me like silk. "This is the best three-week and *one*-day anniversary I've ever had."

CHAPTER TWENTY-SIX

Bond squeezes my knee, and his hand moves higher until it's resting on my thigh. For a moment, I wish I was wearing a skirt, and the Ferris wheel would break down with us high in the air, away from prying eyes.

"How about a picture?" he asks, nuzzling his face into my hair. He rests his chin on my shoulder, and I angle the camera, snapping the picture and saving it to my phone.

I bask in the warmth of his large body pressing against mine, better than any coat at fighting off the cold. Giving him a quick kiss, I whisper, "Thank you, Bond."

I sit up when the ride jerks, restarting, and put a sliver of space between us. Bond sweeps my hair behind my shoulder and places a sweet kiss below my ear. Twining our hands together, he brushes his lips over my knuckles. "Love you, Tuesday."

Every time he says those words, my stomach flutters. I'll never tire of them. "I love you too. We won't have to stay hidden forever. I just need a little longer."

Once we unload from the ride, we make our way back to

the Davis Designs booth for the dollhouse raffle, walking with a *we're just friends* amount of distance between us. I miss the feel of his touch, but it's for the best.

As we stroll past the games of chance, I tally everything that can go wrong if people find out about us—*disappointing my family, having my private business available for public consumption, the possibility of it all falling apart in a spectacular fashion, Dad torching Davis Designs because of me.*

Disappointing my family is inevitable; they'll be disappointed in me no matter what I do.

The lingering fallout from how my last relationship ended —is still ending—has me gun-shy. From what I can tell, Bond is the town's golden boy, and I don't want to tarnish him. The last thing I want is my past on showcase for the people of Trail Creek.

The chance of our house of cards falling around us is the worst thing that could go wrong. I don't think I could come back from losing Bond and everyone I've come to care for in this little sanctuary of a town.

"You guys, the dollhouse and mock-ups are a huge hit!" Morgan's excitement is palpable as she greets us. "We've had several pre-orders for each of the items."

I pull up our socials, excited about the flurry of activity on the posts related to the miniatures. Comments, likes, reshares, along with tagged posts of people posing with the dollhouse.

Bond steps up to Cal and Morgan, a brilliant smile on his face as he turns his attention on them. "Couldn't have done this without you guys."

I stand back from the booth, watching their happy conversation. Whatever he's about to say is drowned out by a familiar, oily voice. "Tuesday Phillips, right?"

Spinning, I find Jacob towering over me, his gray eyes glittering with a smug shine.

When I don't reply, he continues. "Yeah, everyone in town's talking about you. It made it easy to get your name. You'll never believe what I found online."

He flashes his phone, and there on his screen are the pictures. The very ones that haunt my nightmares. The ones I ran to escape.

He thumbs over the screen and zooms in. The image is grainy, taken from a strange angle as if from across the room. The photo of me on my knees has every feeling of violation, degradation, embarrassment, and shame returning tenfold. Seeing them here in Trail Creek, in what's quickly become my happy place, is a fresh stab to an old wound, ripping through scar tissue to slash me deeper.

Heat rushes to my cheeks, and a wave of nausea crashes over me. Bile rises in my throat, and it's all I can do to swallow it back. My eyes are locked on his phone.

"Looks like you have quite the past. What would everyone think if they found out?" He gestures toward the people gathered at the Davis Designs booth, his voice carrying over the tinkling music from the fairway. Jacob's vile words crawl over my skin, and I can't stop myself from scratching at my arms in an attempt to ease the internal itch.

"Why are you doing this? I don't understand."

"You embarrassed me; it's only fair I return the favor." His handsome face twists into an ugly sneer.

From the booth, Bond's eyes meet mine. He quickly reads the situation, the smile falling from his lips. In a flash, he's moving. Coming up next to me, Bond stands, his muscles tense, coiled to strike. From between clenched teeth, he grits, "Get the fuck away from her and close your goddamn phone. You have no right to look at those pictures, and you sure as shit shouldn't be rubbing them in her face."

Scorn darkens Jacob's features. "What are you going to do about it?"

Bond's fist flies forward, catching Jacob squarely in the jaw. As the other man stumbles, Bond strikes again, hitting him just below the eye.

"What I should have done the first night you hit on her in the bar, the night you threw fish guts at us, and the night you left fucking bruises on her skin." Bond stalks forward like a feral animal, a stumbling Jacob his prey.

"This is between her and me. Fuck off, Porter," Jacob sneers, centering himself before rushing forward and swinging for Bond's face.

The thud of a fist against bone makes me cry out. "Stop it! Stop!"

Bond's attention is on me for a split second, but it's all Jacob needs. He lunges, wrapping his arms around Bond's waist and driving him back towards the booth. My stomach lurches as they crash into the table, the momentum too much for Bond to correct. The model dollhouse shatters, demolished pieces falling to the ground like demented confetti.

It's pure and utter chaos. The crowd watches in stunned silence as the fight continues. Bond gains the upper hand, his hits raining down on Jacob. Shock locks me into place, and I'm too stunned to move. I can't believe this is happening.

I ruin everything.

"You stay the fuck away from her, Ashford. You hear me? Doesn't matter who your daddy is; if you come near her, Charli, Waverly, or anyone else important to me, you'll regret it," Bond snarls before Dane and Griff run up to the tumultuous scene and pull the two apart. Jacob has a busted lip and a bloody nose. Bond's left eye is already swelling.

"What is going on here?" Saul's sharp voice cuts through the silence like a whip. "Porter Davis, you should be ashamed of yourself. And Jacob Ashford, don't think your father won't be hearing about this."

The sight of two grown men being scolded by a cranky southwestern Santa Claus dressed in a sweater vest and pleated khakis would be hilarious if it wasn't so awful.

"I'm sorry, Saul, but—"

Without waiting for Bond's explanation, Saul turns to the crowd, and in a move only a lifelong politician—or in his case, town council member—can manage, shoos them all away from the bedlam. "Come along, folks. Nothing to see here. Just two overgrown boys letting off some steam. All part of the fun! Who hasn't ridden the carousel yet? Mmmm, does anyone else smell cotton candy?"

His words trail off as the crowd follows him back towards the midway.

Griff grabs Jacob by the arm. Over his shoulder, he says, "Lottie, you and Wavey ride home with Scott and Lynn. I'll make sure Ashford gets to where he needs to be."

The sight of the Viking dragging the asshole toward the parking lot breaks me from my stupor. I rush to Bond, checking him over for any other injuries. "What the hell were you thinking, Baseball Cap?" My fingers skim over his bruised cheekbone.

"I couldn't stand there and let him talk to you like that and with those, those fucking pictures."

Scott steps into the space behind me and quietly says, "Tuesday, you and Lynn grab a hot chocolate. Let Porter and me get the mess cleaned up."

"I'm going to go home," I mumble, the tears spilling over. It's too much. Everything I've tried so hard to leave behind is nipping at my heels.

Clairy stares at us, her electric blue eyes searching Bond and me for answers. Charli and Waverly watch Griff's retreating back as he hauls Ashford into the dark. To them, I whisper, "I'm so sorry," then bolt to the parking lot.

Before I can escape, Clairy catches up to me. Damn her twenty-nine-year-old, mile-long legs.

"Tuesday, babes! Wait, please!"

The concern in her voice has me stopping. Clairy hooks her arm around my shoulder, and I wince. Everything that happened tonight is my fault. My pictures. My dismissal of Jacob. My stupid, awful past.

Charli catches up to us, stepping up on my other side and looping an arm around my waist. "Whatever you're thinking, I promise you're wrong."

This family. Every time I stumble, there they are.

"Is Waverly okay?" I ask, a tremble threading my words.

"She is. Mom snagged her and hustled her off to The Bee and The Bean's booth. Our parents firmly believe in the restorative power of hot chocolate. We are meeting them there now. Are you sure you won't join us?"

I nod, then look up at the star-filled sky. Was it really only half an hour ago I was at the top of the Ferris wheel with Bond? "Thank you so much, but I really want to get home. Please tell everyone I'm sorry." I give them both a small wave—good to know that even in moments of distress, I'm nothing if not awkward.

Because I'm a glutton for punishment, I spend the first twenty minutes I'm home searching for myself on the internet, cringing and spiraling whenever I come across a site with the pictures. The one of me with my hands being held behind my back. Another of me bent over the bed. A full frontal one catching a hint of my smile.

When I can't take it anymore, I delete my browsing history and close my laptop as if that can magically remove the photos from existence.

A long hour later, a soft knock at the door drags me from where I'm staring mindlessly at the TV, reruns of a comfort baking show playing in the background.

"You know you don't have to knock; that's what the key is for," I say, opening the door to find a slumped-shoulder Bond.

"I wasn't sure how you'd be feeling. If you'd want to see me."

The raw vulnerability in his voice has me reaching for him. "I always want you, Baseball Cap."

He buries his nose in my hair, inhaling me as though I'm the only air he needs. "You've been crying."

It isn't a question, so I don't bother answering. Instead, I twine Bond's hand with mine.

"Let's get some ice on that eye." I lead him to the kitchen and grab an ice pack before continuing to the bedroom. Without speaking, we both undress and crawl into bed.

Positioning the cold pack against the rapidly forming bruise, I hold his head to my chest and pull the light gray duvet cover over us. As he rests against me, the steady, soothing pace of his breathing eases the tension from my body.

"I'm sorry."

He places a kiss over my heart. "What on earth are you sorry for, sweetheart? I'm the one who owes you an apology."

"I hate that you got hurt. And that he found those pictures." My voice cracks when I try to joke. "I should have used my Luna and Sol wish to make them disappear." Pausing for a moment to gather myself, I play with his curls. "I'm not sorry you hit him. He deserved it. But I am sorry my mistakes followed me here."

In a flash, the ice pack lies near my head, and Bond's battered face hovers over mine. "You listen to me, Tuesday Phillips; nothing that happened tonight was your fault. Hey, I mean it." His lips are light against my jaw and cheek. "Say it back to me, Tuesday. Say it's not your fault."

"It's not my fault," I mumble.

He gives me a quick tickle. "That wasn't very convincing, sweetheart."

Sighing, I say, "It's not my fault." After a moment, I add—through a sound that is half laugh and half whine—"You could have hit him in a slightly less public place and without breaking the only model we had."

Bond groans, burying his face into the crook of my neck. "Shit. The dollhouse. I fucked up."

I snort. "Well, this is one way to get the word out about our expanding business."

"Ha ha, very funny."

I pinch my thumb and index finger together. "A little funny. What does it say about me that even with the fight and the pictures, this was still the best three-week anniversary I've ever had?"

"Peach, if I have my way, every milestone we share from here on out will be the best one yet." He raises his head and shoots me a small grin. "Luckily, I set the bar pretty low with corny dogs and fist fights."

"How about a couple more kisses?"

"Now that I can do."

We make it two and a half hours into the workday on Monday before my dad and brother summon us to an emergency video call. Which is wonderful. Precisely how I hoped the week would start.

Bond strides to our office door, closing it before pulling me into his arms. "Hey, whatever happens today, you and me? We're fine. There's nothing your dad can do to us. He's hundreds of miles away."

"He could express his clear disdain for everything about me. Oh, wait, he's already done that." I attempt to smile but fail.

A quick knock has us breaking apart. Morgan sticks her head in. "I've got the conference room ready to go."

Mere seconds later, Bond and I sit side by side at the small conference room table, our knees bumping. The single point of contact provides a modicum of comfort. Whatever's coming isn't good. Bond's black eye is clearly visible, as are the cuts on his knuckles.

Before we've even had a chance to exchange perfunctory pleasantries, a derisive scoff sounds. *Ladies and gentlemen, my father.*

"Congratulations, Tuesday." He sneers the words. "Davis Designs has officially gone viral."

I cringe; my old friends *worthlessness* and *inadequacy* rearing their ugly heads.

Before I can reply, Bond cuts in, his voice firm and commanding. "If you're referring to the video from the carnival, it has nothing to do with the business or Tuesday."

"Tuesday has a proven history of this sort of behavior. She's been with you less than a month and has already caused another public relations disaster. What is this, Tuesday, number three for the year?"

My heart aching, I look around the room into the surprised faces of Morgan, Cal, and Charli. Embarrassment seeps from my pores.

"With all due respect," Bond says, though his tone holds nothing but contempt, "Mr. Phillips, the situation was my fault. The other man and I have a history going back many years. Tuesday had no part in it."

Dad narrows his eyes, the cold weight of his disdain tangible despite the miles between us. "Are you saying the photographs of my daughter available online aren't what prompted this altercation? A brawl that took place, might I add, around families and with branded materials clearly visible in the background."

Bond's hand flexes, and without thinking, I slide mine up his thigh, squeezing it once, then twice, until he relaxes.

"Look, Mr. Ph—"

As if I've borrowed strength just by touching him, I raise my head. "Dad," I say, my words clearer than expected as I cut Bond off. "The local man Porter mentioned caused this unfortunate situation. It escalated quickly, and of course, we hate that there may be anything out there that reflects poorly on Phillips Construction." My father snorts, and despite the sting in my chest, I power on. "However, the overall response, at least on our verified channels, has been overwhelmingly positive. Porter and his father, Scott, the original owner of Davis Designs, reached out to many who witnessed the disagreement to ensure no children were upset. We had multiple orders for the miniatures come in over the weekend after the video footage was posted online, in addition to those placed prior to the disruption. We've also contacted the raffle winner with the promise of a replacement dollhouse as soon as possible." I do my best to respond in a way he might understand, detached and void of personal connections.

"Tuesday, that's very short-sighted. Just because this isn't impacting the local business doesn't mean it won't impact the greater company interests." This comes from my brother, who won't even look at the camera.

"You've got the ventriloquist act down pat, War. I didn't even see Dad's lips move."

War frowns then stares at the floor. Maybe he's actually ashamed this time. I roll my eyes. Doubtful.

My father flicks his hand as though he's wafting away a sour smell. "It's irrelevant. You'll be coming home soon."

Mom's perfectly polished face pops onto the screen, an unwanted curveball. "Tuesday, you look absolutely bedraggled. When's the last time you had your hair done?" Without waiting for me to answer, she blusters on. "I'll make you an appointment with Calla. She'll take care of," waving her hand vaguely in my direction, "whatever is happening here. There's no more need for you to stay in that ridiculous little town."

"What on earth are you talking about?" I ask. My flicker of bravado is stomped out by their words, and everything tightens as if I'm being compressed.

"We can't afford any more embarrassment where you're concerned. This newest development simply cast the final ballot. We're settling with Duncan."

My father's words echo in my ears. All the blood drains from my face and black spots dance in my eyes. "Wh-what?" I stutter, unable to catch my breath.

There's a screech of chair legs scraping against wood. Large, calloused hands holding me. A deep, resonant voice calling my name and for Charli.

I shove the hands away from me and stand, my chair falling over in a clatter. My palms slam on the wood table, and I lean into the camera. "If you settle, we are done. Do you hear me? If you pick him over me, we are nothing. And I am home. This *ridiculous little town*, as you call it, is where I belong."

Mom gasps, and Dad glowers. "Tuesday Jane Phillips, you will not speak to me in that manner. There is no need for your dramatics. It's already decided. I pushed through the payment for the settlement last night. This is simply a courtesy call."

My voice goes ice cold, and I draw from a well inside me I never knew I had. "Are you dissolving my position at Davis Designs?"

"Not officially—" Dad starts.

"Then I will be staying here. If you decide to terminate the position, I will still stay here. I have the money. I have a house. And nothing you have left to say to me matters." My voice is flat, totally devoid of emotion. Without another word, I stride out of the conference room.

I make it two steps into the hall before the black spots are back in force, and it's only when Charli stops me from hitting the floor that I realize I'm falling.

"Tuesday? Can you hear me? If you can, squeeze my hand twice." When I do as she asks, she continues, "Good. So good. Now breathe with me. In for four, out for three."

"Wh-where's Bond?" I'm shivering, goosebumps breaking out over my skin.

"Shh, he's coming. He's finishing up the call with your... with Mr. Phillips. Breathe with me."

"Did you hear?"

"That your dad is an asshole? Yeah, I heard that."

A small laugh comes unbidden from me. Closing my eyes, I follow the pattern of breathing Charli demands. She grips my hands, her grasp surprisingly firm, and I focus on that until my pulse no longer rings in my ears and my chest isn't collapsing like a dying star.

"I've got her, Charli Horse. I take it we can count on your discretion?"

"Of course, Runt. Take her home. I've got things here."

"Come on, Peach."

If Morgan finds it odd that I'm being carried through the

Davis Designs lobby, she's polite enough not to say anything. Flashes of Bond's lips against mine, the snap of the seatbelt, and the rumble of the engine are all I retain from the drive to my house. The slam of my front door pulls me from my fugue state.

"There you are, sweetheart. Let's get you into something comfortable. I texted Mom and Dad. They're coming with Ava's enchiladas and two slices of Sweetheat."

"They know?" I don't expand on what I mean, but Bond understands.

"Yeah, they know. But they won't say anything."

Like a docile doll, I nod and allow him to remove my sweater and pants and slip his oversized sweatshirt over my head. A soft pair of sleep shorts later, and I'm bundled in his arms as he cuddles me on my couch. Bond's scent—that heady combination of earth and air, pines and sky—mixes with the warmth of his body, and I drift off into comfortable numbness, blotting out the ugliness from the carnival and today.

"Tuesday?"

"Hmm?"

"It's going to be okay. You know that, right?"

With a dry chuckle, I say, "We had a good run. Going to have to get one of those signs factories have." At Bond's blank look, I clarify. "You know, X number of days since our last accident. But ours will say *X number of days since Tuesday's last breakdown.* Guess we're back at zero today."

Manic giggles bubble up and out of me before escalating into uncontrollable peals of hysterical laughter and finally morphing into sobbing tears.

"How cou-could he do that?" I whimper, my breath catching.

"I don't know, sweetheart." Bond's rough hands, steady and sure, cradle my cheeks as his thumbs wipe away my tears.

"Al-all my fault."

"Abso-fucking-lutely not. You listen. Nothing that happened Saturday night and nothing that happened today is your fault. You aren't responsible for Ashford's actions or my reaction. You aren't responsible for your father."

"If I ha-hadn't hooked up w-with Dun—"

"Stopping you there. Duncan cheated on his wife. He took and released those pictures. And he sued your family. What's the common thread?"

"Him," I answer quietly.

"Exactly." He kisses my nose, which I wrinkle in response.

"I'm all snotty and bl-blubbery."

He gives me a soft grin and dabs at my face with a tissue. "Yeah, you're pretty gross, but you're still cute. And I love you, snot and all."

"Don't be adorable while I'm mid-meltdown."

"Can't help it."

A soft knock at the door has Bond scooching me over and going to answer it. Seconds later, I'm engulfed in the best, and to my memory only, mom hug I've ever had. Lynn holds me like she can stitch all my broken pieces together with the strength of her arms alone. And in small ways, she is.

"Tuesday, I don't know what happened today, but Bond said you needed comfort and comfort food."

"My Dad...the Phill-Phillipses decided to settle and strongly suggested I return to Dallas."

Lynn's sharp gasp and the fire that burns in her eyes match the ferocity of the way she says, "I don't care what your father says. You belong here."

"I'm so-sorry, Lynn."

"Sweet girl, why on earth are you apologizing to me? None of this is on you."

I laugh, but it's more akin to a gurgle than anything else. "Bond said the same thing."

"He's a smart man. Mostly." She shoots her son and husband a smirk while they are talking together in the kitchen. "Between you and me, he gets that from my side. Now, we'll leave you to eat and rest. Ava may have added some sangria to the order. And I may have added some extra ice cream for the pie. Just saying."

"Thank you."

"Of course, Tuesday. You're family." She kisses the top of my head, and Scott squeezes my arm as they leave Bond and me alone.

Crawling into Bond's lap, I cry every ounce of sorrow out of my system. For myself, for the loss of the people who should have loved me unconditionally, and for the gift of finding new ones who do.

CHAPTER TWENTY-SEVEN

"Tuesday, sweetheart." I softly kiss my sleeping Peach, trying to wake her as gently as possible. After crying in my arms for over an hour, she crashed, emotionally and physically exhausted. I busied myself with canceling work for the rest of the week. It was an easy decision. We always give the team Wednesday through Friday off for the holiday. After the video chat with her dad and brother, my Tuesday deserves Tuesday off as well.

As I sip my whiskey—the rich caramel color of it perfectly matches Tuesday's eyes—my gut churns. I think about the anger and derision on her father's face when he told her they were settling the case against Duncan. No parent should ever look at their child that way. The way he hurt his daughter in that moment, and in so many before, is unforgivable. I relished the stunned silence that followed her standing up to them. Warren the Elder sat there, impassive as a statue, while her mom stormed out. Warren the Younger, War, was the only one who looked even remotely ashamed of himself and their actions.

I didn't keep my opinion to myself, resulting in the video being cut off mid-rant. Apparently, Mr. Phillips doesn't like being called an egotistical, inconsiderate bastard whose daughter deserves better.

Fuck, I've got to find a way to get my company back from that prick.

The outdoor fireplace is bright, as are the stars overhead, but there's a bite in the air. Snow's coming. Settling into the pile of cushions and blankets, I stare at the sky, enjoying the weight of her, the silence of the night, and the simplicity of this moment.

Finally deciding she's slept long enough, I whisper, "Peach, wake up." I kiss her nose, eyelids, cheeks, and lips, earning me an eye flutter and a small smile.

"Tuesday, it's past dinner time. You need to eat something, then I'll let you go back to sleep."

"Promise?" she grumbles, her eyes still closed.

"Yes. I've got cheese enchiladas and a slice of Sweetheat waiting for you."

"Mmm, pie."

"Yes, mmm, pie. But you have to wake up."

"Can't wake up. Just feed me pie and let me sleep." She opens her mouth like a baby bird.

"You little brat." I can't resist blowing a raspberry into the crook of her neck, enjoying her laughter as she squirms. I needed this. The ugliness of the past couple of days has no place in the life Tuesday and I are building together. I want this world to be perfect for her—happy, safe, loving, and full of carbs and orgasms.

Everything she deserves.

"Happy Friendsgiving!" Clairy bursts through Tuesday's door, acting like she didn't spend the entirety of yesterday hanging out here with Charli and my girl. Charli and I stand in the entry with slightly more restraint, waiting for her to welcome us in. But, if I'm honest, I'm fighting the urge to run in as well. It doesn't matter that I spent the morning in bed with her; the two hours I went home to prepare my dish for the meal and pack a fresh week's worth of clothes was too long.

Tuesday insists it's suspicious if I'm here before everyone else arrives. Her belief we are convincing people nothing is going on between us after the fistfight at the fair is sweet.

"Hey guys, come in, please, and make yourselves at home," she says with a laugh as she jerks her head towards my little sister, who already has her coat and shoes off and a cracker with dip in her mouth.

"What?" Clairy asks around her snack.

Charli nudges me. "I noticed it yesterday but didn't get to ask. This is your lot, isn't it? Your dream house?"

I nod once, my eyes on Tuesday.

"Well, shit, Runt. Talk about fate."

Clearing my throat, I give Charli a loaded look. "No fate. We're just friends."

She rolls her eyes and flicks me in the forehead. "You're going to end up with a lie bump on your tongue if you keep this up."

"You sound like a mom. Ouch!" I yelp as she pinches me.

"Everything okay over there?" Tuesday asks.

"Yes, just my baby brother being a menace," Charli answers before ignoring me and turning to Tuesday. "Do you need any help? If you'd like, I can unpack the things we brought and get them into the oven."

A smile lights up Tuesday's face. "That would be great. I'm not great in the kitchen, but your mom brought food over earlier this morning with very specific instructions for me to follow. I suspect we have more than the nine of us can eat."

I snort. "Don't count on it." At her puzzled expression, I say, "Griff eats like he's training for the Olympics."

Charli adds, "If we have leftovers, we'll take them to town hall. They do a Black Friday Feed-A-Thon where they deliver plated meals all around town to anyone who has to work, like the hospital, the police station, and the retail stores. People take their leftovers and make casseroles and hashes and stuff like that. It turns into a giant, town-wide potluck."

"Another of Saul's schemes?" Tuesday asks, a sparkle in her eyes.

"Spoken like a true Trail-Creekian." Clairy laughs.

I love seeing them like this, like a family. Tuesday fits so perfectly with my sisters. With me. A few minutes later, there's a knock at the door, and Mom, Dad, and Wavey walk in.

My mom hugs her. "Tuesday, your home is lovely. It is so nice of you to offer to host all of us here today."

Tuesday grins at the praise. My girl wants so badly to be loved. "You've all been so welcoming and supportive. It's the least I could do."

"Where are your friends, Porter?" Mom asks as she pops foil-covered dishes into Tuesday's double oven.

"They should—" Another knock cuts me off.

This time, it's a race between Clairy and Waverly to see who can get to the door first. Again, the rightness of this, of being in this house with everyone I love, settles over me.

"Hey, Wavey, Clairy." Griff's voice reverberates through the house. I watch as he beelines for my older sister, hugging her while whispering something in her ear. Pink blossoms over Charli's cheeks, and she giggles before glancing over her shoulder, catching Waverly and me watching her. With a small shove, she untangles herself from Griff's arms and returns to the salad she's making.

Dane ambles in, his eyes flicking to Clairy and then away while she studies him like he's an upcoming exam. Once again, my friends and sisters remind me that Tuesday and I aren't the only ones hiding things in this house.

Dad snags my elbow and motions with his head toward the patio door. I nod and follow him out. The crisp air bites through my thick sweater and jeans, but I love it.

"How is she?" my father asks, concern etched into the lines of his face.

"Better today. Charli, Wavey, and Clairy invaded her house yesterday, and they had a girls' day. She sounded like herself when I came over late last night after they finally went home."

"Charli filled in the details for us. That man should be ashamed for the way he spoke to her. How he can't see what a beautiful gift his daughter is baffles me."

I pause and pull my dad into a hug. "Thank you."

"For what, Porter?"

"For not being like that asshole. For loving Charli, Clairy, and me, especially when we make things difficult. I was so angry with you when you sold Davis Designs without explanation, but it feels like fate now."

Taking a breath, I step back and clap him on the shoulder. "She makes sense here, Dad. With us."

Mom sticks her head out the door, a smile lighting her face. "Come on, you two, I can only hold Griff back for so long."

As we gather around the dining room table, everyone I love in one place, I say a thank you to the universe. And when Tuesday's pinkie brushes mine, I say another.

CHAPTER TWENTY-EIGHT

Hours and copious amounts of food later, Mom, Dad, and Wavey have gone home for the night, leaving the six of us alone. After everything that happened on Monday, Charli decided Tuesday needed a game night. Griff and Dane are Davis holiday regulars, so it was no stretch to make it happen.

We gather in Tuesday's living room. Everyone settles around the room. Like always, Griff and Charli end up next to each other, as do Clairy and Dane. I sink to the floor as close to Tuesday's legs as possible without anyone noticing. Occasionally, I brush my fingers over her bare ankle because I enjoy watching her squirm.

Rising from her seat, Clairy comes around, topping off everyone's drink. While she pours, she asks the question that's been nagging me since my Peach and I met. "So, I don't want this to come out rude, but how'd you get the name?"

"What?" Tuesday scrunches her nose, and her cute eyebrows furrow. *Nothing proves you're gone for someone like thinking their eyebrows are adorable.*

"You don't meet a lot of Tuesdays. In fact, you're the first," Charli says, tapping her chin as she speaks.

Groaning, Tuesday takes a long draw from her sangria before answering. "So most of you know I have a twin. He's older by seven minutes. Anyway," she waves her hand in the air, "I don't know how true it is, but the story goes that my brother and I were born on a Sunday, but my mom couldn't pick a name for me. My brother, the chosen one, was immediately given my father's name—Warren James Phillips. But apparently, I was difficult from the start, and nothing fit until my father stormed into the hospital room and yelled, '*It's Tuesday! Just name the baby,*' and my mother swears I opened my eyes and cooed. I guess the involuntary noises of a two day old are the same as putting time and effort into picking a name for your child."

No one misses the bitterness in her voice, and she quickly excuses herself. The room is tight with tension. I've got to find a way to get to her without drawing too much attention.

"Way to go, Clairy," Charli scolds, the two whispering and bickering near the leftover pie. Dane and Griff step onto the porch, and I'm alone in the living room. Taking advantage of the distractions, I step away from the group and make my way down the hall.

Tuesday comes out of the half-bath as I round the corner. My arms shoot out, catching her from falling when she bumps into my chest.

"What are you doing?" she asks, looking around me to see if anyone is paying attention.

"Going to the restroom." I coil my finger around the end of a soft, reddish wave. "You're beautiful." Wrapping more of her long hair around my hand, I press my lips to the delicate skin below her jaw.

She flushes, a moan slipping from her lips. I love creating

competing sensations in her, the tension as I pull on her hair battling the featherlight kisses I place on her neck.

"What are you really doing back here?" she breathes, her voice husky.

With a sigh, I release her hair and kiss the center of her throat. "I know we are in our friend roles tonight, but you are so goddamn irresistible. I can't go without a little taste, even if it isn't the taste I want." My eyes drift down her body.

"Tuesday! Where are you?" Clairy calls from the living area.

"We'll finish this later." I wink at her and step to the side so she can pass by. Waiting a few minutes, I follow her and sit near her feet again.

Clairy stretches her legs out over Dane's lap in the loveseat, using the armrest to prop herself up. "Let's play Truth or Dare!"

"Aren't we a little old for that?" Charli asks, curling up on the end of Tuesday's couch.

"You are," Clairy coughs to cover up her answer. Poorly.

Leaning back to look at Tuesday, I whisper-shout, "How many more drinks before Charli takes Clairy down?" Her loud, uncontrolled laugh breaks out as a cheese cube flies across the room and hits Clairy in the forehead.

Griff shrugs. "It'll be fun. We've got booze. Nowhere to be in the morning. Wavey Gravy is with your parents." He tugs on a strand of her hair. "You aren't scared, are you, Lottie?"

"Of course not!"

Clairy laughs, "You go first, then Charli! Get the ball rolling."

"Fine." She narrows her eyes at each of us, finally settling on Dane. "Truth or dare?"

"Truth."

"What's the worst thing you've ever done at work?"

Dane frowns, a familiar look for him, but this one is deeper than usual. His dark eyes cut to my sister. "I was doing inventory in the storeroom a couple of months ago and ended up sleeping with someone I know is off limits."

Clairy clasps her hand over Dane's mouth while making a buzzer sound. "Dane meant to say sleeping on the clock. I think we *all* misheard him." Then there's a small yelp, and Dane rubs his arm where my little sister pinched him.

Rolling my eyes to the ceiling, I beg the universe to wipe this moment from my memory.

Still rubbing his arm, Dane nods at Griff. "Truth or Dare."

"Dare."

"I dare you to let Charli write her name in permanent marker on your body somewhere that isn't already tattooed."

"Shit, man. You know I'm covered everywhere but my face and my…"

Smirking, Dane nods. "And your…"

A loud laugh bursts from me. "What I wouldn't give for the gift of forgetting. If this is how the game is going, I'm going to need something stronger than sangria."

"It's fine, Lottie. I've got the perfect spot for you to sign." Charli and Griff step out of the room, returning a minute later, a massive smile on Charli's face.

"Where'd she sign, then?" Dane asks, his dark eyebrows raised.

"Right here," Griff answers, pulling his long blond hair into a bun at the top of his head and pointing to a teeny tiny signature on his earlobe.

"Well played, Anderson. Well played. It's your turn, then."

Griff nods his head at Tuesday. "New girl, Truth or Dare?"

Tuesday scoffs. "New girl? Really? I'm disappointed, Viking. If you're going to give me a nickname, at least make it a good one."

"Fair enough, Nickname Pending, what'll it be?"

With a snort-laugh, she says, "Dare."

"I dare you to let Bond take a body shot off your stomach."

After a few seconds, she pokes me in the shoulder. "I'm game if you are."

Fuck yes. I will never turn down a chance to put my lips on her. Tuesday dashes into the kitchen, digging through her cabinets and fridge until she finds everything we need. She sets it all on her coffee table before laying back on the floor and lifting her festive sweater to show off her soft stomach. When I slip the lime between her lips, she wiggles her eyebrows at me.

Brat.

Sprinkling the salt above her belly button, I set the tequila shooter next to her hip. With a wicked grin, I lower my head, licking the salt off her stomach, loving the goosebumps that arise. As I move my head to grab the shot glass with my mouth, I let my tongue drag across the exposed skin. Once the shooter is empty, I toss it aside and lean forward to suck the lime in her mouth, lingering far longer than necessary.

"Damn, that was fucking hot," Griff grunts from his seat on the couch. I pull back, my heart pounding, steadily pumping blood straight to my cock. Shifting my obvious hard-on, I help Tuesday to her feet, the wanting look in her eyes only making me ache more. *Soon, Baby Girl.*

"Earth to Bond, it's your turn," Clairy calls, pulling me from where I've fallen into Tuesday's gaze.

I shake my head to clear out the horny fog and ask, "How about a different game? Pictionary? Charades?"

"Aw, come on! I didn't even get a turn," Clairy whines, her red sangria dangerously close to the edge of the table.

"How about 'I Never'?" Tuesday suggests.

"That's just Truth or Dare without the dares." Clairy pouts as Dane subtly shifts her cup toward the center.

"Yes, but with more drinking," Charli says.

"Oh, that's true. I wish we had a batch of Flamingos."

Tuesday turns green at the mention of the pink drink. "I think I'll stick with sangria for the foreseeable future."

I chuckle, thinking of her last Flocked Up experience. While the others top off their drinks and raid Tuesday's liquor cabinet to make them stronger, I wrap my fingers around her ankle, stroking the delicate bones. With each pass against her skin, she scoots closer until her knee presses into my back. Shifting, I settle between her thighs, my head sinking back against her. When she plays with my hair, I close my eyes.

This is what our life will be. Spending time with my best friends and family. Laughing, making memories. Together.

"Okay, I'm starting us off since I didn't get to go last round," Clairy crows, charging back into the room, fresh drink in hand and Dane right behind her.

Her sudden entrance has me reluctantly lifting my head off Tuesday's leg. How much longer until Tuesday will be comfortable with me showing the world how much I love her?

"Never have I ever searched for myself on the internet." Griff and Charli both drink, and from behind me, Tuesday hums, the movement of her cup visible out of the corner of my eye. Stabs of hurt and anger pummel my heart at what she must've found.

I go next, staring at Dane. "Never have I ever seen a ghost." Dane is the only one to drink this time, and laughter comes from around the room.

He curses under his breath about people not believing him. "You won't be laughing when you get haunted."

"I've got one," Tuesday says. "Never have I ever dated someone younger than me."

Everyone except Tuesday and Clairy drinks this time.

"Charli Horse, who did you date younger than you?" Clairy squawks, her voice growing louder with each sip she takes.

"Um, I...no one you know," Charli stutters, gulping her drink too quickly. Under her breath, my older sister mutters, "Never have I ever had a secret relationship."

It doesn't escape my notice that everyone in the room drinks, even as we all pretend we didn't hear her.

Snores rouse me from where I'm sleeping, Tuesday's head resting on my chest. At some point, she ended up on the floor next to me when Never Have I Ever turned to drunken karaoke, which gave way to watching movies. In the glow of the television screen, I can just make out the hulking shape of Griff with Charli curled up next to him and Clairy and Dane lying almost nose to nose, him frowning even in his sleep. After tonight, I officially know too much about my sisters' and friends' dating lives. We may need to take some time apart.

With a groan, I shift and stretch. I'm too fucking old to be passing out on the floor. Shit, we all are. There are going to be six grumpy-ass adults here in the morning. Post-thirty back pain is no joke.

"Peach, let's go to bed."

"What time is it?"

"After one." I guide her to her feet, loving the sleepy noises she makes as she rubs her face against me. Holding her hand, I lead her up the stairs and to her room.

Once the door shuts behind us, she yawns and zombie walks to the bathroom. I trail after her, the two of us standing side by side as we brush our teeth and wash our faces.

Leaning against the sink, I cross my arms and study her. She looks beautiful, standing in the soft glow of her nightlights and the stars. "I never did get my taste, Baby Girl."

"And you want it now?" Her pretty brown eyes widen.

"Yeah, now. Everyone downstairs is passed out. They won't even notice we're gone. Plus, thirty-six is too damn old to sleep on the floor."

She rolls her eyes but grabs my arm and pulls me through the door to her bed. She undresses me, stopping to kiss different parts of my body as she removes each item of clothing. "Thank you. For sharing your life and those wonderful people downstairs with me." The vulnerability in her words and on her face has me pulling her into my chest.

"Tuesday, those people would love you with or without me. Families come in all shapes and shakes. Some of us need to build the one that fits us best. And that's what you're doing."

As we talk, I return the favor, undressing her piece by piece, my hands and lips exploring her body as though this is my first time seeing it. When she's bare before me, I rub my face against her hair. "They aren't like your parents or brother. You know that, right?"

"I've never had people in my corner like this."

"You've got us all. Now, no more serious talk. I need to love you."

Her indelicate laugh, the one I love so much, is my answer, and together we melt into the sheets. My weight presses her into the mattress as I slip my tongue between her lips, tracing along her teeth. I savor every exchange of breath, the coil of our tongues, the heat we pass back and forth. When her legs lock around my waist, I thrust against her, drinking in the whimper of need that pierces the air. Eventually, I break the kiss, sitting up and staring at her.

She makes no move to cover herself, and I bask in the sight

before me. That she deems me worthy of this is something I will never take for granted. Each mark, freckle, wrinkle, and scar imprint in my mind. The latitude and longitude of my Peach. It doesn't matter how often I map her body with my tongue, fingers, or eyes; it's never enough. Starting at her collarbone, I work my way down, my lips wandering nomads across the desert of her skin.

When I get to the small oasis between her thighs, I stop.

"Bond?"

Kissing her hip in reply, I roll onto my back next to her. "Peach, I said I want to taste you." I grin, wiggling my eyebrows and patting my mouth. Not being subtle, don't give a shit. "Come on, sweetheart. Climb on up here and suffocate me. Want to drown in that pretty pussy."

She clambers to her knees and crawls forward until I'm directly beneath her.

"Use the headboard." While she grabs the padding, I grab her knees. "Now sit."

Being the good girl she is, she sinks down, her delicious heat perfectly placed. Like a convert clinging to an altar, I worship.

My hands skate up her thighs to her hips, where I grip her, guiding her rhythm as she fucks herself against my lips and rides my nose. I tease her, keeping her right on the edge of coming. Each time she gets close, I shift her weight just enough to stop the momentum. At one point, her hand comes off the headboard and tangles in my hair, trying to force me to give her what she wants.

"Bond, please." Her words are desperate, exactly the way I want them.

I swat her ass and lift her long enough to suck in a breath and bark a demand. "Lick my palm." She twists as I bring my hand to her lips. Fuck, I almost lose it from the rasp of her tongue against my hand.

"Spit on it."

She gasps, and I bite the inside of her thigh. "Do it, Peach. Spit." When she follows my command, I grasp my aching cock and give myself a firm stroke. "I can't talk the way I normally do. Not with my mouth so full of you. If you want to come, sweetheart, I need those words. Now get back on my face and ride me."

She drops her weight back onto me, and I'd happily suffocate here in her perfect pussy. Nonsense pours from her lips, mixing with my name, please, love, and come. Her thighs are shaking, and I know she's right on the cusp of it being too much.

The only downside of her sitting on my face is that I miss watching her as she breaks apart. There's nothing in this world like the sight of Tuesday in the throes of pleasure, the wash of ecstasy and freedom written on her face. And no greater purpose for my tongue than this—bringing her to her mindless end.

I work my cock, waiting for the obvious plus to this position. The one I'm about to reap. As I lick and love my girl the way she deserves, I wrap my lips around her clit. No sooner do I apply that pressure, a small bite down, does she come for me, drenching me in her release.

Best fucking shower of my life.

Her release triggers mine, and I spill over my stomach.

Tuesday crumbles, spent, but I'm there to catch her. The same way I'll always be from now on. No matter how far or hard she falls.

CHAPTER TWENTY-NINE

"Care to share where you and Bond disappeared to Thursday night?" Clairy asks, her face all but pressed against the display case inside The Bee and The Bean.

"I don't think they like it when you drool on the glass," I snark, giving Clairy a hip bump.

"As this place's future owner and manager, I'll allow it. Now answer the question."

"Wait. What?"

"Two sea salt croissants, one order of beignets with serrano strawberry sauce, a sweetheat fritter, two large pecan coffees, and one smoked caramel latte with extra whipped cream." While Pippa, the sweet woman who works here most days, makes our order, Charli turns back to me. "Clairy has been working with Auntie B, sorry, Belinda, to take over the bakery. She's teaching her all the secret recipes."

Batting my lashes at Clairy, I say, "Have I ever told you that you're my favorite Davis?"

Clairy's cheery laugh and Charli's sarcastic snort fill me with a sense of belonging. We settle in a small booth near the windows so we can watch the town wake up on this sleepy Saturday morning.

"And once again, you've dodged my question, babes. So spill. Where did you two run off to?"

The sting of holding back aches in my chest. Just a little longer. I'll come clean and admit they've been right all along. All while apologizing, hoping they won't toss me aside for my deceit.

I shrug and quirk my lips into a half-smile. "If you mean early Friday morning, I went to bed, and he said he was too old to sleep on the floor." There. Not a lie. "While we're on the topic of the other night, how did you two sleep?"

The morning after Thanksgiving was a mess of epic proportions. You've never lived until you sit at a table with six adults, all pretending they aren't hungover or sore, eating left-over potato casserole. Oh, and that they didn't all get caught sleeping next to the person they love. Totally normal adult behavior.

When neither sister answers me, I wiggle my eyebrows at them. "Oh, now, who's avoiding the questions?"

Before either woman can reply, Pippa brings out our order. "Saved by the carbs, C-Squared." I blow them a kiss as I drizzle honey over my croissant. "Okay, officially changing the subject. Remind me again why we're out shopping."

Charli doctors her coffee with a bit of milk and sugar. "Because it's Small Business Saturday, and you only have a week to find a dress for the Twinkling Trail Gala unless you have an evening gown."

"I do, actually, but I'm all about doing my part to support the local economy." Or that's what I try to say, but it comes out garbled thanks to my mouthful of carby deliciousness.

"I think I caught the gist of that," Charli deadpans.

"Eat up, ladies. You'll need your strength to dress hunt." Clairy holds up her latte, and we clink our mugs together.

An hour later, with full stomachs and aching sides from laughing, we make our way around the downtown square. Charli stops in front of a cute shop with a brick exterior and a striped awning. A dulcet chime marks our entrance as we step out of the cold and into Pines and Needles.

"Whoa." The most beautiful dresses I've ever seen fill the tiny store.

"Right? I swear I don't know where she goes to market, but Hazel always has the best finds," Clairy says, already draping dresses over her arm.

"And she'll custom fit anything in the store to you. It's a lifesaver if you aren't quite as blessed in the height department as some people." Charli sticks her tongue out at her much taller little sister.

Considering Charli has an inch on me, I definitely feel her pain.

Together, we walk through the color-coded racks, oohing and awwing over the gorgeous gowns. Once we all have sizable stacks, we stagger to the fitting rooms. The first one I try is a total nope. The color washes me out, and the cut flattens my chest while emphasizing my stomach. Numbers two through four are also misses. They are better than the first, but still not quite right.

I'm having my very own Goldilocks moment here.

As soon as I slip into the jewel-toned teal gown, I know it's the one. It's the perfect blend of sexy and elegant. Made from satin with a subtle shimmer, the dress has a slit almost to my hip and a fitted silhouette that highlights my curves. The criss-cross sweetheart neckline hugs my chest, showing just enough cleavage, but I won't offend anyone's Memaw.

I step out of the fitting room to check out the dress in the tri-fold mirrors. It's easy to picture myself on Bond's arm, his thick, strongman body clad in a fitted black tux, a matching teal bowtie contrasting with his tan features and stunning eyes. I imagine his hands gliding over my ass and back, the heat of his palm penetrating the satin to seep into my skin.

"Wow, babes, you are a smoke show!"

Clairy's voice snaps me from my fantasy, and I preen at her words. "Thank you!" I spin, catching sight of the jaw-dropping ruby number she's wearing. The open back and column cut accentuate her lithe figure. "Speaking of smoke shows, good gravy, Clairy, if you're trying to melt Dane's face off with how hot you are, this is the dress for the job."

Her cheeks turn pink. "I don't know what you mean." Her hands flutter over the dress, smoothing out non-existent wrinkles. "He made it clear I'm just Bond's sister to him."

There's a melancholy tone to her voice, and she shakes her head, her long dark curls fluttering across her bare back. I hook my arm with hers. "I've seen the two of you together, Clairy. He can't keep his eyes off you."

"Well, the same is true of you and Bond. Is this your way of telling me there's something there?"

"That's different. We're just friends." The uncomfortable bubble of regret in my stomach expands. *Say it, Tuesday! Admit you're madly in love with their brother.*

Clairy snorts. "Yeah, the same way Charli and Griff are just friends." Her shoulders droop. "Dane and I...we have a complicated past. I've known him my entire life and loved him for the same amount of time. We've had more than one, um, encounter over the years, but since the last time, he's got me locked in the best friend's baby sister box and doesn't want to let me out."

I nibble my lip. She's being so open; this is my chance. But I take the coward's path and hug her. Giving advice is always easier than taking it. "Then break that box apart. And the first step to doing that is reminding him of what he's missing, and this dress," I sweep my eyes from her toes to her chin, "is the right tool for the job."

"What are you two plotting over there?" Charli asks as she steps into the open viewing space with us.

"Holy balls, Charli. That dress is...wow." And I mean it. She looks amazing.

"It's too much, isn't it?" The plum, one-shoulder lace dress clings to her curves, cinching in her waist so tight it would make a pinup jealous. There's a slit, too, not as risqué as mine, stopping mid-thigh, but the material beneath the lace has cutouts woven throughout, so you get sneaky peeks at her skin. "I'm months away from forty. Is this giving off cougar vibes?"

"Um, no. It's giving off exactly right vibes."

Clairy nods her vehement agreement to my words. "Yeah, Charli Horse, you have to get this one. You'll have every single man in the room on his knees begging for a night with you."

Charli makes a humming sound and blushes. "I'm not sure about that; besides, I don't date."

"Who's talking about dating? I'm talking about getting la—"

"Clairy, do not finish that sentence," Charli groans.

"Why don't you date?" I ask, my curiosity piquing. The dynamic between Griffin and Charli definitely seems like that of a couple.

"Getting pregnant at twenty-three took the wind out of my dating sails. Once Waverly was older, I thought I was ready, but I never clicked with anyone. Until I met Gr—" She coughs and shakes her head. With a deep breath, she says, "Until I met Griff. But he's eight years younger than me. There's no way a just turned thirty-two-year-old man wants an almost forty-year-old single mom of a teenager."

Clairy and I both rush in to hug her. "Charli, I haven't been here long, but every interaction between you and the Viking made me think you were already together. What's the worst that could happen if you told him how you feel?"

"I'd lose my best friend."

The tiny voice saying *tell them* grows to a roar. They've both shared so much.

I open my mouth, ready to blurt it all out, lay the whole sordid tale at their feet, when Clairy gives her sister a quick embrace and gestures towards the counter. "Come on, let's get these dresses to Hazel and go harass Saul at the bookstore for a bit."

The heavy talk about murky relationships fades away, and with it, my chance to come clean.

As I get ready for the Twinkling Trail Gala, I smile at the side of the walk-in closet that has gradually morphed into Bond's section. If I also take a moment to sniff a few of the shirts, searching for a hit of his scent, that's neither here nor there.

Settling in front of my vanity, I turn my head from left to right, making sure my makeup is even. I'm mid-mascara when the buzzing of my phone draws my attention.

SEXY BASEBALL CAP

I can't wait to see you all dressed up for me.

> Who says I'm dressing up for you? I'm dressing for myself.

SEXY BASEBALL CAP

Well fuck me, Peach, that's even sexier.

Biting my lip, I debate with myself. I want to send him a picture—a sneak peek. For once, I have on a matching bra and panty set. I should commemorate this moment.

I trust him and know he will cherish any intimate pictures I share. Deciding to be brave, I hike my strapless bra higher, arch my back, and tilt my hips. Then, I lift the phone to the perfect angle to highlight all my assets. I take several pictures before releasing my breath and the pose. Thumbing through the images, I pick the one most likely to set his socks on fire.

Just as I'm about to hit send, another text pops up. But this one drains all the happiness and playfulness from me.

DO NOT REPLY

Aren't you going to congratulate me? How does it feel knowing your family sided with me over you?

Along with the text is a link to a news article. *High-Profile Ceasefire: North Texas Building Baron Settles Dispute with Daughter's Former Flame*

I quickly delete his message and all the risqué pictures, his ill-timed text sucking all the life out of my plans for sexting fun with Bond. Tossing my phone away as if it burns, I blink, trying to not smudge my makeup. *Not crying. Not crying. Not crying.*

So what if my family paid off the man who humiliated and extorted me? Who cares if the sordid details of my relationship and that I have a series of freckles on my lower back in the shape of the Taurus constellation are public knowledge. Not me.

Screw Duncan. Screw my family.

I'm not letting anything ruin my night. I have a beautiful gown to show off, a group of friends to spend the evening with, and a handsome man waiting for my arrival.

CHAPTER THIRTY

Stepping out of my car an hour later, I silently beg the universe to give Awkward Tuesday the night off so I don't trip over my dress and fall flat on my face in front of the entire town.

I'm taken aback by how beautiful the venue, The Skyline, is. Its stucco exterior is blanketed in lights with an emerald velvet carpet lining the stairs to the open doors, welcoming guests in from the cold.

Thankfully, the gods of balance and grace smile down on me, and I make it into the party without incident. I snag a glass of Prosecco off one of the passing trays and take a long sip, letting the effervescent bubbles tickle my throat and calm my nerves.

The inside is festively decorated, living up to the fundraiser's name. Twinkling lights twined in winter greenery and bright red berries adorn the walls and hang from the rafters. According to C-Squared, this is the premiere venue in Trail Creek, and by that, they mean the only one. It's beautiful, though, a mix of elegance and rustic charm I now associate one hundred percent with Trail Creek.

I recognize a few faces, people I've met in passing over the last five weeks. There's Shayla, who runs The Nomadic Nosh—the vegetarian food truck—her arm around Pippa's waist. Hazel, wearing a fabulous dress from her store, laughs with Dave and Linda, the HiCo owners. I spot Saul and Sheila; he's in full man of the town form tonight. They are talking to an older couple, a man with steel gray hair and matching eyes. The hard set of his jaw reminds me of Jacob, and I'd bet my weight in croissants they are his parents. The mayor. Makes sense that he'd be chatting with Saul as head of the town council.

A quick scan of the room finds the jackass lurking in a corner, a sneer on his face as he tips his drink to me. I consider flipping him the bird, but the last thing I want is to cause a scene tonight. I just want to enjoy myself. And see Bond in a tuxedo. Is that too much to ask?

Morgan and Cal snuggle together near the band, gently swaying to the music. Her black dress hugs her tiny bump. I'd go greet them, but they are so lost in each other that I hate to interrupt.

"I've been wondering when you'd get here, Peach." Bond's voice purrs in my ear, sending a rush of goosebumps over my skin.

I spin into him, loving how his eyes rake me over from top to bottom, paying close attention to the slit and the way the dress molds to my body like a second skin.

"Your bowtie!"

"Someone may have given me a heads-up on the color of your dress. I hope you don't mind." Bond smooths the already perfectly straight material of his jacket.

"I love it. And you," I whisper.

He takes my hand, grazing my knuckles with his lips before turning my wrist over and placing a sweet kiss on my pulse point. His eyes never break contact with mine. "You are a vision, Tuesday."

"You're not so bad yourself, Baseball Cap." I nibble my lower lip as I soak in the fantasy that is Bond in a tux. The cut accents his broad shoulders and barrel chest while his pants fit perfectly, clinging to his bubble butt and thick thighs. Sometimes, I think about those thighs crushing things in rugby shorts and knee socks.

"What sort of things, Baby Girl?" Bond asks, grinning.

Crap. "Did I say that out loud?"

"Oh, yeah, you did," he chuckles before leaning closer and brushing his lips against my ear. "If you're a good girl, I'll see if I can find what you need to make that fantasy come true."

"Yease." My mind is running wild with the idea now—Bond spending all his free time at my house in nothing but a tiny pair of fitted gray shorts and bright blue knee socks. Yep, I want that.

Bond escorts me to the Davis Designs table, where his parents, sisters, and friends sit. Lynn rises to greet me, pulling me into one of those perfect mom hugs she's so generous with.

"Tuesday, you look beautiful."

"Thank you, Lynn. I love your dress." I linger in her embrace longer than is probably normal, but it's so damn comforting.

Once we're seated, I take in the smiling faces of those around me. Each one a bright star in the new tapestry of my life. Charli and Clairy and their welcoming spirits, befriending me and our instant connection. Dane and Griff, and the knowledge that they are good, kind men who are watching out for me. Lynn and Scott, who support me and care about my welfare.

And Bond. My light. My center. My home.

If you'd given me a hundred guesses about what my life in

Trail Creek would become when I drove out of Texas five weeks ago, being surrounded by people who genuinely love me and want my happiness wouldn't have made the list.

"Tuesday, any news from your family?"

I cringe. "I haven't spoken to my family since my father announced the settlement with Duncan."

She's up and hugging me again, Clairy and Charli right behind her. I'm the filling in a Davis woman sandwich, and honestly, with the exception of Bond, I've never felt so loved.

"Okay, okay, no more sad talk. Tonight is my first Trail Creek party. What should I expect?" I ask, flapping my hands under my eyes to keep them dry.

Lynn gives me a conspiratorial grin. "Sheila will drink too much and try to sing with the band, Mr. Cahill will break out his old wrestling moves, and anyone who drinks a Trail Creek Twist will end up sicker than a dog in the morning."

Throwing my head back, I let out a loud laugh. "Remind me to stay away from those. Charli, where's Waverly tonight?"

"Anytime the town has an event like this, the school does too. So she's at a dance."

Griff slings his arm around Charli. "Did you see the boys watching her when we dropped her off? We're gonna have our hands full."

I raise an eyebrow at his phrasing, but everyone else nods their agreement. We settle into easy conversations, my personality meshing with theirs. *Take that, Awkward Tuesday!*

Bond stretches until his arm rests on the back of my chair and glides the pads of his fingers along the bare skin of my shoulders. Oh, he's feeling playful tonight. Game on.

As the servers place our plates in front of us and everyone's attention turns to the food, I reach under the table and stroke Bond's thigh. Pulling my chair a hairsbreadth closer, I brush my leg against his.

The faint blush on his ears and smile tugging at his lips are the only indicators of what I'm doing beneath the tablecloth. Sliding my hand higher, I graze his cock, loving how it jumps at my touch. Without looking up from my salad, I murmur, "So responsive for me, aren't you, Baseball Cap?"

He grabs my hand before I can linger in my intended destination and shoots me a warning look. I pout behind my glass as I take a long drink of water. That's fine. I can wait.

Throughout dinner, I make pleasant conversation with the Davis-plus clan.

And enjoyable tension with Bond.

My foot inches up his calf during the entrée, and my fingers tease over his lap during dessert. Each touch has him shifting, his eyes flashing. It's the most brazen I've been with him in front of others, but every stolen touch, a public flirtation of our private love, gives me a thrill.

After dinner, a handsome man asks Charli to dance, and the way Griffin grips his drink makes me fear for its structural integrity. The Viking looks ready to swoop in and carry her out of here, his stormy green eyes never leaving Charli as she moves around the dance floor from one partner to another.

"I told you that dress would have every single man in town panting after her," Clairy says, a mischievous grin on her face.

With a grunt, Griff rises and, in a few long strides, cuts in on Charli's latest dance partner.

Clairy and I laugh as the Viking pulls Charli into his arms. I'm about to ask Clairy about Dane when he appears, whispers something into her ear, and guides her from the table. As they walk, his hand rests on her lower back, his thumb brushing against her spine.

These dresses? Worth every frigging penny.

Bond is in deep conversation with a man I don't know, so I explore the venue and find an alcove tucked away from the crowd. I drift closer, drawn to the view from the large window. As I take in the small pond and mountains towering in the distance, a familiar warmth seeps into my skin, followed by the comforting scent of the man I love.

"There you are. I've been searching for you." Bond's hands slide up my sides.

"What do you think you're doing?" I ask.

He spins me and steps us deeper into the alcove so my back is against the window. "A little payback for the teasing you gave me during dinner."

"You started it! I had goosebumps the entire meal."

His devilish grin belies his innocent words. "It was a simple brush of my fingers. I can't help it if you can't control yourself around me."

"Control myself?" A wicked, wonderful idea pops into my head, and I suddenly feel incredibly brave. "What are the odds of anyone else coming back here?"

Bond raises one eyebrow at me. "What do you have planned, Peach?"

"I have an idea, but you have to be oh so quiet."

"You're telling me to be quiet? Tuesday, your noises could wake the dead."

"Maybe you should put something in my mouth so I can't make any."

"You can't say things like that and expect me to walk away." Bond slips his hand into my hair, gently gripping the strands.

Without answering, I attack his lips. Together, we slide his jacket off and toss it to the side. I indulge in kisses to his neck and collarbone, the blush color of my lipstick smudging against his skin and staining the bright white of his shirt.

Sorry, not sorry. Tonight, I'm telling the world he's mine.

I drop to my knees, but I still feel like a queen. The love in his eyes, the passion, the belief that I'm enough shining through—I'm his everything. He subtly shifts us, ensuring I'm hidden from view on the chance anyone wanders into this part of the building. Always taking care of me.

Bond's Adam's apple bobs, and with a grin, I undo his buttons and zipper before reaching in to find my prize.

"Let's play a game...call it a grown-up version of the quiet game," I say as I nuzzle my nose against the length of his cock. I tease my fingers over him before leaning in to lick a drop of precum away.

"Fuck," he grits out.

I pull back. "No noises. That's the rule."

"Shit, Peach. You're killing me."

"Oh, sweet Baseball Cap, I haven't even started yet." A rush of power and desire floods me when he groans, his fingers tensing in my hair. I kiss him from root to tip before taking him into my mouth, loving his salty taste on my tongue.

When he makes another wanton sound, I stop and stand. "I can see you are going to need some extra reinforcements to follow the rules."

Leaning against the cool window pane, I guide Bond's large hand under the slit in my dress from my knee upward until he finds the thin string of my panties.

"I wondered if you had anything on under this." He continues his search, drawn to the heat between my legs, until he runs a finger over the silky material barring him entrance. "You should take these off; they're soaked."

Usually, this is where I snap to do as he says, but tonight, I'm taking charge. "Actually," my voice is lower than normal, almost a purr, "you take them off."

Bond's head jerks, and our eyes lock. "I see. You're in control here."

Hooking his fingers in the thin material on both sides of my panties, he tugs. Slowly. My eyes close, and my mouth drops open when the silken material tickles and teases as he pulls it down.

Picking up the scrap of black silk, I say, "Open your mouth, Bond."

For a moment, I wonder if I'm pushing him too far, his blue eyes boring into mine, his brow furrowed. Then he grins at me. "Go ahead and play; I'll pay you back soon."

He opens up, and I slip the soft material between his lips. I shudder at his moan and blush, thinking about how wet those panties were before I put them into his mouth. "You can spit those out any time, but I will stop if you make any noises. Understand?"

He nods.

"Good boy," I coo. I make a show of kneeling back before him, my fingers lightly touching him the entire time. I toss my hair, and making sure his eyes are on me, I lick the length of his cock before taking him into my mouth.

I start slow, toying with him. Sucking on his crown, rolling my tongue around the tip. I trace the veins, memorizing the shape of him. When he bucks, I run a finger under his balls and give him a light tickle, then a firm stroke.

Gripping his base, I suck, treating him like my own personal popsicle before enveloping him until my lips meet my fist. He thrusts against my face, his cock touching the back of my throat, and I hum around him. The rules don't apply to me, after all.

It isn't long before he grows frantic. His muffled moans, barely audible around the improvised gag, are music to my ears; they serve as the praise he's not able to pour over me with his mouth full of my panties. When he taps my shoulder, letting me know he's close, I increase the pressure, hollowing my cheeks and gently palm his balls, swallowing around him as he spills into my mouth.

I kiss up his body before placing one to the corner of his lips. Only then do I pull the panties from his mouth and capture his lips in a searing kiss.

Say what you will, but a partner who isn't afraid of their own taste on your tongue is sexy as hell.

Breaking the kiss, Bond yanks the panties back from me and shoves them into his pocket. "These belong to me now." Then, with a smirk, our positions are reversed, and Bond is on his knees, head buried beneath my gown. "This belongs to me too." He breathes the muffled words against my mound before burying his nose there.

"Why," I take a steadying breath, "why do you always do that? Sniff me?"

"Because you smell and taste fucking delicious. Has no one ever told you?"

"No!"

He peeks up at me from beneath my dress. "Don't sound so shocked, sweetheart. Remember that night I thought you hadn't showered, and I—"

I push his head forward. "Stop talking, Bond."

The hot breath of his laugh sends a spike of shivers through me. "I don't have time to savor you like the fine-ass meal you are. People will be looking for us, but I'm still gonna make you come so hard you see stars."

Long flat licks, swirling pointed flicks, pressure both gentle and firm—the intoxicating cocktail has me weak in the knees. It takes no time at all before I'm swept away. Bond's mouth is a saint performing a miracle as he laves, nips, and sucks me into oblivion. Two fingers push into me, then three, and I'm biting my lips to keep from crying out. He's a man driven, his fingers curling. Twisting. Hunting.

"Give it to me, Peach. I love it when you come on my tongue. Fuck, you taste like mine."

My body pulses in time with the pleasure fragmenting me. I crumple to the ground, seeking out Bond's lips as we lie in a tangle of limbs, satin, and cashmere. One quick floor cuddle session later, I'm ready. Ready to share our happy news with the people who love us.

Hair mussed, lips swollen, faces flushed in the afterglow, we stumble back into the main room and right into the leering, judging stare of Duncan frigging Wright.

tuesday

I freeze. If I don't move, he can't see me. That never works. But just once, I wish it would.

Duncan. If Schadenfreude had a mascot, it would be his smug face.

"So this is where you ran off to? Warren did a nice job finding a remote little hamlet to stash you in, didn't he?" Duncan's condescending voice grates my nerves.

"Wh-what are you doing here?" I rack my brain but can't think of a single reason he should be in my new world.

"I came to celebrate my successful settlement with Phillips Construction. Didn't you read the article I sent you? I'm a comfortably wealthy man now."

My temper flares, and I snap at him. "Of course, I didn't read the article. I deleted it like every other text you sent me. I want nothing to do with you. Ever."

"Now, now, Tits, is that any way to talk to someone who's seen you naked?" His wolfish grin sets my teeth on edge.

I ball my hands into fists at my side. "I told you not to call me that."

Duncan waves my words away like gnats. "Imagine my surprise when I stumbled upon this viral video. A ton of people sent it to me, including one of the stars of this social media sensation. Jacob Ashford, I think he said his name was?"

An actual growl comes out of Bond's mouth, and I grimace. That frigging guy! I wouldn't mind shoving Bond's baseball cap up Jakey Boy's nose.

"Anyway, this video pops up showing you hiding away from me in this podunk town while two men fight. Is this what you're into now? Big tough guys?" Duncan steps forward, but Bond places himself between us.

"This is a private event. You should leave. Now."

Duncan sneers at him. "Oh? My understanding is that it's a fundraiser. I happily made my donation, so I'll be staying. What's a few hundred dollars when you walk away with a million?"

My jaw drops. What the everloving hell? My family paid him a million dollars?

"Once the ink on my settlement dried, your dad and I discussed the possibility of my return to Phillips Construction —in an advisory capacity, at a higher salary, of course. Wouldn't that be wonderful, Tits? The two of us working together again." He pauses and gives me a lecherous leer that sends chills up my spine. "It could be just like old times," Duncan says in his most charming voice. The one I see now for what it is: a mask. A lie. A way to manipulate and use those around him.

Stepping out from behind Bonds's back, I ask, "Why are you here, Duncan? You got everything you wanted." I cross my arms and narrow a glare at him, waiting for his reply.

"Like I said, I'm here to reconnect. We have some unfinished business to reconcile. Did you really think I would let you slip away and live out some happily ever after?" He turns to

Bond. "Let me guess, you're the local she's screwing? She really is a dynamo in the sack. So hungry for love and affection. She'll do any—"

"Look, asshole, I'm not looking to get into a fight here, but if you keep running your mouth, I will. And I'll win." Raw anger is evident in Bond's voice.

My cheeks burn, and a look around shows Clairy and Dane, Charli and Griff, Lynn and Scott, along with several other Trail Creek locals watching us, their eyes volleying between Duncan, Bond, and me. "Bond, everyone, let's go back to the table." I make it two steps before Duncan's taunting words stop me cold.

"You ruined my life, or at least you tried to. Luckily, your father saw *my* value, and I landed on my feet."

I spin back and step closer, whispering in the hopes no one else will hear. "Ruined your life? Are you kidding me right now? Duncan, you led me on, told me you were single, and when I ended things with you, you leaked pictures of me online."

"That's a big accusation you're throwing around. If you're sure it was me, why didn't you bring up charges? Why didn't Daddy use it as leverage to make the lawsuit disappear? Face it, Tuesday, those pictures could have been taken by anyone in any hotel room in Dallas. And your father knew it. After all, the kind of woman who goes after a married man probably doesn't have any qualms about other things."

I suck in a gasp of air and flinch. "Excuse me?"

He leans in, his breath making my stomach turn. What did I ever see in him? "Aw, did I strike a nerve? Would your new friends be so welcoming if they really knew you, Tits? If they knew you were a home-wrecking sl—"

Bond grips Duncan by the collar before he finishes the word. "You don't get to call her names. Never again. You have thirty seconds to get out of here, or I will escort you to your car, and you won't like it."

Duncan jerks himself from Bond's grasp, shaking out his jacket and straightening the cuffs of his tuxedo. "Your father will be hearing about this treatment of me. You'd think you'd be more welcoming to your future husband."

My knees give out, but like always, Bond is there to steady me. In a shaky voice, I say, "I think my brain must be offline. What did you say?"

"You really don't know?" He makes a *tsking* sound. "I'll have to talk with Warren about his communication skills. Although, perhaps he thought I'd want to deliver the happy news in person when I told him I was coming here to see you."

"I have no idea what you're talking about, but there is a zero percent chance of me doing anything with you. Ever."

"Tuesday, Tits, babe. It's a done deal. Daddy already gave his blessing. You should have seen his face when I pitched the idea. When you get to Texas, we'll start being seen publicly; let the rumor mill fly. After a couple of months, I'll propose in a big scene. The local media will eat it up. Our epic reconciliation, after all the ugliness of the lawsuit."

"Why would you want to marry me, Duncan? You didn't even like me when we were together."

"Let's not pretend this is anything but a PR coup and reputation-rehab business agreement. Oh, and money, of course."

I falter at his brutal honesty. "You already have a million. That isn't enough?"

My ex—seriously, what was I thinking—scoffs. "What's a million compared to what you have in your—"

"Shut up, Duncan," I snap, my cheeks burning.

"They don't know? Another secret you're keeping, Tits?" When I don't answer, he chuckles, an unpleasant simpering sound. "Shame, shame, shame, Tuesday."

Bond moves to grab Duncan, but I settle my hand on his arm. "Bond, look at me."

His electric blue eyes flick to mine before going back to Duncan.

"Baseball Cap. Look. At. Me."

This gets his attention, and he stares at me with a frown. I straighten his wrinkled, lipstick-stained collar, then stand on my tiptoes and kiss him. A gentle brushing of our lips. From behind us, I hear a whispered *it's about damn time.*

"Can you take a breath for me? I need to say my piece." Pressing my forehead to his chest, I say, "If you want to drag him to the parking lot after, I won't stop you, but I have to do this."

Bond's thumb lifts my chin, his eyes searching mine. "Then I've got your back."

Taking a step to the side, he crosses his arms and plants his feet, looking every bit the protective man he is. All Bond has done since I met him is take care of me, and I've let him. But it's my turn to take care of us now.

"Duncan, I don't know what you're trying to pull, but I'm not returning to Dallas. Ever. And I'm certainly not going back with you. I hate giving you even a second of my time or energy. You've drained me dry for the last time." I spit the words, disgust and anger battling for top billing in my tone. "Whatever sick, twisted publicity stunt you and Mr. Phillips plotted isn't happening. Whatever reason you have for being here is irrelevant. You are irrelevant. I may have been naive in thinking you cared for me once upon a time, but my eyes are wide open now. I see how you sold me for parts to salvage yourself. That you would come here and suggest some sort of faux reconciliation to leverage me for money while still laying the blame for your marriage ending on me is barfably laughable. You are a pathetic, delusional piece of garbage."

His face is blotchy and red, anger and humiliation coloring his features. But I don't stop. "For the eleven weeks we were together, you never cared about me. Never loved me. You swooped in with your charming words before tearing me apart. Go back to Dallas and live the life you deserve. And by that, I mean I hope your wife takes every cent to your name. I hope you step on a Lego every morning with your bare feet. I hope your teeth and hair fall out. I hope your dick shrivels up even smaller than it already is. And I hope you never know a day of happiness again."

With my mic drop moment over, I loop my arm with Bond's, and together, we walk towards our friends, leaving Duncan seething in our wake.

"Don't you walk away from me, Tuesday. It's highly interesting that you're sleeping with another coworker, especially on the heels of the settlement. You really can't help yourself, can you? I'll make sure your father hears about this."

Spinning back to him, I snarl, "Then fucking tell him!" I cover my mouth, waiting to be scolded; I just shouted *fuck* in a room full of people. But then I remember my mother isn't here.

Bond's hand settles on my lower back. "Come on, Peach. Don't pay him any more mind. He's grasping at straws now."

All the pretenses fall away, and Duncan's taunts grow louder. "Do the people here know what you did? That you broke up my marriage, got me fired, and let Daddy hide you away because he was too embarrassed to deal with you? Do they know about the pictures?"

His words carry over the din of the party and Bond tenses, but before he can act, I reach out and pop Duncan right in his smug mouth. My hand throbs, especially my thumb, but his wide-eyed disbelief that I hit him almost makes up for it.

Almost.

Duncan is still standing there, bloody mouth agape, when

Bond hugs me to him. His lips brush over my aching thumb and knuckles. "Baby Girl, that was amazing, but we need to work on your form if you plan on punching anyone else." At my small chuckle, he waves Charli over. "Go on back to the table, Peach. Have another slice of dessert. Your ex and I have a couple of things to discuss."

I try to argue, but he cuts me off with a kiss. "Everything is going to be fine. I'm going to make sure the message sinks in and that he finds his way out of Trail Creek."

Bond heads straight for Duncan, and no one watching tries to stop him. Duncan scurries backward, holding his fingers to his busted lip. Before he can make his escape, Bond's arm hooks around his neck, and he drags him from the room. As they walk away, I hear what vaguely sounds like *you and I are going to have a nice long talk.*

Charli's gentle touch on my shoulder keeps me from chasing after him. "He needs to do this, Tuesday. I'm not saying it's right, but that man hurt you, and my brother can't abide it."

I close my eyes and swallow. The weight of all my secrets being laid open for everyone to see weighs heavy on my chest like an anchor. What must they think of me? Not only do they know I'm a liar, but now they know the entire truth about why I'm here. Plus, they just witnessed a messy public display of loathing—a *PDL, if you will. Oh my god, shut up, Tuesday*—at a town fundraiser. I bet Saul is having a conniption.

Sinking into a chair and grabbing a slice of the fancy chocolate cake that isn't nearly as good as anything from The Bee and The Bean, I mumble, "So, how much did you guys hear and see?"

"Enough to know your jerk of an ex deserves the punch you gave him and whatever Bond is about to give him. And that you've both been lying to us for a few weeks, but none of us are actually surprised by that." Charli smiles at me.

"Too fucking true," Dane grumbles as he wraps a few ice cubes in a cloth napkin and holds the makeshift cold pack to my bruised hand.

I take a swig of the untouched Trail Creek Twist next to my plate, immediately regretting it when the alcohol burns a hole in my esophagus. "What is this? Lighter Fluid?" I gasp, reaching for water to chase away the lingering effects of the gut rot.

"Lynn warned you. They make it with piñon moonshine. That drink could take tar off your tires," Dane says, pushing the noxious cocktail away from me.

The familiar laughter of the people I've come to love the most surrounds me, and I remember why I was drinking in the first place. I take a deep breath to steady my nerves and banish the tremble in my voice. "I understand if you want space from me after everything you heard. The things Duncan said, I can't deny all of them, but he twisted them. As soon as I found out he was married, I broke things off and told his wife. I even paid for her attorney. And everything that came after...getting him fired, the pictures, the lawsuit—"

"Tuesday." Lynn's soft but firm utterance of my name stops me mid-ramble.

Here it comes. The disappointment, betrayal, and hurt. I brace myself, but the verbal blow never lands.

"Sweet girl, you don't owe us any explanation. You are still the wonderful woman we love." Lynn pulls me into a hug that chases the chills from my bones.

My heart races. Charli's smile. Dane holding the ice to my hand. Lynn's hug. Does this mean...are they...

Pulling away from Lynn, I look at the others. "I understand if you're mad at me for lying to you, but with everything that happened in the past, I needed...I wanted time. Bond only lied because of me. So if you are upset, you should know it's all my fault."

Clairy breaks into a wide grin. "It's not like the Bond thing was actually a secret."

Dropping my voice, I ask the question that worries me the most. "And the rest?"

Lynn tuts. "Nothing said today changes how I view you. What I heard were the deranged rantings of a very disturbed man who hurt you many times over."

"What Mom said," Charli says while Clairy nods in agreement.

"Coming here, to Trail Creek, wasn't my choice, but I can't imagine my life without all of you in it. In the time I've been here, you've been my safe haven. The fresh air in my lungs providing me with things I didn't know I needed. The warmth, compassion, friendship, and love you've poured into me in the few weeks we've known each other is beyond measure."

The gathering tears in my eyes have me blinking to will away their sting. "And Bond. He is the nightlight of my life, keeping the darkness at bay and bathing me in his warm glow. He's so incredibly thoughtful and loving, a selfless, nurturing caretaker who looks out for everyone before himself. You raised him to be a kind, wonderful man. I want you to know how much you and he mean to me."

Clairy grins. "You really like him?"

"Actually, I love him," I say softly. "I'm going to ask him to move in with me. Permanently." As soon as the words are out of my mouth, an all-encompassing feeling of rightness settles over me.

"What about your family?" Dane asks.

"You guys are my family."

Arms envelop me from all sides, and suddenly, I'm in the

center of a Davis clan group hug. Charli and Clairy whoop together about gaining a new sister, while Griff and Dane tease and grouse about giving Bond hell for keeping things a secret. Lynn kisses my cheeks, and Scott ruffles my hair. It's a jumble of love and happiness.

Then, the group breaks apart, and Bond is there. His jacket is rumpled, and his chestnut waves are mussed. I scan him over and don't see any other obvious signs of a tussle, but there's an excellent chance he walked away without a scratch. With zero concern about who will see us or what anyone may think, I melt into his arms.

"Are you okay?"

"Of course I am." He kisses the tip of my nose. "I take it everyone knows?"

"Um, yeah. Apparently, we aren't as slick as we think."

Bond throws his head back, letting out that barking laugh I love so much. "No, I don't suppose we are."

"Duncan?" I don't need to expand on my question.

"On his way back to Texas with four reminders not to bother us again."

My eyes go wide. "You didn't!"

"I did."

"What if he presses charges?"

Pulling me tighter into his grasp, Bond rubs his cheek against my hair. "Luckily, there were several witnesses who saw him fall."

"Fall?"

"Turns out Duncan is pretty clumsy. He fell four times. Busted his nose, bruised his jaw, jammed his index finger, and sprained his right wrist. Weird, isn't it?"

"Let me see your hand," I demand.

Ignoring me, Bond pulls my chin up, his beautiful blue eyes searching mine. "Are you upset with me for doing it? Because I always keep my word, Peach, and I promised you he'd pay for each picture."

"No. Not at all. Now give me your hand." With a huff, Bond places his hand in mine. His knuckles are red, but there's no other sign of what went down between him and Duncan. I press my lips to the tender skin. "Honestly? I kind of wish I'd seen it. But now we have matching injuries." Bond's smug grin at my reply is too cute for me to resist kissing.

"Awww, that's adorable!" Clairy coos.

Ducking my head, a blush heats my cheeks. "I think it's time to call it a night. What do you say, Baseball Cap? Take me home?"

Before he can answer me, my phone goes haywire. The familiar number rings once, twice, then a third time before switching to video calls. Well hell. Duncan tattled to my dad.

I briefly consider dropping the blasted device into the cocktail glass containing the Trail Creek Twist, but it's time to put on my big girl panties. Figuratively speaking, of course, since my actual big girl panties are tucked away in Bond's pocket.

Turning to my friends and chosen family, I say, "I need to take this."

"We're here for you, sweetheart." Bond takes my hand in his.

Propping my phone up on the table, I take a deep breath and hit answer. There's no warm greeting, no niceties. Nothing but the icy gaze of my parents.

CHAPTER THIRTY-TWO

The massive difference between Bond's parents and mine is jarring. Mere moments ago, I was in the warm embrace of Scott and Lynn while they showered me with love and praise. Now, I sit hundreds of miles away from the people who provided my DNA—a video connection and mutual disappointment the only bond between us.

My parents sit in my father's study, the same looks on their faces as when they initially banished me to the very place that ended up being my refuge. My father's expensive HD camera captures every nuance of their expression. They stare at me like I'm garbage, their lips curled in disgust. If I didn't know better, I might think someone slipped a Trail Creek Twist into their evening nightcap. But no, those scornful scowls are all for me.

Unsaid words hang in the air, heavy like thick smog. Even the buzz of the party feels stifled by the impermeable silence between us. For years, I've endured their harsh judgments, constant disapproval, and relentless attempts to mold me into someone I'm not. *Tuesday, don't be so dramatic. Tuesday, why can't you be more like War? Tuesday, you've embarrassed us again. Tuesday, you're so ridiculous.*

I hate that word.

With a put-upon sigh, my dad cracks first. *Point to Tuesday.* "Can you imagine my disgust when Duncan informed me about your ugly display? We told you we expected you to come back to Texas. You threw a fit like a petulant child. Duncan offered to escort you home, and you again caused a scene. Why is it so hard for you to do what is expected of you once in your life?" My father's cruelly calculated words land like the tail of a whip, leaving a sting in its wake.

"What's expected of me?"

"It would look good for us if you and Duncan reconciled. He really is a handsome man," my mother says, a too-bright smile on her face.

Bond's fingers lace with mine, and he squeezes my hand. I'm not alone. Thanks to those around me, I'm stronger than before. Stronger than the burden of my family lines. For thirty-three years, I've tried to please them, to be the daughter they wanted. But this? This is a bridge too far.

Today, I step out of those shackles, out of their endless shadow.

"Can *you* imagine *my* disgust when Duncan informed me about your plan? To marry me off to the man who lied to me, used me, and violated my privacy."

"Watch your tone." Warren Phillips' biting voice rings out over my tinny phone speaker.

"How could you?"

My father looks at me as if I'm an ant he'd like to smash beneath his boot. "It's business, Tuesday. Something you'd understand if you had a modicum of sense."

"You aren't even going to ask me which part I mean?" I wrap my words in shards of glass, making them as cutting as I can. "Because I could ask why you believe a lying piece of shit over your daughter. Maybe I'm wondering why you agreed to pay him a million dollars. Or could it be how you invited him back to work after all that? Or perhaps I'm questioning the preposterous scenario where you thought you could marry me off to him like I'm an asset you're managing. Did you seriously think I would go along with this?"

When both of my parents meet my questions with silence, I forge ahead. "What is wrong with you? You say I have no sense? How stupid can you be?"

"Tuesday!" my father snaps, the perfect lines of his bespoke suit tense with his body. "All you've done for the past year is cause problems. Thanks to your escapades, the company has lost hundreds of thousands of dollars in business."

"My escapades?" I ask, incredulity filling my tone. I swear my eyebrows have to be touching my hairline. "You think I released those pictures to the media? Shit, do you think *I* took them?" My voice rises as each injustice brought against me by my family flings to the front of my mind. "The only part of this that's my fault is falling for Duncan's nice single-guy act. All the rest is on him, and you fucking rewarded him!"

"Tuesday, language, and lower your voice," my mother scolds, her hands flying to her perfectly highlighted bob as if she can smooth me into place like a fly-away hair.

Her concern about my language and nothing else happening here reaffirms how little I mean to her. Appearances are all that matter, and the moment I shattered the perfect *Phillips Portrait,* I became a liability. Something to be written off and hidden away.

"Hey, Mom, guess what? See all these people here, listening to this very private, very ugly conversation we're having in a very public location? They love me. As I am. They think I'm smart and funny and enough. They don't care if I say shit, hell, or fuck."

"Fuck no, we don't!" Griff calls from behind me.

"They are more of a family to me than you've ever been. In the last five weeks, they've shown me more kindness than I've known my entire life."

"Oh, Tuesday. You're so dramatic," Mom says.

I huff out a sad laugh, pursing my lips and shaking my head. "While we're on the topic of me being dramatic, I should also tell you, Bond, you know him as Porter, and I have been dating the entire time I've been in Trail Creek. He's moving in with me. I'm in love with him."

"You want me to move in?" Bond asks, grinning at me.

"Oh, yeah, sorry. I guess I should ask."

"I promise I'll say yes." His flirty timbre lightens the strain on my soul.

My mom's shrill voice breaks the moment between us. "Tuesday. Stop that this instant. This is ridiculous. You can't possibly be in love with that man. It's too soon."

Frowning at her use of my least favorite word, I shrug. "Is it ridiculous? No. It isn't, and neither am I. Is it soon? Probably. But guess what? It doesn't matter because it's also perfectly right. The greatest truth I've ever known."

My mom rolls her eyes and scoffs. I don't bother trying to explain it further. She'll never understand, and that's okay.

"If you do this, there's no place for you at a Phillips-owned business." The rapidly falling temperature outside has nothing on Warren Phillips.

"Thank you." At my father's raised eyebrow, I smirk. "You've made the choice incredibly easy for me. I quit."

"You'd walk out on your family? After everything we've done for you?"

At that, I can't hold my laugh back anymore. It lacks my

usual loud, boisterous tone. Instead, it's brittle. Biting. "What you've done for me? Let's review that again since you clearly can't retain information. What you've done for me is make me feel like I'm less than. What you've done for me is pick me apart, telling me all the reasons I'm not enough while simultaneously telling me I'm too much. What you've done for me is love me less than I deserve."

Shaking my head, I huff. "You know what? I'm not even going to try to understand you anymore. I'm done. Done trying to be what I think you want. Because it's never enough. I hope Duncan screws you over the way he did me."

"I suggest you mind your words." Dark red splotches appear on my father's cheekbones.

He's big mad. Good.

"I suggest you suck it."

A scandalized gasp from my mother melds with a round of chuckles from my left. *Clairy and Dane.*

"Tuesday Jane Phillips, if you don't—"

"If I don't, what? What could you possibly do to me that you haven't already? How could you possibly hurt me worse than you already have? The answer is you can't. I have nothing to lose."

"That's not exactly true now, is it?" My father's hard eyes narrow. "You're forcing my hand, and I want you to remember that when those people turn on you for bringing this down on them."

His words have me sitting up in my seat. "What are you talking about?"

"I've already drafted a proposal to dissolve Davis Designs and liquidate the company. Maybe I'll look for multiple buyers and sell it off in pieces. Perhaps I'll sell it to someone so inept it will be bankrupt within months. Or I could always call a friend and convince them to clean house and raze it to the ground. So many possibilities." He steeples his fingers together beneath his chin. "Before you think you've got an advantage here, I'd encourage you to reconsider your actions."

Ice floods my veins, all possible words frozen on my lips. He's selling Davis Designs. Everyone who counts on the company for their paycheck and steady work flashes through my mind. Cal, Morgan, and their unborn baby. The team of workers who do the construction and customizations. Charli. Bond. We are nothing but pawns in Warren Phillips' game of life. Meaningless pieces to be flung far and wide on his whims.

Irrational Tuesday spirals in my brain. *I'm useless. I cost Bond his dream twice over. My father is going to win. I've ruined things once again.*

No. Fuck that. Grabbing a massive mental lock, I toss Irrational Tuesday into a box and slam the lid shut. She needs a long timeout.

I glance at the faces of those around me and see nothing but belief in me. Belief that I can stop this from happening. Belief that even if I don't, things will still be okay.

There's no quake or tremble in me when I say, "You can't do that, the contract—"

"Do you think I don't know the stipulations of my contracts? While it was an unusual agreement, I am still the majority owner. I can do whatever I want with it."

Not letting my father's words derail me, I power on. "Fine, if this is how you want to play it, then I'll put in an offer. With my inheritance, I have more than enough."

"What?" Bond asks, his eyebrows knitting together. Around me, the table goes quiet. "You have that kind of money? Tuesday, your dad paid almost two million dollars."

I shift in my seat. "I have it." Cupping his cheek, I whisper, "But I'd give it all up for you."

Bond turns into my touch, his lips grazing my palm. "I'd never ask you to do that."

"I know, which only makes me want to do it more."

Dad sneers. "As touching as this display is, I'm telling you now, you'll never get a bid in. I'm blacklisting you." When my face falls, his sneer twists into an ugly smirk. "Ah, didn't consider that, did you?"

"Why would you blacklist me? The way I see it, it's a win-win. You get your initial investment back for the purchase of Davis Designs. I'm still out of your hair, and you don't have to pretend to care anymore."

"Your mistake is thinking after everything you've put me through, I'd allow you a win."

I recoil, any possible response gone as if slapped from my mouth. Honestly? A slap would hurt less. I make no attempt to wipe the tears away. There's a rumble coming from the table, the angry voices of four men and three women all enraged on my behalf.

Through the blur of my tears, I see my brother push his way onto the screen. "Tuesday, I'll act as a proxy for you."

"Wh-what? War, what are you saying? H-have you been there the entire time?"

"I came in about the time you called Dad stupid. A moment I'm likely to replay anytime I need a chuckle for the next several years."

My mouth drops open before I gather myself. "War, you can't act as my proxy, and you know it. They'll never let you."

"Don't you worry about me." War's confidence and calm smile feed the tiny speck of hope in my chest, and it doubles in size, going from a mere mote to a shiny, sparkling sliver.

"War, what's gotten into you? You dare turn your back on your mother and me? On the company? After all I've given you?"

My brother is calm and collected. He straightens his subtly striped tie. "Don't take it personally, Dad; it makes perfect sense from the business side." War smirks. "I've already messaged my idea to several key board members, and they love it."

For the first time, I see a crack in my father's armor. His face pales. "What plan?"

"To sell Davis Designs back to the Davis family with Tuesday as the purchaser."

My father hisses, "Why would you do that?"

"You should read the replies. Some of the more vocal shareholders are less than thrilled about bringing a person who sued our company back into the fold."

"How would they know about that?" Dad barks.

I watch War and my father volley back and forth, caught in the struggle between them. Even though I'm hundreds of miles away, the tension is palpable. I almost consider taking another sip of the Trail Creek Twist.

"Perhaps someone let it slip that you and Duncan came to a less-than-savory off-the-books agreement. Maybe that same someone raised concerns we stretched ourselves too thin trying to expand into neighboring states and that it would be best for our ROI if we refocused on our local market. And who better to purchase our failed out-of-state venture than your daughter? Spreading her wings with the approval of her loving father. It's a compelling story. The daughter moves to run the out-of-state acquisition, falls in love with the location—and the locals—and expresses her wish to buy back the small company and make it into something of her own. And the benevolent father—"

I snort. I can't help it.

War coughs and continues, "Agrees to give his only daughter this gift." He smiles at me, the camera picking up a twinkle in his honey-colored eyes I haven't seen in years. "At a ten percent increase, of course."

"Of course." I'll happily pay the ten percent. I'd pay double the asking if it got Davis Designs and me out from under my father for good.

"The shareholders will eat it up, and thanks to the quick sale and price raise, Phillips comes out ahead on paper. And this allows us to truly put the entire…"

"Fiasco?" I say.

"Disaster?" Clairy chirps.

"I'm partial to quagmire," Griff adds.

"Let's go with situation." Ah, War, always the PR professional. "It allows Phillips Construction to put the situation in the rearview. I also suspect we'll be revisiting the opportunity for Mr. Wright to consult." There's a strength and firmness in my brother I've never seen before. I'm proud of him, even if it took thirty-three years and a total upheaval of my life for him to come to his senses.

Warren Phillips looks like he ate a lightbulb. "I see. And you've already messaged—"

"Eight out of twelve are on board, meaning if it goes to vote, I win." War pauses, looking at me. "Even if I didn't do this, I know Tuesday—she'll find a way." He winks. "This just ensures smooth sailing. After all, *this* is what's best for the company."

With a bitter sigh, my father nods once. It's the only assent he gives. He and my mother stand without saying another word or bothering to look toward the camera as they leave the room. I can't say it surprises me, but it still stings. There's a piece of me that will always hope for my parents' love. Every movie I watched as a child said even if the parents and children fought, they always came together in the end. But real life is so much messier than fiction.

Bond squeezes my thigh, the warmth of his touch seeping through the satin of my gown. Lynn's hands settle on my shoulders, and Scott stands beside her. Charli and Clairy scoot their chairs closer, and that ache of rejection eases. My family may not be blood, but they are mine.

"Tuesday, Trail Creek looks good on you. It's nice to see you with so many people who love you."

"Thank you." I tilt my head, studying War through my screen. I can't believe it. The golden boy, the chosen child, stood up to our parents. "How did you do this? And why?"

His lips twitch in a sad half-smile. "Sometimes families make difficult choices that are hard to explain—"

"But truly are in everyone's best interest," Bond and Scott finish.

Leaning into the camera, War smiles, this one meeting his eyes. "What they said, and don't worry about Mom and Dad. I'll ensure the board accepts your offer, and they'll be pretending none of this ever happened before the ink dries on the contract."

"Thank you, War. It might be nice if you came and visited. See why I love it here so much."

"I may take you up on that."

He won't. But that's okay. The olive branch between us is more of a vine, but with time, patience, and care, it can grow. And maybe one day, War and I can at least be friends.

"I'll have a lawyer reach out to you by Monday to ensure all the paperwork for the purchase is in place. Take care of yourself, Tuesday."

When the screen goes black, all the air rushes out of my body, and I crumple into Bond's waiting arms.

"I've got you, Baby Girl. You were so strong. So strong."

I bury my head into the crook of his neck and gulp in deep

breaths of his scent. He smells like love. Like comfort. Like home.

The delicate sound of someone clearing their throat has me lifting my head. "So, that was eventful." Charli gives me a small smile. "I won't ask if you're okay, but is there anything we can do? Or anything else you want to tell us?"

Clairy raises one eyebrow. "Like how the next time we need gala gowns, you're picking up the tab?"

A rough laugh rips from me, and I look up at the exposed beams above my head. "That's fair." I shift, embarrassment coloring my cheeks. "My grandparents left my brother and I inheritances when they passed. It's an amount I don't like to think about. Truthfully, outside of donations to charity, I try not to touch it. Using it to purchase Davis Designs is money well spent."

Wringing my hands, I say, "I'm sorry I hid it from you." My eyes drop to the ground, and my shoulders slump. "I've lied to you so many times. Can you forgive me?"

"Babes, there's nothing to forgive. We all have secrets. I'm glad you're finally open to sharing yours with us. We love you, you know that, right?"

Tears prickle in my eyes. "I do. And I'm so frig—fucking thankful."

A roar of laughter and *fuck yeahs* rises from our small group.

"On that note, I think it's time I take Peach to *our* home." The emphasis Bond puts on ours has my heart fluttering. He takes my hand, pulls me to standing, and laces our fingers together. As a couple, we stride through the tables of curious townsfolk. No doubt we'll be the talk of Trail Creek for a while, but that's okay. I have nothing to hide. Not anymore.

When we step into the chilly air, I take a bracing breath. The cold air stings my nose and lungs, but I relish the burn.

Taking another long draw, I snuggle against Bond's chest. "Longest party of my life."

"It was one for the books, that's for sure." He lifts my chin, his blue eyes searching mine. "Tell me a truth."

"I've never felt so free."

Bond's lips brush mine before pulling back, leaving mere millimeters between our mouths. "Do you smell it, Peach?"

"What?"

"Snow."

Taking a long, satisfying breath, the scent of frost, crisp and clean—and a hint of Bond—fills my senses. I tilt my head, giving him access to kiss me along the column of my throat. As his lips run over my skin, I whisper, "Smells like home to me, Baseball Cap."

CHAPTER THIRTY-THREE

Tuesday sits curled up next to me as we watch the warm white lights on our Christmas tree twinkle while snow falls steadily outside. This morning, I snuck out while she was sleeping to get the tree, and we spent our day decorating it together. I also made a pit stop at my old house to pick up a few remaining items. Truthfully, it wasn't much, but there were two things I couldn't bring until today. One, fully charged, waits in a cheery red bag hidden among the couch cushions. The other sits in my pocket.

The fire crackles, and I study Tuesday's face, drinking in her full, pouty lips, the light spray of freckles on her nose, and the brush of her lashes against her cheeks. She's so beautiful.

And so damn bratty.

I narrow my eyes at her as she's mid stolen french fry bite. She freezes and grins like the cat who got the cream. "I'm telling you, yours taste better!"

"And if I swapped our plates?"

"Yours would still taste better. It's just one of those

strange, unexplainable, naturally occurring phenomena." She laughs, unfettered and loud.

"You are wonderful and strange, Peach. Don't you go changing on me."

"Only in the best ways, I promise." She happily goes back to eating all of my fries.

The mountains are barely visible through the flurries, but it's still a stunning view. I was right when I said I smelled snow the night of the gala. Since then, we've had a steady fall blanketing Trail Creek.

It's been a week since the Twinkling Trail Gala and the showdowns between Tuesday and Duncan and Tuesday and her parents. My Peach deserves a sky full of orgasms and every french fry off my plate from now until the end of time for everything she went through that night.

Tuesday, War, and their lawyers finalized the paperwork for the purchase—reclaiming—of the company late last night. Davis Designs officially belongs to Tuesday, Charli, and me in an equal partnership. Tuesday insisted on listing all our names as the owners, despite her being the one to fund the purchase. She even offered a portion to Clairy, but my little sister declined.

My heart swells with gratitude for what Tuesday did. It took a massive amount of courage to stand up to her family, knowing there was a greater than good chance it would sever their relationship permanently. She still hasn't spoken to her parents, and I doubt she will soon. Luckily, my mom and dad are more than happy to step in and give her the love she deserves. She quickly climbed to the top of the Davis family favorites list.

Tuesday turned my dreams on their head and somehow gave them back to me. I can't believe, after everything, I'm walking away with my family business and the love of my life. She saved Davis Designs in more ways than one—starting with her fresh ideas and ending with keeping it from being swallowed up by Phillips Construction.

The ring burns a hole in my pocket, begging me to break it out. As soon as I saw it, I knew it was the one for her. Mr. Mendoza, Dane's dad and the owner of the best—and only— jewelry store in Trail Creek, said the center stone is a padparadscha sapphire. All I saw was the same sunset as Tuesday's hair. The thin rose gold band is set with a trio of round diamonds on either side of an Ascher-cut gem. It's beautiful, a little loud, and perfectly Tuesday.

"What are you thinking about so hard over there, Baseball Cap?" she asks, tossing my hat off my head.

"How you've given me more than I ever could have imagined."

Her face flushes, and she drops her french fry before climbing into my lap. "When you say sweet things like that, it makes me want to kiss you."

"You should give in to that urge."

Tuesday presses her lips to mine, our tongues twining. It's a slow kiss, all soft lips and exchanged breaths. Nothing desperate or urgent. Instead, it's searching, a gentle savoring. It feels like my future.

But I need to pump the brakes before we get so lost in each other that we can't resurface. I've got a plan.

My hands have a mind of their own, though, and roam her body, fingertips dancing along her spine before the tips dig into her plump ass. She moans and rocks against me, the crown of my cock grazing her core, the heat flaring between us evident through my gray sweatpants and her thin leggings.

Fuck the plan.

Breaking the kiss, I fumble for my phone, digging it from my pocket. Tuesday teases her lips up my neck and along my jaw.

"Dane?" I grunt when she nips my earlobe. "Change of plans. Send everyone home. Yeah, I'm sure. No, it's still happening. Hug my momma and my sisters. Tell them they can call tomorrow." With that, I turn my phone off for the night.

"What was that secretive little conversation about?" Tuesday asks, her eyebrows wiggling up and down.

"Tonight, in front of the people who love us the most, I was going to ask you to be mine."

Her lips skim over mine. "I'm already yours, Baseball Cap."

"Yeah, you are." I draw back, kiss the tip of her nose, and pull the small blue box from my pocket. "I thought doing this at the Great Dane made the most sense, seeing as that's where we met, but right here in our home—the home I built for us before I even knew you—this is where it should happen."

Tuesday's breath catches. Her whiskey eyes widen. "Bond? Are you—"

"From the minute we met, Tuesday Jane Phillips, you captivated me. I've never been one to believe in love at first sight or instant connections, but damn if you didn't prove all my theories wrong. But it wasn't just love at first sight, Baby Girl. It was love at first sight and every sight after. Even in the moments of doubt, the times we ran, your heart called to mine. You completely upended the future I expected and rewrote my dreams. You are what I'll crave for the rest of my days."

I snap the lid open and slide the ring onto her finger. "Marry me, Peach."

"Yease!" she shouts, wrapping her arms around my neck and crushing her lips to mine before peppering kisses all over my face. "I love you, Bond. More than I can say. In your arms,

I've found my home—a place where I'm loved exactly as I am. You see me. You're the most caring, wonderful man I've ever known, and I can't believe I get to call you mine."

"Don't forget sexy."

A single tear streaks down her cheek, and she laughs. "Of course. How could I forget? Sexy, charming, with a cock that makes me sing."

Pressing my forehead to hers, I close my eyes and pause, soaking in this moment. "I swore the night I dropped you off at the Trail Creek Inn for the first time to make Davis your last name. I love you so much, Tuesday."

The sweet, tender kisses between us begin to smolder, growing hotter and crackling with need. Pulling back, I grin. "I have one more gift for you, sweetheart. I couldn't help but notice that out of all those toys in that fun little drawer next to our bed, there was one you didn't have."

"Oh?" She holds out her hands in the universal symbol for *gimme.*

"Now hang on. I have a couple of rules you have to follow. Consider this payback for the panties in my mouth."

"Please. You loved it."

I growl and roll us, trapping her beneath me on the couch, before tickling her without mercy. "Damn straight I did." Only when she's begging me to stop do I let up on my ticklish torture. "Are you ready to hear the rules?"

"Ye-yes, Bond," she gasps, breathing hard from laughing.

"Go over to the rug." Once she's standing on the thick white rug before the fireplace, I say, "Rule one, I need you bare before me. You have sixty seconds."

"What happens if I don't meet your deadline?"

"You lose an orgasm. Clock's ticking, Peach."

She throws her baggy sweatshirt over her head and

discards her leggings with a flourish. The lace cups of her bra smack me in the face, followed by a blur of green as she loses her panties.

"Just made it, Baby Girl. You must really want those orgasms." A glance at the clock shows she finished with plenty of time to spare, but I like making her sweat.

"Rule two, when I give this to you, you'll use it to make yourself come. And I want you talking the whole time. Telling me what you feel, what you're thinking, what you wish I was doing. And rule three? You have five minutes to come, or you don't get to come again until I say so. And I will spend all evening keeping you right on the edge."

Tuesday shifts, rubbing her thighs together, her eyes blown with lust and love.

"Talk to me, Peach. Do you want this?"

"Yes."

"That's my beautiful future wife." I dig between the couch cushions and fish out the gift bag before crossing over to where she stands. "Lie down, sweetheart. Knees up and spread. I want to see all of you."

She drops to the plush rug, lying on her back with her legs splayed wide, giving me a perfect view of her pink pussy. "So fucking gorgeous." I grab her thighs and kiss the soft skin so close to where she wants me. With my ring finger, I trace around her clit and delve into her, gathering her slick wetness and bringing it to my mouth.

With a smirk, I open the bag and pull out the cordless wand. "Five minutes. Are you ready?"

Tuesday nods, her head bobbing up and down. Five minutes is no time at all to make a partner come, but I know Tuesday's triggers. Outside clit stimulation sends her there quicker than anything else. All the reviews I read when researching this toy have me thinking she'll have no trouble meeting my time limit.

I turn on the vibrating massage wand, the wide oval head humming and shaking, and then I slip it into her hands. "Time starts now. And don't forget to talk. I want all your words."

A moan tumbles from her lips as soon as the wand head touches her clit, and she shivers. Squirming, she places it where she wants it. Her cheeks flush, the red glow spreading down her neck and chest. She's stunning.

"Keep those legs spread and knees up. I don't want to miss a second of this." My cock throbs with wanting.

"It feels so good, Bond. God, it's hitting me just right."

I watch, enraptured by the sight of her pleasuring herself. "Is it better than me?"

"No, nothing is. I'm imagining you inside me, your fingers filling me up before your fat cock slides in, stretching me wide."

Fuck. I reach into my sweatpants and stroke myself. "Keep going."

"You flip me over and tease me between my cheeks, your thumb pressing in and setting all my nerves on fire. You're still fucking me, hard thr-thrusts in and out. Heat pools in my stomach and lower back; if I don't let it out, I'll turn to ash in your arms."

"Goddamn, you are so fucking perfect. Get there, Tuesday, so I can sink into you and fuck you the way you deserve."

The muscles in her stomach and thighs quiver, tightening as her entire body chases her climax. Her eyes close, and her mouth parts. She's close. Unable to resist, I shed my clothes and lean over her, taking one rosy nipple in my mouth.

"You s-suck and bite me, gi-giving me just...fuck...just the right..." her words trail off as she shudders and moans, "amount of p-pain to offset the pleasure." She's getting harder to understand the closer she gets to coming.

"Look at you, being such a good girl tonight. Following all the rules. Come for me now, Peach. Come so I clean it up before filling that sweet hole."

"Bond!" Her back arches, her breath hitching as she lets out a choked sob.

The wand falls from her hand, and she melts into the rug, gulping down air. Before she can speak, I bury my face in her pussy. I lick up every wondrous drop, lapping her from core to clit. I don't pick my head up until she calls my name.

Resting my cheek on her inner thigh, I say, "I can't fucking wait to marry you."

"I think I'll enjoy being your wife, Baseball Cap."

I need to make love to her. To show her with my body the way she makes me feel. I kiss my way upward, and when my mouth meets hers, I say, "I love you, Tuesday."

"I love you too."

I trail my lips down her neck to her chest, sucking and nibbling on her nipples. My hands never stop moving, gliding along her skin, anchoring her to me. She's my constant. My North Star. The Luna to my Sol.

I take my time pinching and sucking and loving her as though I'll never get my fill. Tuesday's nails dig into my shoulders before she buries her fingers in my hair. A tingle shoots from my scalp to my base. Without thinking, my hips move against her, each bumping slide of my cock against her pussy driving us both higher.

Breaking away, Tuesday wriggles in my arms so her back is to my chest. As I run my hands up and down her side, following the flow of her body, my hips press against her ass, the firm proof of how much I want her solid and hot there.

Fuck, the power she has over me. She needs me, but I need her just as much.

"Bond." That's it: one word, a whispered plea for more hidden in its depths.

I bathe in her touch, her scent, her lips on my skin.

"How did a goddess like you end up with a mere mortal like me?"

Tuesday hooks her leg over mine, opening herself to me. The callouses of my hands leave a path of goosebumps in their wake as I continue kissing anywhere I can reach.

"I want you, always, you beautiful man."

At her words, I reach between her spread knees and tease her, my fingers dipping in and out of her core before circling and putting pressure on her clit. Each time I toy with her, she presses into me, grinding against my cock.

"Please, I'm ready." She pulls my hand away and brings it to her lips, kissing the pads of my fingers. Without a word, I slide into her, spooning her from behind.

"I love everything about you, Peach. Your beautiful body, your gorgeous smile. That cute button nose you always wrinkle." My hands roam her stomach and chest before coming to rest on her throat. My grasp is light, just enough pressure to make her pliant. "Your tight pussy and the way it grips me. Fuck. Touch yourself."

Tuesday melts into me, her fingers nimbly traveling to her pleasure points. She cranes her neck, her lips seeking mine, and I give her what she's searching for. Our kiss serves as an additional point of contact connecting us. Tethering us.

"Lower. That's a good girl. Keep touching yourself." My thumb brushes against her quivering pulse point.

Her fingers glide over where we join, and she spreads them into a V, framing my cock with each pull out and push in. Is this fucking heaven? I think it must be. Her warm, wet pussy grips me, her fingers adding pressure, her skin sweaty and slick against mine.

"Fuck, that feels good. I love your brain, Baby Girl. How clever and funny you are. I love that big, loud laugh and that cute snort. I even love when you snore. I love you from the tips of your hair all the way to your adorable fucking tiny toes."

Tuesday whimpers, the walls of her pussy squeezing me. All the beautiful signs are there, and I savor the fluttering of her innermost muscles around my cock. She's close.

"I can't wait to fuck you on our wedding night, make you cry out my name as Tuesday Davis. To see you carrying my babies, ripe and glowing. To grow old with you."

"Bond!" she cries out my name as the tension building in her snaps. Her hand flies off her clit, and her fingers dig into my forearm, grasping as she shudders and shakes. Fuck, yeah. I'll wear those crescent-shaped marks like a badge.

"The sound of my name on your lips when you come is my favorite sound." My pace shifts as her knee comes forward, allowing me to sink deeper than before. She writhes, her hands looking for purchase in the thick rug beneath us. "Say my name again, sweetheart; tell me a truth while I come inside your sweet pussy."

"I love you, Bond. Every time we...god, every time we're together is the new best I've ever had."

I lose myself in her. There's no more thinking, just sensation. Soft. Wet. Warm. Mine.

With a soul-deep moan, I flood her with my release. I bury my face in my hair before kissing the column of her neck and enveloping her in my arms. I stay inside her, the heat of her pussy holding my cock in place.

"Best engagement ever." Her words are breathy, satisfied, and happy. So happy. It's everything I want for her and more.

I ease out of her, my lips trailing down her spine, paying

extra attention to the kiss-me spots scattered on her back. Each perfect freckle gets the same attention as the one before it. Then, I slide my hand down to gather up the fluids from between her legs. Swirling us together, I bring my fingers to her mouth, and she opens, licking them clean.

"How do we taste, Baby Girl?"

"Like forever."

Like forever. Hell. Fucking. Yease.

epilogue

Four months later

I tug at my collar, the material suddenly too tight as the warm golden rays of the sun cut through the early April chill. Nerves churn in my stomach and chest, but not ones of doubt or uncertainty.

No, these nerves are pure excitement and anticipation. I'm minutes away from marrying the love of my goddamn fucking life. A woman I don't deserve, but get on my knees to praise for slumming it with me every day.

Tuesday and my sisters transformed our backyard into a small oasis. The beautiful mountains I've grown up with my entire life look over us, the trees budding with fresh leaves and pops of green as winter gives way to spring.

My mom and dad sit front and center in the small arrangement of chairs. The smiles on their faces are there for me and the woman I'm about to marry. Everyone who loves us is here today to celebrate. And those who aren't? Fuck 'em.

"You ready for this?" Griff asks.

Dane snorts. "He's been ready since the night he met her."

"You're a lucky man, Bond."

I glance over my shoulder at my friend, but his eyes are on Charli as she and Waverly step under the flower-draped pergola.

"Sure is." This comes from Dane, and I don't even bother looking. I know he's staring at Clairy as he speaks.

Sighing because some things never change, I look up to the sky and thank the universe for my two best friends and my family. The acoustic guitar plays out the final chords of *You Are in Love,* and the Justice of the Peace gestures for our guests to stand.

At exactly 5:01, the notes of...I pause, laughter fighting its way out of my throat. The first notes of fucking *Pony* ring out. If I thought I couldn't love her more, she just proved me wrong.

My Peach is resplendent. She looks like the desert in spring with flowers in her hair and scattered down the length of her blush-colored gown. Did this moment jump to the top of my future fantasy list? Hell yes.

When she reaches me, she offers her hand, which I happily take in my own. Our eyes lock, and I see the same promises of forever in hers that I know are written in mine.

"Peach, from the moment we met—on what I thought was the worst day of my life, but quickly turned into the best—I knew we would end up here. You are the best thing to ever happen to me. I stand before you today, my heart in your tiny hands. I promise to cherish and celebrate everything that makes you, you. From your laugh and snores to your beautiful hair and constant stealing of my french fries."

My vows earn me one of those loud laughs I love so much. Squeezing Tuesday's hand, I continue, "I'll be your anchor in any storm, your light when it's dark. The person who keeps your secrets. I love you, Tuesday."

A tear trails down her cheek, and I thumb it away. The

desire to kiss her is too strong to ignore, and I capture her lips with mine until the sound of a throat clearing has me breaking away.

"Not quite to that part, son." My dad chuckles from his seat.

With a sheepish grin and shrug, I say, "Sorry, I couldn't resist."

Tuesday takes a deep breath. "Baseball Cap, you burst into my life in a way I never expected. I came to Trail Creek hoping for a fresh start but found so much more. I will take care of you the way you do others and love you with my whole heart." Her voice shakes. "I promise to be your partner in all our adventures, to build a world with you that can be our legacy. Here's my truth: in you, I have found my home."

The cheers from our friends and family echo through the air, and in that moment, time stands still. For all I know, it could be just her, me, and the stars. It's finally time to kiss my wife. I'm lost in the wonder of her lips, her body pressed to mine, the love and connection between us.

My wife. My Peach. My good girl. My forever.

The End

If you're so inclined, I would love it if you left a rating and review for Keep This Between Us! As an indie author, your reviews help others learn about my book.

dick-tionary

If you want to skip straight to the spicy parts, or if you want to avoid them entirely, here are the chapters that contain explicit sex. Some of these are small scenes, some are long and detailed. Take care of your needs!

- Chapter 5: solo masturbation scene, includes use of toys
- Chapter 7: oral scene between MCs
- Chapter 9: oral scene between MCs
- Chapter 10: heavy petting that leads to orgasm
- Chapter 18: oral scene between MCs
- Chapter 19: v/p scene between MCs
- Chapter 22: v/p scene between MCs, includes anal play and use of toys
- Chapter 24: v/p scene between MCs, includes light sensory play and light food play
- Chapter 25: hand scene between MCs
- Chapter 28: oral scene between MCs

- Chapter 30: oral scene between MCs
- Chapter 33: v/p scene between MCs, includes use of toys

acknowledgments

A huge massive thank you to everyone who supported me in this endeavor! To the people who listened to me doubt myself and talked me out of deleting everything too many times to count.

Kink, thank you for the many real-talk moments, the time you pour into me, and pictures of your land seal when I need them most.

Ellie, you are an amazing author and CP, and I am so thankful we stumbled into each other's orbits. Your writing is like a warm blanket on a chilly night. Sinkhole lovers and drowned squirrel girls unite.

Krista and Taylor thank you for being fresh eyes and supports as I brought this story to life.

Tiffany thank you for being a life-long friend and rabidly reading the early draft of this in one day.

Melissa I miss you and your encouragement! Thank you for supporting my dream!

Indie Authors Group: Hannah, Bailey, Genesis, Cherry, Miley, Laura, C. Airia, thank for being an invaluable resource and answering my millions of questions. Also for making me laugh and being there when I need you! I am so thankful to have found you all.

To my betas: Jess, Katie, Ash, and Karla. Thank you for your thoughts, support, and insights! You helped make this book better!

ARC readers, thank you for reaching out with your interest in being a part of my debut. I so appreciate you sharing your thoughts about it out into the world.

To all of you reading this now, THANK YOU. Yeah, all caps style. You mean so much to me. This dream felt too big for so long and at the ripe old age of—let's just say geriatric millennial—my dream is coming true. My book exists! And you read it! From the bottom of my heart, I hope you loved the story, the characters, and the way they loved each other.

Albany Archer is the alter ego of an avid reader, turned writer, of sweet and spicy romance. She loves anything with a happily ever after, regardless of the sub-genre. Banter, hair washing, and feisty female characters who know who and what they want are her love language. Her biggest hope is that you walk away with some sort of joy after reading her work. If you'd like to connect with Albany, check out the links below.

instagram.com/authoralbanyarcher

goodreads.com/albanyarcher

amazon.com/author/albanyarcher